Racing Christmas

Rodeo Romance Book 6
A Sweet Contemporary Holiday Romance
by
USA TODAY Bestselling Author
SHANNA HATFIELD

Racing Christmas
(Rodeo Romance Series, Book 6)

Copyright © 2018 by Shanna Hatfield

ISBN: 9781729048047

For permission requests, please contact the author, with a subject line of "permission request" at the email address below or through her website.

Shanna Hatfield
shanna@shannahatfield.com
shannahatfield.com

This is a work of fiction. Names, characters, businesses, places, events, and incidents either are the product of the author's imagination or are used in a fictitious manner. Any resemblance to actual persons, living or dead, business establishments, or actual events is purely coincidental.

Cover Design: Shanna Hatfield

To those who learn the fine art
of forgiveness...

.

Books by Shanna Hatfield

FICTION

CONTEMPORARY

Blown Into Romance
Sleigh Bells Ring in Romance
Love at the 20-Yard Line
Learnin' the Ropes
QR Code Killer
Rose
Saving Mistletoe
Taste of Tara

Rodeo Romance
The Christmas Cowboy
Wrestlin' Christmas
Capturing Christmas
Barreling Through Christmas
Chasing Christmas
Racing Christmas

Grass Valley Cowboys
The Cowboy's Christmas Plan
The Cowboy's Spring Romance
The Cowboy's Summer Love
The Cowboy's Autumn Fall
The Cowboy's New Heart
The Cowboy's Last Goodbye

Silverton Sweethearts
The Coffee Girl
The Christmas Crusade
Untangling Christmas

Women of Tenacity
A Prelude
Heart of Clay
Country Boy vs. City Girl
Not His Type

HISTORICAL

The Dove

Hardman Holidays
The Christmas Bargain
The Christmas Token
The Christmas Calamity
The Christmas Vow
The Christmas Quandary
The Christmas Confection

Pendleton Petticoats
Dacey
Aundy
Caterina
Ilsa
Marnie
Lacy
Bertie
Millie
Dally
Quinn

Baker City Brides
Tad's Treasure
Crumpets and Cowpies
Thimbles and Thistles
Corsets and Cuffs
Bobbins and Boots
Lightning and Lawmen

Hearts of the War
Garden of Her Heart
Home of Her Heart
Dream of Her Heart

Chapter One

"You're going to rock this crowd, Rocket," Brylee Barton assured her horse as he walked around the perimeter of the practice area behind the rodeo arena.

The horse bobbed his head, as though in agreement.

She laughed, aware he didn't understand what she said, but pretending he did. She patted the dapple gray's neck. "You are such a ham."

Brylee urged Rocket into an easy lope. As soon as the last steer wrestler entered the arena, it would be time for her to line up for barrel racing — an event she fully intended to win.

Evening had arrived, yet it failed to dispel the sticky July heat in this small Idaho town, similar to dozens of others she'd been in over the course of the last month. In a little more than four weeks, she'd traveled almost two thousand miles to rodeos.

She'd competed in several Northwestern states, hustled to Canada for two rodeos, then traveled across the Midwest. Now she was making her way back through the Northwest. On a winning streak, she'd placed at all but two of the rodeos she'd entered, and walked away the winner at seven of them.

This evening's performance was the conclusion of a three-day rodeo. She'd ridden Thursday and claimed a spot in the final go-round. She planned to leave as the winner.

It had taken her five years to make a comeback as a professional barrel racer and she had every intention of earning the world championship title in December. More than just bragging rights were on the line, and nothing would stop her from trying to win.

A boom of thunder followed by a streak of lightening spooked Rocket, but Brylee kept a firm hand on the reins and continued loping him around the practice arena.

"Are you two ready for this?" a raven-haired woman asked as she rode up beside Rocket.

Brylee grinned at her friend. "As ready as I can be, Savannah. How about you and Rainbow? Are you gonna give me a run for my money?"

Savannah laughed and patted the neck of her mare. "You know we'll try, but you are the turn and burn queen." The young woman glanced up at the sky as thunder cracked overhead followed by another bright bolt of lightning.

Fat raindrops began to fall, slightly cooling the heavy air, but making it even more humid than it had been.

"This isn't going to be good," Savannah said, turning with Brylee as they made their way toward a shelter near the stable.

"No, it won't be. That arena will be a sloppy mess before long." Brylee frowned as she stared at the darkening sky. The rain was still falling gently. Maybe it would be a brief storm that quickly passed.

Another boom of thunder sounded before a blinding flash of lightning looked like it might strike the flagpole outside the arena. It barely missed, but left her blinking her eyes in shock.

"That's entirely too close for comfort," Savannah said, trying to keep Rainbow in line as the horse pranced and tossed her head. "Just calm down, girl. Everything is fine."

"Yes, it is," Brylee echoed, rubbing Rocket's neck. She needed to convince herself of it as much as she did the horse or Savannah. Since she wasn't going to ride first in the event, she worried about the condition of the arena. All she could do was hope the crew raking dirt around the barrels did a good job between rides and the rainstorm held off until she and Rocket made their run.

"Let's give a hand to our winner in the steer wrestling, folks! That young man is going places!" The rodeo announcer's resonant voice carried over the crowd and through the storm.

"Come on. Let's get lined up. They'll move things along quickly with this rain," Savannah said, tugging down her black hat inlayed with turquoise and detailed embroidery all around the brim.

Brylee thought her friend could have had a lucrative career as a model. Savannah was tall, generously curved, and gorgeous with long black tresses, perfect skin, and eyes nearly as dark as her hair. The woman always looked amazing and today was no exception. Her turquoise sequined shirt glittered in the lights that had kicked on around the arena. Even her horse appeared flashy with a turquoise saddle pad and matching sports boots.

While some barrel racers looked as though they competed in a beauty contest, Brylee had no time nor interest in such things. Not now. Not when so much rode on her success.

She did keep Rocket groomed within an inch of his patience as he endured the ministrations. He always looked sharp when they raced. Primarily, she stuck with black as her color choice for her gear, from her saddle to his boots, and even the breast collar. All that black, accented with silver, looked fantastic against his gray-flecked coloring and black mane.

Rather than worry about having the most stylish outfit, best hair, or flawless makeup, Brylee spent extra time working with Rocket and improving her riding skills. Oh, she made a little effort to not look like a clueless bumpkin. However, compared to some of the girls who were magazine cover-worthy, she might have felt plain and average, if she let it bother her. Most of the time it didn't.

What she lacked in cosmetic interests, Brylee made up for with her ability to ride.

"I have to tell you, folks, you are in for a treat

with the lovely ladies racing the barrels tonight. What a great group of talented women. And they are all purty to boot," the announcer said. "First up is a gal who's made a great showing for her rookie year. Let's welcome..."

Brylee tuned out the announcer. Tuned out the crowd. Tuned out everything as she shifted her thoughts to the pattern of the barrels inside the arena.

She and Rocket had run the cloverleaf hundreds and hundreds of times. Regulations stated they had to take either two right turns and one left or one right and two left. Brylee had experimented with the options and found she and Rocket performed best when they rode into the arena and took a right turn around the right barrel then followed with a left around the left barrel and another left around the center barrel. By the time he came out of the pocket on the third barrel, Rocket would lengthen his long stride and shoot across the arena.

As the women in front of her competed, Brylee closed her eyes and envisioned riding through the pattern. In her mind's eye she pictured each turn, the tightness of the pockets around every barrel, and how she'd stay centered in the saddle.

While she waited for her turn, rain poured down like the skies had broken open, plastering her shirt against her back and soaking through her jeans. She brushed her hand along Rocket's neck to calm them both and watched Savannah plunge ahead for her ride.

Although she cheered for her friend, Brylee purposely avoided listening to her score. She didn't want to know how anyone else had done, how well she needed to do to win. It messed with her ability to focus when she started worrying about beating someone else's time.

When Savannah rode past her, Brylee gave her a high-five and then moved up in position. She was next.

"We've got this, Rocket. You know what to do, buddy." Brylee leaned forward and rubbed his neck then sat back and mentally centered herself as the announcer began her introduction.

"For those of you who've not yet had the privilege of watching this amazing lady, you are in for a treat. Brylee Barton made it twice to the national finals before taking some time off. She's back now and better than ever. This lil' gal can show you a thing or two about balance and training a horse. Speaking of horses, she's riding Christmas Jolly Rocket, better known as Rocket. He's a ten-year-old gelding she raised and trained from the day he was born. And he's a beaut to boot. Let's give a big welcome to Miss Brylee Barton from Walla Walla, Washington!"

Amid the cheers from the crowd in the stands, Brylee made three quick kissing sounds. Rocket raced into the arena and veered toward the barrel on their right.

"Look at that gal ride, folks. Now that's what I'm talking about. Miss Brylee is one of the best when it comes to staying glued to the saddle and maintaining balance," the announcer said as Brylee and Rocket made it around the first barrel.

The ground felt soft and slick as Rocket sped

across the arena toward the next barrel. Brylee kept her focus on the pocket around the barrel instead of staring directly at the barrel. She'd learned years ago when she centered on the barrel, they'd invariably knock it over, adding five seconds to her score. By keeping her attention in the space around it, where she pictured Rocket turning, it helped them make the turn without a penalty.

"This might just be the winning ride of the night, folks! Watch this lady go!" the announcer cheered. "Talk about turning and burning. If rain wasn't pelting down like a hose turned loose from a fire hydrant, there'd be flames shooting out behind her."

The announcer was right about the rain. Torrential sheets of it started pouring from the skies, making it hard to see. Rocket struggled to get a firm foothold in the arena dirt that rapidly morphed into mud.

They reached the third barrel and Brylee breathed a sigh of relief. Rocket had just moved into the turn when he suddenly lost his footing. He twisted his big body as he went down, sliding through the mud into the fence behind them. Pain pierced her leg and stole her breath when she collided with a fence post. Rocket thrashed and squirmed, attempting to get to his feet.

Instinctively, Brylee tried to roll out of the way. However, her right foot was trapped in the fence and her left remained caught beneath the horse. She felt as though she was being sucked down in the mud with no hope of escape.

She squeezed her eyes shut and prayed as

Rocket continued to kick his legs, desperate to get away from the fence. Thankfully, her leg came free of the stirrup when he stood. Rocket tossed his head, trembling with fear, before he raced across the arena.

"Thank you, Lord, for keeping me alive and my horse safe," she whispered.

Brylee opened her eyes and tipped her head back, watching as the pickup men rode into the arena. One went to catch Rocket while the other hastened her direction. The announcer and the clown told a joke as the medical team hustled toward her as fast as they could make it through the mud.

Frustration battled with anger as the pickup man approached. The last person on earth she wanted to see was *that* particular member of the male species.

"Maybe today would be a good day to die," she muttered as she tried again to disentangle her foot from the fence. If she freed it before he reached her, she could crawl over the fence and make her way back to her trailer without speaking to him.

Why couldn't he have gone on ignoring her like he had the last five and half years? Why tonight, of all nights, was he going to force her to acknowledge him? Didn't she have enough to deal with, like missing her opportunity to claim the winning title? Or the undeniable fact she looked like a half-drowned kitten that had been dragged through a pig wallow?

She thought of her wasted entry fee. Not to mention the hours it would take to get all the mud scrubbed off Rocket and her tack.

Wasn't a no-score enough punishment without being forced to face the most arrogant, self-centered, childish man she'd ever known?

Trapped on her back in the mud, it seeped through her clothes, chilling her and making her fight the need to shiver. She questioned how she could exit the arena with even a shred of dignity when her pants oozed soupy muck like a toddler's soggy diaper.

The slap of boots hitting the mud in the arena drew her gaze upward. A handsome face appeared above her as the pickup man leaned over her. Gray-blue eyes twinkled behind thick lashes and a smile full of even, white teeth gleamed in the arena lights. Shaun Price braced his gloved hands on his thighs and offered her an infuriatingly cocky grin.

Why couldn't she have at least passed out and awakened far away from the infuriating, irritating, Adonis-like cowboy?

"Well, Bitsy, I see you're still racing Christmas," he said, his voice sounding as deep and rich as she remembered.

Brylee glowered at him. "You know I hate that name."

"Yep, I sure do." Shaun chuckled and stepped back as the medics surrounded her.

Chapter Two

"Have you talked to Brylee yet?" Jason Price questioned his son as they waited behind the chutes during the barrel racing event. As soon as it ended, they'd ride back into the arena and get ready for the bull riding to begin.

As pickup men for the Rockin' K Rodeo Company, the contractor providing animals for the rodeo, Jason and Shaun spent a good part of the day sorting stock for each event. During the rough stock events they remained in the arena to help get the riders safely off bucking animals and then move the animals out of the arena. After the rodeo ended, they'd be busy loading animals to transport back to the Rockin' K Ranch. There, they'd pick up a new batch of animal athletes and then be on the road to start the process all over again.

And they both loved every minute of it.

Shaun removed his cowboy hat and ran a hand through his thick copper-colored hair before settling the hat back in place. "No, Dad, I haven't. I don't think she'd like it if I tried."

Jason raised an eyebrow and gave his son a pointed look. "That's what you get for going around breaking hearts right and left. You had to know at some point that would come back around and bite you right on the…"

"I get it, Dad. I do." Shaun scowled at his father. "But Brylee's different. She's old history that's so far under the bridge, it's never coming back upstream."

Jason shrugged then reached out and slapped Shaun on the back. "Have I mentioned how glad I am to have you working with me?"

Shaun grinned at his father. "Only about a million times in the last four months." He settled a hand on his dad's shoulder. "I'm glad to be working with you, too. If Uncle Galen hadn't decided to retire as your pickup partner, I don't know what I would have done with myself. When the doctors told me it was either give up bareback riding or end up crippled for life, I didn't feel like I had a lot of choices."

Jason nodded. "I know, son. Your uncle had wanted to retire for quite a while, so it worked out great for you to take his place once you healed up from that last wreck."

Shaun rubbed a hand over the bone that he'd broken not once, but twice within six months. The thought of being permanently crippled was enough to make him give up a career he enjoyed, but he really did love working as a pickup man. It was still physically demanding, but the odds of getting trampled and breaking something were in his favor instead of constantly against him.

"There she is," Jason said, pointing to a blond-haired woman on a big dapple gray horse waiting just outside the gate where the barrel racers entered and exited the arena.

Shaun allowed himself a moment to study Brylee Barton. From this distance, he could see she looked as trim and fit as she had six years ago when he'd first lost his heart to her. They'd been on fire in their careers and for each other that summer. But they'd both moved on. At least he thought he had.

In truth, he'd often thought of Brylee over the years, especially when she seemed to have dropped off the face of the earth. After taking the barrel racing world championship title her first year at the finals, she should have earned it the second year, but he supposed he was partly to blame for her finishing in third place.

By the time rodeo season headed into full swing the following year, no one had seen Brylee since the finals in Las Vegas. Then one year rolled into two, and here it was, five and a half years later.

He'd heard she was back on the circuit and making a name for herself again. He'd even seen her at a rodeo last month, but he'd been so busy with his work, he hadn't found a spare minute to talk to her. Or at least that's what he told himself as he watched her sit with beauty and grace on the back of her horse.

"That girl always could outride anyone," Jason said, pointing toward Brylee again. "You ever hear why she dropped out of rodeo for a while?"

Shaun shook his head, determined to keep his thoughts to himself. The unwelcoming churning in his gut assured him he had played a part in her quitting the business and turning into a mysterious recluse.

He looked away from Brylee, away from the past and memories he'd rather not shake loose. They'd been strong-armed into the far reaches of his mind and he planned to keep them there. "I haven't heard anything, Dad. I don't think it's something she wants to talk about, otherwise everyone would know."

"True. It's not like there are many secrets in this business." Jason leaned forward as the announcer's booming voice introduced Brylee. "I hope she wins this thing."

Shaun remained quiet, although he hoped she did, too. While some girls focused on speed and looking pretty, Brylee worked hard at getting the most out of her horse and herself. He'd noticed Thursday night how much she'd improved her skills since he'd watched her ride at the finals in Las Vegas all those years ago.

"The arena is a mess. Sure makes it hard on those poor girls running the barrels," Jason said, tugging his hat down and flicking moisture off his chaps.

"I'm glad no one got hurt. With the rain making the arena slicker than the end of a bull's snotty nose, it's a wonder one of them hasn't taken a spill." Shaun stood up in his stirrups and watched as Brylee entered the arena. Her horse spun around the first barrel so perfectly, his movements almost appeared fluid. Hooves churned up chunks of mud as he carried Brylee around the second barrel and on to the third.

As though it happened in slow motion, Shaun watched as Rocket started to skid. It looked like he hit a patch of ice for the way his legs went out from beneath him. He twisted his body around before he landed on his side and slid in the mud with Brylee still on him.

"Open the gate!" Shaun yelled above the gasps of the crowd and the beat of the rain. He and his dad rushed into the arena. Rocket flailed around then got up and began running around the arena, but Brylee remained unmoving in the mud by the fence. "Get the horse, Dad!"

Jason nodded and took off to catch Rocket while Shaun rode toward Brylee. When he saw her move her head, he released the breath he didn't even realize he'd been holding. Relieved she was alive and moving, he willed the hammering beat of his heart to slow. He rode up close to her, noticing her foot wedged beneath the fence and caught in the mud. Something must be wrong or she would have jerked herself free by now.

Unsettled to see her and scared she'd truly been injured, he hid his concern. He plastered on his most obnoxious smile and greeted her by the nickname he'd used during the months they dated.

The moment he called her Bitsy and referred to Rocket as Christmas, a name that always annoyed her, he wondered if the sparks shooting from her gorgeous cobalt blue eyes might actually cause him harm.

Before he could further rile her, the medic team mucked their way over to her. Shaun stepped out of the way then swung back on Lucky, his favorite horse. His dad rode up with Rocket, although the horse didn't seem any too happy to be caught.

"Rocket, settle down," Brylee said in a firm, commanding tone as she glanced over at him.

The horse calmed a little as the medics asked Brylee questions and two of them freed her foot from the fence.

"I'm fine," she assured them, struggling to rise from her bed of mud. Two cowboys pulled her upright and she gave them both an appreciative smile before turning to take Rocket's reins from Jason.

"Thank you, Mr. Price," she said, placing a hand on Rocket's saddle horn and wincing as she pulled herself into the saddle.

"Let's hear it for a great lady and a great athlete, folks! Miss Brylee Barton and Rocket!" the announcer said.

Cheers and applause followed her as she rode out of the arena. Shaun stayed by the doctor who'd come out to check her. "Is she okay, Doc?"

"I want to take a closer look at her leg, but she refused to go out on a stretcher." The doctor gave him a speculative look. "You know her well?"

Shaun might have known Brylee well six years ago. But the determined woman with a spine made of steel who just left the arena was a complete stranger. "Not really, Doc."

All during the bull riding, Shaun continued glancing in the direction of the medic trailer, wondering if Brylee was there, if she was okay.

The moment the rodeo ended, Jason rode up beside him. "Go see how she's doing. She might need a hand."

"Who?" Shaun asked, trying to appear nonchalant while feigning ignorance.

His dad laughed. "You know who. Don't play dumb with me, Shaun. I perfected that move when I was far younger than you."

Shaun grinned at his father. "Yes, sir." Before anyone could waylay him, he rode over to the medic trailer where one of the barrel racers stood outside beneath a big yellow umbrella.

"Is Brylee okay?" he asked, dismounting and leading his horse over to her. The girl, a beautiful spitfire named Savannah, was one he recognized from the rodeo circuit.

"The doctor is doing X-rays. I think she's hurt more than she's letting on," Savannah said, tipping her head toward the trailer door. "Rocket is not happy about someone other than Brylee attempting to take care of him, so I left him alone. At least for the moment."

Shaun nodded. From experience, he knew Rocket was just a step below a fire-breathing dragon when he was out of sorts. "I'll go check on him and come back."

Savannah released an exasperated sigh. "Brylee insisted on checking him over before I brought her to see the doctor. I think he's fine, just keyed up. Brylee on the other hand… She didn't want to get the medic trailer all dirty. You know what she made me do?"

He had no idea, but a few guesses entered his mind.

"She made me take a hose and spray off the mud that covered her from head to toe. She was shivering so hard, I thought she might crack a tooth when I helped her over here." Savannah sighed in disgust. "That girl is the most hard-headed, tough, big-hearted ninny I've ever met."

Shaun couldn't argue with her. Not from what he'd seen of a woman he once knew every bit as well as he knew himself. "Is Brylee traveling with anyone?"

"Nope. She's totally on her own," Savannah said, then tossed him a grateful smile. "Thanks for checking on Rocket."

Shaun led Lucky through the dispersing competitors who were in a hurry to get in out of the rain and made his way to Rocket. Brylee had left the horse in a stall in the rodeo stable. Coated in mud, Rocket appeared as though he'd blow flames at anyone who looked at him cross-eyed.

"Rocket, my man, it's been a while," Shaun said quietly. He looped Lucky's reins around a nearby post and slowly approached Rocket's stall.

The horse snorted and swished his tail then kicked at the side of the stall.

"Here now. There's no need to get so worked up, Rocket," Shaun said, cautiously opening the stall door and checking to make sure the animal had both feed and water. The mud coating him from his ears to his tail could wait. He gave the horse a thorough study. No open cuts were bleeding, and there was no swelling anywhere that might indicate an injury. Other than a bad temper, Rocket seemed fine.

"I can't believe Brylee is still riding you, old boy," Shaun spoke in a low, smooth tone, one that had calmed many a scared animal and wooed more than a few girls.

The horse stopped switching his tail and one ear perked forward.

Shaun held back a grin as he took a step closer. "Did you miss that last turn, Rocket? Hmm? Did the nasty ol' mud pull your feet right out from under you? I bet that's not how you or Brylee planned on things going." He reached out and lightly touched Rocket on the neck. The horse twitched once, but didn't move away. Instead, it was as though he suddenly remembered Shaun and all the times he'd brushed him down, fed him, or taken him for a warm-up ride.

Rocket dropped his head and bumped against Shaun's chest. "Hey, boy, you do remember me, don't you?"

The horse pushed against him, as though he'd just encountered a long lost friend.

Shaun scratched his mud-covered neck and talked to him a few more minutes, waiting until the horse appeared settled. "You behave yourself until I get back to check on you." He gave Rocket one final scratch then moved out of the stall. He took Lucky's reins in his hand and headed back to the medic trailer.

He arrived just as the doctor opened the door and looked around to see who was waiting for news about Brylee. When he saw Shaun, he waggled a hand at him, motioning him closer. Apparently Savannah got tired of standing in the rain or had something else she needed to do, because she was gone.

"Is she okay, Doc?" Shaun asked as he moved near the door.

"No. Her leg's broken. I knew we should have carried her out on the stretcher."

"From what I know, she's plenty stubborn," Shaun said. That might be the understatement of the year. Once Brylee set her mind on something, it might as well be cast in stone then encased in cement.

Shaun released a long breath. "I suppose she walked all the way over here from the barn on that broken leg?"

The doctor nodded, clearly unhappy. "She sure did. I'd be shocked by it, but after doctoring cowboys a long time, I already know they are as mule-headed as they come. That applies to cowgirls, too." The doctor released a long-suffering sigh. "As far as breaks go, it could have been much worse. It's clean, small, and easy to treat. She has a stable tibia fracture."

Shaun gave the doctor a questioning look. "Which means?"

"She has a fracture in her shin bone. Fortunately, the ends are lined up together. That's what makes it a stable fracture." The doctor formed two fists then fit the backs of his knuckles together to illustrate what he meant.

Shaun nodded. "I had one of those in high school."

"That doesn't surprise me at all." The doctor grinned then turned serious again. "Brylee's leg is really starting to swell. It would be ideal for her to stay off it and let that swelling go down for about three to five days. My recommendation is for her to get a cast on it for at least two weeks. After that, she can most likely move to a brace. It allows more movement of the knee and ankle while still protecting the break. We've found that patients who wear a cast the whole time have problems with stiffness later, so the brace is a good alternative. Brylee has assured me she has no plans to drop out of competition, but agreed to stay off her feet, at least for now. Until that leg is completely healed, though, no driving for her. At all."

"So what can we do to help her?" Shaun asked, wondering if Brylee would even speak to him let alone allow him to offer her a hand.

"Unless she has someone here she didn't mention who can wait on her hand and foot for the next few days and drive her where she needs to go for the next six weeks, she could definitely use some help," the doctor said.

"Okay. I'll see what I can find out. Will you keep her here until I get back?"

The doctor nodded. "I gave her some pain medication that knocked her out. She's going to be groggy even if she does wake up anytime soon."

"That's good, Doc." Shaun gave the man a grin, mounted Lucky, and then rode through the rain to where Rockin' K employees worked to load the stock into trailers. Since this rodeo was only an hour away from the Rockin' K Ranch where they kept all the stock, they'd head out as soon as the last truck was loaded.

"How's Brylee?" Jason asked as he rode up to Shaun after chasing a load of bulls into a truck.

"Broken leg. She's gonna need some help," Shaun said, leaning down to open a gate and riding inside a pen.

Jason's eyebrows shot upward, nearly disappearing beneath the brim of his hat. "You have someone in mind?"

Shaun gave him a long look. "Yeah, I do. And no, it isn't me."

Jason laughed. "Okay, then. I'll leave you to your plans."

He rode to the back of the pen to herd steers toward the truck while Shaun rode over to his boss, the manager of the Rockin' K Rodeo Company. Kash Kressley and his wife Celia had been friends of Shaun's long before he started working for them as a pickup man.

"Hey, Shaun. Your dad said you went to check on Brylee Barton. Is she okay?" Kash asked as he kept an eye on the bucking horses being loaded into a trailer, glanced at paperwork, and shrugged deeper into the rain slicker he wore.

"She broke her leg and needs somewhere to rest for a few days until they can put a cast on it. I know it's a lot to ask, but she's traveling alone. Do you think she could hang out at your place and have Barb or your dad take her to get the cast put on?"

Kash nodded. "I don't have a problem with that at all." His brow wrinkled into a frown. "You and Brylee used to be quite an item back in the day. Are you two…?"

Shaun raised a hand to stop him. "No! There is nothing going on. I haven't seen her in years or spoken to her, but she's by herself with no one to help her. The doctor said she won't even be able to drive for at least six weeks. Somehow, she'll need to get her rig home. And then there's her horse."

"Man, that Rocket is a great animal. If she ever decides to sell him, I'd sure be interested," Kash grinned at him.

A crooked smile kicked up the right corner of Shaun's mouth. "Get in line. You aren't the first, or the last, to be a member of Rocket's fan club."

"But you seem to be the number one fan of Brylee's," Kash teased. At Shaun's dark scowl, he sobered. "Seriously, what do you need us to do?"

"Just give her a place to stay for the next week. If it's okay with you, I'll drive her rig back to the ranch so she won't be fussing about getting it or worrying about Rocket. Maybe she can figure out a plan from there. The doctor said she's adamant about continuing to compete."

Kash shook his head. "That doesn't surprise me. She's what, third or fourth in the rankings right now?"

Shaun feigned indifference, even though he'd made a point to see where she ranked when he first noticed she was competing again. For someone who'd been out of the game for so long, she was making one remarkable comeback.

If Brylee was anything like he remembered, she'd be eating herself up with worry over this little setback.

Why he wanted to help her, why he cared, wasn't something he cared to examine. He was a guy who always tried to lend a hand when it was needed and that seemed like a good enough reason to do what he could to help Brylee. He wondered if her folks had come to watch her, but then decided this was probably far enough away they'd most likely stayed home in Walla Walla.

"Let's get this last bunch of horses loaded then we can head out. I'd have Celia drive Brylee, but she headed home right after the rodeo ended." Kash motioned to a group of horses in the next pen over. Shaun helped load them then took Lucky back to the trailer his dad would drive to the Rockin' K.

"So what's the plan, son?" Jason asked as he stepped out of the trailer and Shaun led Lucky inside.

"Kash is going to let her stay at his place for a week. Brylee will have to get a cast on in a few days. It just seems like the easiest solution to the problem of her being here alone. I'll drive her rig and take Rocket to the ranch."

Jason gave him a questioning look as they led in the last horse then closed the trailer gate. "And you're doing all this because...?"

"Because it's the right thing to do." Shaun didn't like the way his dad was staring at him or what he was implying. "I already told you that Brylee and I are history. Even if I wanted to resurrect a relationship with her, and that is a colossal if, it's so long dead and buried the bones have turned to dust."

"Whatever you say, son," Jason grinned at him

SHANNA HATFIELD

then opened the door to the truck. "I'll see you back at the ranch."

"Okay, Dad. Drive carefully in this rain."

"You, too. I'm hoping it stops soon. Looks like it's starting to ease up a little." Jason glanced at the sky then climbed into the truck. "Be nice to that girl, son."

Shaun ignored his dad and headed back toward the medic trailer.

Savannah walked up to it from the opposite direction and smiled at him. "The doctor said you were going to find somewhere for Brylee to stay for a few days until she gets her cast. Are you good with that? I could stay with her until then, if needed."

"Kash and Celia Kressley have a room for her at their ranch and it's not too far away. I'll make sure she's taken care of." Shaun smiled at the beautiful woman. Under other circumstances, he might have asked her out, or at least flirted with her. Now, he wasn't in the mood. In fact, he just wanted to see Brylee and make sure she was okay.

Savannah smiled at him. "Brylee has my number. Tell her to call me if she needs anything. I'm not heading out until tomorrow morning."

"Thanks, Savannah. I'm sure I'll see you around at another rodeo."

She gave him a coy laugh and turned to walk away, tossing her black hair over her shoulder in a move that looked practiced and perfected. "I'll count on it, Shaun."

He tapped once on the trailer door then opened it and stuck his head inside. The doctor glanced up from where he wrote something on a notepad.

"How's she doing?" Shaun asked, hesitant to step in and get mud all over the inside of the trailer.

"Still resting" the doctor said. "Did you make arrangements for her?"

"Yep. Kash Kressley has room for her at his place. His housekeeper can keep an eye on her and take her to get the cast on in a few days."

"Perfect. Who's going to drive her there?"

Shaun gave the man a sheepish look. "I guess that'll be me."

The doctor raised a questioning eyebrow, but merely tore a piece of paper off the pad and handed it to Shaun along with second sheet of paper. "That's a prescription for pain medication. The other paper is detailed instructions of what she needs to do going forward. If you bring her rig around here, I'll help settle her in it so you can get on the road."

"I need to load her horse first. Do you have her keys?"

The doctor disappeared and returned with a set of keys. "She said it's a dark blue pickup with a silver trailer parked at the end of the row."

"Okay. I'll be back in a minute." Shaun went back to the stalls and retrieved Rocket, leading him out into the cool evening air. At least the rain had stopped.

He had no problem finding Brylee's rig. It was the same one she'd driven six years ago. He loaded Rocket without incident. The horse seemed to know it was time to go as he settled into the trailer. The poor critter needed a bath even worse than he did, but that would have to wait until later.

Shaun took off the rain slicker he'd pulled on earlier, turned it inside out, and covered the driver's seat before he climbed in the pickup. He drove close to the medic's trailer and left the pickup running as he ran around to the passenger side and looked for something to drape over the seat, assuming Brylee would still be covered in mud. He grabbed a fleece blanket from behind the seat and used it to cover the leather seat then hurried over to the trailer and tapped on the door.

"She's awake and not happy when I told her who was coming to get her. In fact, she tried to walk out of here until I threatened to have her transported to the hospital." The doctor tipped his head to where Brylee rested on a long bench with her foot elevated.

"I'll say it again so you both are clear on the fact that she absolutely must stay off that foot for at least seventy-two hours. If the swelling is down then, she needs to go in and get a cast on it. In the meantime, she should have ice on it for twenty minutes several times a day. Understood?"

"Yes, sir," Shaun said, taking the crutches the doctor held and carrying them outside. He slid them behind the seat then returned and stood over Brylee, ignoring the way her entire body stiffened at his presence. "I know you'd rather have the devil himself help you, but it looks like you're stuck with me, Bitsy. Let's make the best of it, shall we?"

The frost-glazed glare she tossed at him would have left most men frostbitten, but Shaun merely smiled. He bent down, scooping her into his arms before she could protest.

The doctor smiled as she spluttered indignantly, insisting he put her down and let her use the crutches as he carried her outside.

Gently, Shaun set her on the passenger seat, wishing he'd minded his own business. Holding her close stirred up emotions and longings along with a truckload of hopes and dreams he'd long ago buried and didn't want released from their cold, cobweb-shrouded tomb. How could he have forgotten how well she fit in his arms? How much he liked her there? Brylee was the one he never forgot and couldn't get out of his head or heart.

Regardless, it would be an ice-coated, below-zero day during the midst of a summer heat wave in the desert before he'd admit it to anyone. Especially the woman who looked like she'd shoot him stone cold dead if she had a gun in her hand.

"Here's a pillow to cushion her foot," the doctor said, lifting Brylee's leg and setting it on the pillow he tucked against the dashboard. "Remember, absolutely no walking on that until you've been to see a doctor about the cast. Understood?"

Brylee smiled at the doctor and nodded. "Understood. Thank you so much, sir, for taking good care of me. I greatly appreciate it."

Shaun swore frozen sticks of butter would have melted at the warm sweetness of her tone. She gave the doctor another charming smile as the man offered her an encouraging nod and shut the door.

The doctor slapped Shaun on the back. "Good luck with that one," he guffawed, far too gleefully for Shaun's liking.

"Gee, thanks, Doc," Shaun said, his voice dripping with sarcasm. He shook the doctor's hand then hurried around to slide behind the wheel.

When he started the pickup and looked over at Brylee, she sat with one hand clenching the strap of her seatbelt and the other gripping the handle above the door.

"You need something before we go?" he asked, putting the truck in gear.

"I'm fine."

He pulled away from the medic trailer and turned on the windshield wipers since it had started to rain again. "You don't seem fine. Are you sure something isn't bothering you."

"Nothing is bothering me," she ground out, maintaining her death grip with her eyes squeezed shut.

"Sure seems like something." Shaun knew her well enough to know she was ten different kinds of mad. The exact reasons why he had yet to decipher. He wasn't sure if depending on him for a ride, or at missing out on a win, had upset her the most. If Rocket hadn't gone for a skid in the mud, she would have easily captured first place. But that was rodeo life. One day, you were on top, the next you were literally stuck in the mud.

However, considering her polite and courteous manner with the doctor, he had to assume she hadn't moved past her vow to hate him for the rest of his life.

So much for good deeds going unpunished.

His stomach grumbled with hunger. Shaun was

starving and realized he hadn't eaten anything since breakfast. He saw a drive-through just ahead and turned into the parking lot. "Mind if I grab something to eat?"

"Go ahead," she said. Her clipped tone hinted at her underlying fury.

"Want anything?"

She opened her left eye and glared at him. He took that as a no and parked the truck, but left it running as he jogged inside and placed an order to go.

In less than five minutes, he was back in the pickup. He handed her a cup of hot chocolate. She took it with a nod of thanks, but didn't say a word as he peeled the wrapper back on a big, juicy burger and took a bite before pulling back out on the road.

"Want a bite?" he asked, holding the half-eaten burger toward her. "It's greasy goodness between two semi-stale buns."

Her nose wrinkled up on the end and she flapped a dismissive hand at him. "Whatever."

He finished the burger then dug into the paper bag for a handful of fries. "Sure you don't want some?"

"That's okay."

Shaun assumed her annoyed tone meant she could have been dying of hunger but wouldn't accept a single morsel from him.

"Look, Brylee, I'm just trying to help out, you know. Help an old friend in a moment of need." Shaun glanced at her again. The horrified yet livid look on her face made it clear that was the wrong thing to say.

"Wow!" The way she said that one word made him think he was one step away from her reaching behind the seat for a crutch and bludgeoning him with it.

He blew out a long breath and kept his thoughts to himself for the remainder of the trip. Brylee kept her eyes shut, but did intermittently take small sips from the hot chocolate.

Forty-five minutes later, he pulled up in front of the big Kressley ranch house.

Brylee looked at it with interest as Shaun got out and jogged around the pickup. She opened her door and would have stepped down, but he gave her a warning scowl. Before she could protest, he took her in his arms and carried her down the front walk and up the porch steps.

She remained silent, but she clamped her lips together so tightly, he wondered if she'd ever pry them open again. A memory of just how soft those lips had been beneath his, of how delicious they'd tasted, made him take a stumbling step as he neared the door.

Kash yanked it open before he could knock and Celia hurried toward them down the hall.

"I'm so sorry about your accident, Brylee. Kash said you need a place to rest for a few days." Celia beckoned them inside. "We've got plenty of room and Barb will love having someone to fuss over."

"Barb?" Brylee asked as Celia motioned Shaun to follow her up the stairs.

"Our housekeeper," Kash said, walking behind Shaun. "There's nothing she likes more than being able to pamper someone. It'll make her day to find you here in the morning."

"I really do hate to be a bother. I can call my mom to come get me. We'd have to leave her rig or mine here, though, until we can get them both home."

"Nonsense," Celia said, flicking on the light in a guest room. "You shouldn't be traveling with your injury and we don't mind having you here at all. In fact, Kash and I are leaving the day after tomorrow along with the crew for another rodeo, but Barb and Kash's dad will be here. One of them will make sure you get to a doctor for your cast."

"I, um... I..." Brylee's voice cracked and tears filled her gorgeous blue eyes.

Shaun had never been able to handle her tears. Not when each salty drop felt like it clawed away pieces of his heart. He wanted to comfort her, assure her everything would be fine. Instead, he kept silent.

"Hey, don't worry about a thing. After a hot shower you can sleep as long as you like," Celia said, walking across the room and turning on the light in an adjoining bathroom.

Brylee nodded as Shaun carried her into the bathroom.

"Need any help in here?" he asked, waggling his eyebrows suggestively, knowing it would put a stop to Brylee's tears and draw her furious indignation to the surface.

Celia laughed and pointed to the door. "Out! I can take things from here."

Brylee gave him such a dark, hate-filled look, Shaun rubbed his chest to make sure something barbed and wicked hadn't impaled him.

"I'm going, but if you need help, just holler," he said, backing toward the door.

Kash thumped him on the back and the two of them went down the stairs to the kitchen. "Want a piece of cake?" Kash asked as they walked into the large room. "Barb made it this morning."

"Sure," Shaun said. He washed up at the sink then took the glasses of milk Kash poured to the table while his boss cut slices of cake.

When they were both seated, Kash gave him a studying look. "What are you doing with that girl?" Kash asked as they forked bites of the rich, chocolate cake.

"Helping her, I think." Shaun took a bite of cake so he wouldn't have to say more.

"She looked like she wanted to rip your head off then use it for a rousing game of kick ball."

Shaun grinned. "Yeah, she did."

"What's going on with you two?" Kash tossed him a curious glance. "I know you dated at one time, but then you broke up all of a sudden. What went wrong?"

He shrugged. "Just realized we weren't meant to be together, I guess." Shaun had no intention of getting into the nitty-gritty details of what he viewed as the biggest mistake of his life with his current employer.

Kash changed the subject, talking about the stock they'd load for the next rodeo and what time he wanted to have the trucks pull out on Tuesday morning.

Celia breezed into the kitchen and gave Shaun

a disgusted look. "What did you say to that poor girl to get her so upset?"

"Nothing, Seal. Honest." Shaun held up his hands in a gesture of innocence. "She barely spoke to me after we left the medic trailer."

She narrowed her gaze and plopped down at the table. "Well, what did she say?"

Shaun leaned back and recalled their limited conversation once they got on the road. "I tried talking to her, asking her questions. All I got was a string of one or two word answers."

"And those were?" Celia asked.

"Fine, nothing, go ahead, whatever, that's okay." He tried to think if he'd missed any of Brylee's brief comments. "Oh, and it ended with a wow."

Celia looked at Kash and the two of them smiled.

"You are in deep, deep trouble, my friend," Kash said, forking another bite of cake.

"What did I do? What does all that mean, anyway?" Shaun asked, looking from Kash to Celia.

"It means she thinks you are the stupidest man to ever live." Celia reached across the table and patted Shaun on the arm, as though he was as dumb as Brylee's responses indicated. "Don't take it personally, she's medicated and exhausted."

"It sure seems personal, considering she acted all cuddly to the doc." Shaun stabbed his fork into his cake, stunned by his sudden cavedweller desire to pop the doctor in the nose, and for no reason other than the fact Brylee had smiled at the man.

"Maybe it would be best to give her a little time

to get her bearings," Celia suggested. The glance she tossed at Kash didn't escape Shaun's notice, although he didn't really want to know what it meant.

He huffed with irritation. "I have no problem leaving that prickly, opinionated, stubborn woman alone."

Kash coughed to hide a chuckle. "I can see that you don't. Not one bit."

Chapter Three

Brylee awakened all at once, as though she'd fallen out of her dreams and slammed to the floor. Startled, she popped open her eyes and looked around a room she didn't recognize.

Sunlight filtered in through sheer curtains peeking from behind pale yellow drapes that were pulled back and fastened with ivory cords. Based on the bright light outside the window, the morning had to be more than half gone.

Her gaze shifted from the window to the rest of the room. Soft yellow paint and white furniture gave the room a cheery, welcoming feel. A white and cream striped duvet covered the bed. An overstuffed white chair and matching ottoman sat in a corner of the room, next to a small shelf of books.

The prints on the walls featured western landscapes. Near a door she thought opened into a bathroom, a large white-washed metal star hung on the wall.

An attempt to stretch as she visually perused the room made her swallow a cry of pain. Memories of her accident the previous evening and ending up at the Kressley home came back to her.

So did the fact that Shaun Price came to her rescue. Of all the hundreds of men at the rodeo, why did her hero have to be the one man she loathed entirely? Years ago, she'd vowed to hate him until she drew her last breath.

If the tumultuous emotions swirling through her were any indication, she might just make good on that promise.

Yesterday, she'd wished the ground would open and swallow her whole instead of forcing her to face Shaun. Today, she was grateful to be alive and mostly unharmed.

A broken leg was not going to keep her from competing. She'd take a week off, get her leg in a cast, and be back on the road. If she could keep her accident from hitting the gossip feed, no one would even know she was injured.

The doctor was sworn to secrecy, she'd already texted Savannah to keep things quiet, and she knew no one at the Rockin' K Ranch would spill the beans. At least she thought they could all be trusted. Well, everyone with the exception of Shaun. He'd run her trust and her heart through the grinder, spitting out little splintered pieces that would never, ever heal.

But that was long ago. She held no desire to dredge up wounds from the past when she had a broken leg to deal with and a horse that no doubt needed some attention.

Slowly sitting up, Brylee assessed her aches and pains. Her shoulder throbbed from a bruise she'd noticed last night when she took a shower. Her elbow was sore, but not horribly so. Her back hurt a little, but getting up and moving would help that. Then there was her leg. The doctor had wrapped it in a temporary splint until the swelling went down. In fact, she was probably long overdue for an ice pack.

The first thing she needed was clothes, the second her crutches. She glanced around the room and noticed crutches leaning against a chair on the other side of the nightstand. Her bag sat on a small wooden bench by the bathroom door.

Celia had been kind enough last night to let Brylee borrow a set of pajamas, but she looked forward to getting into her own clothes.

She tossed back the covers and reached out, snagging the crutches. She'd never used them before, but if it was either figure out how to hobble on one foot or stay in bed, she'd master hobbling as quickly as possible.

With a crutch in each hand, she used them to leverage herself out of bed onto her good leg, careful to keep her injured one from touching the floor.

"Piece of cake," she muttered. She took a few cautious steps forward to her bag, unzipped it, and took her toiletry bag into the bathroom. After brushing her teeth, washing her face, and applying a little mascara, she braided her long hair and fastened the end with an elastic band. The mud-coated clothes she'd worn last night had disappeared and all trace of the disarray she'd created in Celia's lovely guest bathroom was gone. She wondered if Celia or the housekeeper had tiptoed in while she slept and cleaned away the mud and dirt.

She'd hated to bring such a mess into the Kressley home last night. But they were all tracking in mud, too. That fact made her feel marginally better.

As she dug through her bag for something she could wear over her cast, she took out a tank top and finally unearthed a pair of running shorts. She tossed the clothes on the bed and sat down to get dressed. When she finished, she reached for her purse in the chair by the nightstand, grateful for whoever had brought her things up to the room.

She took out her phone and sent her mother a text that all was well. The last thing she needed was for her mom to worry about her being injured. She hoped to put off mentioning her broken leg until after she was back at one hundred percent. Since she'd be heading home in a month for the local rodeos, it might be challenging to keep the injury completely hidden. By then, though, she should be nearly healed. At least she hoped she would.

The small matter of how she would get herself home, or to the next rodeo for that matter, presented a bit of a roadblock, but she'd worry about that later. For now, she needed to go check on Rocket. He'd been upset last night. Normally, she would have spent all the time needed to clean him up and calm him down. However, Savannah's relentless insistence Brylee go see the doctor had forced her to leave Rocket sooner than she liked. Savannah promised to stow her gear, but they both knew Rocket wouldn't let her brush him down or clean off the mud.

The poor boy was probably covered in filth from the tips of his ears to the end of his tail. The thought that she couldn't do anything to help him in her current state never even crossed her mind.

She tucked her phone into the pocket of her shorts, took a deep breath, and situated the crutches beneath her arms. It took a bit of maneuvering, but she got the bedroom door open and moved into the wide hall. She could see stairs to her right and headed toward them. She almost lost her balance on the second step and decided she'd probably break her neck at that rate.

Brylee took both crutches in her left hand, clutched the banister with her right, and started hopping down the stairs on her left leg. Halfway down, she felt someone watching her. She lifted her gaze from her carefully-placed foot to an older man who bore a strong resemblance to Kash Kressley.

"Good lands, darlin'. Let me help you," the man said, hustling up the steps. Before Brylee could do more than blink, he had her crutches in one hand and his other braced around her back. "Just lean on me like I was a big ol' crutch."

"Thank you, sir," Brylee smiled at him. "You must be Kash's father."

The man grinned and nodded. "That's right. Frank Kressley at your service. And you're Brylee Barton, barrel racer extraordinaire."

She laughed. "More like barrel racer,

incapacitated. It's nice to meet you, Mr. Kressley. Thank you for allowing me to stay here a few days. I hope I'm not an imposition to anyone."

Frank smiled and helped her down the last two steps. "Not at all, honey. And please, call me Frank. Kash and Celia often have company and I like that just fine. Now that I'm semi-retired, it can get too quiet and lonesome around here with just me and Barb."

"Barb?" Brylee asked as she steadied herself when they reached the ground floor. She took the crutches from Frank and tucked them beneath her arms.

"Our housekeeper and cook. She's been with our family for a long time and honestly, she's been more like a mother to my boys than anyone."

Brylee nodded. "How is Ransom doing? Did I hear he got married?"

"That's right. He moved to Portland to work for an arena football team and fell in love with a sweet friend of Celia's." He leaned closer and dropped his voice to a whisper. "Don't tell anyone, but they just phoned yesterday to let me know I'm gonna be a grandpa right after Christmas."

"Oh, that's wonderful news, Frank. Congratulations!" Brylee smiled and followed the older man as he led her past a big living room. Open beams and a tall rock fireplace with a flat screen television mounted above the mantel gave the room an expansive yet rustic feel. Bookcases flanked the fireplace and a patio door opened to the side yard. Windows on each side of the door allowed plenty of bright morning sunlight to spill inside. Massive leather couches, accent tables made of reclaimed barnwood, and lamps fashioned of rope completed the furnishings.

"That's the gathering room. Feel free to make yourself at home there. Kash and Celia have a good collection of movies as well as books." Frank pointed to the room then moved down the hall.

Brylee glanced into a bathroom with barnwood walls and a slate floor. It would have seemed entirely masculine, but Celia had a vase of fresh flowers on the counter and a beautiful framed photograph of a field of wildflowers hanging on the wall across from the sink.

Slowly making her way behind Frank, Brylee passed the ranch office. A bank of windows provided an amazing view of a pasture where bulls grazed on lush grass. A tall leather chair and two side chairs sat on either side of a large desk. The wall to the left of the desk was covered in photographs that bore testament to Kressley family history.

Brylee loved old photographs and hoped she'd have the chance to study those hanging on the office wall before she left.

"That's the office. I still do a lot of the bookwork, so if you can't find me, that's a good place to look." Frank waved a hand inside the room.

He continued down the hall then stepped aside for her to precede him into a light, airy kitchen. Beams of knotty pine ran across the ceiling while windows flanking a deep double sink let in plenty of light.

An older woman wearing a bright pink polka-dotted apron turned from the sink with a smile. "You must be Brylee. I'm Barb. If you need anything while you're here, honey, just say the word. Welcome to the Rockin' K." The woman wiped her hands on her apron then crossed the room and gave Brylee a warm hug.

Up until that moment, Brylee hadn't realized how much she needed a hug. Unbidden, her thoughts drifted to the feel of being held in Shaun's arms last night as he carried her to the pickup and then into the house and up the stairs. All too well, she recalled how those arms felt around her, how much she enjoyed being held close to his heart. Even all these years later, she could close her eyes and summon the walk-in-the-winter-woods masculine scent of him mingled with the aroma of horses and leather. And he smelled exactly the same last night.

She was so, so close to achieving her goals. The last thing she needed was a distraction like Shaun messing with her head. A broken leg was bad enough, but it was something she could handle. The prods and pricks to her shattered heart that came with the mere sight of Shaun was something else altogether.

Despite how much she loathed the man, he had been kind to her last night and incredibly helpful. If he hadn't taken control of the situation, she had no idea what she would have done. Most likely, she'd have spent the night listening to Savannah tell her she needed to call her mother and go home to rest.

That was definitely not going to happen. No more so than she'd allow Shaun Price to turn her head a second time. He'd burned that bridge of opportunity so completely, not even a speck of ash was left from their previous relationship.

Aware that Barb and Frank were both looking at her, Brylee yanked her thoughts in line and smiled at the housekeeper. "It's lovely to meet you, Barb. Thank you so much for the hospitality and making me feel so welcome."

"My pleasure, honey. Now, I'm sure you must be starving. Would you like a big breakfast or just something to tide you over until lunch?"

"Just a little something to eat now would be fine." Brylee glanced at the clock and saw it was almost ten. The throbbing in her leg suggested it was past time for both an ice pack and a pain pill, but she couldn't remember if the doctor had given her any extra medication.

"You sit down at the table, and I'll bring you something along with ice for your leg. Shaun said the doctor ordered you to stay off it for the next few days and to ice it every little bit. He's going to pick up your prescription on the way home from church."

"Church?" Brylee asked as she took a seat at a big square table that sat off to the side in front of another set of windows. From her chair, she could see a hulking red barn and a pasture with horses in the distance.

"Yep. Kash, Celia, Jason and Shaun, and some of the others headed to church in Twin Falls," Barb said, pouring Brylee a glass of milk and bringing her a plate with a raspberry muffin and a little cup of fresh fruit.

Brylee glanced from Barb to Frank. "I'm so sorry. You both must have missed going because of me."

"Don't give it a thought, honey," Frank said, pouring a glass of iced tea and taking a seat across from her at the table. "Kash called the vet to come out to check on one of the bulls, and I volunteered to stay behind so he and Celia could go to church together."

"Is the bull okay?" Brylee asked as she broke open the muffin, amazed by the moist texture. Maybe Barb would be willing to share the recipe.

"He's fine. Just got into a little shoving match last night while they were unloading. Other than a few scratches, he's dandy." Frank took a gulp of his tea then smiled at her. "We had the vet look at your horse while he was here, just to make sure Rocket was fine. The vet said he's in great shape."

Brylee sighed in relief. She'd been worried about Rocket, concerned he might have an injury she hadn't immediately spotted. "That's good news. Please, let me know what I owe you for the vet bill."

"Don't worry about it. He was out here for the bull anyway."

"Mr. Kressley..." At his frown, she smiled. "Frank, I really do feel like I'm taking advantage of you all. Please, let me at least pay the vet bill."

Frank took another long gulp of his tea then shot her a grin. "We'll talk about it later. After you finish your breakfast, if you want, I'll take you out to see Rocket. Then I think you probably better rest up that leg."

"Thank you. That would be great." Brylee offered a silent prayer of thanks not only for the meal, but also for the kind people who'd taken her into their home.

Frank smiled at her. "If you're anything like my bunch, you're probably far more worried about your horse than your leg."

Brylee gave the older man a guilty grin. "Yes, sir, I guess I am."

Barb shook a spoon at them both. "Don't you encourage that girl, Frank. I think she should stay on the couch with her leg up all day, but I've been around you and Kash enough, and even Celia, to know better than to suggest it."

"That you have, Barb." Frank winked at Brylee and took the half of muffin she held out to him. She didn't want to eat too much and miss out on whatever fantastic thing Barb was making for lunch. The smell of roasting meat and yeasty bread filled the kitchen with a tantalizing scent.

After she ate her breakfast, Brylee followed Frank out the back door and waited while he drove a utility task vehicle up to the end of the back walk. He hopped out of the UTV that looked like a beefed up big-brother to a golf cart and hurried her direction. He grabbed a cushion off a chair near the door then stayed close by as she made her way down the steps and out to the vehicle.

"I've seen these UTVs but never ridden in one," she said, sliding onto the seat.

Frank took her crutches and set them in the back, then placed the cushion so she could rest her leg on it, propped against the dashboard. "I got this one last fall. We've got four-wheelers, but this way, I can haul a little more stuff on it when I need to buzz around doing chores. If I'm careful, I can even get two small bales of hay in the back." Frank sat down behind the wheel and started the machine.

He pulled away from the house and answered her questions about the ranch. She knew the Kressley family owned the rodeo stock company, but she had no idea they had so many head of stock or such a big ranch near the Idaho and Nevada border.

Impressed, she loved the rugged beauty of the landscape as Frank drove her past the barn and over to a set of small pens. Rocket was in one by himself, but a few mares were in an adjacent pen. They appeared to be getting along well if the way they stayed close to the panel separating them presented an accurate indication.

"Looks like he's charming the girls," Frank teased as he turned around so Brylee was parked close to the pen.

"Rocket is not shy," she said with a laugh. "He loves attention of all kinds, even if he doesn't like just anyone to touch him." Brylee accepted the crutches Frank handed to her and stood.

Rocket trotted over to the fence and stretched his neck out as he nickered. His ears moved forward, but he looked relaxed.

"Hey, buddy. How are you doing?" Brylee asked, balancing on one crutch so she could reach out and rub a hand over Rocket's face. He nuzzled against her, almost knocking her over. Thankfully, Frank was beside her and kept her steady.

She smiled at the older man in thanks as she continued to pet Rocket. Someone had given him a bath and brushed him down. His coat shone in the sunshine and his mane looked better than her hair. "Did you get a bath, Rocket? Hmm? Did someone make you all pretty again?"

The horse blew air on her, as though he tried to tell her exactly what happened.

"Shaun took care of him this morning. Rocket wasn't too keen on anyone else getting close to him, but he seems to like Shaun."

"Traitor," Brylee whispered as she leaned her head against Rocket's.

"What was that?" Frank asked.

"Oh, nothing. It was nice of Shaun to do that. I suppose I should clean my tack, too."

"Already taken care of." Frank gave her a long look. "Shaun said if you asked to tell you it's all stored in your trailer just like you like it, whatever that means."

Brylee nodded, unable to speak around the sudden lump in her throat. Shaun was the last person she expected to come to her rescue, take care of her horse, and clean her tack. But he had. At the very least, she owed him a heartfelt thank you for what he'd done. Even if she still despised him, he deserved that much. Then she could go back to pretending he didn't exist.

Somehow, she'd obliterate the feel of his hard muscles beneath her hands as he carried her upstairs from her memory, along with the light that glowed in his gray-blue eyes. His eyes were one of the first things she'd noticed about him when they'd met years ago. They held such warmth and humor, and openness. It wasn't like Shaun to pretend to be something he wasn't. He just happened to be a good-looking, muscled, happy-go-lucky cowboy who destroyed her heart one December day when she was too young and stupid to know better than to get involved with him.

A few years ago, she'd been watching television with her mom and little brother when a commercial came on for a new western clothing company. Without a doubt, she knew one of the guys modeling in the ad was Shaun, even when the commercial never showed his face. No one had a caboose that looked quite like his. It annoyed her then that she'd so easily picked him out of the group just by the way his jeans fit.

Not that she actively searched for the details, but she did discover he'd signed on as a model with the Lasso Eight brand. She'd just seen an ad in a western magazine last month with him and Chase Jarrett modeling shirts in an advertisement for the company.

Even though they were both fully clothed, she couldn't help but assume women all over the country were drooling over Shaun and the hunky bull rider. She was surprised Chase's wife had agreed to allow him to continue modeling after they wed, but then again, the photos for the ad were probably taken long before the advertisement appeared.

Brylee had met Jessie Jarrett a few times at rodeos and liked the quiet, soft-spoken woman. She was happy to see Chase so head-over-heels in love with his wife.

He and Cooper James were two people she never expected to marry and settle down. Yet, they both seemed deliriously happy. Paige James and Jessie appeared to spend quite a bit of time traveling with their husbands. Maybe that was the secret to a successful rodeo marriage, sticking together.

Brylee always wondered how couples managed when the rodeo athlete was gone all the time and left a family behind. She knew when her parents first wed, her dad spent a lot of time on the road as a team roper. But when Brylee came along, he hung up his rope and settled into life on the ranch her great-great-great grandparents had started back in the 1800s.

Thoughts of the ranch and her reasons for returning to barrel racing drew her thoughts back to the present. Nothing was going to stand in her way of making it to the finals in December. Not a broken leg and most especially not the man who broke her heart.

Brylee dug into the pocket of her shorts and pulled out the handful of baby carrots Barb had given her before she left the house.

Rocket eagerly nibbled them off her palm. When he finished, she kissed his nose and smiled at Frank. "Thank you so much for bringing me out to check on him. I feel much better about things knowing he's fine."

Frank nodded and helped her back into the UTV. "I figured as much. If it was me, I would've wanted to check on him before I could settle down and let Barb fuss over me while I pretended I didn't

SHANNA HATFIELD

like it."

Brylee grinned at him as they headed back toward the house. "Spoken like a true cowboy."

A snort broke out of Frank. They returned to the house and were making their way down the front walk when three vehicles drove in. Two of them kept going, although people waved from the open windows as they headed for the bunkhouse and trailers parked past the barn. The third vehicle pulled around the house into the garage.

"That'll be the kids, home from church. Let's go on in and get washed up for lunch. Barb made pot roast and that's my favorite." Frank held open the front door as Brylee made her way up the wide porch steps.

Cool air circled around her in a welcoming embrace as she moved inside. She hadn't realized how hot it was outside until that moment. Then again, she'd been so focused on seeing Rocket, she hadn't paid attention to much else.

"Whew. It's gonna be a scorcher today," Frank said as he tossed his hat on a rack by the door then motioned for Brylee to lead the way down the hall. "Go on and get washed up then come to the kitchen. You'll find we're informal around here."

Brylee washed her hands and splashed her face then made her way to the kitchen where Kash set the table. Celia poured iced tea in glasses. Frank carried a bowl of mashed potatoes to the table. It didn't escape her notice Kash set the table for eight. She wondered who else would join them, but hoped it wouldn't be Shaun.

Her hopes fell like a deflated balloon when

someone tapped at the back door and then three men strolled inside. Shaun and his father were there with a man she recognized as one of the bullfighters she'd seen at several rodeos.

"Hey, Brylee, sorry about your wreck last night. How are you doing today?" the bullfighter asked as he stepped around Shaun and made his way over to where she leaned on her crutches just inside the doorway.

"I'm doing okay, Billy. Thanks for asking." She gave him a friendly smile and took a step forward. In spite of how much it galled her to be civil to Shaun, she turned to him and his father and offered them a polite nod.

"Got your drugs," Shaun said, taking a pill bottle from the pocket of his shirt. "Doc said you should take one pill two to four times a day with your meal."

Brylee took the bottle from him and slipped it in her pocket. She'd been in need of relief from the pain ever since she got out of bed, but she wouldn't admit it. "Thank you. Let me know what I owe you."

Shaun raised an eyebrow then turned away from her and walked over to where Barb carved a roast. "How's my best girl today?"

Barb blushed like she was a schoolgirl and gave him an indulgent look. "If you're talking about me, then I'm just fine."

Jason moved close to Brylee and placed a gentle hand on her shoulder. "It's good to see you up and around, Brylee. If you need anything, be sure to let us know."

"Thank you, Mr. Price."

He grinned and Brylee could see exactly where Shaun inherited his charm. "I thought you'd agreed to call me Jason. Mr. Price is my dad and I refuse to feel that old yet."

Brylee smiled. "Jason it is."

She made her way to the table and found herself seated between Frank and Jason, which was fine with her. Shaun sat by Barb and Kash.

Brylee knew she needed to thank Shaun for all he'd done to help her, but she'd rather do that without an audience present.

As soon as everyone finished eating, Celia helped Barb with the dishes while Frank and Jason went to the media room to see what they could find to watch on television. Billy claimed he needed a nap and Kash said he wanted to check on his injured bull.

Brylee rose from the table and balanced on her crutches.

"Here, honey. You take that pain pill and go rest on the couch for a while with some ice," Barb said, handing Brylee a glass of water. Brylee took the pills from her pocket, popped one in her mouth and swallowed a sip of water.

Barb tossed an ice pack to Shaun. "Make yourself useful, Shaun. Help that girl get settled."

"I can take it," Brylee said, reaching for the ice pack, but Shaun moved it beyond her reach.

"I've got it. Barb has spoken and no one around here wears big enough britches to argue with her." Shaun winked at the housekeeper then followed Brylee as she made her way down the hall to the living room. She sank onto one of the leather sofas. Before she could swallow it down, a pain-laced moan rolled out of her.

"Overdid it, didn't you?" Shaun asked as he gathered a few throw pillows and set them on the couch then guided her leg so it rested on top of them. He disappeared down the hall but soon returned with the ice pack wrapped in a towel and carefully placed it on her leg. "Is that okay?"

Brylee felt sparks shooting all the way up to her head from where his fingers had brushed her bare skin. In fact, she thought the electricity must have short-circuited her brain because she wanted him to touch her again.

"It's fine," she said, battling the need to close her eyes and cry. But she didn't have the time or luxury for tears. Besides, if she started crying, she wasn't sure she'd ever stop. From experience in their mutual past, she knew Shaun did not do well with tears anyway.

"Can I get you anything? A glass of water? Some iced tea? A magazine? You want to watch TV?" he asked as he stood staring down at her.

"Really, I'm good, Shaun, but thank you."

"Liar!" the voice in her head accused. She wasn't good at all. In fact, she felt worse by the second. The pain pill, or her emotions, had left her stomach churning. Her leg throbbed, keeping a painful rhythm with her pulse. And her heart — that cold, dead lump that had just taken up space in her chest the last several years — hurt so badly she looked down to see if something had somehow pierced it.

She glanced up at Shaun. The sky-blue shirt he wore made his eyes look the same color. Without his hat on, thick hair the color of a new penny glistened in the light streaming in the window. Unlike many redheads she'd met, not a single freckle dared reside on his taut, tan skin. In truth, she had no idea where he got his unique hair color. Jason had dark hair, as did Shaun's sister. From photos she'd seen of his mother, she also had dark hair. Maybe he was a throwback to an ancestor from generations ago.

Wherever it came from, it was certainly an intriguing shade. He wore his hair a little shorter than he used to, with the sides closely cropped and the top slightly longer with the most enticing little wave right in the front.

Perturbed by the direction of her thoughts, Brylee dropped her gaze from his hair, avoided his eyes, but couldn't help but notice that darn little indent in his chin. How she used to love to trace it with her finger. Then Shaun would flash a crooked grin that made her knees turn to pudding and he'd kiss her.

She winced, recalling how much she'd enjoyed his kisses, how much she'd once loved him.

"Bits, are you sure you're okay?" Shaun asked in a soft voice as he hunkered down beside the couch and took her cool hand in his. His eyes held hers as he pressed a kiss to the back of her hand.

The jolt of his touch rocketed up her arm and made her toes tingle.

"I'm fine," she said, concerned when her hand disobeyed the screams in her head to jerk out of his grasp. She didn't need him doing whatever it was he was doing. There was no way on earth she'd let him work his way past her defenses a second time.

"I'll let you rest then," he said, rising to his feet.

"Wait, Shaun, I, um..." Brylee cleared her throat and swallowed her pride. "Thank you for everything you've done."

He shrugged. "I didn't do much."

"Yes, you did. You took care of me last night, found me a place to stay, made sure Rocket was okay, and even bought my pain meds." She forced a smile. "Thank you. I really do appreciate it."

"You're welcome, Bitsy. I'd have done the same for anyone who needed a hand." He turned and left the room, leaving her alone with her thoughts.

Shaun spoke the truth. He would have done the same thing for anyone who needed a hand. Why, then, did it bother her so much?

Exhaustion, frustration and pain made her eyelids heavy with sleep. When she closed her eyes, a vision of Shaun's smile met her in her dreams.

Chapter Four

"Have you lost your ever-loving mind?" Cooper James asked as he helped Shaun stow his tack in the trailer after the end of a four-day rodeo. The rodeo clown and barrelman had been Shaun's good friend since high school days.

Cooper was one of the few people who knew the majority of Shaun's deep dark secrets, including most of his past with Brylee. There were one or two secrets nobody knew and never would if he had anything to say about it.

With a cocky grin, Shaun continued working. "No more than usual."

Cooper shook his head. "Then why would you even think about doing what you're planning to do?"

A shrug rode Shaun's shoulders as he closed the back of the trailer and unbuckled his chaps. "What is it you think I'm planning to do?"

His friend crossed his arms over his chest and

leaned against the side of the trailer. "I'm just spitballing, but I'd say you're going to offer to drive Brylee around to the next few rodeos until the doctor tells her she can drive herself. Am I close to right?"

Shaun's gaze narrowed. "Maybe."

"What are you doing, man? Do you not remember how messed up you were for months after you tangled with that girl the last time? I honestly thought you'd end up marrying her for the way the two of you couldn't stay away from each other. Then, in a blink, you broke up and went your separate ways." Cooper gave him a knowing look. "It was like you were trying to fill the void she left in your life by dangling your toes off the deep end of crazy."

Shaun glowered at Cooper then released a long sigh. "I know I should stay miles and miles away from her, Coop, but she needs a little help. It's easy enough for me to give it. I'd do the same for anyone else."

"Yes, you would, but it's totally different and you know it. I think Brylee is your one."

Shaun's brow furrowed in confusion. "My one what?" he asked.

"*The* one, you moron." Cooper gave him a look like he was trying to educate a recalcitrant student. "The one that got away. The one you shouldn't have ever let go. The one whose ghost screws up every relationship you've been in since you told her goodbye. The one who grabbed hold of your heart the moment you met and still hasn't let go. The one you think about at night, wishing you'd fought to keep. The one who haunts your dreams. The one who made you want to set down roots and turn your hopes into your future. The one you're going to love until they lay your cold, dead body deep in the ground. *That* one."

Stunned, Shaun stared at Cooper, unable to even formulate a reply. When had his friend gotten so smart? And how in the world had he so accurately described Shaun's feelings for Brylee. Never in a million years would he have articulated them like Cooper had, but they were there all the same.

Rather than admit he was right, Shaun plastered on what he thought of as his joker's smile and slapped Cooper on the shoulder. "Have you been reading Paige's romance novels or something, man? Don't let the others hear you talk like that or you might end up wearing flowers and a tutu at the next rodeo."

Cooper snickered and rolled his eyes. "Are you ever gonna be serious? Even for a minute?"

"Probably not anytime soon, Coop, but I do appreciate your concern." Shaun gave his friend a sincere smile. "It'll be fine, man. It's only for a few weeks, anyway, and that is all contingent on her agreeing to go along with us. In case you've forgotten, I'm her least favorite person."

"I don't know about the least, but you're definitely in the top ten." Cooper smirked and pushed away from the trailer. "Just be careful, Shaun. I don't want to see you hurt again, at least not like you were the last time you two called it quits."

"Thanks, Coop." Shaun shared a brotherly bear hug with him then shoved Cooper toward his trailer. "If I had a pretty wife like Paige waiting for me, I sure wouldn't be out here spouting nonsense. Go see your girl."

"You should give that settling down and falling in love thing a try," Cooper said, grinning as he backed away. "Talk to you soon, man."

"You can count on it. Tell Paige I will definitely model for the holiday ads. She just needs to tell me when and where to show up."

"She'll be happy to hear that. Night, dude." Cooper turned and headed off into the darkness.

Shaun released a long breath and took a moment to gather his thoughts as he stared up at the stars. Cooper was right, on more counts than he cared to admit.

It was foolhardy, stupid, and dangerous to offer to be Brylee's chauffeur for the next few weeks. Despite knowing that, the thought had niggled at him until he'd taken out the idea, looked at it from all sides, and decided to run with it.

His dad had been oddly close-mouthed about it, but Shaun was grateful he'd decided to refrain from meddling. Most likely, his father doubted Brylee would ever agree to go with him in the first place.

Shaun climbed in the truck and started it, ready to get on the road and head back to the Rockin' K. Back to Brylee, if he cared to own up to it, which he most certainly did not.

A week ago, when he'd packed her out to her pickup, he'd thought he could offer his help, move on, and try, again, to forget about her. All he'd done was knock the lid off a box of memories that buzzed around him like he'd kicked a hornet's nest.

Six years ago when they met, she hadn't even been twenty-one. She had big blue eyes, and gorgeous golden hair, and a smile that could bring him to his knees. The first time he'd noticed her was in Las Vegas at the finals the year she'd taken the world champion title in barrel racing. He'd thought she was cute, but she'd looked so young and inexperienced, he'd stayed away from her. Then he'd bumped into her when they were both registering at a rodeo in June that following summer. The attraction between the two of them sizzled brighter than the fireworks that had gone off that night at the end of the rodeo.

From that moment on, he'd been a goner, but he hadn't wanted to admit it. Even later, when he was in so deep with her he was dreaming of what they'd name their first baby, he refused to acknowledge that he loved her completely.

In the end, love hadn't been enough. Not nearly enough. If it had, he wouldn't have walked away when he did. He knew it would break her heart, because it had destroyed his. The only excuse he had was being young, stupid, and scared of emotions he couldn't identify or process.

As he pulled onto the freeway and headed toward Twin Falls, Shaun considered what would happen if Brylee did agree to his plan. Would the buffer of having his dad there be enough to keep things on an even keel? Was it possible to set aside their differences and the wounds from the past long enough to make it through a few weeks of attending rodeos together? Could he leave her alone? The moment he'd gazed into her eyes he felt that same inexplicable tug for her he'd felt all those years ago. It defied description or reason, but was there just the same.

It didn't help matters that she'd gotten prettier in the years since he'd seen her. Her eyes seemed bluer. Her hair glistened with a deeper golden hue. And those curves of hers. Man, they had filled out to magnificent proportions. The other day when he'd walked in the house for lunch after church, his mouth had flooded with so much moisture he thought he might drown before he got control of himself.

She'd stood in the doorway of the kitchen wearing a form-fitting tank top and a pair of shorts that showcased the fact she'd kept in great shape. Incredible shape if his reaction to seeing her tanned legs was any indication.

Shaun was still contemplating the what-ifs of his plan when he arrived at the ranch a few hours past daybreak. After he unloaded the horses, fed and watered them, he took a shower then climbed into bed and slept for a solid four hours.

When he awoke, he dressed, brushed his teeth, and combed his hair then stepped out of the trailer he and his dad shared both at the ranch and on the road. He made his way toward Kash and Celia's house.

Brylee was sitting on the porch with her casted leg propped up on a pillow while she sipped tea from a glass filled with ice. The shorts she wore provided a great view of her tanned legs while the tank top made him think thoughts he quickly chased away. Her hair looked like spun gold as it hung in waves around her face and down her back.

"I heard you pull in this morning," she said, holding the glass in the direction of his trailer. "How was the rodeo?"

"Good. Dad and the rest of the guys decided they wanted to head home as soon as it ended rather than wait until daylight. We won't have to leave again until Tuesday morning." Shaun lowered himself into a chair beside her and stretched out his legs. "See you got the cast on. How are you feeling?"

"Antsy and ready to do something besides sit around. When Barb was busy cooking yesterday and Frank was gone to town, I snuck out and saddled Rocket. We went for a slow, careful ride, but my boy is ready to race."

Shaun grinned. "I'm sure he is. Rocket always did love competing and running." He glanced over at her. "I can take him for a run later if you want me to work off some of his energy."

"I'd appreciate that, Shaun, but you don't have to. I really do need to get in some practice if I hope to go to a rodeo this week. The doctor forbade driving, but since my pickup is automatic, I think I could handle it."

Shaun made a grunting noise that clearly expressed his disapproval. "I have a better idea and I'll share it with you if you promise to listen to it before you start calling me names that might hurt my feelings."

Her gaze narrowed as she turned to look at him.

"I'm listening."

"I don't know where you're planning to ride the next few weeks, but if you want to enter the rodeos where we'll be working, you can ride along with us. We can make room for Rocket in one of the trailers. You won't have to worry about driving and we'll be around to help you if you need it because I'm fairly certain the doctor told you it's probably best to stay off that foot as much as you can. Am I right?"

She lifted her chin stubbornly, but didn't argue with him. "The doctor may have said that." Brylee shifted her leg. Although she didn't wince, he saw the pain in her eyes.

The woman had no business competing, but since she would refuse to listen to reason, he hoped she'd at least have sense enough to take him up on his offer. Kash had told him his plans were fine with him. Celia had even offered to help Brylee if she needed it. Shaun just had to get her to agree to go with them first.

Brylee set her glass on the small table between her chair and Shaun's and gazed out over the ranch. She remained so still and quiet, he couldn't help but wonder what thoughts tumbled through her head.

Finally, she released a resigned sigh. "I'd really appreciate the help, Shaun. Thank you. And it should only be for a few weeks, until the cast comes off. After I get a brace on, I'll be fine on my own."

"You're welcome to come along with us as long as you need to. Kash and Celia don't mind and neither do the rest of us." He tossed her a rascally grin. "Maybe you'll add a little class to our entourage."

Brylee laughed. "Yeah, I don't see that happening."

Shaun smiled and took a drink from her glass of tea. She scowled at him but didn't say anything when he set the glass on the table between them. "Is there a reason you haven't asked your mom or dad to help you out?"

Brylee's face turned white and she swallowed twice, like she had to work past her emotions.

Shaun knew she had a good relationship with her parents, at least she had when they'd dated. It had been clear to him, though, that she and her dad were remarkably close. He always assumed it was because they were so much alike. And she adored her little brother. Maybe something had happened to change that. To change her.

"Shaun, my dad... um... Dad passed away four years ago."

He leaned toward her and placed a hand over hers where it gripped the arm of her chair. "I'm so sorry, Brylee. I had no idea. Brad was a great, great guy."

Slowly, she nodded. "Dad was one of the best. I miss him every single day."

"What happened?"

"He was working on a flat tire on the pivot and it blew up. They said he died instantly, but it was such a random, freak accident. We'd just had breakfast together. I'd gone out to move a pivot on the other side of the hay field and heard the explosion. He was... it was..." Brylee drew in a deep breath. "It's been hard on all of us, but especially Mom."

"I really am so sorry, Brylee." He squeezed her hand again, wishing he hadn't asked, but glad he knew. "Doesn't your mom need your help on the ranch?"

Brylee nodded her head. "She does, but she needs the money from my winnings more."

Shaun gave her a questioning look, waiting for her to continue.

"My dad didn't have much in the way of a life insurance policy. He took a mortgage out on the ranch a few months before he died to upgrade the irrigation systems and put in a new barn. Ours had burned down in the spring thanks to faulty wiring." A hard, sardonic sound burst out of her. "Ironic, isn't it? The equipment he went into debt to acquire is what killed him, and is currently killing my mother one painful day at a time. Between one thing and another, she got behind on payments and was afraid to tell me. The only reason I found out was because I intercepted a phone call from the bank, warning her about foreclosure if she doesn't get on top of the payments. Mom is determined to save the ranch for Birch and me, but it's going to take money and a miracle to make it happen."

"That's why you're back on the circuit? To win the money to pay off your debts?"

Another nod.

"I have some money saved up. I could give you…"

Her head snapped up and she glared at him. "No, Shaun. Absolutely not. It's kind of you to offer, but no. I have to do this on my own." She sucked in a shaky breath. "I appreciate you making it possible for me to keep competing the next few weeks. I'll try not to get in your way."

"You'd never be in my way, Bitsy."

She cringed when he used her nickname, but he couldn't help himself. Brylee wasn't as tiny as Paige James, but she was small-framed and on the shorter side of average for a woman. He'd called her Bitsy the first time he took her on a date because the name fit her so well. She was petite, even with those sweet curves, but full of fire and sass. He sensed she was even more fiery and sassy now.

Desperate to chase away the uncomfortable silence lingering between them, he changed the subject. "Tell me about Birch. How's he doing? He's got to be what, thirteen now?"

Brylee's face softened and she smiled. "Fourteen going on thirty."

Shaun chuckled. "That sounds about right. Is he still planning to follow in your dad's footsteps and be a team roper?"

"Yes. That hasn't changed a bit. He's getting really good, Shaun. You should watch him rope sometime. In fact, he's been begging and pleading with Mom to let him rope at the Walla Walla rodeo, at least in the slack."

"If he's still as persuasive as he used to be, I bet she'll have a hard time telling him no."

Brylee grinned. "He is and she will. Birch is a good kid, though, and he's grown so much this summer. I saw them on the Fourth of July. I think he's shot up three inches since spring."

"Have you been on the road that much?" Shaun took another drink of her tea, wondering how she could stand to spend so much time alone. Then again, Brylee had always been more of a loner and Shaun was the one who loved hanging out with his friends. He was surprised she'd struck up a friendship with Savannah, who lived somewhere in Florida. The two seemed like complete opposites. Regardless, he was glad she'd had someone to talk to and keep an eye on her.

"I headed to Texas in January and haven't been back to Walla Walla more than a handful of days here and there." Brylee took the tea glass from him and drained it, setting it back on the table.

"I'm sure your mom and Birch miss you."

Brylee gave him a sideways grin. "Birch and I text back and forth several times a day and I do a video call with them every Sunday evening." She sat up straighter and sighed. "Look, Shaun, things are hard enough on my mom without her finding out about my leg. I don't want her to know. Honestly, I don't want anyone to know who doesn't have to. Is my break something we can keep quiet?"

"Fine by me, but it's gonna be a little hard to hide that hot pink cast isn't it?" he pointed to her leg.

"Frank and I came up with a plan," she said, grinning at him again. "If nothing else, the accident gave me the opportunity to get to know Kash's dad and Barb. They are both awesome." She leaned toward him and dropped her voice to a whisper. "But if I keep eating all the food Barb shoves at me, I won't be able to get in any of my clothes, let alone haul myself up on Rocket."

"Then I guess we better get you back out on the road," Shaun said. He battled the urge to pull her onto his lap and wrap his arms around her luscious curves or bury his face in her hair. She smelled the same as he remembered — a decadent blend of sunshine and wildflowers. His eyes dropped to her lips, the bottom one slightly fuller than the top. He'd often mused she had the sexiest pout he'd ever seen, mostly because she had no idea that's what men thought when they watched her lips move. Dang it all, but did he ever want to kiss her. To see if she tasted as sweet as his memories claimed.

Before he gave in to the urge, he stood and took a step down off the porch. "So, we'll plan to head out Tuesday morning. I'll get you a list of the rodeos we'll be at and you can decide if you want to enter them or not."

"Thanks, Shaun. I really do appreciate it."

He nodded once then turned and left, shoving his hands deep into his front pockets. If he didn't, he was afraid he'd give in to the temptation to hold her and most definitely to kiss her.

And that would never, ever do.

Chapter Five

"Are you sure you don't want to ride up front a while, Brylee?" Jason asked as they drove across Montana on their way to a rodeo in North Dakota.

"I'm sure, Jason. You guys made me a nice, comfy place to rest my leg back here and I'm doing great," Brylee assured him.

Shaun glanced back at her over the front seat of the truck. "Anytime you want to trade, just holler. Do you need an ice pack or anything?" he asked.

"I'm fine, thanks." Brylee held back a smart remark and shook her head. Shaun and his dad had been fussing over her like two old women the moment she climbed in the back of their truck early that morning. Their really nice truck.

She knew Kash paid his employees well, but she also knew what the Price men made as pickup men couldn't pay for a truck with all the bells and whistles or the fancy horse trailer hooked up behind them that accommodated eight horses and provided living quarters that were nicer than many hotel suites she'd seen.

She hadn't asked about their snazzy wheels when she got in, but five hours into a fourteen hour trip, curiosity was about to get the best of her. "So, how long have you guys had this outfit?"

Jason glanced in the rearview mirror and grinned. "Pretty nice, isn't it?"

At Brylee's nod, he tipped his head toward Shaun. "The kid won this set up two years ago in a bucking contest along with a nice purse. He got to choose a horse trailer and matching truck and kindly got this for me and his uncle to use. Now that my brother is retired, Shaun's probably glad he made that decision."

"Every day we head out on the road in this thing, Dad. Every single day." Shaun grinned at his dad then glanced back at Brylee. "You must not have done much traveling in the past since you're driving the same pickup, although you downsized the trailer."

"No, I mostly stayed at home."

Brylee didn't want to talk about all the things she and her mother had sold trying to gather the funds to pay their bills. The nice horse trailer her dad had helped her buy was one of the first things to go. They had two other trailers, albeit without living quarters, that would do for ranch work. When Brylee decided to return to rodeo, she took the smaller of the two trailers. The first week she was in Texas at a rodeo, she met Savannah. That girl traveled in style and invited Brylee to make herself at home in her posh trailer.

In exchange for that, Brylee cleaned the trailer, did the cooking, and took care of the laundry. It was the least she could do in trade for Savannah giving her a place to sleep and shower. If she hadn't befriended the big-hearted girl, she had no doubt she would have spent the last several months sleeping in her pickup and showering at the barns or a truck stop. She shuddered at the thought.

No, there was no way she'd tell Shaun all that. Not today, maybe not ever. She hated that she'd spilled her guts to him the other day, telling him why it was so important to her to win this year. The look of pity on his face was almost more than she could stomach.

She didn't want his pity or his sympathy. She didn't even really want his help, but until she could drive, she'd gratefully accept it. If getting to the next rodeo so she could compete and win meant swallowing her pride, then so be it. No matter how bitter that pill, she'd down a whole bottle if it helped save the ranch.

She and her brother had both tried to tell her mom it was okay if they had to let the ranch go, but Jenn Barton set her jaw and refused to listen. Brylee knew part of her mother's determination was because it made it easier to hold onto her father's memories. Her mother also wanted to preserve the legacy Brylee's ancestors had started when they'd taken the ranch out of sagebrush and turned it into a successful, prosperous wheat and cattle operation. It's too bad her father decided to mortgage the place. If only he'd invested in a decent life insurance policy. Or sent her to fix the tire on the pivot.

Looking back only turns you away from where you should be headed, baby girl.

Her dad's voice echoed in her thoughts as she watched the miles glide by. Sometimes she'd hear his voice so plainly in her head she could picture him sitting right beside her. Even after her disastrous breakup with Shaun, her dad still called her baby girl. She'd loved hearing him say it.

Unlike her mother who was always so serious and focused, her dad had been the fun one, the one who made her feel like a princess and encouraged her dreams. If it wasn't for him, she never would have gotten into barrel racing in the first place. He'd practically begged her to go back when she announced she'd never go on the rodeo circuit again, but on that one point, she wouldn't budge.

Not until it was the only means available to save the ranch and all the dreams her family had poured into it for the future — her future and Birch's.

Her phone pinged and she took it out of her pocket. She grinned as she read the text from her brother and sent him one in return.

A few minutes later, it pinged again.

Brylee tried to tamp down a laugh but it came out as a half cough, half snort. She quickly tapped out a message while Shaun watched her from the front seat.

"Are you having some hot text session with your boyfriend back there?" he asked. The slightly pinched tone of his voice seemed at odds with the easy-going smile on his face.

Bored and still filled with enough lingering anger at Shaun to cause him some torment, she gave him what she hoped looked like a sweet, dreamy smile.

"Busted."

Shaun's eyebrows shot upward and the smile dripped off his face. "You have a boyfriend?"

"Sure do. He's a real sweetheart. And he adores me. He tells me he loves me every night and starts my day with the best messages."

Shaun turned around and stared out the passenger window.

Jason glanced at her in the rearview mirror and she winked at him. He gave her a slight nod before Shaun turned back around to glare at her. "You mean this whole time that you've been hurt, you have a boyfriend who hasn't bothered to come to see you? Send you flowers? Nothing?"

"Oh, he doesn't have a driver's license, so it would be impossible for him to visit me."

Shaun's gaze narrowed. "You're dating a dude who can't drive? What's wrong with him? One too many DUI's?"

"Of course not!" Brylee pretended to be affronted.

"Then what's his deal?"

"Maybe he's blind, son. Ever think of that? What if Brylee's boyfriend is a super nice guy who just can't see to drive." Jason glanced back at her. "I'm sure he's real nice, honey."

"He is nice, Jason, and a great guy, but he isn't blind."

Shaun returned to glaring at her over the seat.

"If he isn't blind and didn't lose his license, then what's wrong with him?" When she remained silent, his jaw dropped open. "It's some old geezer too old to drive. Is that it?"

The scowl she shot him that time was not in jest. What did he take her for? Some pathetic loser? If she was going to date a senile, perverted old coot, she sure wouldn't be in the back of their truck with a broken leg, wishing she hadn't dumped out the last of her pain pills with every pothole they hit in the road. She'd talk the sugar daddy into paying off their debts.

However, Brylee would never, ever do such a thing or even consider it.

Although, at that very moment, she might have preferred the perverted old coot to the handsome lunkhead in the front seat who could infuriate her faster than any human on earth.

"You are sick, Shaun," she glowered at him. "Sick in the head."

Jason chuckled. "She has a point, kid. Get your mind out of the gutter."

"Sorry, it's just I can't think of a reason an adult male of reasonable intelligence, which I assume he has since he is capable of texting you, who isn't blind or unable to drive for legal reasons would stay away from his girl if he could get to her. If I was dating Brylee and she was hurt, I'd do anything I could to get to her. Something as trivial as the lack of a driver's license wouldn't stop me."

The frosty feelings Brylee held for Shaun thawed slightly at his comment.

"That's for sure. Remember when you were

fifteen and you took Galen's truck on a joyride to impress a girl." Jason looked at him. "What was her name?"

"Heather Ann Morris." Shaun leaned back against his seat and relaxed slightly. "I thought she was the cutest girl at school. She had legs that seemed ten miles long in her gym shorts and the prettiest black hair."

"You thought she was great until a new girl moved to town after Christmas and Belinda captured your interest."

Brylee giggled. "So he's always been fickle with the attention span of a loopy gnat?"

Jason laughed so hard he almost missed swerving around the mashed remains of what looked like a deer splattered across the highway. "That's a good one, Brylee, and so very accurate."

Shaun scowled at his dad. "Whose side are you on anyway?"

"No sides in this vehicle. It is a judgment-free zone." Jason looked back at Brylee and grinned.

Brylee smirked at Shaun. "I heard your past girlfriends have formed a support group that meets online once a month. Maybe you can get me the contact info. I'd like to hear what they all have to say about you. I've got plenty I can contribute."

Jason looked like he might rupture something as he tried to hold in his humor.

Shaun ignored the comment and glared at her, circling back around to the person texting her. "Who is this boyfriend? Why haven't you mentioned him before? Where does he work? He is employed, isn't he?"

"No, actually, he isn't, unless you count helping out on his family's ranch. Right now his focus is on his studies."

"He's a student?" Shaun gaped at her again. "How old is this dude? Shouldn't he be out of school already?"

"He's almost fifteen."

Brylee reveled in the look of shock then horror that passed over Shaun's face while his father's shoulders shook from trying to contain his mirth. Finally, a big guffaw burst out of Jason while Brylee erupted in giggles.

"What in the heck is so funny?" Shaun demanded, looking from one of them to the other.

"Here, you can read his last text." Brylee held her phone up so Shaun could see the screen.

Miss u 2, sis! Don't give Shaun 2 much trble. Dude is doin u a solid. Txt me when u get to ND.

A look of relief settled over Shaun's face as he read the message then lifted his stormy gaze to hers. "Birch? All that was about Birch?"

Brylee nodded. "And you fell for it hook, line, and sinker." She reached over and smacked the arm he had draped over the back of the front seat.

"Hey! What was that for?" he jerked his arm over the seat, out of her reach.

"For thinking I'd date an old pervert or a dude with too many DUIs or a kid. If you must know, I don't have time for dating anyone right now. What kind of weirdo are you?"

"A big one," his dad said, still chuckling.

Shaun glared at them both then turned around and stuck earbuds in his ears, effectively blocking them out.

An hour later, Jason pulled up at the fuel pumps outside a small convenience store.

"We should be in Billings in about two hours and can have lunch there," Jason said as he cut the ignition and turned around to look at Brylee. "Want to stretch that leg of yours a few minutes?"

"I do, Jason. Thank you." Brylee grabbed her purse and started to open her door, but Shaun opened it and offered her his hand.

Annoyed as she was to accept it, she couldn't help but admire his nice manners. He'd been a gentleman when they were dating, too. Up until that disastrous last night that ended so badly.

Brylee derailed that train of thought before it gathered any steam. After all, she was stuck in Shaun's company for the next two or three weeks. It would make it easier on them all if she forgot how much she loathed him and made an effort to get along.

The moment she placed her hand against his hard, calloused palm, a familiar electrical spark zinged up her arm and down to her toes. Good thing it didn't generate real sparks or Jason might have needed to put the fuel nozzle up and pull away from the pumps.

"Going inside first?" Shaun asked as she stepped down from the truck and slipped the strap of her purse over her shoulder.

"Definitely. Your dad makes rest stop breaks even less frequently than you," she teased as they walked across the parking lot toward the door. Shaun hadn't yet relinquished her hand and something haywire in her brain kept her from yanking her fingers out of his clasp.

He let go when they reached the door to the store. A sign read "pull" so Shaun gave the handle a tug. When nothing happened, he tugged again then stared at the handle and back up at the neon sign that assured customers the store was open.

"What in the...?" He pulled on the door handle a third time.

Brylee reached out and gave the door a push inward. It swung open. They were greeted by the cackles of an old man who looked like he might have settled there right after the first tumbleweeds blew through the area. Tufts of white hair randomly dotted his liver-spotted head. The teeth he wasn't missing appeared chipped and stained. And his shoulders were so hunched he was probably half a foot shorter than he'd been as a young man.

He slapped the counter in front of him and released another amused guffaw. "That pull sign is the best five bucks I've ever spent. You'd be amazed how many people it fools in a day."

Shaun didn't see any amusement in the sign, at least not since the old man was laughing at his expense.

"It is a little funny," Brylee said, nudging Shaun in the side.

A grin kicked up the right corner of his mouth. "Maybe a little." He nodded to the old man. "May we use the restrooms, please?"

"Sure can. You head through that door to your

right, son. The little lady should walk down that hall there by the soda machines. You'll see the door, darlin'."

"Thank you," Brylee said, offering the old man a smile as she turned and made her way to the bathroom. Unlike most gas station restrooms, it was clean and smelled fresh. A tiny table near the door even held a bouquet of wildflowers. Glad Jason decided to stop there instead of some public facility on the side of the road that didn't even have running water, she took a moment to finger-comb her hair and let the tension in her shoulders relax.

She didn't know why she felt like she was strung so tightly. Shaun had been courteous and kind. He'd not made any attempt at discussing their past or if she'd forgiven him, which she hadn't. At least not entirely.

If they could just keep things on an impersonal acquaintance-like level, she'd be fine. Perhaps these next few weeks spent in his company would provide the opportunity to finally forgive him and move on with her life.

Years had come and gone. Years riddled with more anguish than she thought herself capable of enduring, but she had. Yet, some days the memories of what she'd had with Shaun, of how much she'd loved him, would wash over her with such paralyzing pain, it left her gasping for breath.

She didn't have time for those memories or the accompanying pain. Her entire focus needed to be on winning.

Winning isn't everything, baby girl.

"If you didn't want me to focus on winning,

Dad, you shouldn't have left us in debt," she whispered then strode out of the bathroom and into the store.

Shaun was grabbing a large bottle of water out of a cooler and glanced up at her. He held up a bottle and she nodded.

The bag full of snacks Barb had packed for them that morning was in the pickup, but Brylee was out of gum. She picked up two packages along with a little tin of breath mints and went to the counter to pay.

Shaun was already swiping his card to pay for the water and tried to add her stuff to his purchase. She shook her head and took out money to pay. As Shaun finished his transaction, she glanced at a shelf near the cash register and noticed a variety of touristy items, like shot glasses, a little stand with postcards, and a stack of road maps. The cutest little mouse with huge ears sat on top of the maps, staring at her.

Brylee almost reached out to touch it, sure it was a toy. Then it blinked just as she handed the old man her money.

She gasped and pointed to the shelf. "Is that supposed to be there?"

"What's that, darlin'?" He leaned forward and looked in the direction she indicated.

The mouse chose that moment to launch off the shelf and onto the counter behind the cash register.

"Dadgummit!" The old man yelled, scrambling around the counter with a purple flyswatter. "You are gettin' it this time, Dumbo."

"Let's get out of here," Shaun said, taking

Brylee's hand and propelling her toward the door. She snatched her gum and mints off the counter, glad she'd given the old man exact change. The store owner was shouting and whipping the flyswatter around, chasing the mouse.

Outside, she glanced up at Shaun and they both started laughing.

Jason strolled over and gave them both odd looks. "What's so funny?"

"Push the door and watch out for the mouse," Shaun wheezed between laughs as he and Brylee tried to curtail their amusement.

Jason shook his head and went inside the store. The old man's shouts as he whacked at the mouse trickled out to them. Brylee caught the word "varmint" and "big-eared freak show." Giggles spilled out of her all over again.

"Come on, giggle box. Let's leave this stuff in the truck and take a little walk while we wait for Dad." Shaun set the water bottles in the front seat while Brylee left her things in the back. She shoved her hands in the front pockets of her denim shorts and fell into step with Shaun as he meandered around the parking lot.

"I'd suggest walking down the road, but that gravel on the edge wouldn't be good for you to walk in and I'm fairly certain the mouse in the store is hiding from whatever's out here in the brush."

"I've never seen a mouse that looked like that before." Brylee glanced up at him. "Have you?"

"I have, but they were in Arizona. Maybe that little guy hitched a ride and got dumped off at this fine establishment." Shaun grinned as they circled the parking lot and began another lap. "I kind of feel sorry for the little feller, stuck in there with that ornery ol' coot."

"Oh, I doubt he'd really smash it. Chasing it around is probably the most excitement he gets in a day." Brylee stopped and looked up at Shaun. "Speaking of ornery ol' coots, how is your grandpa?"

Shaun grinned. "He's good. We celebrated his eightieth birthday back in May."

"I'm glad he's well, Shaun. I enjoyed visiting with him the few times I saw him."

"He liked you, too, Bitsy. In fact, when I saw him a few weeks ago, he asked about you."

"He did?" Brylee asked, surprised.

"According to him, I'm the biggest fool in the world for letting you get away." Shaun waved at his dad as he walked out of the store grinning from ear to ear.

"You didn't exactly let me get away, Shaun. If you recall, you ran out on me."

Before he could respond, Jason was there, laughing over the old man and the mouse.

"Did he catch it?" Brylee asked as Jason opened the passenger door and gave her a hand inside, leaving Shaun to drive.

"No, but he was teetering after it, hollering about it spreading the plague around his store." Jason glanced back at Brylee. "I got the idea this is a daily routine for the two of them."

"I bet he has a little feeding area with cheese for it in a back room," Brylee said, glancing at the store one last time as they pulled back on the road.

"And a bed with a pillow. Something big enough to support those ears," Shaun said, looking in the rearview mirror with a grin.

Brylee ignored what his grin did to her insides and focused on the road ahead of them. They still had a long way to go before they could call it a day.

Chapter Six

"How did we manage before Brylee joined us?" Jason asked as he and Shaun rode into the rodeo arena. They'd finished the rodeo in North Dakota then headed to one in South Dakota before they drove back to the Rockin' K.

In the past week, Brylee had filled in gaps neither man even realized existed. Since they insisted she stay in the trailer with them, she cleaned it, did their laundry and pressed their clothes, and she cooked meals. Not just sandwiches, but real food. It might be late when they ate it, but there was always something delicious waiting for them when they finished up each night. One night, she'd even made meatloaf with mashed potatoes and gravy, served with hot rolls and green beans. Shaun couldn't remember when a meal had tasted so good.

On top of that, Brylee helped with their horses. Generally, Shaun and Jason switched mounts halfway through the bareback riding and did the same thing during the saddle bronc riding. It was such exhausting work for the horses, they didn't want them to overdo. Bull riding wasn't generally as taxing, so they only rode one horse during that event, usually the one they rode first during the bareback event. At any rate, they needed four horses saddled and ready to ride during the course of the evening.

Brylee had taken it upon herself to make sure their mount changes were ready to go when they needed them. She would ride one and lead the other, warming them up as the bareback riding began. The moment they'd head out the gate to switch, she'd be there with them. She'd take the two they dismounted back to the trailer, switch the tack to a new set, then cool down the two who'd just been working.

Truthfully, she deserved a paycheck from the Rockin' K for all the help she offered without expecting anything in return. When Shaun mentioned it to her, she gave him a dismissive look. "I wouldn't be here competing if it wasn't for you guys. Just accept what I do as my thank you."

Shaun thought she did far more than was necessary, but he wasn't going to argue with her. In fact, he'd done his best to keep a friendly distance, even when everything in him begged to draw closer to her, to love her.

Who was he trying to kid? Since Brylee had entered his life again, it had become crystal clear to Shaun he'd never stopped loving her, never gotten over her. And he wasn't sure he wanted to.

Regardless of his feelings, Brylee would rather take a filthy pocket knife from a hobo on the street and carve her heart right out of her chest than let him have a second crack at breaking it. She'd made no secret of her thoughts on the matter, although they hadn't actually gotten around to discussing the past and the stupid, stupid mistake Shaun had made that ended the best thing to ever happen to him.

With his thoughts about to suck him down to a place he shouldn't go, Shaun shook them off and focused on the rodeo. He needed be fully present to do his job, and that meant keeping Brylee out of his head, at least until the rodeo ended and the stock was settled for the night.

"She's been a good helper," Shaun said, realizing he never answered his dad's question. They watched as the first bronc rider of the evening climbed on the back of one of Kash's prized horses. Shaun mentally went through the rider's every move. After so many years spent participating in the sport, sometimes it was hard for him to be on this side of the gate instead of on the back of a bucking horse.

In spite of dreams that came to an end sooner than he liked, he really did love his job. It kept his mind and body busy. Although he and his dad were primarily tasked with keeping the rider as safe as possible, they did their best to ensure animal safety, too. They also chased the stock out of the arena, loosened and removed flank straps, and kept an eye on photographers and press in the arena. They did their best to make sure the photographers didn't get kicked or trampled. Not all of them were as good as

Celia Kressley at rushing right up to the action then racing out of the way.

The job of a pickup man involved a complex combination of moving parts and pieces. They had to be constantly alert, focused on the animals, the riders, everyone in the arena, and, in some cases, the crowd, too.

Not only that, but Shaun had learned right away that a pickup man couldn't be sensitive about people touching him. When those cowboys reached out looking to get off a thousand pounds of bucking bronc, they weren't too particular where they grabbed. Shaun had suffered bruises on nearly every part of his body at one point or another since he went to work for the Rockin' K. Even so, it wasn't anything like the beating he took when he rode broncs.

He nodded to his dad that he was ready as the gate swung open and the horse leaped into the arena. They remained back the first buck or two, giving the horse and rider plenty of room. Then they hurried to catch up to the horse, staying a few feet away, but close enough they were ready when the rider needed them.

The rider made it the full eight seconds and pumped a fist in the air before he reached behind him and loosened the flank strap. Shaun rode in close to the bronc on the left while his dad circled around on the right. The rider hooked an arm around Shaun's shoulders and pulled himself off the still bucking horse. Jason edged the bronc forward and the rider dropped to the ground. Shaun gave him a quick glance to make sure he was on his feet and safe before racing ahead to guide the bronc through the open gate.

"Good job, Lucky," Shaun said, patting his horse on the neck once the bronc trotted down the alleyway. The big bay shook his mane, as though he congratulated himself for doing well.

Pickup men might work long, hard days with little acknowledgement for their efforts, but their horses really went the extra mile. Without a doubt, Shaun knew the horses he and his dad rode were the most versatile in the arena. Their mounts had to be able to turn on a dime, stop in less than a second, and control their action while other horses kicked at them and cowboys jumped onto and off of them. The horses had to be smart, intuitive, adaptive, and confident, rather like the cowboys who rode them. The pickup men and their horses had to be willing to race into a situation that others ran away from, like a bull charging into a crowd or a bucking bronc gone rogue.

Thankfully, Shaun hadn't faced too many bad-case scenarios, although his dad and uncle had experienced their share over the years. The first time a cowboy got hung up in his rigging, though, Shaun had battled the urge to panic. As a rider who'd had that happen, he knew it was terrifying. Instead, he'd stayed glued to the horse and helped the rider get loose. It took until the end of the event for his heart to settle back into a normal beat, but he'd survived and learned a few things, too.

Today, there were twenty bareback riders competing, so when the tenth one fell off at three seconds in, he and his dad chased the horse through the gate then rode over to where Brylee waited with their mount changes near the bucking chutes.

She swung off Buster and moved to his far side. Shaun and his dad rode alongside the two horses and slid from their mounts onto the fresh ones. In a matter of seconds they were back in the arena. They'd never done it as quickly as they had with Brylee there.

"Thanks, honey," Jason hollered at her as he rode back into the arena.

Shaun tipped his hat to her and followed his dad. He could think of a hundred things he could have said, most of which would have embarrassed her, so he kept his mouth shut.

He grinned as he thought about the old boot she wore to hide her cast. Anyone who saw her walking would just think she had a slight limp, thanks to the cowboy boot Frank Kressley had unearthed. In fact, the man had found two matching boots of different sizes that had once belonged to Ransom and Kash when they were boys. It seemed Frank never got rid of anything. In Brylee's case, it turned out to be a good thing. The boots were well worn, but they at least gave her something to wear that kept her cast clean and covered.

Why she thought she needed to keep the break a big secret was beyond him, but they all agreed to abide by her wishes. Maybe she thought if people knew she was riding with a broken leg, they'd pity her, which they would. Or they'd judge her incapable of competing, which was a distinct possibility.

He turned back and looked at her as she led

away Lucky and Jingo. Even with the cast impeding her walk, she still had that little sway in her step that always made Shaun's internal thermostat spike.

"Head in the game, son," Jason said as he rode up beside him. "I can't blame you for getting distracted by our girl."

The fact his father referred to Brylee as "our girl" hadn't escaped Shaun's notice. He didn't know if his dad did it just to irritate him or remind him of what he'd lost — what he could possibly have again if he worked hard at it.

A part of Shaun knew, though, that winning Brylee's heart a second time was going to be an even bigger miracle than her winning enough money to save the ranch.

He wished she'd let him help. Despite his reputation of living wild and free the past handful of years, the hype was exaggerated. He'd saved a good portion of his winnings as well as the money he made modeling. As much as he enjoyed his work, he didn't want to do it forever. Shaun hoped to someday have a ranch of his own or at least build a house on the back of his family's property, of which he owned a quarter, where he could settle down with a wife and raise a few kids.

Stunned by thoughts of standing still long enough to grow deep roots, Shaun had no idea where they'd come from. Sure, he'd thought about what he'd do when he retired. That's why he'd been saving his money. But never, not even once, had he envisioned a house with a family. And why, exactly, did the wife in his vision look exactly like Brylee?

Trouble.

Brylee was pure, unadulterated trouble when it came to his head and heart. Shaun forced himself to focus on his work and chased after a bucking bronc with his dad, wondering how he'd survive until Brylee could return to traveling on her own.

A little while later, when it was time for the saddle bronc riding, he and his dad rode into the arena to the sound of Joe Diffie singing "Pickup Man."

Cooper James just happened to be the barrelman at the event and stood in the middle of the arena clapping his hands and encouraging the crowd to sing along.

After the rodeo-goers joined in singing, "there's just something women like about a pickup man," the music faded and the announcer's voice boomed throughout the grandstands. "Folks, let's give our hardworking pickup men and their highly skilled horses a hand. For those of you who don't know, Jason and Shaun Price are a father-son team. And for you ladies who are wondering, they are both single."

Jason and Shaun removed their hats and waved them to the crowd. Shaun glanced around and saw Brylee watching over the gate as she sat on the back of a black horse they called Coal. She looked so tiny up on the big beast, but she rode him with confidence and ease. He waggled his hat at her before he slapped it back on his head and got down to business.

Later, when they switched horses halfway through the saddle bronc riding, Brylee smiled sweetly at Shaun through the handoff as she took the reins to the two horses he and Jason dismounted. Just as Shaun rode back into the arena, she snapped the reins in her hands with a loud pop.

It startled Coal so badly he started to buck and caught Shaun by surprise. The crowd roared with laughter as Shaun worked to keep his seat and bring the horse under control. Angry and embarrassed, he forced himself to wave good-naturedly when Coal stopped bucking.

"Maybe ol' Shaun should come back to bronc riding, folks," the announcer teased.

"Ride 'em cowboy," Cooper shouted, racing around in a circle on a stick horse.

The crowd continued to hoot and cheer. Jason rode up beside Shaun and shook his head. "What'd you say to rile Brylee now?"

"I don't know, but she can expect full retribution."

Jason's eyebrows shot upward. "I don't think that's a good idea, kid. After all, things have been pretty peachy with her along. You sure you want to get on her bad side, more than you already are?"

His dad had a point, but Shaun didn't take being humiliated lightly. He had no trouble playing a prank on someone else, but he didn't particularly enjoy it when the tables were turned on him. And he especially didn't appreciate it when he was working.

As soon as the saddle bronc event finished, Shaun left the arena and made a beeline for their trailer where he knew Brylee would be getting Rocket ready to ride.

She had a brush in her hand, combing Rocket's tail when he swung off Coal, and marched over to her.

"What was the big idea? You could have done some real damage, you know." He moved so close to her he could see five different shades of blue flecks floating in her remarkable eyes. Too irritated to fully think about what he was doing, he bent down until their noses practically touched. "You can do what you like to me in private, Bitsy, but don't mess with my horses or me when I'm working. Understood?"

"Perfectly," she said, leaning back from him, as though he'd eaten raw onions with a side of Limburger cheese for lunch. Come to think of it, he'd had a burger with onions and spicy mustard.

He straightened and rested a hand on Rocket's withers, absently scratching him. "What did I do to invoke your wrath in this particular instance? If you tell me nothing or that everything is fine, I'll yank that ugly boot off your foot and let everyone see your pretty pink cast."

Her gaze narrowed as she glared up at him. She stopped brushing Rocket's tail and fisted her hands at her hips, drawing Shaun's attention to her chest. She wore a T-shirt that said, "Love is in the air, try not to breathe." That seemed rather appropriate, even if seeing her wear it left him perturbed.

Love shouldn't be something she made fun of or avoided, or despised. She used to be such a hopeless romantic, full of more dreams than one heart could possibly hold.

Had he really been the reason she seemed so

SHANNA HATFIELD

broken now? Surely not. If she'd loved him as much
as she professed back then, she would have forgiven
him long before now. Especially when he'd tried
multiple times to apologize, to set things right.

"Did you or did you not tell your buddies the
reason I'm travelling with you guys is because I got
one too many DUI's and had my license revoked?"

Shaun tried to rein in his smirk, but failed. He
used his forefinger to push up the brim of his hat. "I
may have alluded to something along those lines. A
few of the guys were pestering the daylights out of
me, wanting to know why you're with us and
what's up with your limp. I told them you had a
wreck, which you did on Rocket. I can't help it if
they think it was a vehicle. The subtle implication
of the involvement of some wicked sauce was not
actually stated. If you think about it, though, the
rainstorm that night did make for a nasty soup."

"Ugh!" Brylee clenched the brush in her hands
like she considered swatting him with it. "You are
such a... a..." She appeared to struggle to find a
name to call him. Finally, she huffed and wagged
the brush at him. "Shaun Michael Price, you know
for a fact that I do not drink. Not ever. Why would
you spread a rumor like that?"

"Oh, calm down. I didn't spread any rumors. I
told Joe and Curtis this afternoon. That's all."
Shaun gave her another pointed look. "I'm just
trying to honor your wishes of keeping your cast a
secret."

"I appreciate that, but couldn't you find some
other way besides concocting wild tales that involve
me being a drunk?" Brylee returned to brushing

Rocket's tail. If she kept going at it in a mad fury, the poor horse wouldn't have any hair left.

Shaun took the brush from her hand, drawing another disgusted glare from her. "I'm sorry, Brylee. Do you have a script written out I should memorize for every possible question and scenario? I figured if I told the two biggest blabbermouths at this rodeo a sketchy story, people would take it with a grain of salt and assume there was some kernel of truth in the tale, which there is. You wrecked because of a deluge of liquid."

She took a deep breath, like she prepared for verbal battle, and then slowly released it. "Thank you."

Convinced she was about to flay the hide right off him with her sharp tongue, he didn't know what to say to her contrite gratitude, so he continued staring at her. His gaze lazily drifted from her eyes to her lips. The berry-ripe color made him ponder if they'd taste every bit as sweet, like they used to.

In an effort to corral his wayward thoughts, he let his eyes travel over her shirt and down to her feet in those stupid brown boots then back up to the word "love" emblazoned across her chest. Perhaps she'd stolen the form-fitting shirt from Birch. The longer he looked at the words, the faster wayward thoughts zipped through his mind. Mouth suddenly dry, he gave her a brief nod and started to leave.

"Shaun," she called after him.

He stopped and glanced over his shoulder.

"I'm sorry. It was childish and dangerous to scare Coal like that. It won't happen again."

He nodded a second time and walked off,

wondering who this woman was because she was nothing like the Brylee he'd known and loved.

While she got dressed then went off to ride Rocket around the warm-up arena, he stayed far away from her. But the moment the barrel racing started, he swung on the back of his horse and rode over to the gate near the bucking chutes where he could watch her.

She was the third one to compete. He held his breath as she and Rocket shot around the barrels. She favored her right side, but unless someone knew she was hurt, they probably wouldn't even notice. He grinned as they came out of the pocket on the third barrel and she leaned forward on Rocket's neck. The horse lengthened his stride and Brylee's hair bounced around her back in shining, golden curls. Despite her leg being in a cast, she clocked an impressive time. In fact, he thought she had a good shot at winning that day's event and making her way to the final go-round on Saturday.

The next three competitors tipped at least one barrel, adding penalties to their scores. Two of the following six came close to Brylee's score, and the last one finished with the exact same time. At least Brylee would have a chance to win on Saturday. He knew she'd be irritated she hadn't gone just a tenth of a second faster to claim the top spot today, but he could see her riding up to the gate to congratulate the girl that tied with her.

Brylee might twist him in knots like a food court pretzel, but she had class and sportsmanship to spare.

That night, after he and his dad had eaten the

casserole she'd made for dinner then washed the dishes while she rested with her leg propped up in a recliner, Shaun had gone to bed. Being around Brylee but keeping his distance was exhausting.

He took a quick shower in their tiny bathroom then turned in. Although he and his dad had both tried to convince Brylee to take the bedroom in the trailer, she refused. Shaun generally gave the room to his dad and slept on the bed at the front of the trailer that required crawling up into it.

Brylee had insisted it was more than adequate for her, so Shaun ended up bunking with his father. The king-sized bed was big enough to give them both plenty of room, but his dad's snoring was legendary. Tired of listening to a sound that he could only describe as a moose with a bad case of whooping cough bugling for his mate, he got out of bed and stepped into the other room, closing the bedroom door behind him to block out the noise.

He expected Brylee to be in bed, but she sat on the couch wearing a pair of pink flowered pajamas, watching TV. All the lights were off, except for the little night light they left plugged in by the sink.

"What are you doing up?" Brylee asked as he sat down next to her on the couch and stretched out his legs.

"I couldn't sleep. Dad is about to saw through concrete with his snores. I'll give him a little while to stop before I consider suffocating him."

Brylee grinned and glanced toward the bedroom, where the sound could still be heard even with the door closed. "He does seem to be extra noisy tonight." She held out a bowl with grapes and whole strawberries.

Shaun helped himself to a few grapes and leaned back on the couch, making himself comfortable. "So, what are we watching?"

"It's one of those explorer shows on the Discovery Channel." Brylee pointed to the TV screen. "See, that guy is the lead explorer. They just found a hidden cave. They had to repel down into it with ropes and once they moved past the opening, it is totally dark down there. They're hauling in lights right now."

"What are they searching for?"

"Hidden treasure, of course." She grinned and bit into a strawberry.

Shaun watched as a droplet of juice clung to her bottom lip. He had the most insane and nearly uncontrollable urge to kiss it away. In fact, he started leaning toward her when she pointed to the screen again.

"It looks so creepy down there. I bet they run into a snake."

A sudden recollection of how much Brylee hated snakes came back to him. When they first started dating, he'd been convinced she was fearless until they visited a zoo one day. He thought she was going to climb over him and anyone else in her way in her effort to get out of the reptile house when he dragged her inside. Knowing she feared something like that had made her seem so much more real to him. Up until that point, she'd been more a dream than a reality.

He turned his focus from her back to the show. "It's a cave, deep in the ground. There's not going to be any snakes down there. What would they eat? Nope. No snakes."

Brylee shook her head. "There's always a snake. Haven't you paid attention during the Indiana Jones movies? It never fails, there's always... Eww! A snake! Did you see it?" She covered her eyes and turned her head his way.

Shaun chuckled. "How could I miss it? The explorer dude is holding it up to the camera by the tail. Looks like a boa constrictor."

"Don't tell me more. Is it gone yet?" she asked, pressing her forehead against his arm.

He was half tempted to tell her the explorer uncovered a whole nest of reptiles and the rest of the show would include an in-depth examination of each and every one. If he did that, he could hope she'd stay pressed up against his side. Instead, he placed a hand on her back. "It's safe. They've moved on to crawl through bat poop."

She lifted her head and turned her gaze back to the show. A shiver rolled over her, as though she couldn't get the sight of the snake out of her mind.

Shaun settled his arm around her shoulders and drew her closer. He fully expected her to shove him away, but she merely sighed and sank against him.

"We should go to a pet store sometime so you can get up close and personal with a snake. Maybe it would help you get past your fear of them if you held one." Shaun took another grape out of the bowl and popped it in his mouth.

Brylee tipped her head back and looked up at him like his brains had just trickled out his ears. "The day you see me get that close to a snake you better be ready for the end of the world to arrive. The only reason I would touch a reptile is if doing so was the one thing standing between the end of civilization as we know it and the arrival of a complete apocalypse."

Shaun laughed and kissed her on top of the head, immediately swamped by her soft fragrance and how good it felt to hold her close once again.

As though she sensed his thoughts, she pulled away and handed him a strawberry. "Watch the show. What usually comes after bat poop? Big spiders?"

Amused, yet desperately fighting his attraction to the beautiful woman beside him, Shaun nodded his head. "Definitely spiders, and maybe a scorpion or two." He didn't care what came next, as long as Brylee stayed beside him a little while longer.

Chapter Seven

"I don't understand why I can't drive," Brylee said. She watched as the doctor slid a long gauze tube over her leg.

"Because it's going to put pressure on your leg that is unnecessary and besides, you're still in the middle of healing." The doctor stopped what he was doing and glared at her. "Stop pushing yourself so hard. In fact, if you don't promise to behave, I'll put a new cast on instead of the brace."

"I'll behave," she said with a huff. She didn't want to, but she would.

"You're healing extremely well, considering you won't stay down and stop racing. Honestly, Brylee, you're lucky you haven't done anything to cause more damage. I know it's pointless to tell you to stay off a horse until you're completely healed, so please continue to be careful. Deal?"

"Deal," she said, giving him a small smile as he fastened a brace on her leg. Although it felt big and clunky, it was definitely an improvement over the cast.

"Go ahead and stand up. We'll see you how do," the doctor said. He moved back as Brylee got to her feet and took a few steps.

She felt like she could walk with a natural gait instead of the uncomfortable limp she'd had the last few weeks with the cast. "This is so much better, Dr. Gunderson. Thank you."

"I'm glad. I've got your file ready for you to take with you and I've contacted your doctor in Walla Walla. You have an appointment to see him as soon as you get back into town in a few weeks. Make sure you keep it."

"Of course I'll keep it. Maybe by then, I'll be able to get rid of the brace." She smiled at the doctor as she slipped a sneaker on her foot and stood again. "Thanks for taking good care of me."

"You're welcome. I'll be watching to see your name taking the world title in December."

"I'm planning on it, sir."

She walked into the waiting room where Frank Kressley mindlessly flipped through a magazine. The Rockin' K crew had returned to the ranch late Sunday evening and they wouldn't have to head out until Wednesday morning for the next rodeo, which was less than an hour away. Frank had volunteered to drive her into Twin Falls for her doctor's appointment Tuesday morning.

"Look at you, honey. No more cast. That's great!" Frank said as he got up and opened the doctor's office door. They stepped outside into the broiling August heat. Brylee was glad to have the heavy cast off for a multitude of reasons. If felt wonderful to have air flowing through the holes in the brace and the thin gauze on her leg. She'd thought she might go crazy when the itching inside the cast grew almost unbearable.

If she hadn't been so utterly distracted with Shaun, she wasn't sure how she would have survived some days. Not that her thoughts of Shaun didn't come with their own exquisite form of torture, but she could handle them.

Since the night they'd sat and watched TV together while Jason practically blew the roof off the trailer with his snores, they'd reached some sort of neutral ground of friendship. In some ways, it felt like the easy, amazing relationship they'd shared back when they were dating. In other ways, it felt forced, like they both knew they couldn't go forward or back, or even to the side, so they stayed in that hesitant, wary state.

Truthfully, being around Shaun had reminded her of all the reasons she'd fallen in love with him in the first place. He was smart and funny, gentle and kind. Shaun was quick to lend a hand, crack a joke, and offer encouragement.

Then he'd turn around and do something stupid, like tell his loose-lipped friends she'd turned into a drunk. She understood why he'd done it, but it still aggravated her that he concocted the wild story.

Brylee hadn't lied about her leg and wouldn't if anyone asked her directly. She certainly didn't expect anyone else to lie for her either. Shaun hadn't exactly lied, but he had manipulated the truth into something so foreign from the facts, she didn't recognize it.

His powers of manipulation were one of the reasons she remained cautious around him. In spite of her determination to keep him an arm's length away, she felt her all-consuming anger toward him slipping away. It was hard to hate someone who brought you coffee just the way you like it every morning and went out of his way to make you smile.

Regardless, she still wouldn't give Shaun the opportunity to scale the fortress she'd erected around her heart. If she did, no doubt existed in her mind she'd end up in even worse shape than she'd been the last time he broke her heart.

"Is that okay, Brylee?" Frank asked, drawing her from her thoughts.

"I'm so sorry, Frank. My thoughts were wandering." She smiled at the older man as he unlocked his pickup and opened the passenger door for her.

"That's okay, honey. You were probably thinking about how good it felt to get that heavy cast off."

"I was thinking about that," she said, not willing to elaborate on the rest of her thoughts.

Frank climbed behind the wheel and started his pickup. "I asked if you'd like to have lunch then we can pick up the supplies and head back to the ranch."

"I would like that, Frank. Thank you."

After they enjoyed a pleasant lunch at a family restaurant, they went to pick up a list of supplies

Kash had given Frank. With the back of the pickup loaded, they headed toward the ranch.

"So, did things go okay with you and the Price boys?" Frank asked as they drove south of town.

"They did. Jason is just awesome. In some ways, he reminds me of my dad." Brylee glanced over at Frank. "Although he can snore like nobody's business."

Frank chuckled. "I can't comment since Kash and Ransom swear I sound like fighting bears have taken up residence under my bed."

Brylee grinned. "It was far, far worse than that."

"How about Shaun. You do okay with him?"

"Yes, sir." Truthfully, Brylee had done okay with Shaun. If the fluttering in her stomach every time he called her Bitsy was any indication, she'd done better than okay. But those thoughts were only going to get her in trouble, so she packed them away.

"You and Shaun have a little history, don't you?"

Slowly, Brylee nodded. That was putting it mildly. "We do, indeed."

"Well, it's none of my business, but you both kind of look like you're maybe moving beyond whatever is in the past. It's always a good thing when you can do that because you can't ever get to the future and where you're supposed to be if you keep looking back at where you've already been."

Brylee smiled and placed a hand on Frank's arm. "That sounds exactly like something my dad would have said."

Frank nodded. "I met your dad a few times when he was roping partners with Myles Smith. He really was a good guy. Sure am sorry to hear about what happened to him. Those unexpected accidents are sometimes the hardest to move past."

"Yeah, they are." Brylee sighed and looked out the window. "Sometimes I'll be in the barn or out working in the fields and expect to turn around and see Dad there."

"He's there with ya', honey. He'll always be there in your heart." Frank gave her a warm, fatherly look. "I bet he's smiling at you, proud as punch over how hard you work to be successful."

Emotion clogged Brylee's throat, so she nodded her head and forced back the tears as Frank pulled up at the house. He let her out before he drove the supplies down to the barn.

That night, as the family and all the employees gathered in the shade of the backyard trees for a barbecue dinner, everyone congratulated Brylee on getting rid of her cast.

"I suppose you'll be burning up the road now that you can drive," Jason said, smiling at her as he took a seat beside her.

Brylee shook her head. "No, I won't be. The doctor said I still can't drive. Not until the brace comes off."

"Brylee, I'm sorry," Celia said, leaning around Jason to squeeze her hand. "You know you're more than welcome to continue traveling with us."

"Thank you. I truly appreciate the offer and will most likely take you up on it. I'm just trying to figure out how to get my pickup and trailer back home. It would be great if I have them there when I get the okay to take off my brace, but I'm not sure how to make that happen." Brylee toyed with the glass of lemonade in her hand. She didn't want to ask anyone to drive it for her. She already felt like she'd been a huge imposition to them all.

"I'll drive it home for you," Shaun volunteered. "After the rodeo next week, we'll come back here to switch out stock. Dad can drive the truck without me for a day and I'll drive your pickup. We can leave it at your mom's place then head on to the rodeo in Kennewick before we come back to Walla Walla."

"Sounds like a plan to me," Jason said, bumping shoulders with Brylee. "I'd hate to lose our great cook."

Brylee shook her head. "I'm far from great, but I'm glad I can do something to be helpful."

"Are you kidding?" Kash asked from across the picnic table. "You've helped the guys with their horses, you worked the stock pens with us, and you even helped us load at the last rodeo. You've more than earned a place with us."

Brylee blushed at his praise and ducked her head.

Jason patted her on the shoulder then looked down the table at Frank. "Did I hear you say you had your eye on a new bull?"

Grateful the conversation shifted away from her, Brylee finished eating then helped Barb and Celia carry the food inside. The guys set the yard to rights and cleaned up the garbage from the paper plates and cups they'd used.

She was on her way into the house with a bowl that held only a few crumbs of chips when she turned the corner to go into the house and smacked into Shaun.

"Oh!" She would have fallen if he hadn't reached out and caught her. Even with the bowl between them, she felt too close to him. Too intimately near with the night shrouding them in darkness and the murmur of voices creating a soft background serenade on the breeze.

"Sorry. I was looking for you," Shaun said, releasing her and stepping back. He shoved his hands in his pockets and stared at her. She didn't remember him being someone who went around with his hands in his pockets all the time, but he sure seemed to be doing it a lot lately.

"What can I do for you?" she asked, taking another step away from him. Away from the decadent fragrance of him that smelled like leather and winter mountains and all man.

"I just wanted to check and make sure you were okay with my suggestion. I really don't mind driving your rig for you." Shaun stepped to one side, as though he just realized he blocked her path to the house.

"No, I'm fine with the plan and very grateful for the help, Shaun. I... um... I really do appreciate it, and all that you've done the past few weeks. Thank you."

He smiled, his teeth glowing white in the evening darkness. "My pleasure, Bitsy. See you in the morning."

Before she could say another word, he strolled

off, whistling a tune she thought she recognized but didn't want to. If she wasn't mistaken it was the song that had been playing the first time he kissed her.

Maybe she would let him take her to a pet store to touch a snake. She'd vowed she'd be poised on the edge of oblivion before she ever forgave Shaun for what he'd done. Either the world was about to end, or she was finally letting go of the past.

The next morning, Brylee packed her bag, including a pair of cowboy boots with short shafts that fit over her brace. She carried her things down to the kitchen and hugged Barb then Frank before she went out to stow her things in Shaun's trailer.

Distracted by thoughts of Shaun and the upcoming rodeos, she stepped inside. When she turned to stow her bag on her bed, she dropped it as a snake's head poked out from beneath the mattress by her head.

Badly startled, she gasped for breath and spun around to leave. It was then she noticed a second snake coiled around the faucet of the sink.

Brylee screamed and raced out of the trailer, stomping the ground a few times, as though the snakes had slithered beneath her feet. The sound of laughter finally penetrated her panic as Shaun and some of the other guys watched her from nearby.

"What is so funny?" she shouted, pointing toward the trailer door. "There are two snakes in there. How did they get...?" Her panic gave way to fury. "You put them in there, didn't you, Shaun?"

He shrugged. "Maybe they slithered in on their own." He stepped into the trailer and retrieved the two rubber snakes that looked entirely realistic, especially to a girl with a great fear of reptiles. "They aren't even real, Bits. Just made of recycled tires."

Shaun held the head of one between his thumb and index finger and wiggled it toward her face. "Totally harmless."

Brylee grabbed it out of his hand. "The snakes might be, but I'm not!" She smacked him across the arm three times with the snake while the guys around them hooted with laughter. "Do not ever play a snake prank on me again. Ever!" She hit him once more as he pretended to crouch from her in fear of dire injury. Exasperated, she tossed the snake in his face and limped off with her leg aching from the abuse she'd given it after jumping out of the trailer and stamping her feet.

"Reckon you best leave those snakes at home, Shaun," she heard Billy tell him as she walked around the pickup.

"I reckon Billy is right," she muttered, hurrying away before the guys caught her smile. As angry as she was at Shaun, she knew she'd most likely looked like she was trying to invent a few new dance moves in her reaction to the rubber snakes.

At least with Shaun around things were never dull.

And revenge was going to be so sweet.

Chapter Eight

Brylee quietly opened the trailer door and stepped inside. She knew Shaun had hurried in to take a shower before the rodeo began. All three of them had spent what seemed like half the day sorting stock in the heat. While Jason showered and changed, Brylee helped Shaun saddle the horses they planned to use during the bareback riding then went to brush down Rocket.

She glanced at her watch, figuring how long it would take Shaun to shower. She wanted to be in the trailer when he finished because she'd figured out a way to finally get back at him for his little prank with the snakes.

It had taken her a week to come up with an idea and a few more days to implement the plan, but she could barely contain her giggles as she thought about Shaun's face when he figured out what she'd done.

When a giggle threatened to roll out her lips,

she pressed her hand to her mouth and waited. Shaun was singing to himself. She could just picture him belting out one of his favorite songs while toweling dry.

Then the picture shifted in focus from him singing to the toweling dry part. Rats. Why couldn't she just focus on being ornery to him instead of his incredible body? Since she'd moved into the trailer with him and his dad he'd run around in front of her without a shirt enough times that she should be used to seeing him that way. But each time she saw those muscles on display, it made her want things she would never, ever have.

The first time Shaun had yanked off his shirt in front of her, she'd gaped at the scars he bore on his sides, back, and chest. He looked like he'd battled a knife-wielding madman and barely survived the experience. He'd had two scars when she'd been dating him, but he'd added quite a collection in the ensuing years.

As though he sensed her perusal, he pointed to a red gash on his side that appeared to be the newest. "Occupational hazard. It's a good idea to avoid getting a spur in the side," he said, then left her gaping after him as he made his way into the bathroom to shower.

Today, though, she tried not to think how enticing he looked without his shirt and center her attention on his reaction to her joke. She shifted a step closer and a floorboard squeaked.

The bathroom door opened and moist air rolled into the rest of the trailer. Shaun stuck his head out and smiled at her. "I thought I heard someone out here. I'll be finished in a minute."

"No hurry," Brylee said, leaning against the counter in the tiny kitchen. "I just came in to get out of the heat."

"It's like being in a broiler out there today. I hope it cools down before the rodeo gets started," he said. Shaun stepped back into the bathroom then reappeared with his toothbrush in his hand. "Is Rocket ready to win tonight?"

Brylee smiled. "Of course. He's always ready to win, whether we do or not."

Shaun nodded as he brushed his teeth then disappeared into the bathroom again. He returned with a can of aerosol deodorant in his hand. He gave the can a hearty shake then lifted the opposite arm over his head and sprayed his armpit.

Brylee bit her lip to keep from laughing as he switched hands and sprayed the other pit. Suddenly, his eyes widened and he glanced from one armpit to the other, then at the can in his hands.

"Hey, this isn't my deo," he said, looking from the can back to his armpits. The hair stood out all stiff and sticky. "It's hairspray!"

Brylee could no longer contain her laughter. When it burst out of her, Shawn offered her a sharp scowl, making her laugh all the more. Tears rolled out of her eyes and she held on to the counter to remain upright. "Need a little mousse to go with that?" she wheezed between snickers.

Shaun took a step toward her, pointing the can her direction. "You did this, didn't you?"

Before he sprayed her with the hairspray, she took the can from him. She'd had to wait until she could catch a ride with Billy to the nearest superstore to find a can of hairspray that so closely resembled Shaun's deodorant he wouldn't notice the difference at a quick glance.

She giggled again, unable to stop herself. "Guilty as charged. The next time you think about scaring me half to death with snakes, remember this moment."

"I'll remember it all right, Bitsy." His menacing glower did nothing to dampen the humor she found in the situation.

One second Shaun was pouting at the bathroom door and the next he'd picked her up with one arm and held her against his damp, solid chest. Shaun yanked the hairspray out of her hand and sprayed it all over her head. He tossed the can behind him, out of her reach, and then ran his fingers into her hair, making it stand up all over.

"Maybe you better remember who got the last laugh, darlin'."

"Oh, I will," she said, squirming against him. Both of them were laughing as he tried to tickle her sides. The more she wiggled to get away, the closer he held her until their lips were nearly touching.

His eyes looked like a summer sky right before a lightning storm, a mixture of swirling grays and blues. The sparks dancing in them ignited. She braced herself, sure the wildfire about to explode between the two of them would set the trailer ablaze.

Unable to fight whatever insane force drew her to him, she half-heartedly pushed at him to let her go. He tossed her over his shoulder and popped her on the backside, but at that moment the towel he had wrapped around his waist started to slip. Left with the choice of setting her down or baring all his assets, he clutched at the towel and bent down to let her slide onto her feet.

"I'll go check on the horses," she said, and raced out the door before she did something stupid, like kiss that smug cowboy.

Jason walked up and mounted Jingo, giving Brylee a strange look. "Shaun ready to go?"

She shook her head. "He's having a technical issue." Giggles erupted again as she told Jason about switching the deodorant with hairspray.

He hooted with laughter.

"Oh, honey, I wish I'd seen his face when he figured it out. He doesn't have time to take another shower, so he's just going to have to work with sticky pits." Jason rode around the trailer and leaned down from the horse enough he could open the door. "Shaun, get a move on. Time to get to work."

"I'll be there in a minute," he hollered. "And if Brylee's out there, tell her we are a long, long way from being done with this."

She snickered and Jason laughed again as he shut the door.

He gave her a high five. "Does him good to have his cage rattled once in a while." Jason was still chuckling as he rode off toward the arena.

An hour and a half later, Brylee had showered and changed. She sat on the back of Coal outside the gate near the bucking chutes as Shaun and Jason waited for the saddle bronc riding to begin.

Cooper strutted into the arena wearing a

rainbow-colored foam fifty-gallon cowboy hat that sported a smattering of gold glitter across the crown.

"What is that thing on your head, Cooper?" the announcer asked.

"A hat. Have you lost your spidey-vision?" Cooper made his way over to Shaun and Jason then struck a pose. "I look pretty cool, don't I?"

"You look…" the announcer's voice trailed off, obviously distracted by something going on in the announcer's box.

Cooper swung up behind Shaun and swept off the hat, fanning it back and forth beside him. "Don't you think my hat's something, Shaun?"

Shaun chuckled. "Absolutely, Coop. You better hang onto that hat with both hands. If you don't, one of the barrel racers might wrestle it away from you. It's just colorful enough with the right amount of gaudy flair one of them might want to wear it."

The crowd laughed and Brylee joined in their amusement. Shaun wasn't wrong in saying some of the barrel racers got pretty wild with their outfits, hats included. She didn't have the time or money to invest in flashy outfits, even if she'd wanted to, which she didn't. Her black hat and favorite navy shirt were good enough for her.

Over the course of the past few months, she'd picked up a few sponsorships which made a huge difference. Although when she started out this year with a dream and determination, it seemed like a long shot to make enough money to pay off the debt and save the ranch. Now, with sponsors on board, and more than a hundred thousand dollars in earnings, she could see a light glimmering at the end of what had been a pitch-black tunnel. If she could just make it through another six weeks of competing and stay on top, she'd have a solid chance at the finals in December.

"Say, Shaun, I heard from the fellas that you've come up with a new way to beat the heat." Cooper's voice took on the tone he used when he was about to completely humiliate someone.

Shaun gave him a cautious glance over his shoulder. "I have?"

"Way I heard it," Cooper said as he slid off the horse and plopped the hat back on his head, "was that you discovered hairspray works great as an under arm barrier to sweat. Did Miss Clairol spray that on your pits for you and did you go for Aqua Net?"

The crowd laughed while Shaun tossed a dark scowl at Cooper then whipped around to glare at Brylee. She was as horrified as he appeared. She hadn't told anyone other than Jason. Her gaze flicked to his. He was laughing so hard, he was about to fall right off his horse.

Cooper held his arms stretched out with his pinky fingers in the air then made an exaggerated pirouette in the arena.

Before anyone else could share any comments, the first rider charged out of the chute.

Brylee watched Shaun and Jason work. It always amazed her how attuned they were to each other and to everything going on around them. While Shaun rode up on the left side of the rider, Jason closed in on the right and loosened the cinch strap. Shaun took the bronc rein and snubbed it around his saddle horn while holding out an arm for the rider to grab hold of and launch himself off the bucking horse. The rider whipped over the back of Shaun's horse and landed on the other side of him. Shaun looked to make sure the rider was fine before he turned and headed toward the gate with the horse.

The two Price men made the work look so easy, but she knew they both were extremely talented and good at what they did. They had to be good ropers, intuitive to the stock and the riders, and be able to confidently react to situations on the fly.

Truthfully, Shaun was perfect for the job and he'd learned from his dad who was one of the best in the industry.

Brylee was glad he'd given up competing in bareback. She'd never admit it to anyone, but she had kept up on whether he made it to the finals every year or if he'd been in any major wrecks. She knew he'd missed several months of competing last year when he'd broken his leg twice.

Maybe she and Shaun were both right where they were supposed to be. Thoughts of how hard she fought to keep from falling for him again made her question if she was where she belonged. It couldn't be true. Not when she needed to stay focused on her goals.

Besides, even if she'd decided to forgive Shaun for what he'd done in the past, it certainly didn't mean she was willing to give him a second chance. From what she'd observed, he didn't seem particularly interested in one anyway. Women flocked around him like seagulls on a spilled bag of peanuts.

Not that he was entirely to blame for the attention cast in his direction.

The jeans he wore from Lasso Eight fit him like a glove, perfectly molding to his backside and heavily muscled thighs. Brylee's heart pitter-pattered just thinking about how good he looked in them.

Her gaze settled on him as he worked. Halfway through the event, Shaun and Jason rode over to switch horses. Shaun glowered at her as though he'd like to toss her to the wolves.

"I didn't tattle, Shaun. Don't be giving me the stink eye." She glanced at Jason and he snorted with another round of laughter.

"I told Cooper, but only because I was laughing so hard, he had to know the cause," Jason said, doing his best to contain his chortles.

"Not cool, Dad. Not cool at all." Shaun slid onto Coal and rode him into the arena.

Brylee led the two horses back to the trailer and took care of them. When she finished, she swung onto Rocket and rode him to the warm-up arena.

She walked him around it twice then increased his speed. When the announcer said it was time for the barrel racing to start, she rode him out of the pen and over to where the other girls were lining up. Brylee was riding last. She glanced skyward. At least it wasn't going to rain.

Her leg felt better and without the cast hampering her movements, she had more control with the brace. She was still careful and tried to keep her weight off her leg as much as possible, but that first turn on the barrel to the right never failed to make her leg throb with pain.

Two girls remained in front of her when she caught a whiff on the breeze that made her look back. Only one person on the planet carried that mouth-watering, luscious scent. She watched Shaun approach. He'd lost his scowl and replaced it with a smile as he approached her and settled a hand on her leg just above her knee. Electricity jolted through her at his touch, but she ignored it.

"Just wanted to wish you luck, Bitsy," he said, letting his hand drop slightly until he fingered the edge of her brace. For some reason, he was concerned she'd take it off to ride and had gotten in the habit of checking to make sure she had it on before she competed.

When the next girl rode into the arena, Brylee gave him a knowing look as she moved Rocket forward. "Thanks for the good wishes."

"You'll win this thing. Rocket won't let you down." He scratched Rocket just behind the ears and the horse practically purred.

Brylee grinned. "You always did know just what Rocket likes."

Shaun cocked an eyebrow upward and tossed her a flirty look. "Used to know what his owner liked, too."

Her smile melted and she moved Rocket forward as the last girl in front of her went through her pattern.

"Go get 'em, Brylee." Shaun patted her thigh

then stepped back as the announcer called out her name.

With Shaun's scent lingering in her nose, she forcibly blocked him from her thoughts while she and Rocket zoomed around the barrels. Brylee settled her mind on what she wanted Rocket to do, which was win. The horse stretched out his legs after they rounded the last barrel and raced across the arena. She yanked back on the reins as soon as he shot past the electronic eye that timed the event.

"Ladies and gentlemen, Miss Brylee Barton is our winner!" the announcer boomed. "Did you see that girl, go? That is what I'm talking about! Give Brylee and Rocket a big hand!"

Shaun beamed at Brylee as she pulled Rocket up outside the gate and took him to cool off. He jogged over to mount Lucky and entered the arena for the bull riding.

As soon as she had Rocket settled, she made her way back to the trailer and decided to make taco salad for dinner. She'd just finished cooking the ground beef when Jason and Shaun came in, both laughing at something Cooper had said during the bull riding.

"That smells good, honey." Jason smiled at her as he made his way past her and into the bathroom. He emerged a minute later with clean hands and the arena dust scrubbed off his face.

"I heard there's a dance tonight. Anyone want to go?" Shaun asked as he moved past Brylee toward the bathroom.

She shook her head. "If you're asking if I want to go, the answer would be no. I'm barely walking somewhat normally with the brace on my leg. I have no interest in trying to two-step with it."

"Aw, come with me. It'll be fun," Shaun gave her an imploring look. "I'll slow dance with you and you can pretend you're taking a break on the fast dances. Please?"

Brylee prepared three plates with the salad and set them on the table. "Are you trying to tell me you don't have a line of girls from here to the freeway willing to go with you?"

Jason smirked. "There are a few who would go with you, son."

"I don't want to go with them. I want to go with our barrel racing champ," Shaun said, winking at her before he ducked into the bathroom. He was still wiping his hands on a towel when he stepped back out then tossed the towel onto the counter. "Come on, Bitsy. Celebrate a little. You deserve it."

"My idea of a celebration would be a good book, a box of rich chocolate, and a bubble bath." Brylee couldn't remember the last time she'd enjoyed a box of expensive chocolates. Or allowed herself the luxury of spending a few hours reading. And a bubble bath? The idea of taking one sounded purely indulgent.

She glanced at Shaun and saw a streak of interest, a spark of something in his eyes she'd rather ignore. She averted her gaze and sat down at the table.

Jason asked a blessing on their meal then pointed his fork at Shaun. "If Brylee doesn't want to go, leave her alone. Keep pestering this poor girl and who knows what she'll do with your toiletries."

The man cleared his throat twice in an attempt to subdue his chuckles, but Brylee heard him muttering something about hairspray and groomed armpits.

Shaun ignored the comments and looked at Brylee again. "I'll quit begging, but I really would like you to go with me, just for a little while. Cooper and Paige will be there and so will Jessie and Chase. Kash and Celia already headed back to the ranch or they would have come, too."

"If it makes you more comfortable, Brylee, I'll go along as a chaperone to make sure my boy behaves himself," Jason offered.

"Good grief, Dad, you make it sound like I'm sixteen and about to steal your car." Shaun stabbed his fork into his salad and took a bite.

"If memory serves me correctly, you did sneak out in your grandma's car one night when you were supposed to be grounded." Jason waggled his fork at Shaun. "You've always been a handful."

"The apple didn't fall far from the tree, old man," Shaun said without looking up from his food.

Jason veered the subject away from the dance to the work they needed to do in the morning to be able to pull out early and get back to the ranch. They could have gone that night, but Kash told them not to worry about loading in the dark. Brylee would have been just as happy catching a ride back with Kash and Celia, but she felt obligated to stick with Jason and Shaun. Despite the many assurances she wasn't expected to help them, she needed to out of her own sense of duty and responsibility.

Jason and Shaun made short work of the dinner

dishes then the two of them stood at the door staring at her, as though waiting for her to get ready to go along with them.

"Oh, fine. I'll go to the dance for a few minutes, but don't expect any fast moves from me. The first time you say something to irritate me, I'm coming back here," she said in warning to Shaun.

"Don't you need to primp and fuss?" Jason asked as she tucked her phone into her pocket and grabbed a packet of gum from her purse. She took a piece then held it out to the two guys. They each took a piece while she rubbed lip balm over her lips.

"Consider me primped and fussed," she said, motioning to the door. "Let's get this over with."

"Boy, Bitsy, you are just a ball of fun," Shaun said dryly as she preceded them outside.

She gave him a frost-laced glare and moved back toward the door. He held up his hands in front of his chest, as though demonstrating his innocence.

"Strike that. I said nothing."

Jason chuckled and held out his arm. "May I escort you to the dance, Miss Barton?"

"You may, Mr. Price. Thank you." Brylee looped her arm around his and the two of them walked over to where the dance was being held in a roped off section of the parking lot.

They arrived at the dance to see the familiar faces of several friends. Cooper danced in front of them, twirling Paige and making her laugh. Chase stood with his arms around Jessie. Brylee could only assume he'd have nearly as hard a time convincing the shy girl to two-step around the dance floor as Shaun would her.

She moved away from Jason and walked over to the couple. "It's nice to see you guys here," she said in greeting.

Jessie smiled with genuine warmth brightening her face and expressive eyes. "It's great to see you, too, Brylee. Congrats on that amazing win."

"Thank you. Rocket deserves most of the credit."

"Not true," Chase said, grinning at her. "That's a team effort and we're cheering for team Barton all the way to the finals."

"I really appreciate that. I'm cheering for you to take the championship again this year, Chase." Brylee laughed as Cooper broke into some sort of disco move and Paige merely stood beside him and rolled her eyes.

"He really can't turn off his tendency to be a clown, can he?" Brylee asked.

"Not most of the time. He's lucky Paige puts up with it." Chase kissed Jessie's cheek. "I don't think my wife would appreciate that kind of attention."

Jessie blushed. "For gosh sakes, don't even think about it. You try something like that while I'm dancing with you and you'll be wondering why you're sleeping on the couch."

Brylee laughed and felt Shaun's presence behind her before she glanced back at him. He settled a hand on her shoulder as they watched the dancers. The warmth of it seared through her blouse and threatened to brand her skin. If there hadn't been an audience around them, she would have pulled away from him. Away from the temptation she found harder and harder to ignore or resist.

"Come on, Bitsy, they're playing our song." Shaun grabbed her hand and led her on the dance floor without giving her a chance to argue. The song was a new one she'd heard on the radio a few times, so it definitely was not their song. She rather doubted Shaun even recalled they'd once had a song.

Before she went down a road that only led to bitter memories, she redirected her thoughts and watched their friends. Chase led Jessie out on the dance floor and she smiled at the couple. They were so deeply in love it was adorable to see them together.

"Aren't they the sweetest couple?" Brylee asked as Shaun took her right hand in his left then placed his other hand on her waist.

He glanced over at his friend and nodded. "Yeah, they are. That first year they were married seemed kinda hard on them, but they didn't know each other before they wed."

"Oh, I think I heard about that. It was supposed to be a publicity stunt but the minister really married them. Is that right?"

Shaun nodded as they swayed in time to the music. "Chase was fit to be tied at first, but I think he took one look at Jessie and lost his heart. It can happen to the best of us."

Brylee looked up at him and measured his words. "If you're implying you suffered the same fate, don't bother trying to fool me. I don't think you ever really loved me, Shaun. Not like that."

"Oh, I did, Brylee. You were all I could think

about from that first time your hand touched mine." Subtly, Shaun drew her closer. "You have no idea how much I loved you."

"If you add in that you still do, I'm walking out of here and leaving you hanging on the dance floor."

Shaun grinned at her. "You sure know how to deflate a fella. When did you get so hard-hearted and cruel?"

"When the boy I loved more than life itself walked out on me." Brylee gave him a pointed look. "Let's talk about something more pleasant, shall we?"

"We shall." Shaun edged a little closer.

Brylee enjoyed being in his arms too much to step back. No matter how much she'd objected to attending the dance, she couldn't think of anywhere she'd rather be at that moment than right there in Shaun's arms.

He looked down at her and gave her a half smile that weakened her knees. "Are you gonna sabotage my toothpaste next or do I need to be afraid of my shaving lotion?"

Brylee laughed. "I promise I won't mess with any of your toiletries again."

"That still leaves a whole slew of things you might mess with, though."

"I'm thoroughly insulted you'd think I'd do something so devious, Shaun. My feelings are hurt."

He chuckled. "Darlin', you and I both know you can and most likely will do something."

"Maybe I'm retiring from playing pranks and giving up all childish behavior." She batted her eyelashes at him and tossed him an innocent smile. "I'm far above such ill-mannered nonsense, you know."

He shook his head. "That's a load of something if I've ever heard one. You can take a bucket of manure, wrap it in pretty paper, and tie it with a bow, but it's still just a bucket full of…"

She placed her hand over his mouth. "I get the idea."

Shaun kissed her fingers and she moved her hand back to where it rested on his broad shoulder. The strength she felt there beneath the cotton of his shirt made her long to explore it. He had more muscles than she recalled from years before. Shaun seemed even larger than life now than he had back then.

The song ended on a soft note. Brylee would have pulled away, but another slow song started to play.

He grinned at her. "You said you'd give me the slow dances."

She tipped her head and studied him. "What did you do? Bribe the band?"

"I'm wounded you'd even suggest I'd resort to such tactics." He took a half step closer to her. One more step and they'd be dancing far too intimately for her preferences.

As Shaun moved her around the dance floor, she wasn't surprised to discover he was still an excellent dancer. He'd always liked to dance when they were dating and he'd taught her several moves, none of which she'd danced since they split up. In fact, unless chaperoning Birch's school dances counted, she hadn't been to a dance since the last one she'd attended with Shaun.

When the band began playing another slow song, some of the crowd looked a little disappointed, but Shaun winked at her and they kept dancing.

Truthfully, she hadn't wanted to go to any dances without him, even when the very thought of him made her bristle with anger. Shaun was the only man she'd ever enjoyed dancing with, the only one she wanted to dance with, except maybe her dad, but that was totally different.

Thoughts of her father made her heart heavy. She could almost hear him whispering in her ear. *Live in the moment, baby girl. Don't waste it wandering around in the past. You've got no business squandering today's gift on yesterday's heartache.*

"Hush," she said, realizing too late she'd spoken aloud.

Shaun pulled back far enough he could look at her. "I wasn't even talking. Don't tell me you can read minds now?"

She grinned at him. "I also have an eye in the back of my head, so you better watch out."

"I already know I'm in big, deep trouble where you're concerned, Bitsy." His eyes looked stormier than usual as he gently slid his hand from her waist to move up and down her back. "You have to know…"

"May I cut in?" Jason asked, with a teasing smile.

"Of course," Brylee said, not giving Shaun a

chance to answer as she turned to his dad and started dancing with him.

Shaun wandered off in the direction of the concession stand.

Brylee watched him go. He'd not touched a bit of alcohol since she'd been traveling with him, but he sure looked like he was considering something now.

"Does Shaun still drink?" she asked his father.

Jason shook his head. "No. He stopped right after he broke up with you. Never said why, but I haven't seen him touch a drop since then. It's probably a good thing. The direction he was headed could have ended badly."

Brylee nodded in agreement. Back in the day, Shaun could party with the best of them. They'd been two stupid kids back then. It's lucky they'd both survived with nothing more than a few scars and, at least in her case, a broken heart.

"I think he really loved you, Brylee. He, um... he had a hard time after you broke up. It wasn't easy for him to find his way out of it."

Brylee kept her thoughts to herself, even though she couldn't imagine Shaun struggling more than she had. He'd moved on with his life with ease compared to the heartache and torture she'd endured.

The song ended and Jason walked her off the dance floor. A fast one began so she glanced around to see if she could spy Chase and Jessie. She wouldn't mind visiting with them until Shaun claimed her for the next slow dance.

She'd been looking over at the concession

stand to see if they'd gone over there when she felt someone grab her arm and propel her toward the dancers.

Brylee glared at the overweight, middle-aged man who tried to force her onto the dance floor. "I'm not interested in dancing," she said, trying to pull out of his grasp.

The man was twice her size and obviously on his way to being blind drunk. "I wanna dance with the champion racer," he slurred. "I bet you've got all kinds of moves, baby."

His hand released her arm only to grab her by the waist and jerk her roughly against him.

Brylee pushed against his chest and turned her face away from his foul breath, but couldn't break his hold. If she'd had two good legs to stand on, she would have kicked him and gone on her way.

She considered how much damage it would inflict if she kneed him where it counted when she saw Shaun shove two bottles of pop into his dad's hands and stride toward her. She'd never seen him look so angry, like he wanted to rip the man's head right off his beefy shoulders.

"Get your hands off my wife," Shaun's voice sliced through the music and silenced the sounds of the crowd.

Chapter Nine

The man either didn't hear Shaun or was too drunk to realize a hurricane of wrath was about to descend upon him. When Shaun laid a hand on the man's shoulder and spun him around, the drunk looked shocked.

"Last warning. Get your hands off my wife!" Shaun's chest heaved with fury and he held his right hand in a tight fist.

The drunk backed away. "I don't want trouble, man. I didn't know she's married."

"You're what?" Jason asked as he strode up beside Shaun. He voiced the question almost everyone appeared to be dying to ask. In fact, even with the music still playing, the noise around them had died to utter quiet.

Shaun disregarded his dad's question and settled his hands on Brylee's shoulders. "Are you okay? Did he hurt you?"

Brylee didn't know whether to hug Shaun for

rescuing her or slug him in the gut for calling her his wife. He'd lost the right to use that title when he left her. She pulled herself up to her full height and gave him a look so full of pain, indignation, and resentment, Shaun took a step back. "You don't get to call me that anymore, Shaun."

"What do you mean anymore?" Jason asked, clearly unwilling to let the matter drop. "You two were married?"

Brylee shook her head. "No, not really."

"Yes, we were!" Shaun looked around, noticing the eyes of the crowd focused on them. "Dad, let's move this little interrogation somewhere other than the middle of the dance floor." Shaun cupped Brylee's elbow and guided her through the crowd surrounding them.

Jessie reached out and gave Brylee an encouraging pat on the back as she moved past her and Chase. With her head held high, Brylee continued walking and didn't stop until they reached the trailer.

The minute the closed door muffled the sounds of the crowd outside, Jason gave them both long, pointed looks. "What is going on? I want the whole story, right now."

"Dad, it's not... I don't..." Shaun tossed his hat on the counter and forked his fingers through his hair.

Brylee sank onto the couch and pulled up the leg of her jeans so she could adjust her brace. Shaun hunkered down and reached to help, but she slapped his hand away. "I think you better answer your dad's question. I've got a few of my own I'd like answered."

Jason sat down on the end of the couch and pinned Shaun with a hard glare. "Did you or did you not marry Brylee?"

"I did."

Shaun stood and started pacing the small space between the couch and the kitchen, back and forth, until Brylee considered sticking her foot out and tripping him just to get him to stop.

"Sit down!" Jason finally barked.

Surprisingly, Shaun obeyed and took a seat next to Brylee.

"Are you still married?"

"No, of course not," Brylee said, rushing to answer the question.

"Start from the beginning," Jason said, looking to Shaun.

"Brylee and I fell in love six years ago, you knew that." Shaun jiggled his foot and drummed the fingers of his left hand against his thigh, a sure sign he was nervous.

"Everyone knew that. It wasn't exactly a secret." Jason moved from the arm of the couch to lean against the counter where he could better glare at his son. "When did you get married?"

When Shaun remained silent, Brylee spoke up. "In Las Vegas, during the finals that year."

Jason rolled his eyes. "Let me guess, it was a spur of the moment thing?"

Shaun nodded. "It was Friday night, before the last day of the finals. Brylee had won the barrel racing that night and I had the top score for bareback riding. I might have had a little too much to drink, and may have coerced her into drinking a glass or six of champagne to celebrate. It was a sure thing we both were going to take home the championship titles, or so we thought." He sighed. "One thing led to another. We ended up in one of those little wedding chapels saying I do."

"Then what happened?" Jason asked. From the look on his face, Brylee could see he tried to piece the puzzle together. The problem was that Shaun was the only one who knew the answer to that question.

Brylee had nearly turned herself inside out trying to figure out why she'd awakened the morning after Shaun married her to find an empty hotel room and a note from him telling her it had been a huge mistake to wed. He'd left instructions for her to call an attorney he'd contacted to move forward with an annulment.

"I, uh... well, I woke up the next day and realized it was a mistake. Remember Will Johnson, who used to ride? Well, his brother is an attorney. I got in touch with him and he took care of the paperwork." Shaun got up and started pacing again. His father stopped him halfway across the floor by placing a hand to his chest.

"Let me get this straight. You got drunk, then talked Brylee into getting tipsy, married her, had the honeymoon, then decided you weren't ready to be a grown up." A vein began throbbing in Jason's neck. He turned to Brylee. "What did he say to you when he left?"

She shrugged and shifted to a more comfortable position on the couch. "He didn't say anything. I woke up to an empty hotel room and a note to call his attorney. The note said he was sorry, but he couldn't be married to me."

"That's it?" Jason gaped at Brylee in surprise.

"That's it. I've known the who, what, where, and when, but I've spent the last five and half years wondering why. Why a boy I loved more than anything just walked out on me like that."

Jason appeared even more infuriated as he glowered at Shaun. "You snuck out of the room like a coward? You didn't even have the decency to tell this poor girl in person?" Jason settled a hand on Brylee's shoulder as he scowled at his son.

Now that Jason was mad and they all were upset, Brylee wished they could have avoided this discussion. As much as she wanted to hear the truth, Jason's sympathy was about to push her beyond her ability to control her emotions. She absolutely refused to cry in front of Shaun.

"No, I didn't, Dad. There's a lot of stupid mistakes I've made through the years, but leaving Brylee that morning is the one I'll always regret the most." Shaun gave her a look so full of remorse she almost opened her arms to him. But doing so would open her heart and that was never going to happen.

Shaun dropped down to his knees in front of her and took her cold hand in his. "I'm truly sorry for what I did, Brylee. Dad's right in saying I was a coward. I acted like a scared boy, not a man, and I've regretted it every day since then. I wanted to explain, to apologize, but by the time I fully realized what I'd done, you'd already changed your phone number and you never answered the letter I sent to you."

"I don't know anything about a letter, but you made it perfectly clear you didn't want to be with me, Shaun. Your attorney wouldn't give me any details as to the reason why, though, other than to say it was a mistake and you were sorry. Well, sorry didn't quite cut it when you left my heart in a thousand splintered pieces in that hotel room. I gave you everything I had to give and you tossed each one of those precious gifts back in my face." She dropped his hand and stood, letting the emotions she'd tried so hard to keep tucked away bubble to the surface. "You have no idea how much you hurt me, how much damage you caused, how many tears I cried. I assumed spending one night as my husband was so traumatic it made you run off without so much as a decent goodbye. I loved you, Shaun, as completely as a human heart can love." *And I still love you!* her traitorous heart cried. "But that wasn't good enough. If you want to know why I disappeared, it's because I never wanted to see you again. Not when you destroyed my heart right along with my dreams."

She turned to Jason. "I don't know what I did so wrong that Shaun decided he couldn't love me and at this point I don't care. It just doesn't matter anymore. This summer gave me the opportunity to finally let go of the bitterness and forgive him, but don't expect me to ever forget because I can't. I can't and I won't."

Suddenly feeling suffocated by the two men, she pushed past Shaun and opened the trailer door. "I need some time alone. Good night."

"Don't go. I'll leave," Shaun said, moving to the door, but she shut it in his face.

Brylee walked past their trailer and turned toward the stables. Emotions and memories she'd buried washed over her bringing an onslaught of pain that left her gasping for breath. She leaned against the end of a trailer for support. Tears streamed down her cheeks and she pressed her hand against her mouth to keep from sobbing aloud.

"Brylee?" a soft voice asked as a hand gingerly touched her arm.

She peered through her tears at Paige and Cooper James.

"What's wrong, Brylee?" Cooper asked, giving Paige a worried glance before he looked back at Brylee.

She shook her head, unable to speak with emotion lodged like a lump of paste in her throat.

Paige settled an arm around her and Cooper moved to her other side. "Let's get you back to your trailer.

"No!" Brylee frantically shook her head, pulling away from them.

"Then come to ours. We've got plenty of room," Cooper said, leading the way as she leaned against Paige for support.

How had a simple dance or two with Shaun ended like this?

Shaun stared at the door Brylee had just slammed in his face, wondering how an evening of fun had so quickly turned into a nightmare. He hadn't meant to blurt out that she was his wife. When he'd seen the drunk manhandling her, though, something protective and primitive took over in his brain. The next thing he knew, he was clenching his fist, ready to knock the guy into next week.

It was bad enough he'd called Brylee his wife once, but he'd said it twice. And the worst part of it all was how much he liked the way it sounded. If he could trade everything he owned for a machine that would take him back in time to that morning when he'd made such a fateful decision, he wouldn't run away from Brylee. Instead, he'd gather her close and never let her go.

But no magic means of time travel existed and from her reaction, she would never, ever get over what he'd done. Even if she had forgiven him, she wouldn't ever trust him again. She had once and all it had gotten her was a broken heart.

"Why, Shaun?" his dad asked from behind him. "Why?"

Shaun took a deep breath and turned around to face his father. "Why to which of the many questions I know you're thinking."

"Start with why you didn't tell me the truth." Jason sank down on the couch, as though he was too weak to stand.

For the first time since he'd become an adult, Shaun thought his father looked old. Old, tired, and weary.

"I didn't want you to think I was a lunkheaded, irresponsible kid, which I was. I guess I was ashamed and embarrassed, and scared." Shaun sat beside him and leaned back. "I woke up with Brylee beside me. At first, I couldn't even remember how we'd gotten to her hotel room or how I'd finally talked my way into her bed, because I hadn't tried before. She was a good girl and I knew it, respected it. Brylee was nothing like the other girls I generally ran around with before I met her." A sigh rose up from his soul and he slowly expelled it. "Then it all came back in a rush. Fear and guilt flooded over me at what I'd done, we'd done, until I couldn't breathe. I was overwhelmed and didn't know how to handle it all. I got out of bed, noticed the ring on my finger, and panicked, Dad. I panicked and called Will and he put me in touch with his brother. After a five minute conversation, I wrote a note with the attorney's info and left."

Shaun glanced at his dad, aware of the censure on Jason's face, and shook his head. "There isn't anything you can say that will make me feel any worse than I already do. What I did was stupid and wrong and hurtful. I'd give anything to go back and undo the mistake I made. That evening, the last night of the rodeo, I hid out so I wouldn't have to see Brylee. As you know, I didn't make my ride and lost the championship. She was so upset she knocked over two barrels and lost her title, too."

His foot began to jiggle as he recalled every horrible moment of that day. "I didn't want to see the look on your face that's there right now, Dad, so I decided to just tell people Brylee and I broke up, which we did, but it was all on me. Before a week had passed, I felt like I'd die without her. I wanted more than anything to take it all back, to confess how much I loved her and beg her to forgive me. By that time, she'd changed her number. I even tried calling her home phone, but her mother refused to let me talk to her or even tell her I'd called. So I wrote a letter. If I thought she would have seen me, I would have driven to her house and pleaded in person, but I figured her dad would rather shoot me than let me apologize."

"I would have shot first and asked questions later if someone had treated your sister like that," Jason said. His tone didn't hold quite as much disgust and his face had softened slightly.

"I know and I wouldn't have blamed him a bit. I tried to get over her, to get over how much I missed her. It hurt so much to know I could have had the best thing in the world and I threw it away because I was a scared, cowardly boy."

"But what were you scared of, son? The responsibility of being married? Being faithful to her? What were you so afraid of?" Jason pressed.

"Brylee! I was afraid of Brylee and how much I loved her!" Shaun struggled with the emotions threatening to suck him under. "I loved her so much, Dad, it scared me spitless. I had no idea love like that existed. Oh, I'd known from the moment I met her I loved her, but holding her in my arms that night made it perfectly clear that she had an indescribable power over me. I needed her so much, loved her so deeply, it terrified me. No one had ever made me feel what I felt when I was with Brylee.

Marrying her just made it all so real, so incredibly beautiful and genuine and amazing. The awe of it all just seemed too much, the possibilities too painful. That kind of love was too big for my heart to hold, or so I convinced myself at the time. No one's made me feel that way since and I don't think anyone but Brylee ever can."

"Is that why you quit drinking? Because of what happened? I was worried about you then, about the direction you were headed."

Shaun nodded. "I can't tell you how many times I wondered if I hadn't been drinking, and hadn't talked Brylee into drinking champagne, if we would have waited and gotten married in a proper ceremony with our family and friends around us. Not some five minute exchange of vows in a chapel with a bunch of strangers gawking at us because it sounded like a good idea at one in the morning. If we'd both been sober, if we'd waited, we might right now be married with a baby or two and living our happily ever after."

"You never listened all the times I told you nothing good ever happens after midnight." Jason gave him the beginnings of a smile.

"I know, Dad. And I'm sorry I didn't tell you everything years ago. I just wanted to put it behind me and forget it happened, but I won't ever be able to forget. Cooper wisely informed me that Brylee is my one." He made quotes in the air with his fingers as he said the word. "I hate to agree, but he's right. There won't ever be anyone for me because she is the one I'll love forever."

Jason squeezed his shoulder and gave him a

fatherly smile. "Anyone with eyes in their head can see you still love her, you idiot. The question is what you are going to do about it. If I get a say in whom my future daughter-in-law is going to be, Brylee gets my vote hands down."

Shaun ran his hands through his hair. "There's not much I can do about it, Dad. You heard her. She might have forgiven me, but she's never going to love me again. Never."

"Never is a very long time, son. Brylee isn't the type to hold a grudge for eternity." Jason grinned. "Besides, I don't think she'd hate you so much if she didn't still have some feelings for you. She wouldn't play that hairspray trick on just anyone."

Shaun looked to his dad, feeling the faintest stirrings of hope. "Really?"

"Really. Now let's talk strategy. We're good at solving problems and Brylee loathing you until you draw your dying breath is definitely a problem we need to overcome."

A grin kicked up the corner of Shaun's mouth. "Okay, Dad. I'm all ears."

"The first thing you need to do is tell her the truth. Why didn't you tell her what you just shared with me? That you loved her so much, it scared you into leaving."

Shaun shook his head. "Because she doesn't want to hear the truth, Dad. Not now. Maybe not ever."

Jason grinned again. "Oh, she'll be ready to hear it by the time we're through. However, we might need to enlist your sister's assistance."

A groan rolled out of Shaun. "I suppose

desperate times call for desperate measures."

Jason chuckled. "They do, indeed. I think you need to take it slow and easy with Brylee, don't rush anything. Treat Brylee like you would a rescue animal that's been beaten down and abused. Or think of her as a high-spirited filly that's never been haltered. You have to be careful, not make any sudden moves, earn her trust, and..." Jason winked at him. "Show her your love. Telling isn't going to be good enough. You've got to show her in a hundred different ways that you love her."

Shaun studied his dad. "How'd you get so smart about women?"

"I had a very happy marriage with your mother until the day she died. That relationship didn't happen overnight or because I was afraid to try."

"I'll do whatever it takes to win her back, Dad. If I have to crawl on my knees through fire, I'll do it."

"I'll bring the firewood and a torch."

Shaun gave him a sarcastic grin. "Thanks, Dad. Nice to know you've always got my back."

Chapter Ten

"I haven't seen Lisa in years, or your dad. It'll be fun to see them again," Brylee said as Jason took an exit at Baker City, Oregon, and turned onto the highway.

"Lisa and Pop are looking forward to seeing you, too." Jason smiled at her across the pickup cab.

Brylee glanced in the rearview mirror to see Shaun following behind them. Since the night Jason had demanded the truth about their marriage, Brylee had tried to stay away from Shaun as much as possible. He kept his promise to drive her pickup and horse trailer home for her, but instead of riding in it with him, she'd climbed in with Jason. After all the heartache and anguish she'd carefully packed away had been dumped out of the murky recesses where she'd kept them, she hadn't wanted to talk to Shaun. It was painful enough just to see him.

To his credit, he'd left her alone, giving her a wide berth, although he'd continued to be helpful and kind. He'd bought a bag full of her favorite snacks and candy, leaving it on the seat of the truck for her to find. He'd taken extra care with Rocket so she wouldn't have to. She'd even found her boots all polished yesterday morning, ready for her to pack.

Since they would drive right past Baker City on their way to Walla Walla, Jason had called his daughter and let her know they'd be at the Price family ranch for lunch.

Brylee looked around with interest ten minutes later when Jason turned off the highway onto a paved road that wound around the side of a sagebrush-covered mountain. She'd been to the ranch a few times with Shaun when they were dating, but it had been a long time since she'd visited.

Jason took a right onto a graveled road and they bounced across the cattle guard. Above them, a Circle P Ranch sign swung from a crossbar attached to two towering timbers on either side of the cattle guard. She grinned at the massive rack of antlers set into a rock base that held their mailbox.

"It looks just like I remember," she said, smiling at Jason.

He grinned at her. "Nothing much has changed, other than we've all gotten older."

"You look just the same as always," she said. Other than a little gray at his temples, Jason Price probably looked just as handsome and fit as he had thirty years ago.

"Flattery will get you everywhere," he said with a grin.

She took in the beauty of the rugged landscape around her as they drove up a small rise. "The ranch has been in your family for a long time, hasn't it?"

Jason nodded. "My grandfather started the ranch. My wife had deep roots here, too. Her relatives on the Jordan side of the family came during one of the gold rush periods. Actually, her great-grandmother, I think it was, came from England as a bride to her great-grandfather. She was of English nobility. A Lady, I think it was."

"Really? That's amazing. I bet life here in Eastern Oregon was unexpectedly different for her," Brylee said. She tried to imagine what it would be like to leave everything that was familiar to venture into the unknown, all for love. "She must have loved Mr. Jordan very much."

Jason shook his head. "From the stories I heard, she hated him when they first got married. It was one of those marriage of convenience things, something to do with an inheritance, but I forget the details. Anyway, she hated him, hated the house, hated the dust and primitive conditions."

"But she stayed?"

Jason nodded. "Yeah, she stayed. Once she quit fighting against building a life here, she fell in love with the land and her husband."

Brylee sensed an underlying message in Jason's story, but kept her thoughts to herself.

Jason looked over at her. "Judy used to say Shaun got his hair color from the Jordan side of the family. Several of them had auburn or copper hair."

"I always found it odd he and Lisa look nothing alike."

Jason guided the pickup around a curve. "Lisa resembles the Price side of the family, although Shaun has more of my personality."

Brylee held back a gasp as they drove on top of a hill. Below them, cattle grazed on acres and acres of green pasture. Mountains covered in pine trees loomed in the distance. A creek weaved through the landscape like a sparkling silver ribbon.

She smiled at Jason. "It's so beautiful. What a spectacular view."

He took a deep breath and drank in the sight of his home. "I never get tired of seeing it." Jason drove to a two-story farmhouse that looked like it had been built in the early 1900s, although it was well maintained. A white picket fence around the yard kept out most critters, although two dogs barked and trotted off the porch to the gate.

"Is that Lucy?" Brylee asked, recognizing Shaun's old cowdog.

"Yep. She's in retirement, along with Linus." Jason cut the ignition and unbuckled his seat belt.

A little girl with red curls flying every direction raced down the sidewalk. Her face lit with happiness as Jason hurried around the truck and lifted her in his arms.

"Papa! You're home! I missed you!"

"I missed you, too, Dani. Have you been a good girl, sweetheart?" Jason kissed the little one's rosy cheeks then shifted her to one arm and walked over to where Brylee got out of the truck.

"Who's that, Papa?" the little girl smiled at her. "I'm Dani and I'm five and I live here with Pops and my mommy and Uncle Galen. Who are you?"

Brylee grinned at the adorable chatterbox. "I'm Brylee Barton. I, um…"

Dani squealed and wiggled to get down. "It's Uncle Shaun. Let me down, Papa! Let me down, please!"

Jason set her down and she took off running to where Shaun walked toward them after parking Brylee's pickup. He scooped the little girl up in his arms and tossed her in the air, making her giggle.

"Do it again!" she begged.

"She's beautiful, Jason. The pictures you showed me of her don't do her justice." Brylee watched Shaun play with his niece while a lump the size of a grapefruit lodged in her throat.

"She's a little firecracker and definitely takes after the Jordan side," Jason said, pride evident on his face and in his voice as he watched his granddaughter. "Since Lisa and Tyler both have dark hair, they might have wondered where that mop of curly red hair came from, but she looks a lot like Shaun."

"She does," Brylee croaked, overwhelmed with thoughts of what might have been if Shaun hadn't destroyed her dreams.

"You sound like you're parched. Let's get in out of this heat and have a glass of iced tea." Jason motioned for her to go up the walk.

Brylee took two steps before Lucy and Linus bumped into her. "Do you two remember me?" she asked, stopping to pet the dogs. Lucy licked her hand and Linus' tail kept up a steady rhythm as he beat it against her leg. "I hear you two are in retirement. Does that mean you keep Mr. Price company?" She scratched both dogs behind their ears.

"You know better than to call me Mr. Price, sweetness. We agreed you'd call me Pops a long time ago," Mike Price said from where he stood on the porch steps. "Now get on up here and give me a hug."

Brylee grinned as she hurried up the steps and hugged Shaun's grandfather. Although he looked older, he hadn't lost the twinkle in his eye or his charming smile — a smile he'd passed on to his son and grandson.

"How are you, Pops?" she asked, stepping back when he released her. She kept a hand on his back as his gnarled fingers rested on her waist.

"Fit as a fiddle and twice as creaky."

She laughed. "It's so good to see you," she said, walking with him inside the house.

"Who's that lady, Uncle Shaun," she heard Dani ask. Shaun's response was muffled as Pops led her down the hall to a sunny kitchen where Lisa set a bowl of salad on the table.

"Brylee! Oh, my goodness." Lisa gave her a big hug. "You look incredible. Congrats on such a great season."

"Thank you, Lisa," Brylee offered her a smile full of genuine warmth. "You look as beautiful as I remember and Dani is adorable. She told me she's five."

"Some days I think she'll soon turn thirty for the things that come out of her mouth." Lisa picked up a potholder and opened the oven door, taking out a pan of perfectly browned rolls. "You all go wash up and I'll have the food on the table when you get back."

Brylee made her way to the bathroom that looked the same as the last time she'd been at the house. The Price family had done their best to preserve their heritage. Even the faucets on the sink were original to the house, although they'd been restored a few times. She loved the old claw-foot tub and pedestal sink, as well as the tile on the floor that had to be a pain to keep clean but gleamed like it had just been mopped.

She rushed back to the kitchen where Jason sat at the table with Dani on his knee, listening to her tell a story about her pony. Pops carried a bowl of potatoes to the table, but Shaun was nowhere in sight.

"What can I do to help?" Brylee asked as she stepped beside Lisa. She'd always liked Shaun's older sister. They'd gotten to be friends and Brylee had missed her when she cut off all contact with Shaun, his friends, and family.

"Fill the glasses with ice and pour tea?" Lisa asked as she spooned creamed peas into a bowl.

"This all looks so good, Lisa." Brylee took glasses from the cupboard and filled them with ice. "Are you still working in town?"

"Yes. I'm the manager of the bank now, instead of a teller."

"Congratulations. That's fantastic. How about Tyler? Jason said he's still in the service."

Lisa nodded. "He'll be finished in March then he's promised to come home for good."

Brylee knew it had been hard on Lisa when her

husband enlisted. From what Jason mentioned, Tyler was on a tour of duty in Afghanistan. "I'll be praying for him to stay safe until he's back here with you."

"Thank you," Lisa said, giving her a gratitude-filled smile.

"If you're the bank manager now, how did you sneak away long enough to make lunch?" Brylee asked as she poured tea into the ice-filled glasses.

"I told them I was taking a long lunch today and not to call unless there was an emergency. In Baker City, that doesn't happen too often." Lisa grinned. "I confess I picked up the meat at a great new barbecue place that opened. Pops did the potatoes while I cooked the peas, but the rolls and pie are from the bakery. Dad and Shaun won't know the difference."

Brylee laughed. "No, they won't. They eat first then forget to ask questions later."

Lisa giggled. "So true." She glanced down at Brylee's leg, encased in the brace. "How are you doing? Is the leg healing?"

"Yes, it is. I have to check in with my doctor next week, but I think it's doing well." Brylee glanced up as Shaun returned to the room. Dani stood on Jason's legs then leaped at her uncle. He caught her and kissed her cheek then whispered something in her ear that made the little one grin. "He's certainly good with her."

"Shaun is fabulous with kids. I never expected him to be, but he's been a huge help with her when he's home. The four Price men all dote on her. I'm afraid she'll turn into a little diva before long."

Brylee laughed. "You'll keep her grounded." She looked around. "I forgot about Galen being here. Is he joining us for lunch?"

"No. He's at a cattlemen's meeting in Salem today, otherwise he would be."

Brylee studied her a moment as Lisa placed the rolls in a basket. "I... uh... I just wanted to say I'm sorry about not staying in touch, Lisa. I really did appreciate your friendship before, when Shaun and I were together."

Lisa gave her another hug. "I completely understand. Don't worry about it. Shaun wouldn't tell me anything other than it was his choice and his fault."

Surprised to hear he accepted the full blame for the disaster that was their unbelievably brief marriage, she carried the tea glasses to the table. Shaun sat next to Jason, attentively listening to Dani tell him all about riding with Pops on the four-wheeler down to the creek to watch the fish play. Her heart turned into warm syrup when he glanced up at her with a sweet, tender smile.

The annoying grapefruit returned to her throat and she spun away before emotion overtook her good sense.

When Lisa set the last bowl on the table, Shaun pulled out a chair for Brylee then sat back down with Dani perched on his knee.

"Shaun, she can sit in her own chair," Lisa said, pointing to the chair beside him that held a ladybug booster seat.

"I know she can, but she's fine right here. I haven't got to see my little Dani bug for weeks and weeks." Shaun kissed the little girl on her nose, drawing out her infectious giggle. He filled a plate for his niece and set it next to his.

Brylee didn't know what was wrong with her, but seeing his copper head bent over Dani's bright red curls did things to her heart she couldn't even begin to identify let alone explain. Mercy, she never expected to see Shaun holding a child so lovingly. She certainly never expected to find it more appealing than anything she'd ever experienced or witnessed.

Yet, as he buttered Dani's roll and helped her with her meal, Shaun was infinitely more alluring to her in that moment than he'd ever been to her before. And that was dangerous. Far more dangerous than any flirting or joking he might do. In truth, she'd missed his teasing since the night she'd walked out of the trailer and stayed with Paige and Cooper.

Thank goodness for good friends. She was in no shape then to face Shaun or Jason. The next morning, it took her an hour after a pep talk from Cooper to convince herself to go back to the trailer. Cooper James could be persuasive when he wanted to be and Paige had offered her own soft words of encouragement.

Brylee had known things would be different now that the secret of her ten-hour marriage to Shaun was out in the open. Jason treated her with even more kindness and compassion, but Shaun seemed to understand her need for space and time to think. He gave it to her without question, or at least as much as he could, considering they traveled together.

Dani pulled Shaun's head down, whispered something and then giggled.

"Danielle Marie, you know better than to whisper at the table," Lisa gave her daughter a warning look. "If you have something to say, you say it to everyone."

Dani's lip puckered into a pout and she leaned against Shaun's chest.

Shaun looked at Lisa and started to say something, thought better of it, and snapped his mouth closed.

Dani pointed to Brylee. "All I said was Brylee is a pretty lady. I like her hair. She looks like the princess in my storybooks."

Lisa smiled at her daughter. "She does look like a princess."

"And she is very pretty," Pops said. He winked at Dani before smiling at Brylee. "You think she'd let me be her Prince Charming?"

Dani giggled and shook her head. "No, Pops! You're too old."

"What about your papa? Would he be a good prince for Brylee?" Pops asked, leaning closer to Dani and tweaking her nose.

She giggled again. "No. No. No. The prince has to be young and handsome and not have his own kids. You both gots kids. Uncle Shaun should be her prince." Dani clapped her hands together. "Oh, I know!" She jumped off Shaun's lap, took three steps, then turned back to her mother. "May I be scused, Mama? Please? I'll be right back!"

"Sure, baby." Lisa grinned as her daughter ran

from the room. Her footsteps pattered down the hall. A few thumps echoed from the front room, then her little feet thudded back to the kitchen.

She held a storybook in her hands and climbed on Shaun's lap with it clutched to her chest. "See, right here," she said, opening the book and pointing to a picture of Cinderella dancing with her prince. "He gots red hair like Uncle Shaun, and she gots pretty yellow hair like Brylee. They're perfect."

Jason hid a laugh behind a cough while Pops chuckled. Brylee tried to cover her emotions, a mixture of horror and humor sprinkled with a helping of truth.

"I thought Prince Charming had black hair," Brylee said, glancing at the book Dani held up for everyone to see.

"Nope. He gots red hair, just like my uncle."

"Yes, I can see that he does," Brylee said, wondering who'd mixed up the ink at the printer because she'd never noticed Prince Charming having red hair before. And the handsome cowboy grinning at his niece like she was the best thing since the invention of cowboy boots made her wish he really had been her prince charming. For the longest time, she was convinced he hadn't even made frog status, but she might give him that much credit now. More, if she cared to admit. Which she didn't.

The rest of the meal passed with Lisa asking questions about the rodeos they'd attended and people they'd seen while Jason and Shaun asked about the ranch and friends in the area.

Thankfully, no one seemed to expect her to

jump into the conversations. She ate her meal while surreptitiously casting stolen glances at Shaun and Dani. The more she studied the two of them, the more her heart ached for what might have been.

Quit fussing about what you don't have and focus on what you do.

Brylee swallowed back a sigh as her father's words marched through her thoughts. She'd been eleven and desperate for a dirt bike because the neighbor boy had one. After begging nonstop for a week, her dad looked at her and said those exact words. It made Brylee mad, but then she took the words to heart and looked at all the wonderful things she did have, like a perfectly good bicycle, and her own horse as well as plenty of other things to keep her occupied in her free time.

Her dad was right then and now. Maybe things wouldn't be any different if Shaun hadn't run out on her. Maybe they would have divorced in six months if they'd stayed married. Maybe they'd have two or three beautiful babies with curly red hair and incredible gray-blue eyes and be happier than she could imagine. There was no way to know what might have been and no sensible reason to dwell on the "what ifs."

Another look at Shaun and Dani made Brylee take a long drink of her iced tea, emptying the glass.

"Mama, can I go outside for a while?" Dani asked. She wiped her mouth with the napkin Shaun handed to her and slid off his leg.

"Yes, but stay in the yard unless someone else is out there with you."

Dani hummed an energetic tune as she

wandered around the table, patting Pops and Jason on their arms before she stopped next to Brylee's chair and looked up at her. "Want to come with me?"

"I'd love to," Brylee said, pushing back from the table. "Everything was delicious, Lisa. If you want my help with the dishes, just let me know. "

"You go on with Dani. These guys can handle dish duty." Lisa grinned when Shaun groaned in protest.

Dani took Brylee's hand and led her down the hallway toward the front door. On the way there, Brylee slowed her steps, studying the dozens of photographs lining the walls. There were photos of Shaun and Lisa, as well as their younger sister. Megan, along with Shaun's mother and grandmother, had gone to Boise on a shopping trip and were killed in a three-car pileup on the freeway. Shaun had only been fifteen at the time, but he'd told her how hard it was to lose all three of them in the same day.

Brylee thought his family had been so overwhelmed with grief and loss that they'd forgotten about him for a time. Not that anyone could blame them, but she often wondered if Shaun didn't have some issues he needed to work through because of it. Then again, he really did seem to have matured and grown into a good, strong, kind man these last few years. Clearly, he still loved to tease and play a joke, but he was hard-working, dedicated, and committed to his career. He was also gentle, protective, and loyal to those he loved.

She couldn't see the Shaun she'd come to know

the past month behaving like the boy she'd married. For all the ways he was the same, there were twice as many that illustrated how much he'd changed.

Regardless, she wasn't giving him, or anyone, the chance to trample all over her heart again. She'd sworn off love, relationships, and her dreams. Right now certainly wasn't the time to change her mind.

"Come on, Brylee," Dani said, tugging on her hand and pulling her out the front door.

They stopped for a moment to pet Lucy and Linus before Dani took her hand and led her out the front gate and down the graveled lane toward the barn.

"We probably shouldn't go too far, Dani. I'll have to leave soon."

"It's okay. They can see us from the house. Mama will yell if she wants us to come back." Dani smiled up at her, baby teeth glistening in the sunlight. The pink sundress she wore swished as she hopped and skipped in a pair of hot-pink sneakers.

Suddenly, she stopped and jerked on Brylee's hand. "See the snake?"

Brylee had seen it. In fact, she'd already started backing away from it when Dani yanked on her hand again. "It's okay. It's a bull snake. The bad snakes make a rattle sound like this." Dani offered her imitation of the buzzing noise a rattlesnake made as she continued toward the barn, dragging Brylee along with her.

Even when they were well past the snake, Brylee turned back to make sure it wasn't pursuing them.

"Are you scared of snakes?" Dani asked,

looking up at her as they neared a fenced-in pasture close to the barn.

"Yes, I am."

Dani fisted her hands at her waist and vigorously nodded her head, sending her curls flying every direction. "I thought so. Your eyes are this big." She made circles with her thumbs and index fingers. "Your face looks funny, too. Kinda white, like Jimmy was at the fair before he got sick and puked all over his shoes." She wrinkled her nose. "It was so gross."

Brylee wasn't sure how she felt about the comparison, but meekly followed Dani as she continued over to the pasture where a fat pony grazed with half a dozen horses.

"That's S'mores." Dani pointed to the pony. "Papa got him for me."

"S'mores is a great name for a pony." Brylee knelt down by Dani as the little girl leaned against the pole fence. "Do you ride him often?"

"Pops and Uncle Galen help me ride him, but not every day. Pops doesn't always feel like going for a ride."

Brylee looked over at the lively child. "Does Pops watch you while your mom is at work?"

"Sometimes. I go with Uncle Galen sometimes, too. The rest of the time I go to Sally's house."

"Who is Sally?" Brylee asked, pulling a handful of grass and holding it through the fence. The pony spied it and slowly meandered toward them.

"She's my babysitter. There are other kids at her house, too. Mama drops me off there on her way to work."

"I see," Brylee said, relieved that Dani wasn't left in the care of a busy rancher or her aging great-grandfather. She drew the grass back a little as the pony stretched his lips out to nibble it. Dani reached out and patted his neck while Brylee pulled another handful of grass and gave it to the child to hold.

"He tickled my fingers." The little girl giggled. Dimples popped out in her cheeks as she grinned and watched the pony eat the grass she'd fed him. "I like petting him and I like you!" Dani threw her little arms around Brylee's neck and gave her a squeeze.

The grapefruit was back, firmly lodged in her throat and making tears sting her eyes. "I like you, too, Dani."

The little imp leaned back and looked into Brylee's face, as though she searched for something. She patted Brylee's cheeks and tipped her head to one side. "Do you like my grandpa?"

Brylee smiled. "I like Pops and your papa. They're wonderful."

"I think so, too," Dani said, placing an arm on Brylee's shoulder and leaning against her as they watched S'mores wander back toward the other horses. She turned her gaze to Brylee's. "Do you like Uncle Shaun?"

Brylee wouldn't lie to the child. "I do like your uncle Shaun."

"Enough to let him be your prince?" Dani asked, full of innocence.

"Oh, sweetheart, a long time ago your uncle Shaun was my prince and I loved him very much."

Brylee stood and took Dani's hand in hers.

The little girl looked up at her with a pout, eye's starting to fill with tears. "He's not anymore?"

How to simplify so much pain and heartache into an answer suitable for a child? "No, sweetie, he's not now."

"Do you wish he was your prince?" Dani stared up at her with eyes so like Shaun's it made Brylee's heart pinch.

"Sometimes, more than anything, I wish he could be my prince again." Brylee bent down and lightly tapped Dani on the nose. "But that's our secret. Okay?"

"Okay!" Dani giggled and started skipping up the lane back toward the house.

Shaun stepped out onto the porch when they returned to the yard. He grinned as Dani ran to him and swung her in the air. "I was just about to come looking for you. Your mom has pie and ice cream inside."

"Yay!" Dani wiggled down. "I love ice cream!" She raced inside the house, leaving Brylee alone with Shaun.

She stopped to pet the dogs again, hoping he'd follow Dani. Instead, he hunkered down and joined her in giving the dogs some attention.

He cleared his throat and glanced over at her. "Dani seems taken with you."

Brylee smiled. "She's the cutest thing, Shaun. That curly hair and those dimples are delightful. She could be the new Shirley Temple."

Shaun chuckled. "Don't give her any ideas. She already thinks she's the queen bee of the Circle P.

And the kid really can't sing or act. A career in showbiz is not in her future."

"But you love her anyway," Brylee said, standing and brushing her hands on the seat of her denim shorts.

"I sure do. Every single one of the Price men are wrapped around her little bitty fingers." Shaun stood and motioned for Brylee to precede him inside. "Seems to be a thing with the women we love."

Brylee ignored his comment and made it back to the kitchen where Lisa served slices of warm peach pie with mounds of vanilla ice cream. When she finished eating her piece, Brylee grinned at Lisa. "I may not need to eat for a week after all this good food. Thank you so much."

"My pleasure." Lisa smiled at her. "I'm so glad we got to see you, Brylee. Please don't be a stranger."

"That's right, honey. We'd sure like to see you around here again," Pops said, leaning over to pat her arm.

Brylee didn't know what to say. Jason seemed to sense her struggle because he stood and carried his plate to the sink. "We better get on the road. After we drop off Brylee's rig, we still have to head to Kennewick and help unload the stock."

"Thanks for a great meal, sis." Shaun gave his sister a hug then gently patted his grandfather on the back. "You did good with those spuds, Pops."

The old man laughed. "A lot of years of practice, son. Your grandma used to have me help her peel them sometimes. Never really minded because I'd steal kisses each time I finished one."

"No wonder it took forever to get dinner sometimes," Jason teased.

Pops shook an arthritic-plagued finger at Jason. "Oh, you be quiet. I caught you and Judy smooching in the kitchen plenty of times."

Shaun smirked at his sister. "That's nothing. I caught Lisa and Tyler..."

The glare of death Lisa shot at him made him close his mouth before he finished tattling on her. "Don't you need to get going?" she asked, giving Shaun a playful push.

"I don't want them to go, Mama," Dani said, wrapping her arms around Shaun's leg. He swung it in an exaggerated motion as he made his way toward the front door.

Pops held out an arm to Brylee and she took it with a smile, walking with him to the door while Jason and Lisa spoke quietly in the kitchen.

Outside, Dani insisted on Shaun giving her a piggyback ride, which he did, before backing up to the porch and setting her down when Jason walked outside with Lisa.

"Come on, sweetie, give me a kiss," Jason said, swinging Dani up in his arms and raining kisses on her cheeks.

She giggled then wrapped her arms around him, giving him a big hug. "I'll miss you, Papa."

"I'll miss you, too, honey. You be a good girl and I'll see you in a few weeks, okay?"

"Okay!" Dani went from Jason to Shaun. She kissed him on his cheek then pulled back and gave him a studying glance. "Don't be a frog, Uncle

Shaun."

At his baffled look, the little girl turned to Brylee and gave her a hug. With her arms wrapped around her neck, she whispered in her ear. "Maybe he'll be your prince again if you believe in him, just like in the fairytales."

Brylee smiled and hugged the little girl back before setting her on the porch between her mother and great-grandfather. She hugged the old man and Lisa then backed toward the truck. "It was so good to see you both. Take care!"

As Jason turned the vehicle around and headed toward the road, Brylee pictured Shaun's head bent over Dani's bright curls. He looked so natural with the little girl, so perfect in the role of doting uncle, her mind toyed with how well he'd do as a father.

The rest of the way home, she could think of little else.

Chapter Eleven

The fight or flight response surging up in Shaun urged him to keep going straight. Instead, he turned off the road and followed his dad and Brylee as they drove beneath the Blue Hills Ranch sign that marked the entrance to the Barton family ranch.

He looked forward to seeing Brylee's brother, Birch. However, he had an idea her mother might load him full of buckshot if he so much as set foot out of the pickup, which he had to do since they were leaving it there.

The last time he'd spoken to the woman, her feelings toward him had been undeniably clear. If she could have reached through the phone and choked the life out of him, he thought she would have gleefully done it.

Brylee's dad had always been easy going and fun, but her mother seemed just the opposite. She was serious and, from what he observed, a little harsh and judgmental. He always thought Brylee and Birch took after their father, but with him gone the past four years, he wondered if Jenn Barton's rather negative outlook at life had rubbed off on her kids. He could certainly see her influence when he'd stepped in to help Brylee a month ago.

Now, the girl riding with his father seemed much more like the Brylee he'd fallen in love with. She'd loosened up, found her sense of humor again, and actually had fun when she let go of her relentless determination to hate him while winning as many rodeos as possible.

Jason stopped in front of the single story ranch house. A long porch out front and vibrant flowers hanging in pots along the porch eaves gave a welcoming appearance. Horses raced in the pasture across from the house and someone waved from the barn.

By the long, gangly limbs, Shaun assumed it had to be Birch.

Brylee jumped out of the pickup and rushed toward her brother. The two of them embraced and Birch swung her around before he set her down then looked at her leg. Shaun drove past the two of them and parked Brylee's pickup near the barn.

He'd barely stepped out when Birch was there, holding out a hand in welcome with a big grin on his face.

"You've grown by at least two feet!" Shaun said as he shook the boy's hand. He gave him a brotherly slap on the back hug. "I can't believe it's you, Birch."

"It's good to see you, sir." Birch practically beamed at him.

Shaun recalled the golden-haired boy with Brylee's cobalt eyes and a smattering of freckles on his nose dogging his every step when he'd visited the ranch six years ago. Birch had been just eight and always looked at Shaun like he was a hero.

Too bad he hadn't lived up to the kid's expectations. However, with the way Birch grinned at him, he hoped he hadn't fallen completely off his pedestal where the boy was concerned.

"Drop the sir. It's just Shaun to you, kid. Are you lifting weights? Playing sports? When did you get taller than your sister?" Shaun asked.

Birch laughed. "Dude, I've been taller than her since I was eleven. In case you haven't noticed, Brylee is vertically challenged."

Shaun grinned. "Yeah, but she makes up for it in other ways."

Birch nodded and ducked as Brylee playfully swatted him.

"So what's new in your world?" Shaun asked the boy.

Birch's chest puffed out a little. "I'm on the freshman football team."

"Hey, congrats. That's awesome," Shaun said as he gathered his things out of Brylee's pickup and pulled the keys from the ignition.

Brylee walked over and took the keys from him. "I'm going to run in and grab a few things. I'll leave the keys on the rack by the phone, Birch. Do not take it for a joyride."

Birch slapped a hand to his chest. "Me? I wouldn't do such a thing. That's more your style."

Brylee reached up and affectionately tapped her

brother's cheek. "Don't be so lippy, young man."

He ruffled Brylee's hair, making her huff in irritation as she headed toward the house.

Jason wandered over to where Shaun stood with Birch.

"Dad, this is Birch Barton. I don't know if you remember meeting him. Birch, this is my dad, Jason."

Jason grinned and shook Birch's hand. "I do remember meeting you, young man, but I wouldn't have recognized you. You were just a little guy then." Jason held his hand out at his side to indicate how small Birch had been the last time they'd seen him. "You look a lot like your dad. I'm sorry to hear about what happened."

Slowly, Birch nodded his head. "Thank you, Mr. Price. It's, um... been hard on all of us."

Jason glanced over the property around them. "From the looks of things, you're doing a great job with the ranch, though."

Birch pointed toward a field in the distance where men appeared to be working on a piece of equipment. "Thanks to Brylee's winnings, we were able to hire a couple of guys to help this summer."

"That's great," Shaun said, keeping an eye on the house. He half-expected an explosion when Jenn Barton realized he was standing outside. "Is your Mom here?"

"No, she's still at work." Birch glanced at his watch. "She usually gets home about half past five."

"At work?" Shaun asked. When he'd been around the Barton's, Jenn had been a stay-at-home mom who spent her spare time working alongside

Brad on the ranch.

"Yep. She got her realtor's license a long time ago, but she never did much with it. Now, she works at it full-time and does well. Walla Walla's a growing wine area and a lot of people are looking for weekend or vacation property." Birch pointed to a vineyard visible on the hill behind them.

Shaun nodded. "Seems like a boost to the economy. It's great your mom can capitalize on it."

Jenn Barton wasn't exactly the people person he envisioned a successful realtor might need to be, but more power to her. He wondered, though, who managed the ranch with her in town and Brylee on the road.

An older man Shaun recognized ambled out of the barn and grinned as his bow-legged gait carried him their way.

"Mr. Barton, it's great to see you!" Shaun reached out and shook the old man's hand. Brylee's grandpa looked like a wizened old elf with white hair peeking from beneath the band of his dirty, misshapen hat. Wrinkles carved canyons across his weathered face. He had to be past ninety if he was a day. "I thought you moved to Arizona."

"Well, Shaun, it's nice to see you again, son. I was living down there where it's always warm and sunny, but I came for a visit at Christmas and somehow ended up staying." The old man turned to Jason. "I think we might have met a time or two. Ace Barton."

"It's nice to see you again, sir," Jason said, shaking his hand. "We did meet a few times, back in the day. You used to help with the rodeo here in town quite a bit, didn't you?"

"I did for about forty, fifty years. Then I decided to let someone who could move a little faster than me take my place." Ace grinned and settled a hand on Birch's shoulder. The boy, who was tall for his age, smiled down at his grandfather. "Me and Birch take care of the ranch while the girls are busy bringing home the bacon."

"That's great, sir," Shaun said, giving his watch a quick glance. If they left in the next five minutes they could avoid an encounter with Brylee's mother. Otherwise, Shaun might stuff his shin guards down the back of his britches and hope Jenn didn't have ready access to a gun.

He was about to suggest Birch run in the house and see if Brylee was ready to go when he heard a door shut and looked over as Brylee came out of the house with a duffle bag on her shoulder. She'd changed into a pair of jeans and a cotton blouse the same shade of blue as her eyes. As she hurried over to them, he watched her every move. The way her hair swung in the ponytail she'd fashioned at the back of her head. The quick stride she took with just a bit of a hitch where the brace still encumbered her ability to walk. The enticing sway of those curvy hips.

Ace cackled and slapped Shaun on the shoulder before he ambled forward and held out his arms to Brylee. "There's my gorgeous girl! How are you, sunshine?"

"I'm good, Grandpa. How have you been? Birch said you've made him tow the line all summer." Brylee kissed her grandpa's cheek then hooked her arm around his as she turned and walked toward the truck Shaun hoped to escape in before Jenn Barton arrived at the ranch.

"Birch is coming right along. We'll make a rancher out of him, yet, if we can get him to stop roping everything in sight." Ace looked back at his grandson. "He's getting purty good at it."

"Maybe next week we can do a little practice together," Shaun said to Birch as they followed Brylee toward the truck.

Birch stopped and stared at him. "Are you kidding me?"

"Nope. We'll be back on Monday. Maybe we can do a little roping Tuesday. When do you have football practice?"

"I get done at four and then ride the bus home."

"How about I pick you up at school? We'll see what you can do."

Birch's eyes were almost as wide as his grin. "You mean it, Shaun? Really? You'll rope with me?"

"Yep. I will. I'll be at the school at five minutes past four. Don't be late." He grinned and tugged on the brim of Birch's ball cap.

Brylee was hugging her grandfather and reminding Birch to behave when a small SUV pulled up and parked in the carport beside the house. She shot Shaun a warning look and he nodded his head in agreement.

Jenn Barton strode over to them and wrapped Brylee in a hug. "What are you doing home, Brylee? I didn't expect to see you until next week." She released Brylee and stepped back. Her gaze moved to Jason then stopped like she'd slammed into a concrete wall when she noticed Shaun.

The welcoming smile melted right off her face, replaced by a hard, cold glare. "What is *he* doing here?"

Brylee moved between Shaun and her mother, placing a hand on the woman's arm, as though that might calm her. "Mom, you remember Shaun and his dad, Jason."

"It's nice to see you again, Jenn." Jason stepped forward with his hand out.

Jenn took it and offered him a half-hearted smile. "It's been a while, Jason. How's your dad?"

"Ornery as ever. We had lunch with him, my daughter, and granddaughter earlier today."

Jenn nodded. "That's good. Glad to hear he's doing well." Her gaze shifted back to Shaun. "I didn't expect to ever see you on our ranch again."

"Didn't really expect to be back here, ma'am." Shaun tried to be polite, but the venomous daggers the woman was shooting at him could have rivaled any Brylee had launched his way. If they decided to gang up on him, they might actually send him to the emergency room.

Jenn gave him a dismissive sneer then turned back to Brylee. "What is going on?"

"Well, Mom, I had a little accident and needed a bit of help. Shaun and Jason offered their assistance." Brylee met her mother's glare with one of her own. "I wouldn't have been able to compete the last month if it hadn't been for them."

"What kind of accident, Brylee Elizabeth Barton?" Jenn's icy tone turned demanding. "I insist you tell me what happened, right now."

Shaun held back the urge to tell the bossy woman to mind her own business, but he wisely kept his mouth shut.

"I broke my leg and couldn't drive. Shaun and Jason invited me to travel with them. If they hadn't offered, I would have been forced to come home. I owe them, Mom. They've been good to me, a huge help."

Jenn glared at Brylee for a full minute before she turned to Jason. "Thank you for taking care of our girl. I appreciate it." She pinned Brylee with a frigid look, the condescension unmistakable on her face. "It was stupid of you to ride with a broken leg. I warned you when you went off on this harebrained scheme you'd end up hurt, in more ways than one. Here you are living up to exactly what I predicted."

"Give it a rest, Jenn. The girl's ranked number one and a shoo-in for the finals. Let her be!" Ace said, glowering at his daughter-in-law while placing a protective arm around Brylee. "If she thought this was the best thing to do, then support her choices, not belittle her after the fact."

Ace kissed Brylee's cheek then waved at Shaun and his dad. "I need to get back to my chores, but thank you boys for taking care of our girl. We appreciate it. It was sure good to see you both."

"Nice to see you, too, Mr. Barton." Jason called after the old man as he hobbled back to the barn.

"I better help, Grandpa." Birch looked at Shaun like an excited puppy about to get a treat. "Later, man."

Shaun gave him a fist bump then watched the

boy run into the barn.

Jenn took two steps closer to Shaun and shook a finger in his face. "You stay away from my son. You've done enough damage without dragging him into trouble, too. I want you off my property, right now!"

"Mom!" Brylee shouted, grabbing her mother's hand. She pushed between her and Shaun, as though she intended to protect him.

He didn't need to hide behind Brylee, but her mother had turned into one cold, mean woman. Hate and animosity practically rolled off her like angry waves battering the shore.

Brylee released her mother's hand and opened the back door to the truck, tossing her bag inside. "I don't care what you know, or think you know, Mother. There's no reason to be rude. Shaun and Jason have both been kind and helpful."

Jenn looked like she was about to say something, caught the shake of Brylee's head, then turned and marched into the house. The slamming of the front door resounded as her goodbye.

Brylee held her head high as she climbed onto the back seat of the truck. Shaun closed her door then slid onto the front seat while Jason moved behind the wheel and started it.

As they pulled out on the road, Shaun looked back at Brylee. She stared out the window with tears glistening in her eyes. He sighed. "I take it your mom knows I left you in Vegas?"

Brylee nodded.

Desperate to make her smile, he grinned. "I heard she's a secret spy for Santa, plying him with top-secret details." Shaun waggled his eyebrows. "I suppose this means I'm on the naughty list for life."

A choked laugh escaped from Brylee and she rolled her eyes. "That's exactly what it means, you dork."

Chapter Twelve

"Two more weeks?" A frustrated sigh worked its way free from Brylee as her doctor fastened the brace back on her leg.

"I just want to be sure it's healed, Brylee. It's not like you've been sitting around taking it easy. Congrats, by the way. I see you're leading the ladies heading to Vegas in December." The doctor smiled at her as she rolled back her chair and got to her feet.

"I'm in the lead today. That could change by the end of the week. Nothing is guaranteed in this business." Brylee got off the exam table and slipped her sneaker back on her foot.

"I know. As frequently as injuries occur, anything can happen between now and then." The doctor walked her out of the exam room and toward the waiting room door. "I'm cheering for you to take the world title again this year. What's it been? Six years since you won?"

"Close to seven, but who's counting?" Brylee grinned at the doctor. "Thanks so much, Kelly. I'll check back in two weeks."

"Great. Just make an appointment on your way out so you're on the schedule."

Brylee made the appointment and added the date and time to her phone calendar then walked into the waiting room. Shaun sat jiggling his foot and watching a pair of toddlers fight over a baggie of cereal. When the cereal spilled on the floor, the little ones went after it like they hadn't eaten in a week.

Shaun grimaced and Brylee tried to hide her disgust. She couldn't even begin to consider the germs the little ones were shoving in their mouths, but their mother didn't seem to care as she flipped through a magazine.

He glanced up and saw her heading his way. Quickly rising to his feet, he glanced at the brace and gave her a sympathetic look. "Another week or two?"

"Two," she said, walking out the door he held open for her.

"And still no driving?"

"That's right. Days like this make me wish Birch at least had his learner's permit, but his birthday isn't until November."

"I remember. Right before Thanksgiving, isn't it?"

Brylee nodded, shocked Shaun paid that much attention to her younger sibling. "Birch hasn't stopped talking about you picking him up today. It's nice of you to practice with him."

"My pleasure. I don't get to do much roping just for fun. It'll be great." Shaun held Brylee's door as she slid onto the seat. "I thought your mom would put the kibosh on it."

"Grandpa had quite a talk with her. More accurately, according to Birch, they had a shouting match and Grandpa won. Mom's still plenty furious I didn't tell her about my broken leg or traveling with you and your dad, although Birch and Grandpa both knew." Brylee leaned back in the seat as Shaun drove her pickup out of the parking lot and turned toward downtown Walla Walla.

"I can only assume you didn't tell her because you knew she'd react exactly as she did. Better to seek forgiveness than ask permission. Is that it?" Shaun asked as they waited at a stoplight.

"Something like that, although at my age, I don't think I should have to tell her everything. Since Dad died, it's like a compulsion for her to be in charge of everything and everyone."

Shaun reached over and squeezed her hand. "It's because she loves you, worries about you. Her methods might need a little work, but the underlying reason behind it is good."

"She doesn't deserve your kindness, Shaun." Brylee wasn't sure she did either. After the rodeo in Kennewick, Jason and Shaun had driven her home then went to the Walla Walla rodeo grounds. The Rockin' K would provide stock for the rodeo although Shaun and Jason weren't working as the pickup men due to a contract with another stock company.

Shaun seemed pleased at the idea of having a

little more free time than usual. Brylee had mixed feelings about him being around all week. She was surprised that Jason didn't want to head back to Baker City, but then she found out that he'd gone home that morning. He'd be back Tuesday morning so they could head to the next rodeo a few hours away in Idaho. Since Brylee couldn't drive, she'd offered Shaun use of her pickup in trade for him taking her to her doctor's appointment. She hoped he'd be game to continue chauffeuring her around until the doctor cleared her to drive.

"Where are we headed?" she asked as Shaun turned a block before Main Street and parked in front of one of the trendy restaurants downtown.

"Lunch. I'm starving." He got out and hurried around the pickup, offering her a hand, which she accepted without thinking.

When he held on to her hand, she started to pull her fingers back. Then he looked down at her and gave her a half-smile that did crazy things to the solidity of her knees. He opened the door to the restaurant and she walked inside.

An hour later, they sat in a booth, laughing over a text Cooper sent Shaun with a video of him humiliating a guy at a rodeo the previous week.

"Cooper will be here this week won't he?" Brylee asked as she sipped the last of her raspberry lemonade.

"Yep. He's picking up Paige and they'll be here later tonight."

"I really like her, and Jessie Jarrett, too. She and Chase live around here, don't they?"

"Hermiston," Shaun said, pulling up a photo

Chase had sent him a few months after he and Jessie had wed. It showed the two of them standing in the snow with her wrapped in a Pendleton wool blanket.

"That's incredible," Brylee said, staring at the photo. "They really are just the cutest couple."

"They are pretty darn cute. So are Cooper and Paige. He'd do anything for that woman, even give up his illustrious modeling career."

"I heard about him being the um… representative of Lasso Eight when the company's fashions debuted. I believe there's another cute guy I know among the roster of models." Brylee gave him a pointed look as the server brought their bill.

Shaun smiled. "So you found out I've been modeling on the side."

"It's not like I didn't recognize your…" Brylee stopped herself before she said anything incriminating and snagged the bill off the table. "Your chin."

Shaun chuckled and tried to take the bill from her, but Brylee refused to relinquish it.

"It's my turn to buy and you're going to let me."

He scowled, but let her pay. Outside, she started for the pickup, but he took her hand and tugged her in the opposite direction. "Let's look around. I haven't wandered through downtown for a while. Anything new or different?"

"Always." She smiled and led the way down the street and over a block.

When they made it back to the pickup, Shaun carried a bag of warm caramel corn from the candy store, while Brylee had a new paperback she'd picked up at the bookstore.

"Hey, I want to run something by you," Shaun said as he climbed behind the wheel and handed her the bag of caramel corn.

"Go for it." She popped a few pieces of the sweet treat in her mouth and grinned.

Shaun took a handful then started the truck before backing out of the parking space and heading toward Blue Hills Ranch. "Would you have any interest in being a Lasso Eight model? The pay is ridiculously good and you only have to work a few days a year. Paige is in charge of choosing the models. She's coming with Cooper because the company is doing a big photo shoot in two weeks at Chase and Jessie's place. It's for the holiday campaign that will debut during the finals. I think Paige would love to work with you, if you're interested."

Brylee gaped at him. She'd heard ballpark figures from Jason about how much Shaun made as a model. That extra income would go a long way toward paying off the ranch debts and getting them back on track. "I don't know that I've got anything Paige can work with, but I'd love to give it a shot if she's willing to let me try. I've seen ads for their women's clothing line and it's all very tasteful. Isn't Celia's sister-in-law one of the models?"

Shaun turned off the road onto the ranch driveway. "Yeah, she is. You remember Tate Morgan, don't you?"

Brylee nodded. "Sure, he retired a few years back, but he was an amazing saddle bronc rider."

"He lives near Kennewick with his wife. Kenzie Morgan is the other tall model in those ads."

"That's awesome. I do remember hearing something about him getting married."

"He and Kenzie are another of those cute couples you talk about. They even have two little ones now."

Brylee tried to picture Tate Morgan and his partner in crime, Cort McGraw, as fathers and role-model husbands. All she could envision was them playing pranks on each other and chasing young cowboys away from Celia.

"Do you really think Paige might be interested in hiring me?"

"Only one way to find out." Shaun parked the pickup near the ranch house and took out his phone. He tapped a message to Paige and hit send before Brylee could tell him she'd changed her mind.

"So, what's the plan for the rest of the day?" Shaun asked as they sat in the cool interior of the pickup, reluctant to step out into the late August afternoon heat.

"I rode Rocket this morning, so I'll probably just help Grandpa for a while."

Shaun nodded. "Do you want to come with me when I pick up Birch?"

"No. He's looking forward to having you all to himself." Brylee smiled at him. "For the record, it's sweet of you to do this for him. He misses roping with dad and Grandpa just isn't up to doing much these days. As you know, I was never very good at it."

"You roped me in just fine, Bitsy." Shaun lifted

her hand to his mouth and kissed her fingers.

Before she slid across the seat and did more than let him kiss her fingers, she opened the pickup door and got out. "Have a good time with Birch. You're welcome to stay for supper, if you like."

"That's funny," Shaun said, giving her a look that made it clear he thought she'd lost her mind. "If I'm in the same room with your mother and weaponry, like kitchen knives, it's likely there will be a murder scene at the ranch."

Brylee grinned. "Suit yourself. You'll pick me and Rocket up in the morning, though, won't you?"

"You bet. And Birch, too. Won't he be at the fair with his FFA projects?"

Brylee nodded. "Yes. Thankfully, Mom has appointments all week and won't have time off until Saturday. The fair will be a hound-free zone until then." She shut the pickup door and waved once as Shaun turned around and left.

With her mother constantly reminding her of how stupid she'd been to get mixed up with him once before, she wasn't eager to make that mistake twice.

Despite her head telling her she was being smart and cautious, her heart whispered at her to give Shaun a second chance.

Chapter Thirteen

"I don't belong here," Brylee whispered to Shaun as they waited for the photographer to position everyone for the next pose.

"You're doing fine, Bitsy. Paige is so excited you agreed to model for the company. She said she'd thought about asking you, but didn't want to bug you since you're so focused on racing right now." Shaun's hand trailed along her back, igniting a fire all the way down her spine. "You look amazing."

Brylee glanced down at the paisley-printed cotton dress she wore. The blue in the print exactly matched her eyes. Regardless, she thought the other women looked glamorous — not her. Jessie Jarrett, Kenzie Morgan, and Kaley McGraw were all tall brunettes with fabulous figures. Compared to them, with her blond hair and short stature, she felt like the stubby stepsister.

For whatever reason, the women voted her as

the official model of the blanket-patterned miniskirts. Brylee tended to think her legs were hideous from the numerous times she'd knocked into barrels. Nevertheless, the woman who worked with Paige to decide how each outfit should look gave her a pair of tights that hid her bumps and scars.

She stood in the sweltering heat wearing a skirt that barely reached her thighs with dark tights, knee-high laser-cut cowboy boots, and a fringed leather jacket, trying to envision the snowy background that would appear in the promotional pieces when they debuted in December.

Brylee wasn't accustomed to wearing heavy makeup either. She generally stuck with mascara, maybe some eyeliner, and a little lip-gloss when she ran barrels or had an interview. The makeup artist had gone all out, accenting her cheekbones, giving her smoky eyes that enhanced the bright color of them.

In fact, when she walked out in the miniskirt to where they'd do the first shoot, Shaun had gawked at her like he'd never seen her before. She didn't know whether to be flattered or irritated. The way he kept making excuses to touch her, and continued to compliment her, she concluded she should just enjoy his obvious appreciation of how she looked.

Despite her mother's protests and heated warnings, both she and Birch had spent a lot of time with Shaun during the fair and rodeo in Walla Walla. Shaun had helped Birch with his FFA projects and was front and center to cheer him on when he showed his steer and horse.

She didn't know how he managed it, but Shaun had even arranged for Birch to help Cooper one night during the rodeo. Her little brother couldn't stop grinning when he found out he got to put on makeup with a crazy outfit and go into the arena with Cooper.

Her mother had been so furious, she hadn't spoken to either of them for two days. Grandpa had thought it was wonderful, especially when Brylee took first in barrel racing.

She placed third at the rodeo last week, though. She blamed it on the rain. It had started to fall during the steer wrestling. By the time it was her turn to run the barrels, the arena was a mess. She held Rocket back, fearful of taking another spill. The horse must have been a little wary, too. In spite of going slower, they still had a good time, just not the best.

However, she intended to come in first at the Pendleton Round-Up this weekend, provided she didn't die of either heat or embarrassment during the photo shoot.

Shaun's hand continued to sear her skin through the fabric of the knee-length dress she currently wore. She still had on the knee-high boots and a long, dangling silver necklace with a chunky silver bracelet.

"Your eyes look like something from another world, Bitsy. They are just gorgeous," Shaun whispered before the stylist stopped in front of them and positioned them in poses. The photographer wanted four couples positioned with two feet between them. An old weathered wagon rested in the background with a handful of horses a few yards beyond that. Brylee was sure it would look spectacular in the photographs, but she still felt out of place.

"Mr. Flynn is quite excited to have a world champion barrel racer posing for his ads," the stylist said, grinning at Brylee as she twisted her hair into a rope and draped it over one shoulder.

Brylee smiled. "I appreciate this opportunity, although I'm afraid I don't measure up to the other models."

The woman stepped back and gave Brylee a surprised look. "Are you kidding, girlfriend? Regardless of your height, many women would kill for a figure like yours. Flaunt it while you got it is what I say."

Shaun smirked. "You heard the woman, flaunt it."

Brylee would have smacked him if she hadn't been told to stay still. Somehow she survived the photo shoot and talked herself into returning the next day for the second and last day of the Christmas modeling gig.

She found herself situated between Shaun and a cowboy named Gage at the bunkhouse. The two men stood on the ground, putting Brylee a step above their height as she posed on one of the steps. The cowboys faced the bunkhouse, showcasing a new style of jeans for men. She leaned her forearms on their shoulders, modeling a beautiful blanket-print winter coat with a shearling collar. The reds, greens, and blues in the coat definitely made her think of Christmas.

A kissing ball of mistletoe dangled on a red ribbon from her finger against Shaun's broad back. She couldn't wait to see what sort of advertisement it turned into. Paige promised it would be classy and fun. Since she trusted the woman and her decisions, she hoped it turned out well.

As she stood draped over the two guys, Shaun kept whispering jokes to her. She had to work to keep from breaking into a broad smile. When they finished, she smacked him with the fake kissing ball, making everyone laugh.

"Bring in the kids," the photographer said, flapping his hand at an assistant.

Brylee stepped back and watched as Tate and Kenzie Morgan came over to the bunkhouse with their son, Gideon, and baby daughter, Marley. Lasso Eight had decided to add a line for children and the Morgan and McGraw youngsters would serve as the first models. Cort and Kaley McGraw joined them with their son, Jacob, and daughter, Grace. Grace was far more interested in playing with Marley than any pose they wanted her to be in. The photographer finally got them all where he wanted them. Brylee's heart melted at how cute they all looked. And it pricked a little as the what-ifs stole into her thoughts.

Warmth enveloped her from behind along with Shaun's delicious scent. She leaned back as he placed his hand on her shoulder and bent close to her ear. "They are a bunch of nice-looking kids. That Grace has got way too much McGraw in her, though. I feel sorry for Kaley."

Brylee grinned. "She does seem quite earnest in

her opinions."

Shaun chuckled. "That's putting it mildly, Bitsy." He gave her a gentle squeeze. "Are you having a good time?"

Although her first inclination was to say no, she nodded her head. "I am having fun. Thank you for suggesting this. Not only do I get to hang out with some awesome people, I get paid for it."

"And you don't even have to brush down a horse or scoop any poop to do it."

She glanced over her shoulder at him. "You always could put such a lovely spin on things."

"I do what I can, Bits. I do what I can."

Once the photographer had what he needed and all the models had changed back into their own clothes, Jessie and Chase invited everyone to join them for dinner. Brylee enjoyed getting a tour of their house and admired the special touches Jessie had added to make it into a home.

Later, after everyone had eaten, Chase and Shaun played with the kids, letting them crawl all over them on the grass as they pretended to be horses. Shaun had Jacob and Grace on his back while Chase carried Gideon. Marley toddled over and babbled to them in her own language, as though she was letting them know she wanted in on the fun.

Shaun said something to Jacob, then picked up Marley with one arm. He continued on as a three-legged ride for the two on his back. Marley squealed with delight and waved her hands in the air. Shaun grinned and kissed the baby on her rosy cheek.

An ache that had started earlier in the day

gained force and breadth until Brylee thought she might collapse beneath the weight of it. Shaun would make a fantastic husband someday for some lucky girl. Tears sprung up in her eyes knowing that girl wouldn't be her.

"Want to join me in the kitchen?" Jessie asked, looking at Brylee with sympathy in her gaze.

Brylee nodded, grateful for the excuse to leave Shaun's presence and the shattered dreams stirred by seeing him with the kids.

"What can I help with?" Brylee asked as they walked into the kitchen.

Jessie poured two glasses of tea and motioned to the counter. "I just thought you could use a break from everything."

Brylee accepted the glass Jessie held out to her and took a seat on a barstool at the counter. She had an idea Jessie included Shaun as part of everything. The woman might be quiet, but she was uncannily perceptive. "I could, Jessie. Thank you. This whole modeling thing is new to me, but kind of exciting, too."

Jessie smiled. "I about died when Chase and Paige talked me into modeling at not one but two fashion shows in Vegas last year. I guess, though, it wasn't any worse than marrying Chase in front of hundreds of his adoring fans."

"I can't even imagine how hard that would have been." Brylee might not be shy like Jessie, but she was a private person. Being in the spotlight in front of that many people for an intimate event like a wedding wouldn't have been something she would have wanted to do. Then again, she'd married Shaun in front of a dozen strangers.

Jessie took a sip of her tea and rubbed her finger over the droplets of moisture the glass left behind on the counter. "It wasn't easy, that's for sure. In the end, I got Chase and that's all that really matters."

"You two met at the altar, didn't you?" Brylee asked, knowing the story, but wanting to hear it from Jessie.

The woman nodded. "Yes. My friend entered me in a crazy contest that Chase's cousin held. One lucky woman would win the chance to marry him for a day. It was supposed to just be a publicity stunt, but the minister performed a real ceremony. Ashley, that's Chase's cousin, claims she had no idea how it happened, but we're convinced she hired a real minister on purpose."

Brylee's eyes widened in surprise. "That's a little…"

"Ashley. It's a lot Ashley, actually," Jessie grinned. "But whether she conspired to make it happen or it was an accident, I'm blessed every day to wake up with the man I love beside me." Jessie smiled at Brylee. "I'll even tell you a secret. Neither Chase nor I wanted to stay married, but Ashley talked us into doing it for a year. By the time Chase left for his first rodeo in January, I was already so in love with him, my heart ached with every breath, but I was convinced he didn't love me back. He felt the same way, loving me from afar but afraid to tell me how he really felt. It took a disastrous experience at a fashion show in Vegas for us to finally get together. I was so mad at him, I flew home to pack my things and leave."

"What happened?" Brylee asked, leaning toward Jessie, eager to find out more of the story.

"Let's just say a desperate cowboy who confesses he's an idiot and can't live without you can talk you into or out of just about anything." Jessie grinned at her again. "It's none of my business and I won't pry, but I know from what we overheard a few weeks ago at that dance that you and Shaun were once married. I don't think it's a secret to anyone that he still loves you."

Brylee shrugged. "Our very brief marriage ended so badly, I've sworn off love for life."

Jessie gave her a studying glance. "Love or Shaun?"

"Both, since to my head and heart those are one and the same," Brylee admitted.

"Have you considered giving him a second chance? From what Chase said, Shaun, like so many of the guys in their group of friends, has grown up considerably in the last few years. Maybe things would be different now."

Brylee shook her head, unwilling to even consider the possibilities. "And maybe things would be exactly the same. I don't have enough pieces left of my heart to risk letting him destroy it a second time."

Jessie placed a hand on her back and gave it an encouraging pat. "I'm sure things will work out just like they are supposed to when the time is right."

Brylee was saved from answering when Chase popped his head inside and motioned for them to come outside. "You've got to watch Grace. She's serenading Shaun."

"We'll be right there," Jessie said, giving her husband a loving smile.

"I'm gonna go, Jessie," Brylee said, unable to spend one more moment watching Shaun that night, especially with the adorable kids flocking around him. Grateful she'd just been given permission to drive again, she could escape without waiting for someone to drive her home.

"Take care, Brylee. We'll see you later this week in Pendleton." Jessie gave her a hug and walked her to the front door.

Brylee got in her pickup and left, wondering why she kept torturing herself by hanging around Shaun and his friends. Each moment she spent with him just made it that much harder to deny how much she wanted him, needed him, and loved him.

Chapter Fourteen

"Rain, rain, go away," Shaun chanted under his breath as a steady drizzle fell from gunmetal-gray skies during the last day of the rodeo in Pendleton. The clouds that gathered and loomed that morning gave way to rain before the rodeo was half over.

Now that the barrel racing was set to begin, the moisture had done a number on the arena. The football field-sized grassy infield surrounded by a racetrack was roughly twice the size of a regular rodeo arena. The surface of the track, where the barrels were set up, quickly turned into a goopy mess while the grass morphed into a surface slicker than a sheet of ice coated in cooking oil.

While Shaun wasn't one of the pickup men working the event, he had tagged along to help with the Rockin' K stock participating in the rodeo. Mostly, he wanted to be there to cheer for his friends, especially for Brylee.

Shortly after the rodeo started, he'd gone up

into the bleachers and ate a hamburger while he visited with the McGraw and Morgan families. Jessie Jarrett held little Marley Morgan while Cooper and Paige James helped keep Grace McGraw corralled. Cooper wasn't working this rodeo, so he hung out in the stands with his wife to support their friends. Next to them, Brylee's grandpa and her brother anxiously awaited her turn to ride. Birch was so excited to watch his sister compete, he could hardly sit still.

However, as the time neared for barrel racing, Shaun shared the worry of Ace and Birch Barton about how the rain would affect Brylee's run. He knew she held back when it rained, fearful of another wreck. He couldn't blame her, since she'd just gotten rid of the brace and been cleared to drive again last week.

Regardless of the rain, she had some stiff competition today and would have to give it her best if she planned to win. She was sitting in second place, but all that would change once the girls began turning and burning around the barrels.

Wryly, Shaun contemplated how much burning there would be with the soggy weather. Barrel racers sometimes referred to the run in the Pendleton arena as the Green Mile. Right now, it looked more like the waterlogged bank of a bayou.

He made his way down to where six teenage volunteers waited to go into the arena. The boys would rake around the barrels between each ride. He slipped twenty dollars to one of the boys and took his place, wanting to be nearby if something happened to Brylee.

He walked out with the others and helped set the barrels, grinning at one of the men in the arena who razzed him about stealing jobs away from babies.

"Just call me multi-faceted," Shaun said as he made his way out to the third barrel at the far end of the arena. He'd watched Brylee compete enough to know she never had a problem with the first barrel and rarely the second. For some reason, if she knocked over a barrel or if Rocket acted up, it was always on that last one. So he stood there in the rain and leaned on the rake, waiting with a fourteen-year-old who couldn't stand still.

"Didn't you used to ride broncs?" the kid asked.

Shaun grinned at him. "I sure did."

"And you won a world championship?" the boy took a step closer.

"Three of them." Shaun watched as the first rider entered the arena.

"And now you're volunteering to rake dirt around barrels?" The boy shook his head. "I think you peaked too early and went downhill, man."

Shaun chuckled, amused, yet also insulted by the teen. He watched as the first barrel racer slid into the second barrel, earning a five second penalty. The second rider took a mud-driven dive into the bucking chutes, but got up uninjured.

His gaze latched onto Brylee when she and Rocket entered the arena. Rocket pranced sideways and tugged against her hold on the reins, ready to run. Suddenly, the horse exploded into action and took the first barrel with no problem. He slipped a

SHANNA HATFIELD

little going around the second barrel, but it stayed upright.

Shaun cheered as loudly as anyone in the crowd as she raced to the third barrel. "You've got this, Bitsy," he shouted as she circled the barrel. "Run, baby, run!"

Rocket stretched out his stride and raced across the arena. He'd almost reached the electronic eye that timed the ride when his feet went out from under him. The horse went into a deep slide. Brylee ended up under him in the mud.

The crowd gasped and Shaun took off running across the grass, slipping twice and almost falling. He was only halfway across the arena when Rocket got to his feet. A nearby group of cowboys stepped in to help. One caught Rocket's reins, even though the horse fought against him. Two others helped Brylee to her feet while a third retrieved her hat out of the mud.

Shaun didn't even realize he was still holding the rake until he reached her. He tossed it to one of the boys who'd been standing around and the teen took off running back in the direction Shaun had come.

"Brylee, are you okay? Anything broken?" he asked, placing an arm around her back for support when she seemed to have trouble standing on her own.

"I think she got the wind knocked out of her," a cowboy named Chet said, moving back as Shaun looked at Brylee.

"Do you need the medic team, Bitsy?"

She shook her head, but didn't seem in a hurry

to move.

"Give Brylee Barton a hand, folks," the announcer boomed. "That little gal has had quite a season. Regardless of her score today, you'll see her competing in Las Vegas at the finals. Are you okay, darlin'?"

Brylee raised a mud-coated hand and waved to the crowd.

"Can you walk?" Shaun asked as she took a halting step.

She didn't answer, but took another step that made her wince.

Shaun started to pick her up, but she shook her head. "I have to walk out of here on my own, Shaun. Just give me your arm to lean on." Brylee took his forearm in a death grip and he inwardly cringed with each painful step she took.

The crowd cheered her on with the help of the announcer.

Once they disappeared out of sight beneath the bleachers, Shaun swept her into his arms and headed straight for the sports medicine trailer.

Brylee leaned her head against Shaun's shoulder, too weary and disappointed to fight against him. Truthfully, she was grateful he'd run to her side then picked her up when she didn't think her legs would continue to hold her. Her ankle felt as though someone had put it in a vise and cranked the pressure one too many turns.

She wanted to scream at the injustice of making it through the barrels with what surely would have been a first-place time only to have Rocket go down at the last possible second. The poor boy was probably scared and in need of attention, and here she was getting carted off to the medic trailer.

Why, of all days, did it have to rain today? The weather the past week had been warm and gorgeous. Rain wasn't even in the forecast. If it had been, she probably would have spent several days freaking out instead of the forty-minutes she had between the time it started raining and when the barrel racing began.

Disappointment rolled over her in violent waves that made her feel nauseous, or maybe that was from the pain radiating from her ankle up her leg. If she'd damaged her recently healed break, she knew she'd be out of competing for a long while. As in no-trip-to-the-finals recuperation time. Months spent out of the game meant no winnings from finals to pay off the ranch debt.

Fear threatened to choke her as Shaun carried her to the trailer. Mud dripped off her, much like it had the last time she and Rocket had taken a fall in the rain, but she wouldn't be the only one tracking a mess into the medic trailer.

Shaun set her down inside. The doctor took one look at his anxious face and shook his head. "Go find something to do while I see what's injured."

Brylee grabbed Shaun's hand. "Please, go check on Rocket. I'm worried about him."

Shaun squeezed her hand, then rushed out the

door.

"You ought to be more worried about you, young lady," the doctor said, helping her back to a private area to do the exam with the help of a volunteer nurse. When he finished, the doctor gave her a smile. "Your leg is fine, but you've got a dandy sprain on that ankle, Brylee."

"But nothing is broken, right?"

"No breaks, that's the good news. The bad news is, you need to baby that sprain. Stay off that foot for at least two weeks. I'm not kidding around. Completely off it. No walking anywhere you don't have to, and absolutely no riding," the doctor warned her as he gently rotated her foot to show her where it was already starting to bruise. "I can give you a prescription for pain pills if you need them."

"I'll be fine without them," she said. Her foot had already swollen to the size of a cantaloupe. She certainly couldn't get her boot back on and walking all the way out to where she'd parked her pickup and trailer seemed like it might as well have been five miles away.

She heard the door open and someone else enter the trailer. A female volunteer appeared in the exam area carrying a sack from one of the vendor tents across the street.

"A cowboy left this for you," the woman said, handing Brylee the bag. Inside was a new pair of jeans and a blouse, along with a pair of socks.

The doctor smiled. "Glad to see someone is watching out for you. Go ahead and get changed out of those wet, muddy things. When you're ready, we can help you out of here."

Brylee took off her muddy shirt and used the inside of it to wipe away as much mud as she could from her hair. She pulled an elastic band from her pocket and twisted her hair into a loose bun and secured it with the band, hoping to keep the mess from spreading too much on the new clothes. Two white towels from a nearby stack turned grimy as she used them to clean up as best she could. She pulled on a pair of jeans that fit her perfectly and a navy blue blouse with little white hearts that looked like polka dots. She'd eyed it earlier in the morning when she'd gone through the vendor tents with Birch. Had he purchased the clothes for her? Most likely, she could attribute the gift of clothing to Shaun.

However, if her brother was waiting outside for her, he could help her get to the pickup. She'd asked her grandpa to drive it up closer, but she didn't want him trying to walk through the mud.

When she was dressed, she wadded her muddy clothes into the shopping bag, pulled on her left boot, and hobbled to the front of the trailer. Shaun and Birch both waited there for her.

"You sure like to play in the mud, sis," Birch teased before giving her a hug. "You about scared me and Grandpa half to death. I'm not sure he's calmed down yet. I left him sitting in the bleachers with Tate and Cort because he was shaking so bad, I didn't think he'd make it down the steps without falling."

"I'm okay, Birch. Nothing's broken." Brylee forced a smile for her brother's benefit. "Why don't you go back and help Grandpa out of the stands and

I'll see about getting the pickup."

Birch made no move to leave.

"And just how are you planning to drive?" the doctor asked, giving her a pointed look.

Brylee glanced down at her right foot and sighed. "I... um..."

"I'll make sure you and your rig make it home then have someone pick me up," Shaun said, taking out his phone and texting someone a message. His phone pinged with a return message. He tapped out another one and hit send then stuck it in his pocket.

Brylee shook her head. "All the way to Walla Walla? No. I don't want to be an imposition. Besides, I need to get Rocket loaded and..."

Shaun placed his fingers over her lips, making a shiver wash over her. She blamed it on the cold mud that still coated a good portion of her body and not the good-looking cowboy who seemed determined to make things easier on her.

"It's less than an hour to your house. Honestly, it isn't a problem. Besides, Rocket is already loaded and ready to go. I had the vet check him over and he's perfectly fine, even if he looks like he took a mud bath." Shaun tipped his head to the doctor. "Thanks for taking care of her."

"That's what I'm here for, Shaun. Just make sure this girl follows my orders."

Shaun grinned. "I'll do my best, but she's tougher and meaner than me." Before Brylee could protest, he handed the bag of muddy clothes and her boot to Birch, and then swept her into his arms.

"Birch, get the door, please," Shaun said. He stepped outside and people seemed to stop to watch as he carried her toward a side gate. Jessie and Chase stood outside a nearly new SUV with the back door opened.

"What's going on?" Brylee asked.

"Chase and Jessie thought you might be more comfortable in their SUV. I'll bring Birch and Ace in your pickup. Okay?" Shaun asked as he set her down on the fleece blanket Jessie had spread across the back seat.

Jessie folded the blanket around Brylee and patted her on the arm before moving back. "We'll follow you, Shaun."

"I don't think I've ever been out to Blue Hills Ranch, although I've heard you have some incredible horses there," Chase said, smiling at Brylee.

Tears stung her eyes and she wanted to bury her head in her hands and weep. Instead, she drew in a deep breath. Pain shooting up her side jogged her memory about the bruised ribs the doctor mentioned. She held a hand to her side and did her best to give Chase and Jessie a watery smile. "Thank you both so much for helping."

"Our pleasure, Brylee. Really, it's no trouble at all. It gives us an excuse to duck out on all the fan stuff going on after the rodeo." Chase grinned at her. "Can't say I mind a bit."

"Did you guys...?" Birch started asking questions, diverting their attention.

Shaun leaned inside the SUV. He brushed a hand over Brylee's cheek then cupped her chin. "You scared at least ten years off my life back there. I'm glad you're going to be okay."

She nodded and tried to swallow the lump of emotion stuck in her throat. "I'm glad nothing is broken this time, but Shaun, I didn't even get a score. It's not how I envisioned today going at all."

"Life is seldom how we plan it, Bitsy, but always worth the ride." He kissed the top of her mud-streaked head then shut the door.

She watched him and Birch jog off toward the area where the contestant trailers were parked.

Chase held Jessie's door before hustling back around to the driver's side and sliding behind the wheel.

Jessie turned around and gave Brylee a compassionate look before handing her a water bottle. The woman smiled at her husband and started asking him questions about who won, what late season rodeos were left, and the rankings for the events other than barrel racing.

Brylee appreciated Jessie's efforts to keep the conversation light and offer her a chance to remain quietly in the backseat, contemplating her loss of the day as they drove her home. Her ranking was solid and she knew she wouldn't get bounced so far down that she'd miss out on Vegas before the season ended, but it rankled that she missed the opportunity to win today. If Rocket had remained on his feet just a tenth of a second longer, she probably would have come in first. If not, it would have been a close second.

In spite of the rain and her worries about Rocket getting hurt or her breaking something, she'd raced him like everything was on the line. They'd been so close to winning, so close to taking another championship title. Yet, here she was, riding home with a foot twice the size it should be while Shaun once again came to her rescue.

Since she wouldn't be competing anywhere for a while, it seemed like a good time to tell him goodbye, again. She felt indebted to him for all he'd done — all he and his dad and the Rockin' K crew had done — but part of her resisted letting him go. In the past two months, she'd grown accustomed to having him around.

He made her laugh and see things from a different perspective. Brylee had come to realize the years she'd spent at the ranch listening to her mother's negativity day in and day out had taken a toll on her. She used to be a happy, upbeat person, but disappointment and pain had left her feeling like an embittered empty shell.

It was only after she'd decided to forgive Shaun that she started feeling more like herself. Not like her old self, because that naïve, clueless girl no longer existed, but a grown-up version of the person she used to be. One that had finally come out on the other side of a horrible experience.

Brylee breathed a sigh of relief to see her mother wasn't home when they arrived. Although they'd all invited her to go with them that morning, she insisted she had work to do and houses to show to a couple flying in from Seattle, intent on buying something before they returned to the city Sunday evening.

Her mother had been so different when Brylee was growing up. Not that she'd ever been lighthearted and full of fun like her dad, but her mom hadn't been so harsh and soured on life. Brylee noticed a change in her mother after she started competing in rodeos. When she went pro and was gone for weeks at a time, she could almost feel the negativity and bitterness as a palpable force anytime she came home. Then Brylee returned to the ranch with a shattered heart. A year and a half later, her dad passed away, and things had gone from bad to worse.

Despite how much her mother complained about having to work in town to keep things afloat on the ranch, she'd gotten her realtor's license several years ago. She dabbled with it, selling a house or two a year, until necessity forced her into doing it full-time. And Jenn loved it. She loved finding just the right house for people and didn't even mind the mountains of paperwork. But her relationship with the ranch and its occupants seemed to be a love-hate thing, with a lot more hate than love lately.

Brylee had no idea what made her mother tick, what her hopes and dreams were, now that her father was gone. Sometimes, it seemed like her mother just struggled to get through one day at a time.

She hated that her grandfather had to come back to the ranch to help them out, but someone who had a clue about ranching needed to be there to oversee the seasonal help they hired. Birch was far too young for that kind of responsibility. Brylee's mother seemed to have no interest in work on the ranch anymore. Her only interest in Blue Hills Ranch was to make sure it stayed intact as a legacy for Brylee and Birch.

"I can't thank you enough for driving me home," Brylee said as Chase parked the SUV at the end of the front walk. "I really am sorry to be such a bother."

"You aren't a bother at all, Brylee. I'm just sorry about the way the day ended for you." Chase looked over the seat at her then glanced outside.

"Is that King? Your dad's roping horse?" Chase asked as he noticed the horses in the pasture across from the house.

Brylee smiled. "Sure is. If you come in the house and get a handful of carrots, you'll be among his favorite people for life."

Chase grinned at Jessie then hurried out of the SUV. He opened Brylee's door. "How do you want to do this? I can carry you, or you can walk between us and we'll support you," Chase glanced at Jessie for a suggestion as she stepped beside him.

"I think if you just help me hop to the door, I can make it with no problem." Brylee untucked the blanket from around her and swiveled so both feet were flat on the floor instead of one propped on the seat.

"I've got her," Shaun said. He stepped forward and scooped Brylee into his arms before she could protest. Not that she really wanted to.

Birch and Ace led Rocket out of the horse trailer and over to the barn. He was still covered in mud, but Brylee knew her brother and grandpa would take good care of him.

Shaun carried her up the steps and handed Brylee her pickup keys to unlock the door. He bent down so she could reach the doorknob. She gave it a push and he walked inside.

"Where to?" he asked as he stood inside the tiled entry, looking around.

The house hadn't changed much since the last time he'd been in it nearly six years ago. Brylee pointed to a hall just past the ranch office.

"If you wouldn't mind carrying me to my room, I'd really like to wash off all this mud before I do anything else." At the teasing, suggestive look on his face, she popped him on the shoulder. "And no, I don't need any help. While I do that, would you run into the kitchen for some carrots? Chase wants to meet King."

Shaun grinned. "For the record, I don't mind carrying you anywhere. You don't weigh as much as a sack of feed, but sure are more fun to hold." He waggled his eyebrows at her as he stepped into her bedroom.

Unlike the rest of the house, it had changed greatly from the last time he was there. The girlish posters and prints on the walls were gone. She'd put away trophies and awards she'd won in high school. The room looked more like something out of a home décor magazine with crisp white curtains, white furnishings, and a queen-sized bed with a navy duvet cover. Coral and white accent pillows were tossed across the bed and a white-painted reclaimed wood headboard stood in stark contrast to the navy wall behind it.

"Oh, wow," Shaun said, setting her down just inside the door. "I had an idea, but this confirms navy blue is still your favorite color."

"It is." Brylee looked over her shoulder at him as she hobbled to a dresser and opened the top drawer. "Mom talked me into taking an online class in staging homes. I help her and some of the other realtors in her office from time to time. This was my first project, to see if I was any good at it."

"I'd say you have a talent for it, Bitsy. It looks nice, even if I'd get all that white stuff filthy by the end of the first week."

She grinned at him. "You wouldn't make it past the first day." Brylee hobbled toward her bathroom. "I'll be quick, I promise."

"Take your time. Once Chase starts studying the horses, it might be a while before he's ready to leave." Shaun backed up a step, but shot her the half-smile that made her wish he was truly hers. "Sure you don't need help?"

She laughed and pointed to the door. "Get out of my room, cowboy. Oh, and Shaun, thanks for the clothes. I love them. I'll like them even better when I'm not covered in mud."

"You're welcome. I saw you eyeballing that shirt earlier." He nodded at her then left the room.

Brylee rushed to wash the mud from her hair and body, amazed it was even caked between her toes. She toweled dry and dressed, gulped two pain reliever tablets, and then made her way to the front door with the help of the crutches she'd hoped to never need again.

Through the window next to the door, she could see Jessie on the porch with Ace. Quietly easing the door open, she listened to him tell stories about life on the ranch back when he was a boy during World War II.

Jessie glanced up and noticed her then rose to her feet. "You shouldn't be on your feet, Brylee. Take my chair."

"I'm doing okay," she said, sitting next to her grandpa as he rested on a wicker settee. She removed a throw pillow from behind her and set it on the wicker coffee table, then propped her foot on it.

In the pasture across from them, Birch and Chase straddled the fence, feeding her dad's old horse carrots while Shaun stretched his hand through the poles, scratching King along his neck.

"It's a beautiful place here," Jessie said, glancing over the serene landscape. Now that the rain had gone, the sun gilded the sky with a brilliant array of crimson and lavender. "I love the sunsets in this area. Some of the prettiest I've ever seen have been over the hill by our ranch."

Ace asked Jessie questions about where she grew up and talked about how glad he was he didn't have to spend time in a big city.

Brylee leaned her head back as her grandpa kept an arm around her and closed her eyes, listening to the hum of conversation, the sounds of birds in the trees, and the laughter of the men over with the horses. The crunch of gravel made her eyes pop open, fearful her mother had returned, but it was just Birch walking across the driveway with Shaun and Chase.

Her grandfather gave her a knowing look, as though he, too, worried about the explosion that would take place the moment Jenn returned home.

Brylee preferred her friends not get caught in the crossfire.

"I can't thank you all enough for your help today and taking such good care of me. If I can ever return the favor, please let me know." She looked at Jessie then Chase.

"We were more than happy to help, but we better get going," Jessie said, rising to her feet then bending down to give Brylee a hug. "Take care of yourself. If you ever want to chat or get together, just give me a call."

"I'd like that, Jessie. Thank you. And thank you both again." Brylee smiled as Chase took one of her hands in his and squeezed it.

"Be sure you ice that foot. You probably already know the routine, but ice will take the swelling out. Heat will help relax the muscles." Chase smirked and pointed to her foot. "I've done something similar to that a time or two myself."

"Thanks, Chase." Brylee shifted her gaze from the departing couple to Shaun. She didn't know what to say to him. Goodbye seemed like the smartest choice, but the words wouldn't roll off her tongue.

He bent down and kissed her cheek. "Call me if you need anything. Promise?"

"Promise," she said, although she had no intention of doing so.

Shaun shook her grandfather's hand then hooked an arm around Birch's thin shoulders. "Walk us out?" he asked as the boy fell into step with him. Brylee couldn't hear what was said, but Birch glanced back at her once then nodded to

Shaun.

Shaun blew her a kiss with a wink while Chase and Jessie waved as they climbed in the SUV and left.

Before their dust settled in the driveway, Brylee held out a hand to Birch. "Help me back in the house. I sure don't want to be sitting here when Mom gets home."

Ace laughed as Birch pulled her to her feet. Her brother handed her the crutches then moved back as she made her way into the house.

"I was sure hoping your friends left before Jenn got home," Ace said. "I had Birch send her a text that we needed some groceries so she'd be late getting back."

"Grandpa! I didn't know you had it in you to be so sneaky." Brylee grinned at him. "Way to go."

Ace cackled as he followed her inside and closed the door.

Chapter Fifteen

Brylee parked three blocks away from the real estate office where her mother worked with a dozen other people and took a moment to gather her thoughts. She inhaled a deep breath and sent up a prayer for patience as she opened the door of her pickup and slid out.

She straightened her navy plaid pencil skirt and glanced down to make sure she hadn't gotten any mud on her black high-heeled dress boots.

November wind whipped around her ears and trailed inside the collar of her coat, carrying a frigid bite. Brylee wished she'd remembered to grab a scarf on her way out the door. She'd been so excited when she got the mail and found the check from Lasso Eight for her modeling gig in September, she was lucky she'd remembered to yank on her coat. Paige had warned her it could take eight to ten weeks for the payment to be processed. It had been almost nine weeks since she'd posed with Shaun and the others at Chase and Jessie's ranch.

Today, with the overcast skies and the possibility of snow in the forecast, those golden early autumn days with Shaun seemed like a lifetime ago.

After he'd helped her get home the day she'd sprained her ankle, she'd hardly seen him. She knew the Rockin' K had contracted to do a few late season rodeos. In direct contrast to her mother's orders that she stay home and give her body more time to heal and rest, Brylee had driven to Texas in mid-October for the women's rodeo finals where she came in third. Her ankle had healed quickly and she was more than ready to compete.

She'd been thrilled to discover the Rockin' K crew providing stock at the circuit finals in central Washington the first week of November. In spite of her mother's heated protests about her attending, Brylee had not only participated in the event, she'd also let Birch tag along with her. His presence kept things light between her and Shaun. No matter how badly she wanted to take things to the next level with him, it just wasn't meant to be.

Shaun had texted her nearly every day and called once a week to check on her, but he'd made no effort to move their relationship beyond the solid friendship they'd established during the last four months.

Jason and Shaun had both been a great help and support to her during those final weeks of the summer and into the fall. But Shaun was the one she couldn't stop thinking about. In fact, his friendship had come to mean more to her now than it ever had back when they were dating.

She and Shaun had grown up, changed. Since he was no longer drinking, she didn't have to wonder if she was talking to the real Shaun or Shaun under the influence. And he seemed so much more interested in her as a person.

Before, their relationship was full of flirting and stolen kisses. In a lot of ways, it seemed superficial as she looked back on it. Now, though, they discussed any number of topics, and had meaningful conversations. The two of them could even defend opposing viewpoints without getting angry because of an underlying respect for the other person.

Shaun had grown into an incredible man, one some woman would be blessed to marry. Thoughts of that happening, of a woman other than Brylee becoming his wife, made the hardened lump in her chest she used to call a heart throb with pain. She didn't want to think about him with anyone else. Yet, she couldn't marry him. Not with all that had gone on in their past. Not with things as they were.

Her bond with Shaun wasn't the only thing that kept her awake at night. Brylee's already strained relationship with her mother had grown ten times worse when Jenn discovered Brylee's sprained ankle after the Pendleton rodeo.

True to Grandpa's predictions, the woman had thrown a hissy fit of legendary proportions. It took two days before the dogs could be coerced to come up on the back porch, scared Jenn might still be ranting and raving inside the house.

As she fussed over Brylee's foot and changed

the ice pack, she'd yelled at her, calling her a brainless moron for chasing such a ridiculous, stupid dream.

Brylee did her best to hold her tongue because arguing with her mother never accomplished anything except getting everyone worked up. When her mother started blaming Shaun for her accident, Brylee couldn't hold back anymore. In no uncertain terms, she informed her mother that he ran all the way across the arena just to see if she was okay, bought her a dry set of clothes, and made sure she got home. She reminded Jenn that if it wasn't for Shaun and the help he'd so selflessly given, they wouldn't be looking at paying off the ranch debt by the end of the year.

From there, things were said that shouldn't have been; heated, hurtful words, mostly from Jenn. Birch and Ace tried to come to Brylee's defense, which only made her mother even more difficult to handle.

Honestly, everyone had been walking on eggshells around the woman since September, terrified of setting her off into another tirade. Brylee understood the pressure her mother felt, the gaping chasm in her life that death and disappointment had left behind, but she couldn't understand why her mother chose to deal with everything by wallowing in bitterness and anger.

After today, with one of her burdens lifted, perhaps she'd let go of some of her negativity and move back into the land of the living. Truly, she felt like her mother had been going through the motions of life without engaging in the world around her for far too long.

The saddest part of it all was that her mother had spent the last handful of years missing out on watching Birch grow into an amazing young man. They'd celebrated his fifteenth birthday last week with Brylee taking him and three of his friends to the Tri-Cities for a day of bowling, pizza, movies, barbecue, and a concert. Birch had declared it his best birthday ever, especially when he arrived home to find several gifts awaiting him, including a new rope Shaun had sent with a note he looked forward to helping him break it in.

Regardless of what Jenn said and everything that had transpired, Birch remained a faithful advocate of Shaun. Brylee pondered if her brother thought Shaun actually possessed the ability to rope the moon for the way he seemed to view him as a hero.

Wisely, Brylee had hidden the gift from Shaun until it was time for Birch to open it. Her mother had started to offer a nasty comment about it, but a quelling look from Ace had forced her to shut up.

Brylee didn't know what she'd do without the steady presence of her grandfather beside her. Together, they made decisions for the ranch while she oversaw most of the responsibilities. She'd kept two of their part-time seasonal workers to help finish up the fall work. They agreed to stay until the day before Thanksgiving, but after that, they were heading south for the winter.

She couldn't blame them. The weatherman predicated a long, cold winter. A shudder rolled through Brylee just thinking about it. If she had to spend months cooped up with her mother, she might go insane.

A year and a half ago, when she decided to get back into pro rodeo, she and her mother had faced off in an epic battle. Unbeknownst to Jenn, Brylee had paid her dues, kept her barrel racing membership up-to-date, and participated in just enough rodeo events to remain active the past five years. She knew if the day ever came when she wanted to return to something she loved doing, she needed to be ready. Once the dust settled, she promised her mother she'd only go on the road for a year and would hang up her rodeo spurs once she competed in Las Vegas.

The last thing Brylee wanted to do was quit and return to the life she'd led the last several years. Before her father passed away, she'd been devastated by Shaun's abandonment and the dark days that followed in its wake. Once she'd clawed her way out of that mire, her father had died and she'd been thrust into the role of trying to hold the ranch together while her mother threw herself into her real estate business to bury her pain and bring in much-needed funds to pay the bills.

Commission on real estate sales didn't provide the steady income they needed and in a moment of desperation, Jenn had finally agreed to Brylee's plan of earning the money to pay off the debt through barrel racing. She'd been at the top of the game once, almost twice, before. She knew she could do it again, but she had to get some things settled in her personal life.

And today would put one big concern to rest.

Brylee pushed open the door to the office and smiled at Dot, the plump, jolly-faced receptionist who always made her think of Mrs. Claus.

"Brylee! It's great to see you," Dot said, getting up from her desk and giving her a hug. "Is your mom expecting you?"

"No, I was hoping to catch her between appointments, though." Brylee glanced toward her mother's office door.

"As a matter of fact, her last appointment of the day left about five minutes ago. Go on in." Dot waved her hand in the direction of Jenn's office.

"Thanks, Dot. Great nails, by the way." Brylee knew the woman got a weekly manicure, often with a seasonal theme. This week, she sported falling leaves on all her nails, except for a plump turkey painted on her left thumbnail.

Dot giggled and waggled her fingernails.

Brylee walked over to her mother's office door and tapped once before sticking her head inside. Jenn was on the phone but motioned for Brylee to come in and take a seat. She perched on the edge of a chair and absorbed the warmth of the room. She hadn't realized how cold the temperature had dropped until she'd walked from her pickup to the office.

Jenn wrapped up the call and gave Brylee a studying glance. "It's nice to see you wearing something besides dusty cowboy boots and jeans. Are you staging a house today?"

Brylee ignored her mother's thinly veiled criticism and removed an envelope from her purse. She laid it on the desk in front of her mom.

"What's this?" Jenn asked, opening the envelope.

"Relief," Brylee said with a smile.

"What are you talking about? It's not a roll of antacid tab..." Jenn's voice trailed off and her mouth gaped open as she stared at the check in her hand.

"That's what I earned from modeling for Lasso Eight, Mom. I want you to go with me to the bank so we can pay off our debt. Then you and I are going to make a pact that we never, ever let something like that happen again. Okay?"

Brylee held out her hand to her mother. Tears glistened in Jenn's eyes as she closed her mouth and shook Brylee's hand, giving it a long squeeze.

The woman leaned back in her chair and drew in a rough breath before she spoke. "Brylee, you should keep this. You've worked so hard all year and I know you were disappointed about not winning in Pendleton."

Brylee stood. "No. You and I made a deal and I'm sticking to my end of it. Get your coat and let's go. I want to finish this today so we can close that horrible chapter in our lives and move on. To celebrate, I think we should stop by that place that serves those fancy desserts and eat something decadent."

Jenn smiled and saved a document on her computer before turning it off. Brylee held her mother's coat while she shrugged into it then watched as Jenn gathered her briefcase and purse. Together, they stepped into the hall.

"Dot, I'm going to be out the rest of the

afternoon. Have a good evening." Jenn motioned for Brylee to follow her outside. "Brr. I think it's colder now than it was than when I was out showing a place right before lunch," Jenn commented as they crossed the street and headed back the way Brylee had come to go to the bank.

Inside, it didn't take long for them to deposit the check into the loan account. Jenn held Brylee's hand as the payment was processed and they received a statement that showed the loan balance at zero.

Brylee wanted to cheer, but she settled for beaming a smile at everyone they encountered between there and the dessert shop. Inside, she ordered a chocolate éclair while her mother ordered an almond croissant. Within moments, they were seated at a corner table with a cup of espresso in their hands, relishing the treat.

Jenn leaned back in her chair, appearing content and relieved. "Now that the loan is paid, you can cancel your trip to Vegas. I was thinking..."

Brylee didn't let her finish. "I'm not canceling the trip, Mom. We agreed I'd go when I started this and I'm going." Brylee set down her fork and tried to rein in her temper. She was tired of fighting against her mother over everything. It wasn't like she was a child. She was twenty-seven years old and had experienced more pain and heartache than many people endured in a lifetime. In addition, she'd been in charge of running a large wheat and cattle ranch when her mother refused to deal with it.

Jenn's lips thinned into a narrow, angry line.

"There's no need for it. The loan is paid. It would be foolhardy to press your luck, Brylee. What if you get hurt again? What if the next time Rocket falls he breaks a leg? What if you end up married to that no-good Casanova who broke your heart? It's just like you to run right back to him at the first available opportunity."

Brylee gave her mother such a cold, harsh look, the woman closed her mouth and pressed it back into that annoying thin line. "What if I succeed, Mom? What if I take the championship title again? What if I win as much money there as I have all year? It could happen, you know, because contrary to your ongoing, belittling, ever-negative opinion, I'm pretty good at what I do. As to what does or does not happen between me and Shaun, that's my business, not yours. Not anyone's. Shaun is a wonderful, gentle, caring man and if you'd take five minutes to really see him instead of glaring daggers into his back, you'd realize that for yourself."

Jenn jerked back in her chair as though Brylee had reached out and slapped her instead of quietly stating her opinion. Before her mother could launch into a tirade right there in the dessert shop, Brylee slipped on her coat and gathered her things. "Just once, would it kill you to support me instead of treat me like I'm too dumb to tie my own shoes? I know you blame me, and particularly Shaun, for all the heartache our family has faced the last several years, but it's time for you to let it go and get over it. If I can forgive him and move on, what right do you have to cling to the past and throw it in my face every time I turn around?"

Brylee walked out into the cold, blustery air and used the sting of the breeze as an excuse for the moisture that seeped from her eyes.

Chapter Sixteen

After she'd walked away from her mother at the dessert shop last week, Brylee had sat in her pickup for ten minutes and sobbed. She was just so tired. Tired of fighting with her mother. Tired of heartache and loss. Tired of wondering what might have been. Tired of life feeling like it was in limbo.

By the time she got home, she decided getting back to normal was long past overdue. Whether her mother liked it or not, Brylee was determined to make it happen. Since her father's death, they'd barely decorated the house for Christmas or celebrated the holidays.

With the help of Birch and her grandfather, Brylee prepared a Thanksgiving feast. Her mother slept in then went to the office for a few hours, coming home just in time to eat. She complained that the potatoes were lumpy, but when Ace told her he'd mashed them, she returned to eating the meal without saying another word.

In an effort to make peace with her mother, Brylee asked Jenn if she wanted to hit the Black Friday sales the following morning. Jenn refused. "The office is quiet today. I'm going to catch up on paperwork and prepare some listings for next week."

As soon as her mother left, Brylee packed up the few Thanksgiving decorations she'd set out. Birch and Ace sat at the kitchen table eating leftover pumpkin pie for breakfast. She grinned at them both and motioned toward the back door. "Get your boots on, boys, because we're about to deck the halls at Blue Hills Ranch."

Birch whooped and shoved the last two bites of pie in his mouth. He had on his boots, coat, and gloves, and was running outside to the storage shed before Ace had set down his coffee cup.

"I reckon I better keep an eye on him," Ace said, finishing his pie and coffee before he bundled up and made his way out into the cold.

While Birch and Ace unearthed decorations that hadn't seen the light of day in years, Brylee put away many of the knick-knacks and decorations currently in the house. When she finished, she moved furniture around in the living room so they could place the tree in front of the window.

She'd just gone back to the kitchen and picked up a dustrag when Birch and Ace opened the door and carried in a large wooden sign.

"Oh, you found Dad's sign!" Snow blew in with them so she hurried to close the door against the flurries and the cold breeze. "Where was it?"

Ace stretched his back amid a chorus of creaks

and groans and shook the snow off his hat. "In the loft over the garden shed. We found two boxes of lights and the Christmas tree ornaments there, too."

Brylee gave him a concerned glance. "Please tell me you did not climb up the ladder, Grandpa."

Ace grinned at her. "Okay, I won't." He pulled off his coat and gloves then sat down at the kitchen table with a weary grunt.

Brylee gave the old man a long look then turned to her brother. "Birch, can you carry in the rest of the boxes? I need Grandpa to help me wipe the dust off everything."

"Can do." The boy hurried back outside into the cold.

Brylee made a cup of steaming, fragrant tea for Ace and set it in front of him before handing him a dustrag.

While Birch carried in the decorations, Brylee dusted the wooden sign. Her dad had taken old barnwood and cut it in even lengths then sealed the wood so it wouldn't be rough. He'd attached the pieces together to form a three by four foot sign then took it into town to someone who did custom painting. The woman painted horse heads, one on top of the other, so that it looked like a tree. She added a few stars and, at the top of the sign, "Merry Christmas" was painted in a decorative font. He'd given it as a gift to Jenn for their fifth Christmas together.

"Let's hang it in the entry," Birch said, picking up the heavy sign and following Brylee to where she'd already removed a painting across from the front door.

Brylee helped him heft it up to the hook then the two of them stepped back and studied it. Birch grinned and dropped an arm around her shoulders. "Things already look more like they should around here."

"Agreed. I want to get this all done before Mom gets home. If it's finished and all the boxes are put away, she won't make us take it down."

"Then put some hustle in it, sis," Birch teased as he raced back to the kitchen. Two hours later, the three of them bundled up and drove into town. They went out to eat at Ace's favorite restaurant for lunch, then made their way to the local tree farm. Brylee and Birch held up trees while Ace decided which one he liked best. Brylee made the final decision, selecting a fragrant fir tree. While the attendant made a fresh cut on the bottom and attached the stand they'd brought along, Brylee and Birch went into the gift shop and filled a basket with holly, two loaves of the special apple bread only available during the holiday season, and searched for a new ornament to hang on the tree.

"These remind me of Dad," Birch said as they stared at a display of metal star ornaments. Brylee got an idea and tossed three dozen of them in her basket. Birch shrugged, grabbed a bag of beef sticks from the cooler across from the front counter, and waited while Brylee paid for their purchases.

Brylee shook her head as her brother began gnawing on one of the seasoned meat sticks the moment they stepped outside. "I swear both of your legs are hollow. Where does all that food go?"

Birch grinned. "I'm a growing boy.

Remember?"

"How could I forget? You've grown an inch since school started. Aren't you already six-foot?"

He nodded and bit off another piece of the beef stick. "Yep. The coach measured me last week. Another quarter inch and I'll hit six-one." Birch nudged her with his elbow. "Kind of makes up for you, doesn't it, shorty?"

"Call me that again and I'll send that photo of you dancing around wearing nothing but your cowboy boots to the school to place on the bulletin board." Brylee watched her brother's cocky grin fade, taking her threat seriously.

"Would you really do that? My entire existence at school would turn into a nightmare. Besides, I was only three."

"Call me that again and see what happens."

Birch smirked. "Sure, stretch. Whatever you say."

Brylee playfully whacked him on the arm as they set the bags in the back of her pickup and drove around to where Ace waited with the tree lot attendant to load their tree. Once the tree was loaded, they drove home. Ace offered his opinions as Brylee and Birch carried the tree inside and set it on the plastic tablecloth Brylee had draped over the floor to keep the needles and any leaks from the tree stand from getting into the carpet.

"A little to the left," Ace said, tossing his coat on the back of the couch and taking a seat. "No, you went too far."

"It's fine, Grandpa," Birch said, quickly running out of patience.

"How about now, Grandpa?" Brylee asked as she gave the tree a slight turn with Birch's help.

Ace sighed and settled back into the soft cushions of the couch. "Perfect! I'll just rest a bit while you two put on the lights then I'll help with the decorations."

Brylee had already tested the lights to make sure they worked. It didn't take long for her and Birch to string them on the tree.

Birch reached for a box of their old ornaments, but Brylee took it from him and looked from him to her grandfather. "I have an idea to decorate the tree and want both of you to weigh in. If you hate it, we'll just put these on like normal."

Ace grinned and Birch gave her a knuckle-bump after she shared her idea. Birch went out to the tack room to gather one of the items she needed while Brylee invaded the private domain of her mother's bedroom. She found what she was searching for in a box in the back of the closet, right where she knew it would be.

Lovingly carrying the box to the front room, she set it on the coffee table. She and Birch sang along to the Christmas carols playing on her phone while Ace offered encouraging comments as they twined the rope her dad had used when he team roped around the tree.

They hung the star ornaments she'd just purchased along with all the red ornaments they could find on the tree. Brylee tied strips of bandana fabric on the ends of random branches.

"How does it look, Grandpa?" she asked, stepping back and leaning against Birch when he draped his arm across her shoulders.

"I like it. Looks just like something your dad would love. He enjoyed all holidays, but none as much as Christmas." Ace sniffled and took out a faded blue bandana. After honking his nose, he stuffed it back in his pocket.

"Come on, sis. Let's put on the top," Birch said, carrying over a small step stool they kept in the hall closet.

Brylee opened the box and took out her dad's cowboy hat. The pale gray felt looked like an unpolished pearl. She breathed deeply as she lined it with a piece of plastic to keep from getting sap on it, savoring the faint hint of her father's after-shave that clung to the hat.

She handed it to Birch and he reverently set it on top of the tree.

"That's perfect," Ace said, getting up from the couch and moving so he could stand with his arm around Brylee's waist.

She kissed his cheek then leaned her head against him as he gave her a hug. "I can almost feel dad here with us."

"Me, too," Birch said, stepping off the stool and standing on the other side of Ace. "I'm glad Mom's not here."

"I hate to say it, but I'm grateful she went to work today," Brylee admitted. "The house is so peaceful when she's gone. I know she works too hard, Grandpa, and we don't need a lecture about her being our mother. We love her, it's just she's been so hard to love. The negativity and bitterness is just hard to deal with everyday. I don't know how

SHANNA HATFIELD

you both put up with it when I was gone."

A sob at the doorway made them spin around in surprise. With the music playing and the three of them so focused on the tree, they hadn't heard Jenn come in.

"Mom, we're..." Brylee watched as her mother turned and opened the door, hurrying out to the carport. "Mom! Come back!"

Jenn whipped her car around and raced down the driveway. Brylee thought about chasing after her, but she had no idea what to say. Quietly, Brylee shut the door and returned to the living room.

Ace plopped down on the couch and scrubbed a hand over his face. "Maybe it's good your mom heard what you said. She's been carrying around burdens that she just needs to let go."

Brylee nodded, hoping one of her dad's nuggets of wisdom would pop into her head, but his voice remained oddly silent.

It was late when Brylee got a text from her mother.

Need some time to think. Going to the cabin. Be back Monday night.

Brylee sighed and tossed the phone on the coffee table. She and Birch sat on the couch while Ace rested in his recliner, pretending to watch a holiday movie with them although he alternated between reading a ranching magazine and snoring.

Birch gave her a questioning look. "Was that Mom? Is she okay?"

"Yeah, she's fine. She said she's going to the

236

cabin and will come home next week."

Birch nodded. "I don't know what to say to her besides I'm sorry. She didn't answer the text I sent."

"I know, sweetie." Brylee brushed her fingers through Birch's hair like she'd done every since he was little. He shifted so his head rested on her lap and she placed a comforting hand on his shoulder.

"Mom needs to work some things out on her own," she said, hoping to reassure her brother. "I'm glad she's taking some time for herself."

"Me, too. I just hope she'll be safe."

Brylee tried not to think about her mother driving an hour on treacherous roads up to the cabin located in the northeastern Oregon section of the Blue Mountains. The closest community was Weston. It was a twenty minute drive from there to the remote road that ended at the cabin constructed by Jenn's grandparents back in the 1930s. Indoor plumbing and electricity had been added to it and the cabin had been renovated twice since then. The last time was not long before her grandparents had both passed away. They'd left the cabin to Jenn, but she hadn't been there since before Brylee's father passed away.

Brylee and Birch went there once in a while just for a place to get away. In fact, they'd gone with Ace back in October when she got home from Texas. They spent a wonderful weekend fishing and relaxing, laughing about fun times they'd had there before life had changed so drastically.

Jenn didn't come home Monday as she promised, but Brylee knew she was at work. One of the other realtors had asked Dot to call her about staging a house for him. She'd asked Dot if her mother had a busy schedule that day and the woman confirmed she was booked.

Brylee didn't want to worry Birch, so she kept her thoughts to herself on where her mother was staying. She might have gotten a hotel room, or decided to stay with a friend. She wondered if her mother intended to hide until Brylee left for the finals in a few days.

The night before she was ready to leave to drive to Las Vegas, Brylee had just sat down to dinner with Ace and Birch when her mother walked in and glanced around.

"That smells good. You have enough for one more?" Jenn hung her coat by the door and left her purse and briefcase on the floor.

"Sure, Mom," Brylee said, giving the woman a welcoming smile before she hopped up and got a plate for her mother.

"Everything okay?" Ace asked, placing his gnarled hand on Jenn's back and giving her a gentle pat when she sat beside him.

"I think so," she said, then turned her attention to filling her plate.

The tension and quiet that had descended over them made Brylee want to run out to the barn and hide there until her mother went to bed. Instead, she turned to Birch and asked him how he'd done on his math quiz.

"Aced it, as usual," he said, leaning back with a cocky grin. "Since I'm getting all A's and I'm done with football for the season, I think I should go with

Brylee to Las Vegas. I've never gotten to see the rodeo in person and she might need some help."

"Birch, you can't miss that much school," Brylee said, giving him a motherly frown. "You'd be bored to tears after the third day."

"I promise I'd get my assignments and do them while I'm there and I wouldn't get into any trouble. Honest, Brylee. Please, please, let me go."

She shook her head. "No, Birch, not this time."

"This time?" Jenn asked, raising her head from the food she'd eaten in silence to stare at Brylee. "You plan on their being a next time?"

"Maybe, Mom. I don't understand why you are so dead-set against me doing something I love so much and I'm good at. I'd like your blessing to compete again next year. I know I promised it would be one year, and I'll keep that if you truly need me to stay here on the ranch, but I'd really like the opportunity to see what I can do when I'm not desperate to win because of our financial situation."

"Mom, you have to let…" Birch's pleas tapered off as Brylee gave him an admonishing scowl and shook her head.

Jenn wiped her mouth on her napkin and looked around the table. "Ace, you're the only one who hasn't voiced an opinion. What do you think?"

The old man cleared his throat and leaned back in his chair, as though he needed a moment to gather his thoughts. "I think it's time you let go of your unreasonable need to control Brylee's life and let her do what she's meant to do with whomever she chooses to walk beside her." Ace gave her a pointed look. "You've had a hard time of it, Jenn.

No one is denying that, but Brylee's had her own difficulties to overcome. Fighting you to chase her dreams shouldn't be one of them."

Tears rolled down Jenn's cheeks. "I know. It's just after all we've lost, I want to keep my babies close and keep them safe. I can't lose any of you." Jenn took a ragged breath. "I'm sorry I've been so... horrible to live with. I'll try to do better. Running away last week didn't help. If anything it made it even harder for me to sort out my thoughts. Roger mentioned this afternoon that Brylee had staged a house for him the other day and it just made me realize my stubbornness is costing me the thing I'm most afraid of losing — all of you."

"Mom, it's okay." Brylee hurried around the table and gave her mother a hug then Birch engulfed them both with his long, gangly arms.

Ace dabbed at his face with his napkin and cleared his throat again. "Darn tree is stirring up my allergies."

Brylee grinned then leaned over and kissed his cheek. "Sure it is, Grandpa."

Jenn gave Birch one more hug then patted his chair next to her, indicating she wanted him to sit back down.

"Son, I know how much you want to go with your sister, but she's right. You need to stay in school. However, I did buy a ticket for you to fly down on the Thursday before the rodeo ends. If Brylee isn't opposed to it, you can drive home with her."

"Really, Mom? You're not teasing me?" Birch asked, his face alight with excitement. He jumped up and hugged his mother then looked at his sister. "Will you let me ride with you?"

Brylee grinned. "Of course, you dork. You know I hate driving long distances by myself. It'll be fun."

"Will Shaun be with us?" Birch asked without thinking. He tossed a worried glance at his mother, concerned about mentioning someone who always drew out her ire.

"No, Birch, he won't be, but you will see him there." Brylee glanced at her mother. "Shaun and I are just friends, Mom. That's it."

"Someone very wise told me the other day it's not any of my business what he is to you, and it isn't. My personal feelings are just that — mine. I'll do a better job of not being so vocal in expressing them going forward."

"Thank you."

Jenn took another deep breath, as though she'd been rehearsing a speech and had to deliver the whole thing at once. "As for you competing next year, if you want to do it, go for it, honey. With the debt paid off and the commissions I've earned the past few months, we can afford to hire someone to manage the ranch on a more permanent basis." She turned to look at Ace. "I know I haven't said it nearly as often as I should, but I appreciate everything you've done for us, for me, Ace. You've been a rock when our world was tossed into chaos. If you want to move back to Arizona, I completely understand, but if you'd like to continue living here at the ranch, we'd love to have you stay."

"Well," Ace leaned back again and rubbed his

hand across his whiskery chin. "I reckon since I'm already pretty comfortable in my room here and whoever you hire will need someone to show them the ropes, I might as well stay."

"Yes!" Birch said, doing a fist pump in the air.

"I'm glad you'll be here, Grandpa. I like having you around," Brylee gave him a hug.

She lifted her glass of milk and held it up. "Here's to happier days and many sweet moments ahead for the Barton family."

Chapter Seventeen

"Will pacing the floor help her get here any faster?" Jason asked as Shaun strode across the length of the living area in their suite in Las Vegas, turned around, and retraced his steps.

Shaun had been keyed up since they arrived in town that morning, anticipating the moment he'd get to see Brylee. He'd almost offered to ride with her, but didn't want to push her into spending time with him.

Jason and Shaun arrived in town a few days before the rodeo was set to begin so they could attend industry trade shows and events. Although neither of them would be working as pickup men during the rodeo, it was a good time for them to network about rodeo business and their ranch.

Since Shaun was modeling for Lasso Eight, the company was paying for a suite for him and one guest. His dad was more than happy to give up his standard cheap hotel room in a smoky casino for the posh suite in a swanky hotel.

Brylee would be staying at the same property and Shaun couldn't wait for her to arrive. He hadn't seen her since the circuit finals a month ago. He'd been working that weekend and barely got to do more than say hello and wish her well on her ride, but at least he'd actually seen her. In person. Where her fragrance ensnared his senses and he found himself struggling not to fall into the gorgeous depths of those amazing cobalt eyes.

He had kept in touch with her since then via text and phone calls. From her last text, he knew she anticipated arriving in town around three that afternoon. She planned to head straight to the rodeo venue where she would settle Rocket in a stall before checking in at the hotel.

"Maybe I should go see if she needs help with Rocket," Shaun said, pacing the room again.

"Sit down, son," Jason said, motioning to the two big side chairs across from where he sat on the couch. "You're gonna wear a hole in this nice carpet and you're making me dizzy watching you go back and forth. Brylee is a big girl and can take care of herself. You, more than anyone, should know that."

Shaun frowned. "Why do you say that, Dad?"

Jason rolled his eyes. "I told you to take things slow and easy with her, like you were breaking a high-spirited filly. Dang if you don't act like you're afraid to get close to the fence, let alone the filly."

Shaun scowled and plopped down in a chair. "I'm not afraid of the fence or the horse…" He sighed. "I'm not afraid of Brylee, Dad. It's just that she made it crystal clear I have absolutely no chance at romance with her. We've built a solid, incredible friendship the last few months and I don't want to jeopardize it."

Jason shrugged. "Then so be it."

"So be what?" Shaun said, losing his hold on his patience and temper.

"Friendship. If you're willing to settle for friendship with Brylee, then stop worrying about the rest of it. She'll eventually fall in love with a great guy, settle down, and have two or three kids. You can let them call you Uncle Shaun. Maybe you'll even get to be friends with her husband. Would that be awkward, since you're technically the ex-husband?"

Shaun jumped up and started pacing again. "I'm not willing to settle," he snapped. "I don't want her to marry anyone but me."

Jason hid a smile behind the cup of coffee he held in his hand. "Then do something about it."

"Like what, Dad? March into her room and tell her I can't live another day without her? That I love her more than life itself and I'd do anything for her? That the thought of a future without seeing her smile every morning makes me want to crawl under a rock and die?"

A chuckle rolled out of Jason. "That might be a good start."

Shawn growled and grabbed his hat from where he'd set it on a table by the door. "I'm going for a walk."

"You do that, son. If you happen to go somewhere that has a grocery store, bring back a snack. I'm not sure I can hold out until dinner."

The door clicked shut with a force just short of a slam as Shaun left the hotel room. Rather than wait for the elevator, he took the stairs. It wasn't until he'd gone down five flights that he recalled they were on the seventeenth floor. By the time he reached the bottom and stepped outside into the bright sunshine, the exercise had dulled the edges of his anxiety.

"Thinks he's a regular comic," Shaun mumbled about his dad as he strolled down the sidewalk until he was on The Strip. He turned left and headed toward the heart of it. A few blocks later, he stood on a corner, watching a big video screen overhead play advertisements for various properties and restaurants.

Surprise kept him glued in place as he watched a video clip of Brylee turning Rocket around a barrel. The next image featured what appeared to be a sheet of parchment paper with charred edges. Words slowly appeared. "For the shoppers and bakers..." The text looked as though it had been burned into the paper before segueing to another clip of her riding Rocket. "For the gift wrappers and decorators..." flashed next on another parchment background. The third clip of Brylee showed her and Rocket running full-out across an arena. He smirked when the words "Racing Christmas is hectic" swept across the screen.

The next image made Shaun's jaw drop open. Brylee walked forward like a runway model wearing a blanket print skirt that showed off way more of her legs than he wanted the general male population ogling. A golden braid draped over one shoulder where it bounced, along with other undeniable assets, in slow motion with each swaying step she took. The background of a snowy field faded to a soft blur. Text came into focus on the screen. "Why not do it in style?" Then the Lasso Eight logo popped up along with their website information.

People pointed to the screen. Men grinned like lecherous jerks while women chattered about the great new Lasso Eight fashions.

More worked up after seeing Brylee's ad than he'd been earlier, Shaun turned around and made his way back to the hotel room. He'd just walked inside when his phone pinged with a text. He practically ripped off his shirt pocket in his haste to answer it, making his dad laugh again.

"Brylee?" Jason asked, as he flipped a page in the newspaper he read.

"Yep. She said she just got her room key and needs an hour to unpack then she'll be ready to go to dinner."

Shaun glanced at the clock. It was almost five. He had plenty of time to shower and shave for the second time that day. He tossed his hat on the counter, emptied his pockets and left everything next to his hat, kicked off his boots, and hurried into his room. His father's chuckles floated after him, but he ignored them as he hopped into the shower. Ten minutes later, he dabbed a tissue against a nick on his chin, wondering why he let himself get so worked up about Brylee.

His dad was right about one thing, though.

Unless he could somehow come to terms with the possibility of her falling in love with someone else, he had to do something. Was he willing to risk the friendship they'd built for a second chance with her? Was he willing to walk away if he didn't try? One thing he knew for certain: he couldn't stand by and see Brylee with someone else. Not when he loved her so deeply and completely.

These last few months had taught him many things — things he'd needed to learn and accept. He'd been the world's biggest fool to run out on Brylee six years ago. He had no intention of messing things up with her again. But what could he do to win her back, to gain her trust? Would she even listen if he told her how much he loved her?

Plagued by questions he hesitated to answer, he dressed and gave his dad's annoying observations consideration. Perhaps it was time to step up his game. Maybe tonight was the perfect time to start. After all, Brylee was going to dinner with them. What if he figured out a way to woo her without her catching on to his plans?

Shaun returned to the living room and grabbed the electronic tablet he'd brought along from the end table where he'd left it. He picked it up and began hurriedly scrolling through a website.

"What are you doing?" Jason asked, setting aside the paper and watching as he frantically searched for information.

"Preparing to win my fair lady's heart." Shaun glanced up at his dad and grinned. "At least I'm going to give it my best shot."

"Well, it's about time, son. It's about time."

Twenty minutes later, Shaun's foot nervously jiggled as he waited for Brylee to let them know she was ready. Just when he was about to march down to the front desk and beg for her room number, she sent him a text.

I'm starving. What room are you guys in? I'll be right there.

Shaun texted the room number and then grinned at his dad. "She's on her way." He rushed into his room to make sure he'd combed his hair. Assured all was well, he'd just stepped into the living room when a knock sounded on the door.

Jason stood and picked up the hat he'd left on the coffee table then stuffed his phone in his pocket.

Shaun pulled open the door and blinked twice before he gathered enough of his wits together to smile and move back so Brylee could enter the room.

She gave him a hug then moved over to hug his dad. Shaun swiped his hand over his chin to make sure he hadn't started drooling. The deep teal-colored dress she wore wasn't revealing at all. In fact, it was similar to one his sister wore to church, but the way the tight waist hugged Brylee's figure and accented her curves robbed him of the ability to speak for the length of several heartbeats. The hem was almost to the ground in the back but just brushed her knees in the front, and the skirt fluttered and flowed with each step she took. The wedge sandals on her feet made her seem inches taller than her usual five-three height.

Shaun finally took a deep breath and placed a hand on her waist as he kissed her cheek. "You look incredible, Bitsy."

She glanced down and brushed at an imaginary wrinkle in her skirt. "I had lunch with Jessie Jarrett and Chase's cousin, Ashley, last week. Ashley assured me I needed to bring my fashion A-game to Vegas this year, so here it is."

Shaun would have to remember to thank Ashley later. He loved Brylee no matter what she wore, but he rarely got to see her in anything other than jeans and boots. She looked so classy and feminine in the dress. The long brass necklace she wore had a medallion dangling from the center of it with a horse laser-cut in the metal. Even dressed all girly, Brylee still added a little western flair. He noticed the matching bracelet on her wrist and the small embossed leather clutch she carried.

The young girl who'd first arrived in Las Vegas six years ago with stars in her eyes had been replaced by a breathtaking woman. One who'd completely captivated him.

"Shall we get some dinner?" Jason asked, motioning toward the door while he gave Shaun a knowing look.

"We shall," Brylee said, walking out of the room and over to the elevator. She pointed to a door across the hall. "That's my room if you guys need me for anything."

Shaun made note of which room she'd indicated then shoved his hands in his pockets to keep from wrapping them around Brylee. The effort required to keep his hands to himself was almost more than he could handle. He pushed a button on the elevator as they stepped inside, entranced by the soft fragrance of Brylee that filled his nose.

The elevator stopped and they walked out. Jason held out an arm to Brylee and she took it with a laugh, leaving Shaun to lead the way to a restaurant that boasted a taste of Venice. He'd called ahead and made a reservation, so they were seated quickly at a table that looked out on the Grand Canal Shoppes and the Grand Canal that ran through the property. Brylee smiled as she watched a couple glide by in a Venetian gondola. Shaun maneuvered to sit beside her while his dad took a chair across the table.

Jason opened the menu, shot Shaun a dubious look, and then rolled his eyes. "How are we supposed to read this dang thing? I don't want to end up ordering something disgusting, like snails."

"I don't think you have to worry about that here." Brylee grinned and leaned across the table, pointing to the menu Jason held. "The descriptions are all in English."

"So they are," he said, giving her a wink.

Brylee returned to studying her menu then bumped her arm against Shaun's. "What are you going to order?"

"Beef." He set down the menu and grinned at her. "How about you?"

She returned to studying her menu. "There are so many things that sound delicious. It's going to be hard to narrow it down."

Their server appeared to take their order. Brylee choose gnocchi with a Bolognese sauce while Jason ordered a calzone. Shaun pointed to an item, unwilling to even try pronouncing it. "The beef stew, please."

"Excellent choice, sir," the server said then disappeared with a polite nod.

They ate warm breadsticks and a green salad with a light balsamic dressing while they waited for their meal.

"Did your mom really agree to let Birch come for a few days?" Shaun asked as he finished his salad and leaned back from the table.

Brylee dabbed at her lips with her napkin and nodded her head. "She did. We had quite a conversation the other night."

Shaun knew Jenn had been riding Brylee hard the last few months. Brylee had mentioned having another fight with her mother right after Thanksgiving, but she hadn't elaborated on any details. "Is everything okay?"

She smiled, but her eyes held a hint of sadness. "I think it will be. Mom hasn't really wanted to celebrate Christmas for a while. She made me so mad one day, I decided we'd go all out on the decorations and rejuvenate some of our traditions this year. Mom went to work on Black Friday, so Grandpa and Birch helped me deck the halls. We even went out and got a live Christmas tree. Anyway, while we were decorating it, Mom overhead us talking about how much more pleasant it was when she was gone."

"Oh, that's not good," Jason said, giving Brylee a worried glance. "What happened?"

Brylee toyed with the stem of her water glass.

"She ran off and sent a text she was spending the weekend at the cabin. I don't know if she actually went up there or not, because I know she was at work that Monday. I was helping one of the other realtors stage a house and the receptionist mentioned Mom being there. Anyway, she finally came home the night before I had to drive down here and apologized for the way she's been, some of the terrible things she's said. I know the situation won't automatically get better, but I'm hopeful it will eventually improve. It's a big step in the right direction that she agreed to let Birch come for a few days." She raised her gaze to Jason's then glanced at Shaun. "He was gunning for the whole two weeks, but I told him no way. If I didn't know better, I'd think he was trying to play mind games with us to get what he wanted, which was to come for a few days."

"He probably was." Shaun chuckled. "Birch is one smart kid. You'll have to hustle to stay a step ahead of him."

"Tell me something I don't already know." Brylee smiled at him then sat back as the server appeared with their meals.

Once they'd eaten their fill, Shaun insisted on paying for the dinner. He went to take care of it then returned to the table. Brylee and Jason were laughing together but their amusement ended abruptly as he stepped up to the table. In spite of warning bells clanging in his head, he tried not to read anything into it. He could always pump his dad for specifics later.

"Want to explore a while and walk off that

SHANNA HATFIELD

dinner?" he asked, suddenly flooded with nerves.

"I'd love to," Brylee said, rising from her seat and walking out onto the streetscape of the shopping area. She tipped her head back, staring at the ceiling painted like a summer-blue sky with white fluffy clouds.

"Have you been in here before, Brylee?" Jason asked as they meandered past a statue.

When the statue blinked, Brylee stopped to watch, fascinated the man with his face painted white like marble could hold so still. She took money out of her clutch and left it in a donation box near his feet. As they continued on their stroll, she walked between the two men, taking in the energy-infused atmosphere. "I haven't been here before, Jason. The last two times I was in Vegas were both very busy and hectic. The first time, I mostly stayed at the rodeo grounds, close to Rocket. The second time..." Her voice drifted off.

"If you've never been here, then there's something we have to do," Shaun said, taking her hand and hurrying over to the line for the Gondola rides. The line wasn't long, but Jason backed away.

"I don't do boats, so you kids have fun."

Brylee glanced from the boats docking in front of them back to Jason. "No, let's find something all three of us can enjoy."

She started to leave the line, but Jason settled a hand on her shoulder. "No, darlin'. You two go ahead. I've heard it's lots of fun. I'm gonna head back to the room. There are a few calls I need to make anyway. I'll see you both later."

Brylee stepped closer to Shaun then watched

Jason disappear in the crowd. "Does he really not like boats or is he just trying to give us time together?"

Shaun grinned as the line move forward. "Dad hates boats and being on the water. One time, when I was probably about twelve, we went to the coast during spring break. Dad and I went out on a fishing boat. I thought it was awesome, but he spent the whole time hanging over the back, feeding the fish. That was the last time I've seen him willingly set foot in a boat."

Brylee gave her hand to the gondolier as he motioned for her to step into the boat. Shaun took a seat beside her and then they were gliding down the man-made canal that ran through the shopping center. He slipped his arm around her shoulders and pointed out interesting things as their gondolier serenaded them. They floated beneath bridges, went past cafes, and dipped under balconies along the Venetian-inspired streetscape.

"That was amazing!" Brylee beamed as they left the boat and continued strolling toward the area known as the square in the midst of the shopping center. As they neared it, music trickled out to them.

Shaun grabbed her hand. "Come on, Bitsy!"

They entered the square to find a group of carolers dressed in Dickens-era costumes singing on the small stage.

Shaun bought them each a gelato at a nearby booth then they sat on the edge of a large stone planter, since all the seats were taken, and watched the performance. During the last song, the group asked the crowd to sing along, so Shaun joined

Brylee as they added their voices to a rousing rendition of "We Wish You A Merry Christmas."

Brylee set her gelato dish on her lap and clapped. Shaun wished he could see her that happy all the time. At the moment, she looked like a young girl without a care in the world. When the carolers left the stage, she took the last two bites of her frozen treat, got to her feet, and looked around. "What's next?"

Glad she wasn't in a rush to get back to the hotel, Shaun threw away their trash, took her hand in his, and they meandered their way back toward the entrance.

He pulled her into a shop that sold fancy masks, like one might wear to a masquerade ball. "Try one on," he encouraged, but she seemed hesitant.

Finally, he handed her a sapphire blue mask dotted with pearls. One side of it was shaped like a butterfly made from lace and ribbon.

"What do you think?" she asked, smiling as she tied it in place on her head.

Convinced she didn't want to hear the truth spill out of his mouth, he held back his thoughts. The blue in the mask made her eyes look huge and luminous, drawing out the rich color, while the shape of it accented her cheekbones and smooth skin.

Mesmerized.

The mask gave her an air of mystery, one that was completely mesmerizing, but he couldn't tell her that. Not yet, anyway.

"Let me take a photo," he said, holding up his

phone and snapping a few photos.

When he finished, Brylee removed the mask, then swept the cowboy hat off his head and made him try on a black mask. "You look like Zorro."

He struck a pose that emphasized his chest and made her giggle. "My turn to take a photo."

They stepped out of the shop and both sent photos to Birch, knowing it would make him smile.

"That was fun," Brylee said, wrapping her arm around Shaun's and leaning against him. "Thank you for that."

"You're welcome, Bits." He kissed the top of her head. "In fact, what would you…"

Shaun was interrupted when three handsome young men dressed in suits walked up to Brylee.

"Aren't you the barrel racer that's in the video?"

Brylee offered them smiles, but turned to Shaun with a baffled expression on her face.

He nodded. "A Lasso Eight video ad of you is playing on one of the big screens on The Strip."

"We saw her in the taxi on the monitor that plays a loop of ads," the shortest of the three men said. The interested looks he gave Brylee made Shaun want to concave his nose. "You're even prettier in person."

"She sure is. Your name is Brylee, is that right?" A man who was as tall as Shaun moved a little closer. Although they were close in height, Shaun's broad shoulders and muscled arms made the other guy look like a broomstick.

"That's right," she said, giving Shaun what appeared to be a slightly panicked look. He didn't think she had any idea how popular she was about to become with the Lasso Eight ads playing all over town during the next two weeks. He'd enjoyed his own share of popularity from ads in the past, but the promotional pieces he'd been in didn't usually show much of his face.

"Would you gentlemen like an autograph?" Shaun asked, doing his best not to growl at them.

"That would be great," the third man said, digging in his suit coat pocket for a pen and a small notepad.

Brylee patiently asked each of their names and wrote three notes, one for each of them. "What are you in town for?" she asked as she signed her name with a flourish on the last note. "If you say the rodeo, I'll know you're fibbing."

The shortest of the three smiled. "Banking retreat. We're all from different branches."

"Makes sense." Brylee handed the third banker back his pen and notepad. "I hope you'll think about coming to the rodeo one night. It's a lot of fun."

"We're only here through Friday," the broomstick banker said.

"Get tickets for Thursday. Opening night is always awesome." She smiled again, wrapped her hand around Shaun's arm, and tugged him forward. "Come on, honey, we better get going."

Shaun settled his arm around her shoulders, pulling her closer to his side. "Whatever you say, honey."

Once they were out of the line of sight of the three men, Brylee elbowed him in the side and took a step away, leaving space between the two of them.

"You know I was only saying that for their benefit. Paige didn't warn me about random people wanting autographs. I've even forgotten about the long lines at autograph sessions."

He grinned. "Hope you brought extra pens. If not, you better stock up on them."

"I'll have to get some," she said.

Together, they walked back to the hotel and made their way up to their floor. Shaun paused in the hallway between their two rooms. "Want to hang out with us for a while?"

Brylee shook her head. "I appreciate the invitation, but I'm exhausted. Maybe we can have breakfast or lunch tomorrow."

"Sounds great," Shaun said, walking her to her door, desperate to kiss her, to see if she'd taste like the mint gelato she'd eaten. "Just text or call when you're up and going in the morning."

"I will, Shaun, and thanks so much for giving me such a wonderful evening. I had a lot of fun."

"I did, too." He waited as she unlocked her door. When she pushed it open and stepped inside, he bent down and kissed her cheek. "Sleep well, Bitsy."

Brylee smiled at him and he fought the urge to sweep her into his arms and kiss her like he'd longed to do since July. Instead, he took a few steps back then made his way to his room. His dad was stretched out on the couch watching one of his favorite cop shows that he rarely got to see.

Jason sat up and gave him a curious look. "Well, how did things go?"

Shaun set his hat down then kicked off his

boots. "Pretty well, until three guys in suits went all fangirl on her. She gave them her autograph."

Jason laughed. "I suppose that's to be expected. I saw a Lasso Eight ad featuring her a little bit ago on TV, something about hectic holidays and baking."

Shaun shot his dad a look that let him know he was clueless. "That same ad is playing down the street on a huge display screen and, apparently, on the little monitors in the taxis."

"Really? Our girl is about to hit the big time," Jason said, leaning back and giving Shaun a studying glance. "How are you gonna handle the competition?"

"I've got a plan, Dad. If she hasn't at least cracked the door to her heart for me by the time the rodeo is over, I might as well give up and think about joining a group of monks."

"You? In a monastery?" Laughter rolled out of Jason until he had to wipe moisture away from his eyes. "Just trying to envision if that is even possible, son."

"Whatever, Dad," Shaun said, tossing a pillow at his father. "What were you and Brylee talking about while I paid the bill at dinner?"

"Oh, just this and that. I think she's pretty excited to be back here. Did you know she paid off the ranch debt?"

Shaun nodded.

"It was sure good of you to make the suggestion about her modeling for Lasso Eight. She said without that, they'd still be struggling to figure out how to get that debt settled. Of course, she'll probably do well at the finals and could have paid it, but anything can happen, as you both know."

"I sure do," Shaun said, rubbing his thigh, thinking about the unexpected end to his own career goals.

If he hadn't hurt his leg again he might never have had the opportunity to work with his dad, which had been a big blessing. He certainly wouldn't have been around to connect with Brylee again. That alone was worth any sacrifices or dashed career goals to him. He just hoped the connection they'd made would turn into something far more before Christmas arrived. Maybe he just needed to garner a higher spot on Santa's nice list.

Chapter Eighteen

Brylee slid between the crisp, cool sheets of her hotel room bed and released a weary sigh.

The previous day, she'd left the ranch at noon and drove to Jackpot, Nevada, where she spent the night. Had she been traveling with someone, she would have left early and drove straight through to Vegas, but it made for a really, really long day when she was alone.

The clock on her dash read five that morning when she left Jackpot. She made good time, arriving at the rodeo venue early in the afternoon. It took a little time to get Rocket settled and then she ran into several people she knew who all wanted to talk. She left her pickup and trailer at the rodeo venue in a designated parking area, and then took a taxi to the hotel.

After a quick shower, she unpacked her suitcases while her hair air-dried. When she'd had lunch with Jessie and Ashley the previous week, she attentively listened to the fashion tips Ashley had shared. The woman pointed out the need to look her best at all times because the spotlight would definitely be on her once the Lasso Eight ads started releasing.

In fact, the two women had called Kenzie Morgan and Kaley McGraw to meet them. They'd all gone back to Blue Hills Ranch where the women helped Brylee assemble a great wardrobe with coordinating accessories for the entire time she'd be in Vegas. To keep things simple, Ashley had even tagged the clothes by day and put notes with the jewelry, boots, and belts about which outfit to wear with each item. The four friends had given her suggestions on hairstyles and makeup tips, too.

Brylee could fix herself up when the moment called for it, but she just didn't have many occasions to do so. Thoughts of catching Shaun's eye, though, made her eager to look her best.

Within the darkness of her hotel room, she smiled, recalling how he'd looked when he'd opened the door. Shaun couldn't hide his surprise at seeing her in a dress and sandals instead of the boots and jeans he'd no doubt expected. Admiration had mingled with desire in his gaze and gave her hope that perhaps not all was lost.

She'd had plenty of time on her long drive to Las Vegas to think about her life, about the direction she wanted it to head, about the ranch, her family, and her dreams. No matter how much she wished otherwise, nothing would change the past. But she could make different choices for the future.

One of those choices was to consider how

much she needed Shaun in her life. She'd be the first to admit Shaun was a handsome man with that head of thick copper hair and a swoon-worthy smile. His eyes were the color of a winter sky as the sun shifted behind clouds, not blue or gray, but a fascinating shade in between that sparkled with life, humor and intelligence. Goodness only knew how much he made her laugh and smile.

In prime physical condition, Shaun drew the attention of women everywhere they went, but tonight he acted as though no one existed but her.

She'd seen the jealousy in his gaze when she signed autographs for the three banking executives. If she hadn't been so unsettled by the experience, she might have found it amusing. Brylee couldn't believe anyone would want her autograph, let alone recognize her from the Lasso Eight ads. Paige had sent copies of all the promotional pieces to her, but it was one thing to look at them on her computer at home and something else entirely to find out they were running on a huge electronic screen in the heart of The Strip in Las Vegas.

Brylee grinned as she thought about the conversation she'd had with Jason when Shaun went to pay the bill at the restaurant at dinner. Jason had given her a fatherly look and asked if she was dating anyone.

"No, Jason. Of course not. When would I have time even if I had the inclination?"

He'd grinned and leaned back in his chair. "You ought to take advantage of expanding your dating horizons while you're here. I predict there will be guys lined up at your door if they find out where you're staying. Just pick a few and have some harmless fun."

Brylee had stared at him, aghast at the idea. "With my luck, I'd end up with a crazy stalker dude or a psycho who tries to kidnap me. Thanks, but no thanks."

Jason gave her an intense look. "What if I check them out first, make sure they aren't perverted whackos? I could send you a pre-approved list. Would that make you feel better?"

Brylee's left eyebrow crept upward. "That dials down the creepy factor only slightly. Honestly, Jason, I'll be busy with the rodeo and all the obligations that come with it, not to mention everything going on with Lasso Eight. I don't know when I'd even find time."

"You let me take care of the details. The past year, all you've done is work hard. I think it's time for you to have a little fun. I know you aren't a love 'em and leave 'em type of girl. I'll see if I can round up some nice, respectable fellas for you. Just think of them as arm candy."

"Arm candy?" A laugh rolled out of her that made Jason join in her merriment. They were still sharing their amusement when Shaun returned to the table. Both of them had immediately curtailed their laughter. He'd given them suspicious glances, but didn't say anything.

She'd felt like turning the very same look on Jason when he left them at the gondola ride. Perhaps the man really didn't like boats, but it seemed too convenient for him to leave her alone with Shaun for what many would consider a romantic experience.

The evening from that point on turned into something from a dream, being with the man she loved. It had been nearly euphoric to spend hours with Shaun as the sole focus of his attention. A part of her had hoped he'd attempt to steal a kiss when he left her at her door, but he hadn't even tried.

As soon as the rodeo was over, she would sit down with Shaun and have an honest, sincere conversation with him about their past. There were things that still needed to be shared and discussed, even though she dreaded it. Based on how he reacted to what she needed to say, she'd see if the chance of a future together might exist.

In the meantime, though, it couldn't hurt to have a little fun. If Jason vetted the guys he sent her way, she'd go out with them. Not because she was interested in dating a bunch of different men, but in hopes it might inspire Shaun to move beyond the "let's be friends" stage of their relationship.

After finally quieting her busy mind, Brylee fell into a deep, restful sleep and awakened recharged, ready to take on the day.

She dressed in an old pair of jeans and a sweatshirt, pulled her hair into a ponytail, slipped on a pair of sneakers, and left her room. It didn't take long for her to catch a taxi at that early hour of the morning when most of the town seemed to be sleeping.

The taxi left her near the area where barns were temporarily set up at the rodeo venue. She hurried to feed Rocket his breakfast. While he ate, she cleaned his stall then led him out to the warm-up pen used by rodeo contestants and walked him around the arena for fifteen minutes before she broke into a jog and he trotted along with her. She slowed him back down to a walk for five minutes then took him back to the barn. After making sure he was set for the day, she hurried to where she'd parked her pickup, unhitched it from the horse trailer, and drove back to the hotel.

After leaving the pickup with the valet, she made her way to her room where she showered and did her hair and makeup, then sent a text to Shaun that she was ready for breakfast if he and Jason hadn't eaten yet.

We're starving. Meet you by the elevator in five minutes.

Brylee smiled at his reply and fastened a wide brown leather belt around the waist of her soft ivory dress embroidered with pink roses and soft green vines. She shoved her feet into a pair of plain brown cowboy boots that were comfortable for walking in all day, and slipped on a faded denim jacket. Quickly tucking essentials into a brown leather embossed shoulder bag, she rushed out the door and held back a grin as Shaun did a double take when he saw her.

"You take beauty rest to a whole new level, darlin'," Jason teased as he kissed her cheek and settled her hand around his arm. "That's sure a pretty dress."

"Thanks. It was one Paige let me keep from a photo shoot." Brylee glanced at Shaun as he continued gaping at her instead of stepping onto the elevator. "You coming, Copperhead?"

Shaun gave her that crooked half smile she adored, threatening to dissolve any strength her knees may have possessed, and stepped onto the elevator. "I don't remember seeing you wear that at Jessie and Chase's place."

Brylee glanced up and smiled. "Paige invited me to do a photo shoot last month for the spring line. This dress is from that collection."

"You didn't mention it." Shaun gave her a curious look. "When was that?"

"When I got back from the circuit finals. I made a quick trip to Portland for the shoot. I thought I told you, but life has been so crazy." Brylee shifted over as the elevator stopped and more people got on. Shaun bumped into her from behind and his mouthwatering scent engulfed her every bit as much as the warmth of his presence. She wanted, more than anything to lean back into him, to rest against his strength, but she didn't. She remained next to Jason, wondering what put such a smug look on his face as he tipped his head toward her and gave her a conspiratorial wink.

"Paige mentioned something the other day about posing for the spring ads, but said we could plan it for after Christmas." Shaun put out a hand to hold open the door when the elevator reached the lobby. After they stepped out, they strolled to a nearby restaurant for breakfast.

Since it was early, they had no trouble getting a table and were soon enjoying their meals.

"Do you need help with Rocket this morning?"

Shaun asked as he slathered jam on a piece of toast.

"Already fed, stall cleaned, and exercised," she said, cutting off a bite from a thick omelet.

Both men looked at her and then at their watches, noting that it was barely eight o'clock. "What time did you roll out this morning?" Jason asked.

"I left here a little past five," Brylee said, forking another bite. "Did you guys rent a car?"

"No, we figured we can hoof it, take a taxi, or ride the monorail." Jason waggled his fork at Shaun. "This one thought we should rent a vehicle, but we'll be fine."

"I brought my pickup back with me this morning, so if either of you need to borrow it, consider it yours."

"Thanks, darlin', we might just take you up on that." Jason stuffed a bite of fluffy biscuit smothered in sausage gravy in his mouth while Shaun toyed with a piece of crispy bacon.

"So, what's on the agenda today?" Brylee asked. She was glad she didn't have any obligations. Starting tomorrow, though, the pace would be hectic until the rodeo ended.

"I thought we could..." Shaun's words drifted off as a hunky cowboy approached their table.

He and Jason both stood and shook the man's hand. Brylee recognized him as a steer wrestler. The cowboy had just missed making it into the finals, but he'd obviously come to town to either check out the competition for next year or cheer on his friends. Perhaps a little of both.

"What are you up to, Nate?" Shaun asked,

motioning for the cowboy to take a seat next to Brylee since she'd somehow managed to sit across the table rather than beside him.

"Well, I heard there's a pretty girl looking for something fun to do today." Nate turned a megawatt smile on Brylee. "Some friends and I are doing a helicopter tour over the Grand Canyon. There's room for one more if you want to come along."

Brylee shot Shaun a hesitant glance. Before she could politely decline the invitation, Jason enthusiastically nodded his head. "She'd love to go!"

Her head snapped up and she scowled at Jason, but he merely grinned then looked to Nate. "What time are you leaving?"

"We need to leave in about twenty minutes." Nate glanced at his watch. "I told the others I'd meet them at the airport at nine."

"That sounds fine," Jason said, waggling his fork at Brylee's plate. "Eat up, honey, or you'll be late."

She started to give him a piece of her mind about taking over as her personal assistant and lining up dates for her, but the livid look on Shaun's face kept her silenced. He appeared as though he considered pummeling poor Nate. That wouldn't be an easy task since Nate was a good three inches taller and at least twenty pounds heavier than Shaun.

Brylee pasted on her sweetest smile and turned to look at the steer wrestler. "I'd love to go, Nate. Would you like something to eat or drink while we finish?"

"No thanks. I already had breakfast and my limit of coffee for the morning." He glanced at her outfit. "Do you want to change before we go?"

Brylee glanced down at her lovely dress, hating not to wear it, but not wanting to be uncomfortable. She looked back at Nate. "Do you think I need to change?"

He waggled an eyebrow at her. "Not on my account. You look about as pretty as a dewy rose petal."

Shaun grumbled something under his breath and broke the piece of bacon he held between his fingers into a pile of crumbles.

"Everything okay, son?" Jason asked, feigning deep concern.

"Just dandy," Shaun said, wiping his hands on a napkin and rising to his feet. "I have some things I need take care of. Brylee, will you call me when you get back?"

"Sure." With a coy smile, she turned her attention back to Nate.

The afternoon sun shone brightly overhead when she returned to the hotel. Unable to wipe the smile from her face, she'd abandoned trying. Nate had given her a ride to the airport where they met four other cowboys and went on a helicopter tour over the Grand Canyon. All five of the guys flirted with her, in a fun way, making sure she was warm enough, pointing out things for her to see, and taking selfies with her.

Without a single doubt, she knew Jason had arranged the whole thing. On their way back, she'd crossed her arms over her chest and leveled each one of the men with a knowing glare.

"Okay, who wants to tell me what's going on?"

The cowboys gave each other sheepish looks.

Brylee leaned forward slightly. "I smell Jason Price all over this. Fess up. What's all this about?"

"Jason asked us if we'd take turns going out on dates with you. We had this tour already planned, so it seemed like a good way for you to spend time with us and get to know us a little better," Nate explained. "He said Shaun deserves a little payback for something he did, and asked if we'd all help. Since we've been on the receiving end of Shaun's pranks more than once, we were more than happy to step in. Everyone knows he's sweet on you, Brylee. Jason thought this would teach him a lesson or two."

Brylee kept her face impassive. "It's about time someone gave him a taste of his own medicine." She broke into a grin and the guys started to chuckle.

Nate laughed. "You should have seen his face when I walked up to the table and sat down this morning. He looked like he was about ready to shove me outside for a showdown."

Once the men stopped laughing at Shaun's expense, Brylee sat back and studied them. "So, what are you guys doing after we get back?"

She ended up going with them to a barbecue place for lunch. While the guys lingered after they finished eating, talking about rodeo, horses, and life in general, she walked over to a large mall across the street. With nothing else to occupy her time, she browsed to her heart's content, admiring all the festive holiday decorations and did a little Christmas shopping before taking a taxi to the rodeo venue.

After checking on Rocket and carefully feeding him so she wouldn't get her clothes dirty, she caught another taxi back to the hotel. By then, afternoon gave way to dusk and the evening shadows made the lights of The Strip glow.

Brylee hadn't even fully stepped off the elevator on her floor when Shaun opened the door to his room and hurried her way.

"Did you have a good time today?" he asked, taking the bags from her hands and following her to her door.

"I had the best time. Have you ever done the helicopter tour?" she asked as she keyed into her room.

Shaun followed her and set the bags on the couch. "I have and it was awesome. Didn't you get cold in that outfit, though? It can get pretty chilly this time of year."

Brylee glanced over her shoulder at him as she dug through one of the bags. "No, the guys made sure I stayed warm."

A vein began to throb in Shaun's neck and he muttered something she couldn't hear. She had to turn away to hide her smile. If Jason's plan was to tie Shaun in knots, it appeared to be going well.

In truth, she didn't like tormenting him by letting him think she was interested in someone else, but she did have a great time today. Halfway through the tour, she realized she hadn't allowed herself to fully relax and enjoy anything frivolous for a very long time.

Glad she'd gone on the tour, she looked forward to the "dates" the guys had planned out. Harmless and in good fun, she knew they'd be enjoyable, even if part of her felt guilty about how it would bother Shaun.

Then again, he hadn't expressed his feelings for her. No understanding existed between them, so he shouldn't be upset if she went out with other men.

On the other hand, if he started chasing other women, Brylee might run them over with her pickup and park her horse trailer on top of them for good measure. She knew turn about was fair play, but the whole situation was a plan his father devised. Surely he knew better than anyone how Shaun felt, and how he'd react. Wouldn't he?

Shaun took a deep breath and seemed to shake off whatever was bothering him. He turned back to her with an engaging smile. "Are you free for dinner tonight?"

"As a matter of fact, I am. You have something in mind?"

"I was hoping you'd keep me company. Dad ran into a couple of old friends from his college days and I'm on my own for the rest of the evening. If you're game for it, I have a place in mind."

An hour later, she found herself seated in front of a window at a restaurant high above The Strip.

She'd just finished eating a delicious meal when Shaun pointed out the window and they watched the fountains at the Bellagio come to life. Brylee had stood in front of the fountains and watched them, but looking down on the display provided an entirely different, spectacular view.

"Oh, Shaun, it's amazing!" she clasped his hand and squeezed it as they watched the water dance below them.

After leaving the restaurant, they strolled through the large casino and attached shops. Shaun stopped at a Parisian-themed bakery and bought a small box of pale blue macarons decorated with feathery frosting snowflakes.

"These are good," Shaun said, after sampling one and taking another from the box, "but not as tasty as those cookies you made for us this summer."

"I'm glad you liked them. If you're a good boy, maybe I can make a batch when I get home and mail them to you."

"Or maybe I can come get them in person. You know it's less than three hours from my house to yours." He bit into another cookie.

Brylee finished her cookie and brushed the crumbs from her fingers. "I am aware of that fact. However, the pass could be treacherous and I don't want to worry about you driving on icy roads when you don't have to. You get enough of that with your job."

Shaun gave her a hopeful look. "You'd really worry about me?"

She grinned and pointed to a towering Christmas tree glowing with lights, hoping to distract him. "At least for five whole minutes."

He snorted with mock disdain and took her hand, leading her to see more decorations.

Chapter Nineteen

Brylee stepped off the elevator in the hotel's lobby and almost ran into Shaun as he stood near the doors. "What are you doing up so early?" she asked, taking in the two disposable cups of coffee he held.

"If you don't mind, I thought I'd tag along while you feed Rocket. Kash has two guys who are taking care of the stock, but I thought I'd see if they need any help this morning."

"Sure," Brylee said, turning toward the entrance and handing a numbered ticket to the valet so he could bring her pickup around to the door. She glanced at the coffee Shaun continued to hold. "Are you planning to drink both of those?"

Shaun grinned. "Nope. I figured you could use a jolt of java this morning."

"I definitely could," she said, taking the cup he held out to her. It was black with just a hint of cream and one spoon of sugar, exactly how she liked it. "Thank you, Shaun." She took a long drink then looked at him. "Thanks for last night. The food was fabulous and the company wasn't bad either."

"I could take that coffee back," he said, reaching for it.

With a saucy smile, she held it away from him. "I don't think so. I've already got my cooties all over it."

Shaun took a step closer to her and bent down until his lips nearly brushed her ear. He smelled of leather and coffee with a hint of mint from his toothpaste. "I kinda like your cooties, Bitsy. You can share them with me anytime."

She glanced over her shoulder at him, at the heat smoldering in his eyes, and wondered if he had any idea how entirely alluring he looked at that moment. With a day's growth of scruff on his face, the captivating cleft in his chin, and that sexy half-grin on his face, how was a girl supposed to keep her wits about her?

Before she could gather her rapidly scattering thoughts, the valet arrived with her pickup. On the way to the rodeo venue, they drank coffee and laughed at some of the crazy billboards they drove past on their way there.

While Brylee fed Rocket breakfast, Shaun wandered over to check on the Rockin' K stock. She saw him talk to two cowboys she recognized from traveling with them part of the summer then Shaun walked back as she filled a small stock tank with water for Rocket.

"Billy and Sam get the early bird award today. They're just finishing up feeding," Shaun said. He took the rake leaning against the wall and started cleaning Rocket's stall.

"You don't have to help me," she said, trying to take the rake from him.

"I know I don't have to, but I want to. I'd rather be busy than stand around looking irresistible."

Brylee shot him a dubious glare, but she thought he'd nailed the statement right on the head. Shaun was gorgeous, whether he dressed nice or dressed down. Last night, he'd made her mouth water when he'd worn a pair of new pressed blue jeans and polished boots with a gray and blue paisley shirt that turned his eyes into an incredible whorl of color. Right now, he looked incredible in an old pair of faded jeans that fit him just right and a Wrangler T-shirt that clung to his solid chest muscles and biceps as he worked.

In fact, she had no problem at all standing in the stall door watching him work, especially when he bent over to pick up a bit of baling twine that had somehow found its way into the sawdust on the stall floor.

As though he sensed her perusal, he glanced back at her and winked.

Cheeks flaming from embarrassment, she spun around and kept herself busy while he cleaned the stall and Rocket finished eating.

"You ready for a little exercise, boy?" Brylee asked, fastening a lead rope to Rocket's halter.

Shaun waggled his eyebrows and shot her a rascally grin. "What'd you have in mind, darlin'?"

She popped him on his all-too-cute backside with the end of the rope and led Rocket out of the stall. "I wasn't talking to you, smarty."

Shaun reached up, as though he was covering Rocket's ears. "Don't listen, Rocket. She didn't mean to call you a dummy."

Exasperated, Brylee sighed. "That's not what I meant and you know it."

A chuckle rolled out of him as he pushed the wheelbarrow down the aisle of the make-shift barn to dump it.

Brylee had already walked Rocket in a lap around the warm-up arena when Shaun caught up to them.

"Want me to walk him?" he asked as he fell into step beside her.

"I've got..." One of the other barrel racers waved at Brylee and motioned for her to join her and two other girls. Brylee bit back a sigh and handed the lead rope to Shaun. "If you're sure you don't mind?"

"Not at all. You go do the girly chat stuff," he said with assurance then waved at the girls.

Brylee walked out of the arena and over to where the girls sipped coffee. "Good morning."

"Morning, Brylee. How'd you talk the bronzed Adonis into helping you?" one of the girls asked.

Brylee glanced back to where Shaun walked Rocket around the arena. She shrugged. "He volunteered."

"After the ad I saw yesterday, it's a wonder you don't have guys following your every footstep," another girl commented, giving Brylee a teasing smile.

"I'm nobody important. If they don't know that

already, they will soon enough." Brylee forced a smile. "Is there something you girls needed?"

"No, we just wanted to watch him do that." The third girl pointed as Shaun broke into a jog and ran alongside Rocket.

Between the muscles, tanned arms, long legs, and early morning sunlight glinting off his hatless head, Brylee's mouth suddenly turned dry.

One of the girls bumped her with her elbow and offered a smug smile. "You're welcome."

Brylee grinned and leaned against the fence as the four of them watched Shaun. He eventually slowed to a walk and made two more laps before he joined them. Sweat made his shirt stick to him like a second skin. He handed Brylee the lead rope then tugged the hem of the T-shirt up to wipe his face, exposing washboard abs.

One of the girls gasped and looked like she might reach out to touch them before the girl standing closest to Brylee grabbed her hand.

"Hey, Shakin' it Shaun. You planning any dance contests this year?" the cheeky girl with the wandering fingers asked.

Shaun did a quick two-step, spun in a circle, gave his back end a little shake, then winked at the girl. "Nope. Not unless Cooper holds an impromptu dance-off again."

At Brylee's confused look, he smiled. "When Paige first met Cooper, he played a joke on her by asking me and some of the others to join in a dance-off to showcase our backsides. Anyway, it ended up televised and I somehow got the nickname of Shakin' it Shaun."

"Only because when you shake that thang, it drives the women around you crazy," the cheeky one said, taking a step closer to Shaun with a man-hunting gleam in her eye.

Shaun maneuvered so he stood on the other side of Brylee and took the rope from her hand. "I'll take Rocket to his stall."

Four sets of eyes watched him walk away before Brylee pulled her thoughts back on track and smiled at the other women. "Are you girls going to the autograph session today?"

"Yep. We'll be there at two."

"I'll see you all there. Have a great morning," Brylee forced a cheerfulness she was far from feeling. As she watched the women ogle Shaun, she felt the most insane urge to tell them to keep their eyes and hands off her man.

Only he wasn't hers. Not yet. Although whatever she'd seen in his eyes that morning gave her hope that perhaps all was not yet lost where Shaun Price was concerned.

After they settled Rocket in his stall, Brylee and Shaun headed back to the hotel. When they stepped off the elevator, Shaun walked her to her door. "Breakfast in an hour?"

She opened the door and glanced at the clock across the room. "How about forty-five minutes and if I beat you down to the lobby, I get to buy breakfast for you and Jason."

"Deal," Shaun said, backing down the hall. "But you're really gonna have to hustle it, Bits."

In thirty minutes she'd showered, blow-dried her hair, applied makeup, and tidied her room. It took her another five minutes to dress and grab her purse, then she raced out of the room. She'd gotten as far as the elevator when she realized she'd want a cowboy hat later and returned to the room. From those she'd set on the shelf in the closet, she grabbed a rustic burned straw hat with a quarter-inch strip of cream edging the brim and settled it on her head.

Brylee hurried back out the door and to the elevator, then rushed into the lobby. Shaun and Jason were nowhere in sight, so she took a seat on a nearby chair where she could keep an eye on the elevator. A few minutes later, she watched the two men step out when the doors opened.

"Beat you," Brylee said, walking up to Shaun with a victorious grin. "I get to buy breakfast this morning."

"I won't argue about a pretty lady wanting to feed me," Jason quipped, slipping Brylee's hand around his arm. "What are you in the mood for this morning, darlin?"

Brylee pointed to a restaurant on the other side of the hotel's casino. They made their way through the ringing and buzzing slot machines to the short line at the restaurant's door.

Jason stepped back and gave her a long look then glared at Shaun. "I think we need to ask for a different room."

"Why on earth do we need to do that?" Shaun asked, scowling at his father. "We're close to the elevator and on a quiet end of the building."

Jason wrapped an arm around Brylee's shoulders and gave her a hug. "Because this girl must be breathing in a magical elixir at night. She just gets prettier every day. Our room certainly can't boast that."

Brylee blushed and glanced down at the cobalt paisley dress she wore with brown boots and a chunky turquoise necklace. Although the skirt was long, the buttons in the front of it ended in a placket above her knees. When she walked, the soft fabric swished around her, making her feel ultra-feminine and pretty.

From the look on Shaun's face as he studied her, maybe he thought she was too.

Rather than comment on his father's statement, he remained quiet as the hostess showed them to a table. Shaun didn't add much to the conversation while they ate breakfast, seemingly lost in his thoughts.

Brylee had barely finished drinking a cup of spicy tea that tasted like Christmas when a cowboy she recognized sauntered by.

"Hey, Brett!" she called after him. The cowboy spun around and grinned at her, making his way to their table.

"Brylee. I was looking for you. Are you ready to go?" The team roper tipped his head to Shaun and shook Jason's hand.

"I am ready," Brylee said, pushing against Shaun to let her out of the booth.

"Go where?" Shaun asked. His already sullen features slid into a dark scowl.

"Brett and I are going to go check out the art exhibit where Celia McGraw has three of her photographs on display. The art's going to be auctioned off for the crisis fund." Brylee got out of the booth and straightened her twisted skirt, then leaned over Shaun and grabbed her hat from where she'd left it on the booth seat.

When she inadvertently brushed against him, he stiffened and drew in a sharp breath. She moved back, plopped the hat on her head, and gave the two Price men a smile. "I'll pay the bill on the way out. Have a great day."

Brylee fell into step with Brett. By sheer determination not to make a scene, she didn't smack him when he wrapped a hand around her waist as they made their way to the door. The cowboy was well aware of Jason's joke on Shaun and reveled in making it look like he was truly fascinated with her, at least until they made their way outside.

When you play with fire, don't whine when you burn your fingers.

Brylee ignored her father's voice issuing the warning as it plowed through her thoughts. She hadn't heard his words of wisdom for weeks and now he suddenly popped back into her mind. Rather than listen, she ignored the admonishment.

Three hours later, she dropped Brett off at his hotel. He'd thanked her for a fun morning and the opportunity to torment Shaun before he closed the door and wandered inside. Brett had been fun and she enjoyed going to the art show with him, but she'd rather have been with Shaun. Brylee had just pulled out of the parking lot when her phone buzzed.

"Where are you?" Shaun's voice came across the speaker.

"Driving toward the convention center. Why?" she asked, wondering what he was up to. She could hear traffic in the background, as though he stood outside.

"Will you swing by the hotel and pick me up?"

"I'll be there in a minute," she said, disconnecting the call and switching lanes. She turned and pulled into the valet area in front of their hotel. Shaun jogged over from where he'd stood talking to one of the valets and climbed in the passenger seat.

"Did you have fun with Brett?" he asked as he buckled his seatbelt.

"I did have a good time." She waited for the car in front of her to move. "Did you do anything fun this morning?"

"Oh, just this and that," Shaun said, giving her a look she couldn't interpret. He didn't look upset, but he wasn't exactly smiling, either. "Are you in a rush to get to the convention center?"

"No. I have an autograph session there at two, but I'm free until then."

"Great. Are you game for an adventure?" Shaun asked as she pulled into traffic.

"With you around, I have to be," she teased.

He pointed out the window. "Turn right at the corner."

Shaun had her drive to a casino and resort property that housed a Cirque du Soleil performance. She didn't know how he'd found out about it or arranged it, but they joined a dozen

people in taking a behind the scenes tour of the
stage for the live circus show. Awed and amazed,
she and Shaun recounted all the interesting facts
they'd learned over lunch at a restaurant at the
resort. After Shaun insisted on paying for lunch,
they made their way to the convention center where
she spent an hour signing autographs with other
barrel racers.

She'd just gathered her things when Shaun
appeared at her side. "Mind if I ride with you to the
hotel?"

"Not at all," she said, handing him her keys.
"In fact, you can drive. I forgot how exhausting it is
to sign autographs nonstop."

Lightly, Shaun placed his hand at the small of
her back and guided her through the crowds outside
into the bright, warm sunshine. "I'm sure not
complaining about this nice weather. It's going to
be awful when we head back home to cold and
snow."

"But it'll seem more like Christmas," she said,
setting her bag on the floor and taking Shaun's hand
as he offered to help her inside the pickup. She
didn't really need the help, but appreciated his good
manners and the opportunity to hold his hand, even
for a moment.

Tired, she closed her eyes and rested while he
drove them back to the hotel. As he walked around
the pickup and gave the valet the keys, she handed
the valet a tip.

"Do you and your dad need a ride to the
rodeo?" she asked. "I plan to leave in an hour."

"That'd be great. I'm not sure where Dad is

right now, but I'll check in with him. He's probably up in our room making enough racket with his snoring the housekeepers will think someone has dragged wild animals into the suite."

Brylee laughed and led the way off the elevator. "See you in an hour."

She was almost ready to leave when Shaun sent her a text that he wasn't going to make it and to go ahead without him.

Once she arrived at the rodeo venue, she didn't have time for wondering what Shaun was up to. She fed Rocket, partly due to his crankiness if he didn't get to eat prior to an event and because she wanted to give him time to digest his food before it was time to run the barrels.

After he ate, she groomed him as much as he would tolerate then changed from her chore clothes into a pair of dark jeans with a sapphire blue sponsor-emblazoned shirt, including a new patch with the Lasso Eight logo. The owner of the company had been very happy with how she appeared in his ads and had offered her a sponsorship if she'd agree to model for Lasso Eight in the coming year.

Near the end of the steer wrestling, Brylee saddled Rocket and put on his boots that offered both support and protection. She rode him around the warm-up arena then moved into the alley where the barrel racers lined up to go into the arena.

Brylee looked around at her competition and felt a little pang of jealousy. Most of them had someone there to walk them down to the gate where they'd enter the arena, whether it was a significant other, parent, or a handler.

Alone, she quietly sat on her horse, determined not to let it bother her. She focused her thoughts on what she wanted Rocket to do in the arena — win.

A touch on her knee sent her nerve endings into a frenzied dance. Her gaze dropped and she looked into Shaun's smiling face. He held up a single-stemmed pink rose. The inside of the petals were a pale creamy shade that graduated into blush pink with the very tips of the rose sporting a hot pink hue.

"Oh, my gosh, Shaun! It's gorgeous," she said, taking the rose from him and inhaling the fragrant scent.

"So are you, Bitsy. Dad's right you know."

She gave him a curious look then sniffed the rose again. "Right? About what?"

"You really do get prettier every day." The hand he'd left on her knee slowly slid up to her thigh. "I'm not gonna wish you luck because you don't need it. You and Rocket are an incredible team. Just go do what you do best and don't worry about anything else."

"Thanks, Shaun." Brylee smiled at him as she broke part of the stem off the rose so she could tuck it into her hatband. When she settled it back on her head, she leaned down toward him. "I needed that reminder. What would I do without you?"

"Let's not find out, hmm?" He grinned then brushed a sweet, tender kiss across her lips. "Go show 'em what you've got, Bits."

The announcer began Brylee's introduction. Shaun walked with her until she got to the point where she'd start Rocket's run.

"Give a big Las Vegas welcome to Brylee Barton!" the announcer boomed. Fast-paced music thumped in the background and Brylee made three quick kissing sounds. Rocket tore into the arena and made a perfect turn around the first barrel. He rounded the second and turned the third with no trouble at all. Brylee held her breath as they raced across the arena to the cheers of the crowd.

"Look at that folks. That's a fantastic first run for Brylee Barton," the announcer said. "If you've missed the new Lasso Eight ads, you'll see Brylee featured in them throughout the rodeo."

Brylee forced herself not to glance at the scoreboard. She didn't want to know how she'd done until everyone had raced. Shaun met her at the end of the alley where they waited for the final score. When the announcer said Brylee took the top score by a tenth of a second, Shaun whooped and patted her leg. Then she was off, racing around the arena for her victory lap.

Giddy with excitement and overcome with a wealth of emotions, she rode outside the rodeo arena and over to her trailer. She slid off Rocket on wobbly legs. Instantly, Shaun was there and wrapped her in his arms. He just held her, not saying anything, until she regained the ability to stand with his support.

"You did great, Bitsy. That was a fantastic run for the first night. Just keep doing what you do and you'll win this thing."

"Thanks, Shaun. And thanks for being here with me." She took a deep breath of his enticing scent before pushing back and loosening the cinch on Rocket's saddle. "I was feeling a little left out until you showed up."

His brow furrowed in a frown as he bent down and removed one of the horse's boots. "Why did you feel left out?"

"Everyone had someone with them, except me." She smiled at him as she lifted off the saddle and set it in the tack area of her trailer. "But then you showed up and made everything all better. The rose is beautiful. I'll put it in water as soon as I get Rocket settled."

He glanced at the rose tucked into the band of her hat. "It suits you, soft and beautiful, fragrant and delicate, yet full of surprises."

Brylee blushed, but the evening's darkness hid it. She placed a magnetic blanket over Rocket's back to encourage blood flow. Together, they walked Rocket around the warm-up arena until he cooled down. Back at her trailer, they removed the blanket then rubbed liniment on his legs before taking him to his stall. Once he was settled for the night, Shaun went with her to the awards ceremony at a property south of The Strip. He cheered the loudest as she collected that night's winning buckle for barrel racing.

After he'd talked her into indulging in a celebratory piece of red velvet cheesecake, he walked her back to her room.

"You did good, Bitsy," he said as they lingered in her doorway. "I'm proud of you." He trailed one rough knuckle across her jawline before he kissed her cheek and disappeared into his room, leaving her confused yet full of yearning for another taste of his kiss.

Chapter Twenty

"Are you making any headway with Brylee?" Cooper asked as he and Shaun stood on a busy street corner waiting for the light to change.

"I don't know. Some days I think I am, and others I seem to be backpedaling," Shaun said, adjusting his hold on a box full of coffee and pastries. He and Cooper had volunteered to run out and get breakfast. Paige dealt with last minute fashion show problems and Brylee had disappeared to take a shower after feeding Rocket that morning. Birch, who'd arrived Thursday afternoon, had gone with Jason to see the historic Welcome to Las Vegas sign.

Tonight was the last evening of the rodeo. The last night Shaun had to make it clear to Brylee he couldn't live without her. The last opportunity to convince her to give him a second chance.

He'd tried being supportive of her date-a-day scheme. She'd gone out on a date or adventure with a different guy every single day they'd been in Vegas. Just yesterday, she'd gone ziplining with a guy Shaun generally liked but totally loathed at the moment because Brylee had raved about how much fun she'd had with him.

Shaun sighed in frustration and glanced over at Cooper. "I've tried doing the subtle, romance thing. I took her on a hot air balloon ride. On a picnic in the desert. We went on a gondola ride at The Venetian. We've strolled through the conservatory at the Bellagio, and had dinner at The Paris so she could see the fountain show from up high. Last night, I took her to see the flamingoes. She acted like she loved it. On the way back, we walked through one of the open-air shopping areas and watched a Christmas tree lighting. Fake snow fell all around us and Christmas carols were playing. In spite of it being warm out, I bought her hot chocolate and a peppermint cupcake. I don't know what else to do."

Cooper smirked. "Man, you have got it bad." He looked at Shaun as they crossed the street and continued on their way. "Everyone is talking about the pink roses in her hatband. I've heard about you smooching on her each night right before she rides."

Shaun grinned. "Something must be working, she's only knocked over two barrels the whole time she's been here and her scores are consistently in the top three. She's got a strong shot of winning tonight."

"Yeah, she does, so don't do something stupid that messes with her head between now and then."

Shaun scowled at his friend then released

another long sigh. "I'm trying to be careful, Coop, to not distract her, but with her daily dial-a-date, I'm kind of floundering here."

Cooper laughed. "Dial-a-date. That's a good one." He stopped as they came to another intersection and waited for the light. "You have to admit all the cowboys she's dated are good guys."

"I know that or I would have slammed the brakes on this nonsense long before now," Shaun said. He glanced up at the big digital screen above them. A Lasso Eight ad began to play. This one showed snow gently falling with a bunkhouse in the background. The camera zoomed in on the bunkhouse and three figures came into focus. He and his friend Gage's backsides were in perfect view, then the image panned out and showed Brylee leaning on their shoulders with a ball of mistletoe dangling from a red ribbon looped around her index finger. Shaun had the most besotted, lovesick look on his face as she glanced at him with her deep red lips formed into a seductive pout.

"It Must Have Been the Mistletoe" rolled across the screen followed by the Lasso Eight logo and website. The final screen shot mentioned their booth at the convention center.

Cooper snickered and thumped Shaun on the back. "Well, if that doesn't make Brylee the most popular girl in town today, I don't know what will."

Shaun growled at him and stalked across the street.

"Hey, wait up," Cooper called as he hurried to catch up with him. "Dude, you've got to calm down and get a hold of yourself. How do you think Brylee feels seeing women drooling after your backside like it's one big ol' decadent piece of candy?"

Shaun hadn't given any thought to Brylee being as plagued with feelings of jealousy or irritation by his modeling as he was by hers.

He'd watched her model at a fashion show on Thursday and had to sit on both hands to keep from punching a few guys who made raunchy comments about her. He was proud of her, enjoyed seeing her success, but hated the way men watched her, wanted her.

Then again, he knew what Cooper said was true. Women followed after him, begged for his autograph, propositioned him everywhere he went. Did it bother Brylee at all?

"I don't think she cares, Coop. She'd have to consider me more than a friend for that to be an issue."

Cooper guffawed as they entered the hotel and stepped onto the elevator. "Surely you aren't as dumb as you sound right now. You are the only person on the planet who doesn't know how much she likes you, Shaun. Get your head on straight and your eyeballs examined. If Brylee isn't completely in love with you, I will eat my big, rainbow-colored foam hat."

Shaun grinned. "I'd like to see that, but I hope I lose this bet."

"I hope you do, too." Cooper got off on his floor when the elevator doors opened. "Make sure you all are at the fashion show by eleven or my wife will have a meltdown and no one wants that to happen."

"We'll be there." Shaun went to his room then sent Brylee a text that he had coffee and pastries.

Before she could reply, Jason and Birch walked in. The boy was so excited he could barely contain his enthusiasm or energy.

"Did you get a good photo with the sign?" Shaun asked, glancing at Birch's phone as he held it out. The teen was pointing to the sign with a big grin on his face in the image. "That's great."

"Did you bring back plenty of food? I'm starving," Jason said as he sat on a barstool at the counter in the kitchen and took a cup of coffee from the box.

"There's milk and juice in there, too." Shaun slid the box toward Birch.

Brylee arrived and the four of them shared breakfast.

"Okay, guys, it's the last day in town. What one thing does everyone want to do today before we run out of time?" Jason asked as helped himself to a croissant filled with ham, eggs, and cheese.

"We've done some fun things since I got here," Birch said, wiping his mouth on a paper napkin. "But I'd really like to see the M&M store."

"Not a problem. Totally doable," Brylee said, smiling at her brother then looking to Jason. "Don't laugh at me, but I'd love to see the Titanic exhibit."

Birch snickered and jumped up from the barstool. He held his hands out from his sides, as though he stood on the end of the ship's deck and needed to maintain balance. Shaun moved behind him, recreating a famous pose from the Titanic movie that starred Leonardo DiCaprio and Kate

Winslet. Together, the two goofballs sang the chorus to "My Heart Will Go On."

Jason glared at both of them then patted Brylee on the back. "We'll make that happen, darlin.'" He glanced at Shaun. "What about you, son?"

"I'm game to go wherever you guys want to go, but if we head down to the Titanic exhibit, I wouldn't mind popping by the Christmas vendor show on that end of town." Shaun grinned at Birch. "Then you'll get to see the granddaddy of them all this afternoon when your sister makes an appearance at the Lasso Eight booth."

"Great! When do we leave?" Birch asked, glugging the last of his milk and taking a step toward the door.

"Let us finish our coffee first, Birch," Brylee said, taking a sip of hers and flipping her hair over her shoulder.

Shaun grabbed a maple bar just to keep from reaching out and burying his hands in the fragrant profusion of curls she'd fashioned that morning. Each one taunted and tempted him to touch the silken ribbons of her hair.

He took a savage bite out of the doughnut then shifted his attention to his father. "What about you, Dad? Anywhere you want to go?"

"Nope, I'm happy just to hang out with you kids, but we should get going soon if we want to see everything before the fashion show. If we're late, Paige is likely to string you two up by your thumbs."

Brylee nodded. "Give me ten minutes and I'll be ready to go." She left with Birch tagging along behind her.

Shaun released a sigh and sank down on the barstool she'd vacated. "I'm out of time, Dad, and out of ideas."

Jason offered him a sympathetic thump on the back. "The opportunity hasn't ended yet, son. You've got until midnight to turn her head. If that doesn't happen, you do know where she lives."

"Midnight?" Shaun asked, taking a drink of coffee that had grown lukewarm. His dad grinned and Shaun shook his head. "I know, nothing good happens after midnight. It might if she'd marry me again."

"Then give her a reason to want to marry you, Shaun. You can figure this out, and I know you will."

Jason disappeared into his room while Shaun cleaned up their breakfast mess, left a tip for the housekeeper on the counter, then went to grab a few things he needed before they met Brylee and Birch in the hall.

Hours later, he was no closer to figuring out how to capture Brylee's heart. In awe of her, he stood behind the curtain of the stage and watched her strut down the runway at the Lasso Eight fashion show. She executed a sassy turn before she made her way back to the other models, including Jessie Jarrett and Celia Kressley, standing across the stage.

Shaun studied the navy blue halter dress Brylee wore. The dress style was simple, but looked fancy with a spray of pink and red roses embroidered along the bodice and down to the high slits on both sides of the skirt. Absently, he hoped Paige let her keep that particular dress because he'd sure love to see her wear it again. At home. With just the two of them.

Nervous, he shifted from one foot to the other as Kenzie Morgan and Kaley McGraw walked out on the stage with their youngsters followed by Tate and Cort. The two families earned more than their share of applause from the crowd, especially when little Grace pranced out front and dipped into a dramatic bow.

"That kid is gonna give her dad a run for his money," Cooper observed as he watched Cort pick up Grace. He carried her back down the runway and behind the curtain.

"I'd feel sorry for him, but he probably deserves it," Shaun said, making Cooper, and Chase Jarrett, who'd joined them, snort with laughter as the show ended.

Brylee left the stage and disappeared with the other women. A few minutes later, she emerged in yet another western dress that made Shaun take a moment to appreciate her curves, her smooth skin, and the long curls of her golden hair.

"When are you gonna marry that girl, again?" Chase asked with a teasing grin.

"I'm working on convincing her, I just don't want to distract her before the end of the rodeo."

"Good plan. Distractions aren't a good thing. I think…" Chase lost his train of thought. He grinned from ear to ear as his lovely wife beamed at him and hurried his way.

"So says the man who can't even finish a

sentence when his wife smiles at him," Shaun said, waving at the couple as they left. He knew he'd see them at the Lasso Eight booth soon.

While he and Brylee hung out at the booth, signing autographs, Jason and Birch wandered through the huge cowboy Christmas vendor show. By the time they'd finished their shift at the booth, Birch had accumulated several bags of purchases. Jason volunteered to carry everything out to Brylee's pickup while the rest of them kept shopping.

"Are you spending all your money in one place, kid?" Brylee asked with a teasing smile.

"Aw, don't give me a hard time," Birch said, looping an arm around her shoulders. "I might have even bought you a Christmas present."

"Really?" she perked up at that statement and stretched to see if she could see Jason in the crowd. "Maybe I'll peek in the bags."

"No, you won't," Shaun said, moving to her other side, blocking her in between him and Birch. He looked at the teenager over Brylee's head. "What else do you want to see, Birch?"

The boy pointed to a booth selling cowboy hats. After Birch bought a new straw hat, Jason reappeared and pointed to his watch. "We better get going if Brylee's going to change and get to the rodeo grounds on time."

"Okay," Birch said, staring with longing at the rest of the show he hadn't yet had time to explore.

Shaun gave Brylee an imploring look. "Why don't Birch and I hang out here a while? We can catch up with you later."

Brylee stood on tiptoe and kissed his cheek. "Thank you. I hate to pull him away when he's having fun and he'll be bored waiting around for the rodeo to start. I'll catch up with you guys later. Are you staying or going, Jason?"

"I'll keep an eye on these two," Jason said, smirking at Brylee. "We'll see you later."

"You can count on it." Brylee waved then hurried toward the exit.

"Birch, there's something I want to talk to you about," Shaun said as he and Jason walked with the boy down another aisle.

"What's that?" Birch asked, stopping to look over a booth selling hand-forged knives.

"Do you think you could hang out with Dad for a while after the rodeo? I'd sure like to take your sister on a real date, but I'll postpone it if you have something you want to do with Brylee later."

Birch grinned. "Man, it's about time you took her out. Are you thinking dinner and flowers and the whole thing?"

Shaun smiled. "The whole thing."

"Then go for it," the boy said, turning his attention back to the display of knives.

Jason gave Shaun a meaningful glance before softly chuckling. "Kid is right. It's about time."

When Shaun, Jason, and Birch arrived at the rodeo, they bought barbecue beef sandwiches and strolled through the booths there. They listened to a concert for a while before wandering toward their seats. Shaun didn't plan to stay. He'd go hang out with Brylee as soon as the steer wrestling started. They visited with the Morgan and McGraw families when they filled the row behind them. Cooper and Paige sat down next to Birch while Jessie Jarrett and Chase's aunt and uncle along with his cousin Ashley filed in and occupied seats in the row in front of them.

"The gang's all here. Let's get this party started!" Cooper said, causing Paige to roll her eyes and shake her head at him.

Once the rodeo got underway, Shaun joined in the good-natured teasing going on between his friends. As soon as the steer wrestling began, he hustled out of the stands and made his way to where he knew he'd find Brylee getting ready to ride.

She wore the navy blue shirt he'd bought her the day she'd slid in the mud in Pendleton. Sponsor patches had been sewn along the sleeves and on the pockets. It was a good thing it happened to be a Lasso Eight brand or she might have been in trouble with Paige and the company's owner.

"Hey, Bitsy. Need any help," he asked as she bent down to put on Rocket's boots.

She glanced up and handed him a boot. "I'd love some help."

As he slipped on Rocket's boots, he watched her, watched the way she worked with easy, graceful movements. Watched the way her hair slid over one shoulder, leaving a little portion of her neck exposed. A spot that would be perfect to kiss if he wasn't determined to keep his emotions and yearnings in check, at least until after the rodeo.

"Finished?" Brylee asked, drawing his thoughts back to the moment instead of his plans for later.

"Yep. What else do you need me to do?" Shaun

asked as she checked the cinch on the saddle for what he knew was probably the third, or maybe fifth, time.

"Just keep me company, Copperhead." Brylee smiled at him in a way that gave him hope he might have a shot at winning her back. The few times she'd called him Copperhead made him so happy his heart had galloped in his chest. That endearment, such as it was, carried a wealth of sweet, wonderful memories from the days when he knew she loved him.

As they walked Rocket over to the warm-up arena, he measured his steps to her shorter stride. The air held a cool bite to it, but Brylee didn't seem to notice. She appeared deep in thought as they made a lap around the arena in silence. Finally, she glanced over at him and took a deep breath.

"Shaun, there's something I need to tell you, actually several things. I, um… can we meet after the rodeo? Hopefully, I'll need to attend the awards ceremony, but after that, would you make time for the two of us to talk?"

He grinned and placed his hand at the small of her back, wondering if that light connection affected her like it did him anytime they touched. "You must have read my mind, because I was prepared to beg you for a little of your time later. Dad said he'd keep Birch out of trouble if we want to have dinner and talk. I thought maybe we could order room service so we could speak in private. Would that work for you?"

"Yes, that will be great." Relieved, she nodded and looked as though a weight had lifted off her shoulders as she stopped and turned to face him. "I'm about one step away from being an emotional mess right now, so I'll make this quick. Shaun Price, you've been an amazing friend to me the last few months, and especially the last two weeks. Truly, you are the best friend I've ever had and I appreciate you more than I can ever adequately express."

"Right back at ya', Bitsy. I've got more friends than I know what do to with some days, but you are my best friend. As your best friend, I'm telling you right now to let go of whatever is worrying you and relax. You need to shake off the tension before you climb on Rocket. He'll feel it and it's going to mess up your ride. I want you to win tonight, not just be a champion, because it's your goal, your dream." He grinned and kissed her cheek. "And because I think you're the best and have earned that title."

She gave him a brief hug then shook her arms and legs. "Tension shaken off. Now, what do you say we go win this thing?"

Shaun grinned and walked with her to the alleyway where the barrel racers started lining up. "I'll be back in a minute," he said, then hurried over to the Rockin' K trailer where he'd stashed a little something for Brylee.

When he returned, she was laughing at something one of the other girls said. He stepped beside her and held up three roses, stems already cut short.

"What's this?" Brylee asked in surprise.

"For the head," he said, handing her a yellow rose. She sniffed the blossom then tucked it in the band of her hat.

Next, he handed her a red rose. "For the heart."

Brylee's cheeks turned a deep pink hue as she took the blossom and held it to her nose. She glanced around for somewhere to put it.

"Here, take this," one of the mothers standing with a young contestant handed Brylee a safety pin.

"Thanks," she said, taking the pin and fastening the rose to the front of her shirt, next to the Lasso Eight logo right above her heart. She looked down at Shaun with such love, he almost let out a whoop of victory.

"What's the last one for?" she asked.

"For the spirit." He held up a rose that was orange at the base and faded to a soft shade of coral around the tips of the petals. The woman at the flower shop had told him the meaning behind every shade of rose she had. Pink for admiration, sweetness, and joy. That was the color he'd given Brylee all week.

Tonight he wanted to do something more. The yellow rose meant friendship and new beginnings, or so the florist told him. He thought it was an appropriate symbol of what he hoped would happen when he spoke with Brylee tonight — a new beginning for them, a second chance at love. The red rose he knew signified love and passion. The orange-hued blossom, according to the florist, meant desire. It seemed wildly appropriate, too, considering the direction his thoughts continued to travel.

He wanted Brylee with every breath he took, but it was so much more than a physical longing.

Love for the stubborn, tough, tender girl filled his heart so full there were moments he thought he might drown in the emotion. Instead of running away from it this time, like he had six years ago, he wanted to run into it, to fall into it, and never find his way out of it.

Brylee challenged him, teased him, forced him to think, made him laugh, made him want to be a better version of himself. When he was with her, anything seemed possible. He just hoped the possibility of her opening her heart to him a second time existed.

In a few hours, he'd know.

Brylee took the orange rose and gave him a look so full of yearning, he wanted to pull her off Rocket and lose himself in her arms.

"Thank you, Shaun," she whispered and tucked the rose into the braid she'd fashioned in Rocket's mane. The orange color stood out in bright contrast to the horse's black mane and gray coat. "Now Rocket and I both can have a little reminder of you with us when we ride tonight."

Shaun placed a hand on her knee and gave it a gentle squeeze. "Just go out there and ride for the pure pleasure of it. Win or lose, you're still the best."

She leaned down and grabbed the collar of his jacket, pulling him up until their lips met in a hard, demanding kiss. When she pulled back, the girls around them were gawking and giggling. One of the cheekier girls shouted. "What took you so long to do that, Brylee?"

Although her face was nearly as red as the rose

pinned to her shirt, she gave Shaun a parting glance then rode Rocket forward.

Shaun watched her impressive, skillful ride with a broad smile.

"She's shooting out of the pocket like a rocket on Rocket, folks," the announcer said, clearly amused with his clever turn of phrase.

Shaun held his breath as she flew across the arena and came close to breaking the finals standing record. Even though she didn't quite make it, she did end the night with a ride that she could be proud of. He was certainly proud of her.

As she left the arena amid ear-splitting cheers, Shaun jogged to catch up with her where she stopped at the end of the alley.

Her face glowed from excitement as he reached up and gave her a high-five. "That was awesome!"

"It was awesome, Shaun. Thank you for telling me to do it just for the pleasure of it. I sometimes forget I need to be having fun, not just competing."

He scratched Rocket in that spot behind his ears that the horse loved. "You both did great. I'm so, so proud of you, Bitsy."

She grinned, then they held their breaths and listened as the winner was announced. Shaun wasn't the least bit surprised that Brylee had won.

"Go take that victory lap, darlin'."

After settling Rocket for the night then attending the awards ceremony with Jason and Birch, the four of them returned to the hotel. Jason took Birch out for one last stroll down The Strip and to get dessert. If Shaun knew Birch, they'd quite likely end up at a burger joint getting a second dinner followed by dessert. That boy could eat more food than three adults, but he remembered his own growth spurts and eating everything that wasn't nailed down at home.

Shaun took Brylee's hand in his as they made their way off the elevator. Brylee told him she needed just a minute to freshen up and would meet him in his room. When she knocked on his door five minutes later, he opened it and stepped aside to let her enter. He'd made arrangements before he left the hotel that afternoon to have a special table with a linen cloth set up in front of the living room window where they could look out and see a great view of The Strip.

A bouquet of roses of every color filled a crystal vase and sat in the center of the table while long tapered candles flickered in crystal holders on either side of the bouquet. A cart that had been delivered just a few minutes earlier waited next to the table and held covered plates of steaming food.

"Oh, Shaun," Brylee said. She glanced around the romantic scene, appearing impressed and pleased. "It's so lovely."

"So are you," he said, moving to pull out a chair for her. If he didn't seat her and focus on the meal, he was sure he'd succumb to the need to hold her and love her.

Before that happened, there were things that had to be said. Things that would either draw them closer or drive them apart.

The not knowing, the waiting to find out, might just kill him.

Chapter Twenty-One

Brylee felt like she'd stepped into a fantasy instead of Shaun and Jason's hotel room. The aroma of something delicious filled the air, making her empty stomach growl. She also picked up the nuance of something that smelled Christmassy, like spices and pine trees. Underlying all that, she caught a whiff of Shaun's alluring scent, although it never fully left her nose, even when she was cleaning Rocket's stall.

From the elegant table sitting in front of the window to the vase brimming with gorgeous roses, Shaun had certainly outdone himself.

When he'd presented her with three roses right before her ride, she wondered how she'd manage to race Rocket when her limbs felt as languid as a limp noodle. Brylee had studied the meanings behind flowers for her home staging work. She knew exactly what each flower meant. The way Shaun had presented them to her, she had a good idea he was aware of their meanings, too.

The expensive vase on the table held a rainbow of roses, signifying everything from friendship and new beginnings to passion and gratitude. She picked up the heavy vase and sniffed the flowers before setting it down on the coffee table so it wouldn't obstruct their view while they ate.

A part of her wished Shaun would wrap her in his strong arms and never let her go. Another part of her was glad he merely pulled out her chair and set a covered plate in front of her. He set a second plate across from her then took a seat. From a champagne bucket, he pulled a chilled bottle. Panic set in for a moment until she realized it was just sparkling cider. Champagne six years ago had been the beginning of where things had gone so horribly, terribly wrong. Brylee hadn't touched a drop since and neither had Shaun.

After he poured two champagne flutes full of cider, he took her hand in his and offered a word of thanks for the meal, for Brylee winning the championship title, and for the opportunity for them to spend time together. The sincerity in his voice made tears sting her eyes, but she blinked them away after she said amen and dug into her food. Shaun had ordered steak just the way she liked it. As they ate, they kept the conversation light, talking about the rodeo, the winners of other events, and how happy they were Chase Jarrett claimed the world title again in bull riding.

"I'm not sure who's more excited: him, Jessie, or Ashley," Brylee said, dragging her fork through the toppings on a loaded baked potato.

Shaun grinned. "I think I'd say Ashley. She's got sponsors for Chase lined up around the block. The more he wins, the easier it makes her job."

Brylee nodded. "True. Oh, Jessie said she and Chase are planning a little get-together New Year's Eve. If the roads are good, would you like to go?"

He lifted his gaze to hers and smiled. "Of course. Chase mentioned it this afternoon. I was gonna ask if you wanted to go."

They finished their meals and Shaun set the plates back on the cart. Two more covered dishes were on the cart, but instead of trying to talk her into immediately eating dessert, which she couldn't have even if she wanted to, he sat back down at the table and reached across it, taking both of her hands in his.

"Brylee, I've wanted to say this to you for months. At first, I knew you didn't want to hear it then later, when I thought you might have stopped hating me quite so much, I was afraid to say it."

"Afraid to say what, Shaun?" she asked. The secret she needed to share with him would create a far greater impact on them than anything he could say.

"The morning after we so rashly wed, I woke up beside you and the first thought that entered my head was that I'd died and gone to heaven. Being with you was the one thing I wanted more than anything else in the world. Then alarm and fear set in. I couldn't even remember how I'd gotten to your room, into your bed. I worried I'd talked you into something I shouldn't have, which I kinda did because I was the one who got you to drink all that champagne. That's when I saw the ring on my finger and I panicked."

"I know that, Shaun. We were both young and naive and..."

He shook his head, silencing her.

"It wasn't the commitment or responsibility that freaked me out, Brylee. It was you."

At her confused look, he drew in a deep breath before continuing. "The love I felt for you was beyond anything I'd ever imagined possible. It was so intense, so all-encompassing, so huge and raw and real... well, it scared me so much, I jumped out of that bed and set something in motion I've regretted every single day since. I had no idea how to handle all the feelings and emotions coursing through me. On top of that, the thought of losing you someday like my dad lost my mom just made me race out the door all the faster."

Brylee stared at him, shocked by his admission. She'd had no idea he felt that way, that he'd loved her as much as she'd loved him, still loved him. Before she could comment, though, he cleared his throat.

"I regretted the decision to leave you before I even made it back to my hotel room, but I was too much of a coward to crawl back to you. Then we had to compete that night. By the time I got home from the rodeo, all I wanted was to run to you, to apologize, to beg you to take me back, but you didn't return the dozen messages I left on your phone. I called the ranch once and pleaded with your mom to let me talk to you, but she refused. Many times, I got in the pickup and started to drive to Blue Hills Ranch, but I'd talk myself out of it and turn around. Finally, I sent you a letter trying to explain and begging for your forgiveness. When I never heard back from you, I knew I had to let you go. I shouldn't have given up so easily, Brylee. I should have done everything in my power to get back to you, but I didn't and I'm sorry."

Brylee had no idea he'd called. She'd never seen a letter from him. Most likely, her mother had interfered. In her own way, Jenn probably thought she was helping by keeping both the letter and phone call from Brylee.

In those first weeks after Shaun left her, Brylee would have eagerly taken him back. Would have forgiven him anything. Then everything changed and her love slowly turned to loathing.

"I never received the letter, Shaun, and my mother never mentioned you called. If she had, I would have called you back. And for the record, I didn't change my number or ignore your calls. I lost my phone after riding the last night at the rodeo. I was so upset with you and about losing, my hands shook with tremors. And the tears, there were so many tears. It's a wonder I didn't lose my pickup keys, too. When I got a new phone the next morning, I got a new number." She released a soul-weary sigh. "There was nothing I wanted more than to be with you, but you walked away from what could have been." Tears glistened in her eyes as she squeezed his hands. "I loved you so much, Shaun, and it broke not just my heart, but also something in my spirit when you abandoned me. I thought I'd done something horribly wrong, that there was something so wrong with me that you couldn't stand to be around me. I thought I was unlovable, Shaun, because after I poured out my love to you, you left me. You just left me alone in a hotel room without even a word of goodbye."

Agony filled his features as he released her hands then picked her up, sat in her chair, and held her close to his chest. "No, Brylee, no. Don't think for a single minute you were unlovable, that you were anything less than perfect. Those hours we spent married were incredible, beyond anything I could have hoped or dreamed. You're a beautiful, passionate, giving, loving woman and that's part of what scared me so bad. It wasn't that we weren't a good fit for each other, it was that we fit so well that left me terrified. I know I could apologize every day for the rest of my life and it wouldn't be enough, but I am so, so sorry, Brylee. Sorry for that one stupid decision that brought both of us so much pain."

Brylee nestled against him, relishing the warmth of his arms around her, the steady beat of his heart beneath her ear, the enticing scent of him captivating her senses. "What about now, Shaun? Are you still scared of what we could have together?"

"Not at all."

She heard the smile in his voice before she felt his lips press a kiss to her forehead. She tipped her head back and studied his face from the slight cleft in that handsome chin to the love glowing in eyes that looked like a winter storm brewed there.

"The only thing that scares me now is losing

you, Brylee. I love you with every single bit of my heart. These past months of being with you have taught me a whole new level of love — one of patience and caring and sincerity that I might never have known. I'm grateful for that, but I'm hoping you'll say I can have a second chance to make you fall in love with me."

Brylee shook her head and schooled her features into an impassive expression. "I can't give you another chance to make me fall in love with you..." Before Shaun's happiness completely segued into worry, she grinned. "I'm already in love with you, Copperhead. I've been in love with you for a very long time. In fact, I don't think I ever stopped loving you, even when I couldn't see past the hurt and pain of you leaving me."

Shaun slowly threaded his hands into her hair. In no rush, he lowered his head until his mouth brushed across hers. "I love you so much, Brylee Barton. More than you'll ever know."

"Not as much as I love you."

He kissed her then, like she'd been dreaming he would ever since the day he carried her through the mud when she broke her leg. Gently, softly, his lips moved against hers — teasing, exploring, renewing, remembering. Her hands slid up his arms and wrapped around the back of his neck.

His fingers trailed down her back and traced the most exhilarating circles across her sides as he pulled her closer and continued tantalizing her with powerful, ardent kisses.

Brylee moaned in pleasure, losing herself in the bliss of being loved, once again, by Shaun. The restraint he'd used gave way to a new level of passion as he deepened the kiss. Without a single doubt, she knew Shaun truly loved her. Loved her in a way that matched what she felt for him, what she'd always feel for him.

Finally, he pulled back and rested his forehead against hers. "Does this mean you've forgiven me?"

She released an emotion-filled laugh and hugged him. "Yes, I suppose it does."

"Then I think we should celebrate by eating dessert." He reached over and lifted one of the dessert plates off the cart and set it on the table in front of them.

"Honestly, Shaun, I'm so full from dinner, I don't think I could hold another bite. Maybe we can wait a while and try it later. Or save it for your breakfast. Your dad wouldn't be opposed to pie or cake for breakfast."

He grinned and kissed her nose. "Please, just try one bite. It's going to be really good."

Brylee shifted so she was half facing him, half facing the table. She lifted the lid covering the plate and gasped in surprise.

Blue M&Ms topped a piece of cheesecake. Each piece of candy held a word that spelled out "Will you please marry me, again?"

She glanced from the candy to Shaun.

He grinned and shrugged. "I got those at the M&M store this morning. Will you, Brylee? Will you marry me, again? Will you let me grow old with you and cherish you the way I should have the first time?"

Tears rolled down her cheeks as she placed her

hands on either side of Shaun's face and kissed him. Kissed him with all the love flowing through her at that moment. "Nothing would make me happier than to marry you, Shaun, but there's something I have to tell you first. Something I should have told you a long time ago. All I can say is that you wounded me so deeply, I wasn't exactly thinking rationally at the time. When it was over, I didn't see the point. Right now, I wish I'd been honest with you instead of keeping a secret."

"What is it? Nothing you can say will change how I feel about you. I promise, Brylee. There isn't a single thing that will keep me away from you this time around." Shaun brushed the tears from her cheeks with the palms of his hands.

Unable to think with him so close, with everything in her wanting to fall into his arms and never leave, she rose to her feet and moved to stand in front of the window. Hundreds of lights glittered through the darkness, but she didn't see them as she stared out into the night.

"Don't make a promise you might not be able to keep," she warned as he moved behind her, settling his hands on her shoulders. With her courage about to fail her, she took her phone from her pocket and sent him a text.

She turned and clasped his hand in hers. "Come sit with me on the couch. I don't think I can stand up to tell you this."

Wary and clearly worried, he let her lead him to the couch. "Just spit it out, Bitsy. Whatever it is, it'll be okay."

She took a seat and pulled him down beside

her. "I'm not sure it will, Shaun. What I need to tell you, what I should have told you six years ago, is something you may never be able to get past."

When he started to protest, she tapped his shirt pocket. "Look at your phone, please."

He pulled out his phone and clicked on the link she'd sent in a text. His brow furrowed into a puzzled frown as he stared at the image of a baby.

"Why did you send me a picture of Dani?" he asked, turning his phone sideways to make the image bigger.

Brylee's tears dripped down her cheeks as she looked at the photo of a beautiful, perfect newborn baby sleeping on a fluffy white blanket. A thick thatch of red hair stood out in contrast to the white background while a tiny rosebud mouth rested in a sweet little pucker.

The pain in her chest nearly stole her breath away, but she swiped at her tears and forced herself to speak. "It isn't Dani."

Shaun looked from the photo to her then back at the photo. "If it isn't Dani, it sure could be her twin. Where did you…"

His voice trailed off and he drew the phone closer, blowing up the image of the baby's face and studying it before counting the fingers and toes visible in the photo.

The silence he lingered in as he stared at the photo sent daggers of anguish shooting through Brylee's heart. When he finally raised his gaze to hers, tears glistened in his eyes.

"Mine?" he asked on a croak, clearly overwrought with emotion.

Brylee nodded and took his phone from him, scrolling through photos to show him a picture of a happy baby with red hair and huge blue eyes.

"A month after the rodeo, I got really sick. At first, I thought it was a stomach bug, but it lasted for days. I finally went to the doctor and found out I was pregnant. I started to call so many times to tell you, but then I'd think about waking up to that empty room and your note to call the attorney, and I'd hang up before I even dialed your number. Our daughter was born on the tenth of September with a healthy set of lungs and a head full of red hair. Dad used to joke that her hair certainly matched her temper. He blamed that on you. I named her Michaela Jo."

"Where is my daughter?" Shaun glared at Brylee. He got up and paced across the floor "How could you leave her and go off on the rodeo all year? How could you hide her from me?" He stopped pacing and narrowed his gaze as he pointed an accusing finger at her. "I was in your house, Brylee! Where was she?"

"Gone," she whispered, gaze fixed on the last photo she had of her darling daughter.

"Gone?" he asked. He resumed pacing and forked a hand through his hair in frustration. "What do you mean, gone? How does a five-year-old just go somewhere? Did you leave her with someone when I was there? You had no right to keep my daughter from me."

Indignation and a hint of unresolved pain shimmered in her eyes. "Actually, I did, Shaun. You abandoned me. You left me. From the facts I had at the time, you never attempted to get in touch after the morning you walked away from me, from my love. I know better now, but I didn't then. I didn't have any idea you'd sent the letter or called. If I had, I certainly would have told you I was pregnant."

Shaun sighed and sat next to her, taking his phone and studying the image of a bright-eyed baby. A Santa hat looked comical in contrast to the baby's fancy white dress with red roses embroidered down the front. Birch was stretched out behind her, holding Michaela in a sitting position while they both wore big smiles. The baby's hand rested against Birch's cheek, as though he belonged to her.

"Where is my daughter?" Shaun asked again, scrolling through dozens of images Brylee had taken of the baby.

She placed a hand on his arm and pushed the words out past the expanding lump in her throat. "She died, Shaun. Five years ago."

"Died?" he asked in a ragged whisper. His face wore a mask of misery. "How?"

Brylee leaned her head back and took a long breath, knowing if she didn't tell him everything at once, she wouldn't be able to get through it. "You have to understand we all adored her, even Mom. Birch absolutely doted on her, acting like she was a special gift meant just for him. Michaela was a happy baby, except when her temper got riled. She wasn't sickly, laughed easily, and filled the house with so much joy."

At Shaun's pleading look, she took another

breath and continued. "Right before Christmas, Birch had a special program at school and we all went. I took that photo of her in the Santa hat as we were getting ready to leave the house. Michaela smiled and cooed and charmed everyone at school. After the program, Birch wanted to show her off to his friends. It wasn't anyone's fault she got sick, but kids that age share germs. A few days after Christmas, Michaela woke up sneezing and couldn't stop. Her nose started to run and then she got fussy, which rarely happened. That night, she ran a fever and the next morning she had a horrible, rattling cough. I took her to the doctor and he admitted her to the hospital with a respiratory infection. Normally, it's not a serious thing for babies her age, but it just knocked her down so quickly. The doctor tried several treatments, but instead of getting better she kept getting worse. She was in the hospital for a week, and then she was just gone." Brylee sobbed, relieving the excruciating pain of losing her beloved child. "My baby was gone in a blink and there was nothing I could do to save her or bring her back."

"How could you keep this from me, Brylee?" Shaun appeared stunned as he gaped at her. He rose, making his way over to the window she'd stared out earlier. "How did you keep from dying right along with our daughter? I just found out and the pain of it is too much to bear."

"There were days I didn't want to go on. Days I couldn't force myself out of bed. Days that I needed you so badly, I couldn't breathe." Brylee inhaled a tattered breath and released it. She stood and picked up one of the discarded napkins on the table, using it to wipe away her tears. "Birch is the only reason I survived."

"Birch?" Shaun glanced over his shoulder in confusion.

"He blamed himself for Michaela getting sick. In those first days after she died, Birch repeatedly said if he hadn't brought his friends over to see her, she wouldn't have gotten sick. The truth is, we wanted someone to blame, even if we never said as much to Birch. Mom and I blamed the doctor, the hospital, and the pharmaceutical companies. If there was someone a finger could be pointed at in blame, we did. Birch was so devastated by her death he missed six weeks of school. One cold February day, I looked around me and realized wallowing in the pain and grief wouldn't bring back Michaela. All it was doing was destroying what was left of my family, especially Birch. He couldn't eat or sleep, and moved around like a zombie. For his sake, I had to stop. Dad supported me wholeheartedly and by summer, Birch was mostly back to normal. But anytime anyone mentions Michaela, he gets the most haunted look in his eyes and draws back into a place no one can seem to reach him."

Shaun studied her a moment. "The hospital bills were why you were in debt. Is that right?"

She hated to tell him, but she nodded her head. "Yes. I didn't have much insurance and what I had to pay out of pocket was astronomical. Dad helped me so much with the bills, but that's why, when the barn burned and he had to upgrade the irrigation system, he took out a loan. Every extra penny had already gone to paying off the hospital bills."

Brylee brushed away more tears. "We don't keep photos of Michaela in the house and we never talk about her for Birch's sake, but she's always in my heart and my thoughts. I'm sorry, Shaun, more sorry than mere words can express, that I didn't tell you about her, share her with you. If I'd known you wanted her, wanted to be part of my life, I would never have kept her from you. She was an amazing little sweetheart and I'll always regret that you didn't have the opportunity to know your daughter."

She walked over to him and settled a hand on his back. He didn't pull away, but he didn't turn and take her in his arms to offer the comfort she so badly needed.

"I knew from the moment I saw you this summer that I had to tell you, but I dreaded it. Perhaps I knew all along it would be the thing that kept us apart. If you think you can someday forgive me, I'll be waiting for you. No matter what you might be thinking, I do love you, Shaun, with all that I have to give. I'll always love you, only you. But if you aren't going to love me in return and move past the mistakes we both made, then let me go."

Brylee didn't wait for him to speak. She turned and fled to her room where she cried until no more tears could be shed.

Chapter Twenty-Two

Numb.

Shaun felt numb inside.

Numb from the pain. Numb from the loss. Numb from the devastation of finding out he'd had a daughter then losing her in the same unbelievably excruciating moment.

He wanted to despise Brylee for what she'd done. She'd kept something from him that he had every right to know. She could have told him back in July when they reconnected, but she hadn't. She had so many opportunities to tell him the truth, to tell him he was a father, but she'd remained silent until he'd professed his undying love to her.

It would be so easy to hate her, but he couldn't. How could he blame Brylee when it was his fault. All his fault.

If he'd never been such a cowardly idiot and run away from her six years ago, none of this would have happened. If he'd stayed with her, it was possible they would have a happy, bubbly five-year-old daughter they both adored.

He glanced at the first image of the baby again, cradling his phone on his palm as though he could cradle her. His baby.

Michaela Jo.

With the immediate bond of affection from parent to child that defies explanation or reason, he loved the name just like he loved the baby he'd never know.

Michaela looked so much like Dani did as a baby it was easy to see how he'd mistaken the identity. He thought back to the day Brylee had been at the Circle P with them. She'd been so good with Dani, seemed so attached to her, now he knew why. His niece could easily pass as a sister to his daughter.

Shaun scrolled through the images, grateful Brylee had taken so many. He stopped when he came across a photo of her standing out in the pasture. The trees framing the image hadn't quite changed into the vivid colors of fall. Brylee leaned against a wooden fence with Rocket in the background while she glanced down at the blanket-wrapped baby in her arms. Love unlike anything he'd ever seen glowed on her face.

Brylee looked so beautiful and happy, so content and full of love. And if he'd made one different choice, just one, he could have been beside her, basking in her love, pouring out his own for her and their child.

A father.

Shaun could have been a father. He could have

bought Michaela her first pony. He could have taught her how to throw a rope or whistle for the dogs. As though he could picture every milestone of her life, he envisioned her first day of school, her first dance, the day she got her driver's license, and walking her down the aisle at her wedding.

Overcome with guilt and grief, Shaun sank onto the couch, buried his face in his hands and wept. He hadn't cried since the day they buried his mother, grandmother, and little sister, but he couldn't hold back the tears now if he tried.

Brylee wasn't to blame for the life-altering mistakes he'd made. She'd been wrong to ask for his forgiveness because he was the one who needed to plead for hers, again. How she must have hurt and grieved, and gone through it all alone while feeling completely unwanted and unloved.

He jerked when a hand settled on his shoulder. Through the tears clinging to his lashes, he looked up at his dad's concerned face.

"What in thunderation happened?" Jason asked, sinking down beside Shaun. "I dropped Birch off in Brylee's room, and she's sobbing like the world just ended instead of the fact she won the championship title tonight. I thought you were gonna propose?" Jason's face paled. "Did she turn you down?"

Shaun took the handkerchief his father held out to him and wiped his face and nose. "She agreed to marry me, but said she had to tell me something first. She indicated I might not want to marry her after I heard what she had to say."

"Well, what did she tell you?"

Shaun didn't even know where to start, how to

begin, so he picked up his phone from where it had fallen on the couch beside him and scrolled back to the first photo of Michaela. He handed the phone to his dad.

"I don't remember seeing this photo of Dani. She sure was a cute lil' bug, though." Jason glanced from the photo to Shaun. "What's this got to do with the two of you acting heartbroken, though? It has to be something bad to have you this upset, son."

"It is bad. The worst kind of bad," Shaun said, pointing to the phone Jason still held. "That picture isn't of Dani. That's my daughter."

Jason's face went from pale to completely white as he gaped at the image of the newborn. "Your what?"

"Apparently, our wedding night was all it took for Brylee to get pregnant. She had no idea I'd tried to get in touch with her, thanks to her meddling mother. Honestly, I should have tried harder. For all she knew, I wanted nothing to do with her and had truly abandoned her. So she kept the baby a secret."

Jason sat up and a smile wreathed his face. "I have another grandbaby? What's her name? I reckon she'd be about five now, right? Has Brylee been hiding her from you the last few months when you've been at their ranch? How could she not tell us about her?"

Slowly, Shaun shook his head and had to swallow three times to dislodge the emotion threatening to choke him. "The baby would have been five in September. Her name was Michaela Jo."

"Would have been? Was?" Jason appeared stricken. "You don't mean..."

"She died, Dad. She died right after Christmas when she was three months old."

"Died?" Jason rasped, leaning back and clutching a hand to his chest, as though it could lessen the pain.

"Brylee said she got a respiratory infection and didn't make it."

"Why didn't Brylee take her to the doctor? Why didn't..."

Shaun held up a hand. "She died in the hospital, Dad. Brylee took her the morning after she got sick. In spite of the doctor doing his best to save her, Michaela died. Brylee said it almost killed her, and Birch, too. It seems Birch blamed himself for wanting her to be at a school program where germs always abound. They think that's where she caught something. According to Brylee, Birch missed weeks of school and it took months for him to get back to normal."

"What about Brylee? I know how hard it is to lose a child, to lose someone you love."

"She said she wanted to die then, too. Then she lost her Dad on top of everything else."

Jason snuffled, looking through the images of Michaela. "She's sure a sweet little thing. At least you know now why Brylee disappeared from rodeo. She couldn't have competed while she was expecting then she wouldn't have wanted to be gone with Michaela to care for." He glanced over at Shaun as he brushed a lone tear from his weathered cheek. "She still should have told you, let you have the chance to know your baby."

"She should have, but I can't exactly blame her, Dad. She didn't know I cared. Didn't know I loved her. I'm as mad at myself as I am her."

"Don't be too hard on either one of you, Shaun. Both of you were young and foolish and made some horrible mistakes. You're just gonna have to decide if you can forgive each other and move on, or if you're finally gonna let that girl go."

Jason handed Shaun the phone then rose and shuffled to his bedroom like an old, weary man. Like the way Shaun's soul felt; tired and worn beyond endurance.

Instead of sleeping, Shaun spent the night alternating between prayers and despair. The next morning, his dad took one look at him and pulled him into a hug, patting his back without saying a word.

Jason got them both some breakfast and bracing cups of black coffee. Shaun couldn't eat a bite, but he drank the coffee then silently packed his things and followed his dad outside to hail a cab to take them to the airport. When they landed in Boise several hours later, Shaun still felt as though someone had shoved his emotions through a shredder, leaving them blunt, raw, and frayed.

"Let's go home, son," Jason said as they climbed in the pickup they'd left parked at the airport. Shaun was grateful his dad didn't ask anything of him. He didn't think he had enough functioning brain cells left to make the two-hour drive to their ranch.

An hour out of Boise, snow began to fall. The

freeway grew icier the closer they got to Baker City. They both breathed a sigh of relief when they reached their exit. Soon, they pulled up the lane to the ranch. Lisa, Galen, and Pops had decorated the house both inside and out for Christmas, but Shaun barely noticed. He just felt lost and alone, and empty. So empty.

The only thing that gave him any peace in the following days was holding Dani. He'd clung to her so much, she'd taken a wide berth around him, afraid he wouldn't let her go.

With unwavering clarity, Shaun fully understood the breadth and depth of consequences. He and Brylee were drowning in them and the worst part was that he had no idea how to make it better, to fix what was broken. Nights were spent wide-awake, staring at the ceiling and contemplating his future, reliving his past.

As he forced himself out of bed one morning, he knew he had to forgive Brylee for keeping his daughter a secret and seek her forgiveness for his choices that created the chasm between the two of them in the first place. If he didn't, the pain of it would consume him.

No matter how upset he was with her, no matter how bitter he felt that he'd been cheated out of a chance to hold his child and love her as a daddy would, he still loved Brylee. He always would. It was what he intended to do about that love that left him caught between his anger toward her and his soul-deep love for her.

Since he'd been home, everyone had tiptoed around him like one wrong word would break him.

Even little Dani had been subdued by the tension he carried on his shoulders like a self-righteous cloak.

In need of an escape from his thoughts and the strain he'd inadvertently placed over the entire household, he saddled Lucky and went out to check fences. The day was beautiful with the sun glistening on fields of snow like thousands of diamonds had dropped down from heaven. Overhead, the sky was a vibrant shade of blue. As Lucky meandered through the snow along the fence, Shaun realized Christmas was only a few days away.

For the sake of his family, especially Dani, he needed to pull himself together. It wasn't fair to any of them for him to be a wet blanket on the Christmas festivities.

Shaun finished checking the fence then rode out to the hilltop where he'd always dreamed of building a home. A home he wanted to share with Brylee. He could even picture a red-haired little girl with bright blue eyes helping him build a snowman while Brylee sat on the porch, laughing and sipping hot chocolate. For several minutes, Shaun sat on Lucky just soaking up the sunshine and the quiet of the snow-covered hills around him.

When his phone buzzed, his first inclination was to ignore it, like he'd ignored most calls for the last week. Determined to do better, he pulled it out of his coat pocket and answered it without glancing at the screen.

"This is Shaun."

"Well, who else would it be, you idiot," Cooper joked.

"Hey, man," Shaun said, genuinely glad to hear from his friend. "Are you and Paige all ready for the holidays?"

"Yep. The halls are decked and Paige's sister is here helping her bake cookies today." Cooper chuckled. "Gramps and I are doing our best to eat them as fast as they come out of the oven, but I think we're falling behind."

Shaun smiled for the first time since Brylee had told him about their daughter. He envisioned Cooper and his grandfather harassing the two women as they tried to bake. "Tell Paige I give her permission to take back your Christmas present, then."

"Shoot! You know what she got me?"

"I'm not saying a word," Shaun said in a teasing tone.

"Listen, Shaun, I... um... I talked to your dad. He mentioned you're having a hard time right now. You know if there's anything I can do, just tell me."

"I appreciate that, Cooper. I'll be okay, eventually." Shaun realized he would. There might always be a gaping hole in his heart and life from losing his daughter, but he would be okay. He'd learn to live again, no matter how painful the process might be.

"I know you will be, but just take all the time you need to work through this. Your dad didn't give me the details and I don't need them, but if you ever want to talk, I can shut up once in a while and listen."

"Thanks, Coop. I really do appreciate the offer." Shaun released a sigh, released some of the weight that had made his chest feel like one of Kash's bulls sat on top of it. "So what's up?"

"Well, the reason I called your dad is because you haven't answered your phone lately and someone has been trying to get in touch with you. They finally called me since they know we're friends."

"Who?" Shaun asked, wondering if it was Brylee. Surely, if she wanted to talk to him that badly, she would have just called the house.

"Will Johnson. You remember him, don't you?" Cooper asked.

"Of course. His brother is the one who filled out the annulment or divorce papers or whatever it was when Brylee and I..." Shaun couldn't force himself to say the rest.

"Right. Well, he's been trying to get in touch with you. He finally tracked me down and asked if I'd reach out to you. Will didn't say what was going on but he said it was a very important matter you needed to know about immediately if not sooner."

"I'll call him right away. Thanks, Coop. For everything. In case I don't talk to you before Christmas, I hope you and Paige have a wonderful holiday. Tell your grandpa Merry Christmas for me, too."

"Will do, Shaun." Cooper's voice took on a serious tone. "And remember you can call anytime if there's anything I can do to help you."

"I know, man, and I'm grateful to have your friendship. Now hang up and go steal a cookie for me."

"That I can do." Cooper's amusement carried

over the line as he hung up and sent Shaun a text with Will's number.

Shaun called it, wondering what Will needed to tell him that was so important. On the third ring, the man picked up.

"This is Will."

"Will, this is Shaun Price," he said, watching a coyote slink through the shadows of the trees in the distance. As long as it stayed away from the cattle, he'd leave it alone. "I'm sorry about not returning your calls. What's up, man?"

"Shaun, I'm so glad you called. There's something I need to tell you, well, actually, my brother needs to tell you, but he's too chicken."

A sense of foreboding settled over Shaun. "What's going on?"

"You know when you had Wes help you with those annulment papers?"

"Yes, I very clearly remember that," Shaun said, thinking he could live for a thousand years and never forget it.

"Well, Wes finally got a promotion and was cleaning out his office the weekend before last and he came across an envelope that had fallen down behind the credenza." Will hesitated before continuing. "It was your paperwork, Shaun. It never got filed. I don't know how to tell you this, but you and Brylee are still married."

"What!" Shaun's voice echoed off the hills. The sound caught Lucky off guard and the horse crow-hopped a few steps. Shaun had to work to hang onto the phone and bring the horse under control. "Repeat that for me, would you?"

"I said you and Brylee are still married. My stupid brother misplaced the paperwork all this time and just found it recently. I didn't want to bother you during the finals, but I've tried calling several times in the last week. I figured you'd want to know sooner rather than later, although I suppose after six years a few more days won't make a difference."

"So Brylee and I are still legally married? As in she's my legal wife?"

"That's right. According to Wes, since he failed to file the paperwork, it's like it never existed. You and Brylee are still legally married. He did say if you still want to separate, he can file for a divorce, but honestly, I'd recommend someone else. He only got the promotion because he recently married the boss's daughter."

"I appreciate the info, Will. Truly, I do. Thanks for letting me know. I hope you have a great Christmas." Shaun felt his heart leap in his chest and resume functioning with strong, steady beats after more than a week of stagnation in a dormant state.

"Thanks, man. You, too."

Shaun stared at his phone for a minute after he disconnected the call. Suddenly, everything that had seemed so disjointed and hopeless shifted into place.

He grinned and patted Lucky on the neck. "Come on, boy. Let's get back to the house. I've got places to go and things to do."

Chapter Twenty-Three

Brylee couldn't recall crying herself to sleep after running out of Shaun's room and his life, or awakening in the early hours of the morning with a massive migraine. She had no recollection of returning to the rodeo venue hours before dawn, hitching her trailer to the pickup, or loading Rocket. She couldn't even remember leaving Las Vegas in a flurry of tears as she drove toward home.

According to Birch, though, she did all those things. And when she stopped for gas at a little town a few hours out of Las Vegas, she asked him to drive. The boy had been driving a pickup on the ranch since he was ten, but he hadn't gained much on-the-road experience since getting his driver's permit a month earlier.

Thankfully, the weather was beautiful and the roads clear. Birch managed to get them to a truck stop near Boise with no problem. Although Brylee was exhausted from the miles and miles of tears she'd cried, she climbed behind the wheel and drove the rest of the way home, pulling up at their house just in time for dinner.

The second the pickup rolled to a stop at Blue Hills Ranch, Birch rushed inside the house, warning their mother and grandfather to leave her alone.

Birch had been so excited his last night in Las Vegas before he returned to the room. From the moment he found her teetering on the edge of hysteria as she sobbed and couldn't explain why, he'd gone into a protective mode.

While Brylee appreciated his care and intervention on her behalf, she told both Ace and Jenn of Shaun's proposal and her confession about keeping Michaela's existence a secret.

By the time she finished telling what happened, all four of them were in tears. Grandpa went with Birch to put Rocket in the barn while Jenn sobbed even harder than Brylee, begging forgiveness for her part in making a bad situation worse.

"I forgive you, Mom, but what you did was so wrong and hurtful. If you'd just let Shaun apologize, things could have been different."

"I know, honey. All I can say is I'm sorry. I never even told your father what I'd done," Jenn said, sniffling into a soggy tissue. "I suppose a part of me knew what an awful thing I'd done to both you and Shaun. I didn't want him to know, to think less of me."

"Then why did you do it?" Brylee asked, wanting, for a brief moment, to inflict as much pain on her mother as she'd poured out on her.

"Honestly, Brylee, I thought I was protecting

you. You came home from that rodeo so sad and broken. I decided Shaun didn't deserve to get you back because he'd hurt you so badly."

"But that wasn't your choice to make, Mom. That was mine." Brylee sighed. "I'd like to think I would have done the right thing and let him know I was pregnant."

The next several days were hard for her, but Brylee had spent so much time lost in despair after Michaela died and then her father, she refused to wallow in pity or grief.

She threw herself into preparations for the holiday and pretended everything was fine. She and Birch even painted three old tractor tires green and rolled them down the driveway to the front fence. After placing them just so, she added huge red bows, making them look like giant wreaths. The two of them added more lights to the fences and even around the barn. It was as though they tried to overcome the gloom in their hearts by filling the world around them with as much festivity and light as possible.

Brylee had mailed a hundred Christmas cards to family and friends with greetings from all four members of the Barton family. While her mother worked, she cleaned the house, baked holiday treats, and spent an hour crying when she realized she'd made Shaun's favorite cookies.

She wrapped gifts, and even sewed an outfit for one of the shepherds for the church Christmas program when his mom's sewing machine went on the fritz. Brylee rode her dad's old horse or Rocket around the ranch, breathing in the frosty winter air and hoping the snowy landscape would bring peace to her mind if not to her heart.

One afternoon, she and Ace filled baskets with gifts for the elderly and took them to one of the assisted living facilities. The residents were thrilled and Ace had a fabulous time playing Santa, but Brylee couldn't find the joy in it she'd hoped it would bring.

Five days before Christmas, Brylee awakened and realized her attempts at filling the ache in her heart with busywork wouldn't make the pain go away. For that, she needed time and maybe a bit of quiet. Inspired to see getting away from everything would make her feel better, she packed a suitcase, then went in search of her grandpa. She found him polishing a set of old sleigh bells in the tack room.

"Grandpa, I love you all dearly, but I need a little while by myself. I'm heading up to the cabin for a few days."

"That's a great idea, honey." Ace wiped off his hands and studied her. "Maybe in the quiet up on the mountain you can come to terms with what happened and be ready to start the New Year with a fresh perspective."

She kissed his cheek and gave him a hug. "I promise I'll come back Christmas Eve morning. Will you please let Mom and Birch know that I'm fine, but need to be alone?"

"I will, honey. You drive carefully and enjoy the peace and quiet up there."

Brylee had tossed her suitcase and a bag full of goodies she'd made in the pickup, ran by the grocery store to stock up on food and supplies, then headed up the mountain. She drove past rolling hills that held golden wheat in the summer but were now covered in a blanket of snow.

The snow deepened and the sky looked stormy as she drove higher into the mountains. It was nearing noon when she parked in front of the A-frame cabin that kept snow from accumulating on the roof. A memory of climbing into the slope-ceilinged loft as a little girl and staring out the window at the woods around them made her smile. Life was so easy and simple back then.

She hauled in the groceries and her suitcase, built a fire in the fireplace, and made a sandwich to eat for lunch. After she took a brisk walk around the property to make sure everything was as it should be, she curled up on the couch beneath a soft blanket and went to sleep.

When she awakened hours later, the sky was dark and the cabin was chilly. She turned up the heat on the propane furnace and stoked the fire. Since the power so often went out up in the mountains, the entire cabin could run without electricity. The appliances and furnace ran on gas and a big generator kept the rest of the cabin functioning if the power did go out.

Brylee made pasta and a salad for dinner and sat in front of the fire to eat it. TV reception along with cell service was spotty, so she watched one of the many holiday DVDs she'd packed.

Before she returned home, she was determined to capture a healthy dose of the Christmas spirit. She thought inundating herself with sweet holiday romances couldn't hurt.

Only she'd ended up crying as the couple in the movie admitted their love and got their happily ever after.

Brylee had no delusions that once upon a time she had a chance at a happy future with Shaun. Between fear and faltering steps, it had slipped through her hands before she could grab onto it.

Unable to watch another movie, she retrieved the paperback she'd started reading before she left for the rodeo finals and opened it to find an envelope tucked inside. Taped to the front of the envelope was a note from her mother.

I'm so sorry, Brylee, for the pain I've caused and for the mess I've made of things. I wouldn't blame you if you never forgive me, but I hope you someday will. Despite everything, I really do love you, honey, and I'm so, so proud of you.
Mom

Brylee pulled off the note and saw the envelope was addressed to her in a masculine hand she recognized as Shaun's handwriting. Fingers trembling, she opened the letter, noting the postmark on the envelope was from six years ago. She unfolded the single sheet of paper and read what he'd written.

Dear Brylee,
I don't know how to write this letter or even what to say other than I'm sorry. I'm sorry for running out on you last week. I'm sorry for leaving you to wake up alone in that hotel room. I'm sorry

for acting like a jerk and writing the stupid note to call the attorney.

It didn't take more than a few hours to realize I'd made the biggest mistake of my life — not in marrying you, but disappearing like that.

Contrary to what you probably think right now, I love you with all my heart. I love you so much it scares the bejabbers out of me. But I figured out I'd rather risk the chance of drowning in your love than remain safely anywhere else without you.

I'm sorry we didn't have a proper wedding and I apologize for getting you tipsy, but I won't apologize for loving you. That one night with you was the single most miraculous thing I've ever experienced in my life and I hope we'll have thousands of nights together as we grow old and gray, side by side.

If you think you can forgive this idiotic, lunkheaded, foolish cowboy, I'd like a second chance at loving you. We can even have a real wedding if you like. All I know is that I can't stand the thought of being without you.

So, please, Brylee, forgive me. I'm begging you, Bitsy, please call me, text me, send a carrier pigeon or smoke signals, whatever it takes and I'll come to you.

I'll love you forever, no matter what you decide.

Yours always,
Shaun

Although her tears nearly blinded her, Brylee read the letter twice more before she set it on a side table and collapsed on the couch, once again overtaken with tears.

The next morning, she slept until eight after spending half the night tossing and turning, praying that Shaun would reach out to her at some point. She decided if she hadn't heard from him by New Year's Day, she'd just drive to Baker City and face him in person.

Regardless of the outcome, she had to see him one last time, to tell him again how much he meant to her and how sorry she was about keeping Michaela from him.

I told you keeping secrets from those you love never ends well.

"I know, Dad, but it's a little late to fix things now."

Her father's voice in her head fell silent again, leaving her in a contemplative mood. She bundled up and went outside, going for a walk through the woods. Trees shrouded with snow created a canopy overhead as she meandered on a path most likely made by deer. At least she hoped it was a deer and not something that might try to eat her for dinner.

Too bad no one had ever taught her tracking skills or she might be able to figure out what had been passing through the area. Maybe that would be something good for Birch to learn. She knew someone who worked as a trapper for the state. Perhaps he'd be willing to let Birch tag along this coming summer. She didn't want him to spend all his teen years tied down to the responsibilities of the ranch. He'd have enough of that to deal with when he was grown.

Poor Birch. He'd been nearly as distraught as she was when she told him she and Shaun would not be getting back together. Shaun had become a father-figure to the boy and a big brother rolled into one. The two of them had spent many hours together — roping, joking around, and doing the things Birch so often missed out on with their dad gone.

Foolishly, she'd imagined Shaun learning about Michaela and his reaction going far differently than it had. In her vision, they'd hug and offer words of love and comfort, and all would be well between them.

Instead, Brylee realized how childish and ridiculous she'd been. It seemed she still had some growing up to do. Shaun had every right to hate her, to never forgive her. How could she blame him? If he'd been the one to hide Michaela from her, she didn't know how she'd ever get past it.

Brylee took a deep breath of the crisp winter air redolent with pine and wood smoke. As the stillness of the woods calmed her tumultuous thoughts, she got an idea. She hurried back to the cabin and dug around in the tool shed behind the house until she found a handsaw. She walked through a stand of smaller fir trees until she found one just the right size and cut it down.

After carrying it back to the cabin, she returned the saw to the tool shed and unearthed a galvanized pail. She dragged a sixty-pound bag of sand she used for traction from the back of her pickup and filled the bucket partway full of the sand then lugged it inside the house. She draped an old red and white striped tablecloth over a small table in the corner of the main room then hauled in the tree and set the tree inside the bucket, twisting and turning it until the tree was secure in the sand. She retrieved a plastic pitcher from beneath the sink and filled it with water then dumped it in the bucket, repeating the process until the sand was completely soaked.

"Now for decorations," she said, not even caring that she'd started talking aloud to herself.

She went outside and gathered a sack full of pine cones and made another trip to the tool shed to see what she could find there. With a spool of jute string in her pocket and her hands full of rusty old jingle bells she'd found in a box among nails and bent hinges, she returned to the house, kicked off her snow boots, and set to work.

An hour later, she'd hung pine cones and jingle bells on the tree branches with the jute string.

"It needs some color," she said, searching the cabin, which didn't take long. The house boasted a large main room, a good-sized kitchen, two bedrooms downstairs along with the bathroom, and a loft upstairs. She returned to the kitchen and grinned as her eyes landed on a jar of cinnamon.

Brylee quickly whipped up a batch of salt dough using salt, flour, cinnamon, and water. She found a bottle of red food coloring in a drawer. The food color had probably been there since she was a little girl, but a drop of hot water loosened the thickened liquid. Several splashes of the food coloring went into the dough and she mixed it in until the dough was a cheery red color. After rolling it out on the counter, she used a knife to cut star shapes and then poked holes in the top of each one using the handle of a spoon. She placed the stars on a baking sheet and slid it in a warm oven to dry the dough.

When she took them out a while later, she strung jute through the holes and hung them on the tree. The whole cabin held the fragrance of pine and cinnamon, the way Christmas should smell. She smiled as she settled into a rocking chair by the fire and stared at the little tree.

The beginnings of Christmas cheer trickled into her heart. It grew as she made a bowl of soup for lunch then nibbled a few cookies before stoking up the fire.

Ready to treat herself to an indulgence, she went into the large bathroom and filled the huge bathtub with hot water. The tub was big enough to hold two people and deep enough for a good soak. Family lore said her grandfather hauled the tub in and had it installed when they added on the bathroom to the cabin as a surprise for her grandmother. Brylee grinned, thinking he probably got some enjoyment out of it, too.

She sat on the edge of the tub as she added bubble bath to the water. The vanilla scent held a hint of pomegranate and a spice she couldn't quite identify that gave off an aromatic Christmas fragrance.

Brylee pinned her hair on top of her head and then carried a small side table into the bathroom, leaving it next to the tub. She made a cup of hot chocolate brimming with marshmallows, and left it along with her book and phone on the little table by the tub. She sank into the steaming, fragrant water then pulled up a playlist of mellow Christmas songs on her phone.

Since she was alone and had no worries of anyone spying on her, she left the bathroom door wide open. The view from the free-standing tub was straight across from the big picture window in the main room with a spectacular view of the mountains.

She sipped her chocolate and watched snowflakes fall outside. With the smells of the Christmas tree and cinnamon-laced ornaments blending with the holiday scent of her bubble bath, the sound of carols playing softly accompanied by the crackling and popping of logs on the fire, and a delicious cup of hot, creamy chocolate in her hand, she sat back in the tub and relaxed for the first time in a long, long while.

The heat drew the tension and soreness from her muscles while the atmosphere calmed her spirit. She took another sip of the chocolate and closed her eyes, letting her head rest against a towel she'd folded and placed against the edge of the tub.

Thoughts she'd refused to dwell on surfaced, like how much she'd enjoyed kissing Shaun the last night of the rodeo, how good it felt to be held in his arms again. For a few marvelous moments, it was as though all the pain and loss between them had washed away, leaving behind pure, sweet love. She had such dreams of sharing Christmas with him, of the future holidays they would enjoy together. Now, all she knew is that she'd do most anything to be with him again.

Lost in her thoughts, she drifted in a state of not quite awake or asleep until she heard what sounded like a car door shut. She settled deeper in the water, convinced it must have been a log shifting on the fire.

Then a creak that sounded like someone opening the front door reached her. Her eyes popped open and she stared into the main room, but she couldn't see the door or the entrance area from the tub. The abundance of bubbles provided an iridescent cover for her, but she didn't relish the idea of facing an intruder while she was naked.

The distinctive jingle of spurs caught her attention as footsteps thudded across the floor. If someone was sneaking up on her, they weren't doing a very good job. She glanced around for a weapon and realized all she had within her grasp was her book and her cup of chocolate.

Not willing to sacrifice the mug or clean up a mess if she was losing her mind and hearing things, she set down the mug and picked up the book, pulling back her arm and taking aim for the center of the door.

The footsteps drew closer and she sucked in a frightened breath, holding it as a cowboy hat-covered head came into view along with a crystal vase full of gorgeous red and white roses.

She lowered the book and gawked at Shaun as he stepped into the bathroom with a broad grin on his face. A million questions ran through her head, but she couldn't voice a single one. Not when she could see love glimmering in his eyes and hope dancing in his smile.

"Well, this isn't exactly how I envisioned finding you, but I'm not complaining," he said, holding the vase in front of him as he walked closer to the tub. "It looks like you've been holed up here playing Santa's elf." He sniffed the air. "It even smells like Christmas."

"Shaun! Good grief! You scared me half to death sneaking in here like that." She couldn't believe he was standing in her bathroom looking like he'd just ridden out of one of Lasso Eight's advertisements. It was all she could do to keep from leaping out of the tub and into his arms.

He smirked. "I wasn't sneaking. My spurs and boots made enough noise to wake a deaf dog."

The barest hint of a smile lingered on her lips. "I know you didn't ride Lucky all the way here. Why do you have on spurs?"

He glanced down at his boots then back at her. "I didn't take time to change once I decided to come see you."

That made sense, even if she had no idea what motivated him to drive all the way up to the cabin. "What are you doing here?"

Rather than answer right away, he glanced around and noticed a small stool in front of an old vanity in the corner of the bathroom. He set the vase on the vanity then pulled the stool over by the tub although he didn't take a seat on it. "I need to talk to you about something and a phone call won't do. I'm still mad at you and aching about Michaela, but that's not what I drove all this way to say."

"I'm sorry, Shaun. Truly, I am."

"I know you are, darlin', but I'm the one who needs to apologize. None of this would have happened if I'd never left you, if I'd done everything I could to get you back. I'm sorry, so incredibly sorry."

"And you are forgiven," she said, meaning it. She forgave him because she loved him, but that still didn't explain why he'd come to the cabin. He could have apologized on the phone.

"How'd you find me?" she asked, sinking deeper in the tub and shifting around bubbles to provide strategic coverage. She lifted a bubble-covered hand and pointed toward the door. "Why don't you wait in the living room and I'll join you in a minute."

"I think I like you right where you are," he said. He removed his hat and set it on the vanity then shrugged out of his coat and draped it there, too. When he sat down on the stool and took a drink of her chocolate, she got the idea he didn't intend on leaving the room or her anytime soon.

"Mmm. That's good chocolate," he said, taking another sip before handing the cup to her. "To answer your question, I went to your house, but Ace told me you came up here yesterday then gave me detailed directions in case I'd forgotten how to find the cabin. Although we stopped by a few times when we were dating, his map came in handy. With the snow falling like it's gonna turn into a blizzard, it made it challenging to see the landmarks I thought I recalled."

One of his long, tanned fingers dipped into the

tub and lazily trailed back and forth through the bubbles by her knees.

Brylee glanced at his finger and goose bumps broke over her flesh despite the heat of the water. She needed a distraction from how much she wanted Shaun, wanted him to love her. "Why are you here and where did you find such beautiful roses?"

His shifted his attention from the bubble he'd captured on his finger to her face. Brylee felt the magnetic pull of him as his gaze fused to hers. "I called a florist and had those flowers delivered to your house this morning, but Ace decided it would be a good idea to bring them with me." Shaun grinned. "I think he was right."

"They are beautiful and very much appreciated, but why did you choose red and white?" she asked, knowing the meaning of the combination of colors, but wondering if Shaun did. "Because they look festive for Christmas?"

"No, although they do fit well with the holiday." Shaun walked back over to the vanity and pulled a red rose from the vase then handed it to her before he took a seat on the stool again.

Brylee buried her nose in the bloom, studying him as he sat there looking more handsome than her battered heart could take. "So if it wasn't to spread Christmas cheer, why did you choose red and white?"

"It's the symbol for unity, isn't it?" he asked, trailing his index finger through the bubbles again. "Going forward, you and I are going to be united, Brylee. United in our thoughts, in our dreams, in our hopes, and our hearts, and most definitely united in marriage."

Sure she must have gotten soap bubbles in her ears and hadn't heard him correctly, she stared at him. "You still want to marry me? After finding out about Michaela, about my mother meddling in things and creating half of the mess, you'd still want to spend your life saddled with me and my crazy family?"

Shaun pulled off one boot and let it drop to the floor followed by the other, then yanked off his socks. "I'm not married to your crazy family, Brylee, although I love Birch like a little brother and your grandpa like he was my own. Your mother is going to take a little work for me to warm up to, but given enough time, it will most likely happen." He stood and unfastened his belt buckle then pulled the tails of his shirt from his jeans. "I had an interesting conversation this morning with Will Johnson. It seems his brother never filed the paperwork to annul our hasty wedding. In the eyes of the law, we're still married."

Brylee's eyes widened with shock. "You're kidding me."

Shaun shook his head and unsnapped his shirt, letting it fall to the floor. "I would not kid about something that serious, Bitsy. I spoke to his brother and even had my attorney check to be sure the paperwork was never filed. It wasn't. So you, my beautiful little holiday enchantress, are still married to me. If it's okay with you, I'd like to keep it that way for the next sixty or so years." He tugged the Henley shirt he wore over his head. "If you're tired of loving me by then, we'll revisit the option of going our separate ways, but only by mutual agreement."

Brylee drank in the sight of him, of bulging muscles and the beauty of a rugged hard-working man.

Sparks flickered in his eyes, like lightning across a stormy sky, as he braced his hands on either side of the massive tub and bent down until his lips hovered achingly close to hers. "What do you say, Brylee Elizabeth Barton? Will you remain my wife in sickness and in health, in hard times and happy times, through the birth of the children I hope we have together although no one will ever replace Michaela in our hearts, and the many years ahead when I'll stay right by your side until the good Lord calls us home? Even then, I'll love you still."

Tears of joy glistened in her eyes while happiness unlike anything she'd ever known flooded her heart.

Unable to speak, she nodded her head and pressed her lips to his. Passion and yearning exploded between them, right along with hope and promises for their future together. Promises they both knew they'd always keep.

"I love you so much, Bitsy," Shaun whispered, holding himself up on the edges of the tub while she buried her face in his neck, breathing in his decadent, familiar scent.

"I love you, too, Copperhead. I have since the first moment we met."

"Then, I guess we should do this," he said, digging in the front pocket of his jeans and pulling out two rings. He took Brylee's left hand in his and kissed the tip of each finger before sliding a beautiful platinum etched band with a diamond set in the center onto her finger. "With this ring, to my already wedded wife, I vow to cherish you, protect you, support you, encourage you, to make you laugh, wipe away your tears, and love you forever."

She took the other ring, a wide band that matched the one on her finger, and slid it on his ring finger, kissing it then pulling his hand up to her cheek and kissing his palm.

"With this ring, I promise to honor you, to support you, to do my best to obey you," she grinned at him and he smiled, "to treasure you, to encourage you, to care for you, to laugh with you, and love you with every beat of my heart."

Shaun kissed her again, so tenderly and sweetly, Brylee thought she'd melt into the bubbles that rapidly dissolved around her.

When they stopped to draw a breath, Shaun dropped his jeans and climbed into the tub, pulling her into his arms, into the bliss of being his beloved wife.

Later as they cuddled on the sofa in front of a roaring fire, Brylee held out her hand to watch the diamond sparkle in the firelight. Shaun took her hand in his and kissed her fingers again, making tingles race down to her toes.

"I love you, Bitsy, more than you can know," he said in a husky voice.

She snuggled closer against him, relishing the feel of his hard chest pressed against her back. "I have an idea because I love you just as much,

Shaun. May this be the beginning of a lifetime of happy Christmases we share together."

He pressed a warm kiss to her neck and wrapped his hands more tightly around her waist beneath the blanket that covered them. "I think we should make it a tradition to come up to the cabin every year right before Christmas to celebrate our anniversary."

"That's a wonderful idea," she said, glancing over her shoulder at him then shifting to trail her hand through his hair.

"I also think we should renew our vows. I'm thinking a little ceremony with just our close friends and family. What do you say?" he asked, giving her a hopeful look. "You could have a real wedding dress, and a reception."

She turned over so she could see him better, gaze into the face she so loved. "Your close friends encompass at least a hundred people and you know it." He smirked and kissed her cheek.

Brylee traced the cleft in his chin. "I don't need a fancy ceremony or an expensive dress or a six layer cake, but I think it would be nice to renew our vows. What do you think of doing it New Year's Day? Most of your friends will be in the area for Chase and Jessie's party anyway."

"That sounds perfect, Bits. You invite whomever you like and I'll be there with bells on."

"Leave the bells on the Christmas tree, and you've got a deal," she said, kissing him with all the love she'd held for him in heart for so long. Shaun was finally hers to love and cherish, and she planned to love him with all her heart from that moment forward.

"Merry Christmas, Mrs. Price," he whispered against her lips.

And Brylee knew it would be.

Recipe

Here is the recipe for the meatloaf Brylee made for Shaun. Sometimes, there is nothing like a little comfort food. This recipe is different, but always moist and good.

Not Your Granny's Meatloaf
2 pounds of ground beef
3 eggs
2/3 cup milk
1 tbsp. parsley
1 1/2 cups Panko crumbs
1 tsp. seasoning
dash of salt
1 tbsp. olive oil
1/3 cup celery
1 tsp. onion flakes (or you can add fresh diced onion)
2 cups chicken broth
3 tbsp. butter

Preheat oven to 350 degrees.
Thinly slice celery. Heat olive oil in a small skillet on medium heat and add celery and onion. Cook until celery is softened. Remove from heat and let cool about ten minutes.
Mix celery with remaining ingredients until thoroughly blended.
Line a rimmed baking pan with foil or a piece of parchment (if you're lazy like me) and give it a shot of non-stick spray. Form a loaf in the pan that is about 12 inches long by 5 inches wide by 1 1/2-2

inches deep.

Bake for an hour, until the outside is a nice, deep brown.

About twenty-five minutes before the meatloaf is finished baking, pour 2 cups of chicken broth into a heavy skillet with the butter. You can add a spoon of seasoning, if you like.

Bring to a boil then simmer for about twenty minutes, until it starts to thicken. It will not get thick like gravy, but will be thicker than broth.

When the meatloaf is cooked, remove from the oven, slice, and drizzle with the gravy. We like it best served with mashed potatoes.

Author's Note

The first time I wrote about Shakin' It Shaun in *Barreling Through Christmas*, I knew this cowboy needed his own romance. Shaun is outgoing, full of fun, and doesn't embarrass easily. He's handsome and hunky, and maybe a little cocky from time to time.

I knew to give him his own happily ever after, I'd have to create a girl who was strong enough to balance his character.

That's when I came up with Brylee.

Brylee might be small, but she is mighty and she is fierce! At least that's how I see her. Brylee is one tough cookie but I think the thing I admire about her most is how deeply she loves.

I also had a wonderful time creating the secondary characters like Jason, Pops, Ace, and especially Birch. I'm thinking Birch might need his own story once he's all grown up!

If you caught the mention of the Jordan family when Jason was telling Brylee about his wife's ancestors... yes, I'm referring to Thane and Jemma Jordan from the Baker City Brides series. It's such fun to tie in characters from other series.

I've previously confessed I could spend hours (and hours!) on Pinterest. One day while I was looking at Pins for ideas for this book, I happened upon one that was titled "Five Deadly Terms Used by a Woman." Those terms are "Fine," "Nothing," "Go Ahead," "Whatever," and "That's OK." The word "Wow!" is listed as a bonus word. The descriptions that go with each of the statements are hilarious. "Fine" is a word women use to end an argument when they know they are right. "Nothing," of course, means something and men should definitely be worried. "Go ahead" is a dare, not permission. Men are discouraged from pursuing it. "Whatever" implies the man in question should back off and leave her alone. "That's OK" means she's thinking long and hard about retribution for whatever the man has done. "Wow!" simply points out her amazement that one person could be so stupid.

After reading all that, I, of course, had to find a way to work it into the story and the perfect opportunity arose when Brylee was injured and left at the mercy of Shaun — a man she loathed, or at least tried to convince herself she did.

If you noticed the mention of the sports medicine trailer at the rodeos and the helpful physicians who staffed it when Brylee was injured, those trailers are real. Through the Justin Sportsmedicine Team®, trailers and medical staff travel to rodeos all across the country, providing assistance and care to rodeo athletes. The sportsmedicine team works in conjunction with the Justin Cowboy Crisis Fund. Find out more about the JCCF and why I support it through my *Read a Book, Help a Cowboy* campaign.

One day my niece and I decided to go to lunch at a newly opened restaurant. The door had a "pull" sign, so we pulled. And pulled. Read the sign again and pulled. Then she pushed and the door swung open. The person watching us had the biggest smile on her face. Once we were seated, we watched another unsuspecting customer go through the same experience. Apparently, the sign was switched solely for the entertainment of the staff working there. It seemed fitting to include that bit of humor in the gas station scene with the crazy old coot and his mouse.

I have to tell you the story that inspired the mouse.

I was at a conference in Arizona. It was hot. I was tired and thirsty and wanted to go sit in front of the vent in my room and pretend I was somewhere about twenty-degrees cooler. On my way to do exactly that, I stopped at the hotel's gift shop that carried snacks and cold beverages and loaded up on water bottles and a few little trinkets to bring home.

As the girl at the cash register rang up my purchases, I noticed the cutest little mouse with the biggest ears sitting on a shelf about a foot away from me. It was adorable, and so lifelike. I handed the girl my credit card and she ran it while I continued studying the cute little mouse that would have made a wonderful tree ornament. Then it blinked.

Not wanting to scream at the top of my lungs in the swanky hotel, I took my credit card from the girl and pointed to the mouse. "Is that supposed to be there?" I asked, thinking maybe it was a pet mouse, since I'd never seen one like it before.

"What? Where?" she asked and leaned over the counter. The mouse turned and looked at her, wiggling his long whiskers. She released a blood-curdling scream I'm sure could be heard from the gift shop all the way to the top floor of the hotel.

Frightened, or perhaps knowing he'd been busted, the mouse leaped onto a row of packaged peanuts, charged across candy bars, and scurried under the counter. The girl behind it launched herself upward, screaming while dialing hotel security.

I signed the receipt, gathered my unbagged purchases, and left while she continued screaming and shouting at security to come do something about the mouse.

How could I not include the mouse in a story?

You can thank my awesome friend Melanie and her sweet daughter for the idea for the name S'mores for Dani's pony. Melanie possesses a unique and skillful talent at crocheting. She can make the most adorable crocheted animals. And to my delighted surprise, she sent me a horse she'd created that her daughter named S'mores. He's my little mascot, sitting on top of the speakers on my desk.

Remember the scene where Brylee and Shaun are both grossed out by kids eating cereal off the floor in the doctor's office. That actually happened! I was sitting in the waiting room and a young woman with two children was there, flipping through one magazine after another while the kids screamed and yelled and fought their way over and around the other patients. When they got into a tug-of-war over a bag of cereal and ripped it open, they dropped down and started eating it like wild animals off the floor. All I could think of was the disgusting things they were no doubt picking up right along with their fruity loops.

One year when Captain Cavedweller and I attended the Wrangler National Finals Rodeo, his parents went along with us. We took them around town, showing them some of the most popular "tourist" attractions. After dinner one evening, we decided to stroll through the Grand Canal Shoppes. CC's mom and I were walking along, talking about the stores and decorations when we happened upon a life-sized marble statue. It appeared so real, you could almost feel the body heat coming off it. Then my mother-in-law reached out to touch it and the statue blinked. Of course she screamed, the rest of us laughed, and the guy portraying the statue even cracked a grin. Every time we go to the Grand Canal Shoppes, I think of that moment and smile.

After sharing this next tidbit of inspiration, CC may strangle me, so if you don't hear from me again, that's the reason why. Years ago, it was one of those chaotic mornings when the alarm didn't go off and we were both in a frenzy to get ready so we wouldn't be late for work. Crammed into our small bathroom, I'd just finished combing my hair while CC brushed his teeth. My hairspray can happened to be sitting next to his can of deodorant on the counter. In a rush, he grabbed the hairspray, sprayed it, and then got the most horrified expression on his face. He looked from the can to his armpits to me. That's when I lost it. I started laughing so hard, I had to stagger into the bedroom and plop down on the edge of the bed because I couldn't even stand up straight. For days, the merest thought of the look on his face made me break into spurts of laughter. Even all these years later, I still giggle whenever it comes to mind (like right now as I'm writing this). Although I didn't switch the cans on purpose like Brylee did with Shaun, it truly was comical. (Unless you ask CC, then it wasn't funny. At all.)

In the story I have Jason avoiding boats because he had a bad experience out fishing. That is inspired by a fishing trip CC took with his cousin. From the stories I heard when they got back, the two of them spent most of the time hanging over the edge of the boat feeding the fish while his uncle actually caught fish.

I love roses of any shape, size, and color. It was such fun for me to incorporate a variety of colors into this story and share their meanings. Visually, my favorite is a pale pink rose, or one with graduated pink color like the first one Shaun gave Brylee. But for meaning, there are so many of them that speak to my heart. I might have even gotten a little emotional when I wrote about Shaun bringing her the vase of red and white roses. That whole idea of him wanting them to be united going forward is so sweet. If you are a rose fan, I'd love to hear your favorite color and why you like it best.

Without my wonderful editors and beta readers, this book would never be published. Thank you, especially, to Shauna, Leo, and Katrina for their excellent help in editing the story, to all the Hopeless Romantics who read ARC copies, and to Jill Fletcher and Tonya Lucas for making sure I had my barrel racing facts straight. Also, thank you to my Hopeless Romantics ARC readers. I so appreciate all of you!

My deepest, heartfelt thanks to you, dear

readers, for coming along for the adventure of Shaun and Brylee's story. If you enjoyed it, I hope you'll tell others about the Rodeo Romance series. I hope, too, that you'll join me during the 2019 holiday season when the next book in the series releases.

Wishing you the best and brightest of holidays!

Thank you for reading ***Racing Christmas*** I hope you enjoyed Shaun and Brylee's story. I'd be so appreciative if you'd share a *review* so other readers might discover the heart and hope shared in this series. Even a line or two is appreciated more than you can know.

And be sure to check out the Justin Cowboy Crisis Fund and my ***Read a Book, Help a Cowboy*** campaign!

Also, if you haven't yet signed up for my newsletter, won't you consider subscribing? I send it out a few times a month, when I have new releases, sales, or news of freebies to share. Each month, you can enter a contest, get a new recipe to try, and discover news about upcoming events. When you sign up, you'll receive a free short and sweet historical romance. Don't wait. Sign up today!

And if newsletters aren't your thing, please follow me on BookBub. You'll receive notifications on pre-orders, new releases, and sale books!

Sleigh Bells Ring in Romance — Rancher Jess Milne lost his wife years ago, but he's finally ready to give love a second chance. It's a shame the one woman in Romance who captures his interest is a prickly, wasp-tongued she-devil. She used to be one of his closest friends until he asked her out. Her vocal, vehement refusal made her thoughts on dating him crystal clear.

Widowed more than ten years, Doris Grundy tries to convince herself she's content with her life. Her recently married grandson and his wife bring her joy. The ranch she's lived on since she was a young bride gives her purpose. She's an active member of their close-knit community. But the old coot who lives down the road continually invades her thoughts, keeping her from having any peace. Doris will be the last to admit she longs for the love and affection of her handsome neighbor.

When the two of them are unexpectedly thrown together, will they find a little holiday spirit and allow the love of the season to ring in their hearts?

Turn the page for a fun preview...

Sleigh Bells Ring
IN ROMANCE

"Did he see you sneak out here?" Blayne Grundy asked, peering around the edge of the barn door as he lingered in the shadows.

Janet Moore shook her head and tugged her sweater more closely around her in the nippy November air. "No. Dad is zonked out taking a nap. He's been exhausted since he came home from the hospital. Who would have thought the mighty Jess Milne would sleep more than a toddler after having knee replacement surgery? At least the doctor said he's doing well and should have a normal recovery." She stepped out of view of anyone passing by, moving closer to Blayne. "I never thought we'd resort to holding a clandestine meeting in the barn to discuss the love life, or lack thereof, of my dad and your grandmother."

Blayne chuckled and leaned against the wall behind him, crossing his arms over his broad chest. "Honestly, it's never something I envisioned, either.

It's nice of you to use your vacation time to come take care of your dad while he heals. How long are you planning to stay before you fly back to Salt Lake City?"

"Until the first of December, but then I have to get back home. By that time, Steve and the kids will either have learned how to take care of themselves or be living off pizza and take-out food while dressed in filthy clothes. I'm not convinced any of them know how to turn on the washing machine."

He smirked then tossed her a cocky smile. "You know I had a huge crush on you when you used to babysit me."

Janet nodded. "Since you followed me around like a besotted puppy, I was aware of that fact."

"I did no such thing," Blayne said, scowling at the woman who had been his neighbor, babysitter, and was now a good friend.

"You did and you know it," Janet pinned him with a perceptive glare. "But let's figure out what to do about Dad and your grandmother. Do you have any idea why Doris refuses to speak to him?"

"Not a clue. She isn't the least bit helpful when I've asked her why she turns all lemon-faced at the very mention of Jess." Blayne sighed, removed his dusty cowboy hat, and forked a hand through his hair. "I've done everything I can think of to get those two together. It's obvious to everyone but Jess and Grams that they should fall in love."

"The problem is that they are both too stubborn and opinionated to admit they like each other. We'll just have to get creative." Janet plopped down on a bale of straw. When one of the ranch dogs wandered inside, she absently reached down and rubbed behind his ears. She glanced up at Blayne. "What does your wife think about all this?"

"Brooke is all for whatever makes Grams happy, and Jess, too. She and your dad get along like old friends."

"I'm glad to hear that. Brooke is fantastic, Blayne. You couldn't have found a better girl to marry."

Blayne's face softened at the mention of his wife. "She is pretty special."

Janet remained silent for several moments, lost in thought, before she looked up at Blayne with a confident smile. "What if I suddenly had to return home and no one else could stay with Dad? Could you persuade Doris to take care of him until he's back on his feet? If they had to see each other every day for two or three weeks, maybe they'd get past whatever it is that's keeping them apart."

A slow, pleased grin spread across Blayne's face. "I think, with enough guilt, it might work. I can remind Grams of the number of times she's lectured me about it being not just a duty, but an honor and privilege to help take care of our friends and neighbors in times of need."

"Perfect! I'll see if I can get on a flight tomorrow. If not, the next day at the latest. Steve is going to be thrilled at this bit of news." Janet hopped up and tugged her cell phone from her pocket. "I just hope our plan works. Doris and Dad have too many good years left for them to spend them alone."

"Especially when they clearly would like to be

together." Blayne pushed away from the wall. "With a little holiday magic, anything is possible."

Janet nodded in agreement. "It certainly is…"

Find out what happens in ***Sleigh Bells Ring in Romance***,

part of the *Christmas in Romance* series, available now <u>on Amazon</u>!

RODEO ROMANCE SERIES

Hunky rodeo cowboys tangle with independent, sassy women
in this sweet contemporary holiday series!

Rodeo Romance Series
Hunky rodeo cowboys tangle with independent
sassy women who can't help but love them.

The Christmas Cowboy (Book 1) — Among
the top saddle bronc riders in the rodeo circuit,
easy-going Tate Morgan can master the toughest
horse out there, but trying to handle beautiful
Kenzie Beckett is a completely different story.

Wrestlin' Christmas (Book 2) — Sidelined
with a major injury, steer wrestler Cort McGraw
struggles to come to terms with the end of his
career. Shanghaied by his sister and best friend, he
finds himself on a run-down ranch with a
worrisome, albeit gorgeous widow, and her silent,
solemn son.

Capturing Christmas (Book 3) — Life is hectic
on a good day for rodeo stock contractor Kash
Kressley. Between dodging flying hooves and
babying cranky bulls, he barely has time to sleep.
The last thing Kash needs is the entanglement of a
sweet romance, especially with a woman as full of

fire and sass as Celia McGraw.

Barreling Through Christmas (Book 4) — Cooper James might be a lot of things, but beefcake model wasn't something he intended to add to his resume.

Chasing Christmas (Book 5) — Tired of his cousin's publicity stunts on his behalf, bull rider Chase Jarrett has no idea how he ended up with an accidental bride!

Racing Christmas (Book 6) — Brylee Barton is racing to save her family's ranch. Shaun Price is struggling to win her heart. . . again.

About the Author

Hopeless romantic Shanna Hatfield spent ten years as a newspaper journalist before moving into the field of marketing and public relations. Sharing the romantic stories she dreams up in her head is a perfect outlet for her love of writing, reading, and creativity. She and her husband, lovingly referred to as Captain Cavedweller, reside in the Pacific Northwest.

Shanna loves to hear from readers.
Connect with her online:
Blog: shannahatfield.com
Facebook: Shanna Hatfield's Page
Shanna Hatfield's Hopeless Romantics Group
Pinterest: Shanna Hatfield
Email: shanna@shannahatfield.com
Check out the Racing Christmas Pinterest board to see the images that helped inspire the story!